Gods of Arcadia

DAUGHTER OF ATHENA

ANDREA STEHLE

Daughter of Athena
Copyright © 2014 by Andrea Stehle

First edition, published October 2014

All rights reserved.
This book is protected under the copyright laws of the United States of America. Any reproduction or other unauthorized use of the material or artwork herein is prohibited.
This is a work of fiction. The characters, incidents and dialogues are products of the author's imagination and are not to be construed as real.

Interior Layout by Author's HQ
Cover Art by Howard David Johnson

The Gods of Arcadia

Eons ago the Gods ruled over the dawning of ancient Greece. From the heights of Mt. Olympus they bent mankind to their will. Unfortunately, Olympians are immortal and easily bored. One day they looked away from their children and in the blink of an eye the Earth changed. Mankind forgot the Gods and instead called them myths. To their regret the Olympians discovered no amount of manipulation of human history could bring mankind back into the fold, and so they took the only option left to them – they started over.

Transplanting a small group of human colonists to the distant world of Arcadia, they created a new and perfect utopia. Each Olympian reigns over a cult of followers in a personal city-state where their word is law. To promote harmony, the Great Law of the Olympians forbids all war on Arcadia. For two thousand years the Gods and mortals have lived in harmony, although even the Olympians would have to admit - nothing is ever perfect.

Once every hundred years the Son of Ares is born to upset the delicate balance of their world.

Salutatio

History is written long after the events have unfolded. It is an inescapable reality that the perceptions of the storyteller taint the truth of the story. I not only accept this fact, but choose to embrace the imperfection. I will not pretend that I can keep my feelings (or as an empathy - the feelings of the people around me) from influencing my story.

I want the future to understand the real Ardella and the events that shaped who and what I became in the history books written by others. I want the people of our world to know the true heroes and villains in our struggle against the Gods of Arcadia.

Lady Ardella

Daughter of Athena

Two thousand, six hundred and fifty years *Ab Terra Condita*

Chapter 1

Just as a seedling grows in the shade of the massive oak aspiring to one day stand as tall, so too a child sprouts in body, mind, and soul into a reflection of the parent.

**Hermaenia, 24th Great Mother of the Demeter Sect
One thousand and three years *Ab Terra Condita***

I STOOD PATIENTLY before the massive golden doors of the Goddess' inner sanctum. From within the glistening metal could be witnessed a visualization of the original Great Library of Alexandria. The library's graceful maiden columns, guardians of the knowledge of the past, stood proud and unwavering against the flowing sapphire ribbon of the great mother Nile. The desert winds danced through the fields of wheat that had once been the breadbasket of the Mediterranean. I marveled at this dreamlike image, so symbolic of the world of Arcadia. The vision and its beauty spoke of our society's reverence and admiration for the distant home of our ancestors—a place called Earth.

I smiled as I recalled the day I stood by another door just as symbolic—at least for me. It was the simple wooden door from my childhood home. My mother had been trying to explain the reality of living in the world of the Olympians. I don't recall making it very easy on either of us:

I stood there, a petulant ten-year-old and complained, "I don't understand why I have to go to the Academy, Mother."

My mother's smile was patient despite my outburst. She had long since become accustomed to her daughter's high-strung ways. "It is very unAthenian," she often reminded me. "It is time to go to the Academy to learn the ways of our sect," she said placing her hand on my small shoulder.

"I don't want to go," I whined. I clung to her hand with my little fists. "I want to stay here with you."

"I know, Ardella, but it's not possible." She was gentle but firm.

That wasn't the answer I wanted to hear. It wasn't the answer my young heart was willing to accept. "Tell the Goddess I can't go," I demanded, stomping my foot.

My mother was suddenly quiet. After a moment she whispered, "You are old enough to know that we do not say such things." The sharp timber of her voice startled me as she continued, "You are ten years old, which is the age children are to begin their education at the Academy. That is the way the Goddess wants it."

I would not relent. "You always told me that the followers of Athena have free will. So why do we let the Goddess tell us what to do?"

I felt my mother's body stiffen and the air between us grew cold. I actually heard the sound of the slap even before my mind recognized what she had done. I touched my stinging cheek and looked at her bewildered. That was the only time in my life my mother ever struck me and looking back, I realize it was not anger that I saw reflected in her eyes—but fear.

"The next words you speak will be an explanation of why you will follow the Goddess now and in the future." Her tone allowed for no further refusal.

I knew the answer she expected, and so I repeated an old proverb I had heard her speak many times before: "Free will is a gift to all mankind, but a wise woman will allow the Goddess to guide her steps."

She looked relieved at my words, but I still didn't understand. I didn't want to be guided by the mysterious Olympian who lived in the Tower in the center of the city. I wanted to choose for myself, and most of all—I desperately wanted my mother to choose my wishes over those of the Goddess. Still stunned from my mother's slap, however, I did not give voice to these concerns.

My mother saw the confusion reflected in my eyes. "You know the right words, Ardella, but you still don't understand, do you?" I heard a rising note of panic in her voice.

"I want to understand, Mother," I managed to whisper. My hands were trembling.

She guided me to sit beside her on bench on our front porch. With the patient love only a mother possesses she did her best to explain the delicate balance of Arcadia. "We have the freedom to learn and grow in any way we choose, Ardella. But we also have the wisdom to choose to follow the guidance of others. We are the children of the Goddess of Wisdom. Just as you trust me to help guide your steps, the followers of Athena, we have chosen to submit ourselves to the will of the Goddess."

"Because Athena is like a mother to us all," I mimicked the words I had so often heard my mother speak.

"Yes, darling," my mother sighed. She took me into her warm embrace.

Although my mother seemed satisfied that her child finally

understood, the truth was that for me they were still just words. It was obvious to me they were more than words for my mother, but my young mind was caught up in a maelstrom of doubt and fear that threatened to overwhelm me.

The first tears that rolled down my cheeks startled us both, but soon the torrent began in earnest. I sobbed uncontrollably unable to stop the strange wave of sadness that filled me. My mother held me there in her arms until all my tears were spent. I clung to her like a toddler frightened by a midnight thunderstorm. I didn't understand why I was scared, but I knew I didn't want to leave the shelter of my mother's embrace. Somehow I realized that this moment would be the last time I truly felt safe.

"I don't think I am ready to go to the Academy," I finally confessed with a soft hiccup.

My mother's laugh soothed my soul as surely as her gentle hands were comforting my shaken body. "If it makes you feel better, I think most of us weren't ready to leave home at ten, but we all made the best of it."

A little voice in my head (one that sounded irritatingly like my twin brother) reminded me that my trepidation was not, in fact, universal. "Not everyone is scared to go to the Academy," I whined. "Rafe is ready to leave. He is even excited about it."

"You're right about your brother. He has an inner strength and ambition that I have seldom seen in a boy his age. One would think he was the one with Olympian blood," she mused, and then suddenly looked startled at what she had said. "Just remember that each person grows and develops in his or her own way," she offered. "Perhaps Rafe's presence will help you adjust to life at the Academy."

"I guess it will be alright, if Rafe is coming too," I said softly, and then added, "Besides, he will never let me forget it, if he goes to the Academy and I don't."

My mother chuckled softly. She lovingly stroked my long

brown hair and shared her secret:

"The Goddess herself told me that you are destined to serve in the Tower of Athena. You will one day be allowed the privilege of speaking directly to the Goddess. That is a great honor, but also a great burden. You must always do as the Goddess expects, and you must learn to control your words."

"I will try."

"You must do more than try, Ardella. You must learn control. You must be careful. The gift of free will can be dangerous. You never want your words to displease the Goddess."

Then what is the point of free will? I wondered. But instead of listening to that little voice in my head, for the first time in my young life I followed my mother's advice and kept the erroneous thought to myself. I had always known that my mother was devoted to the Goddess, but that day I realized she also feared the mysterious Olympian in the Tower. I think that is when I began to understand. The followers of Athena had obeyed the Goddess' since we arrived on Arcadia over 2,000 years ago, and the childish whims of one spoiled little girl could not change two millennia of tradition.

"The Goddess guides us, because she wants the best for her children. That is the way it has always been and will always be," my mother said softly. Her word mirrored my own thoughts, and yet they contained something I feared mine never would—a solemn conviction of their truth. I envy her faith to this day.

My childhood recollection ended abruptly as the colossal entrance slowly began to swing open, indicating the Goddess was ready to begin my audience. Although well beyond the threshold, instinct compelled me to retreat even further from the massive metal barriers. Driven by the will of the Goddess, I knew that those enormous golden doors would not stop moving until they had slammed into the wall with an earsplitting roar of thunder.

As the sound echoed through the marble hall of the entrance, I took a deep breath and reassured myself, as I always did, that I could control my words in the presence of the Goddess. I walked slowly and reverently into the inner sanctum and assumed a self-assured, calm demeanor that did not reach my inner core. The soft lights along the recessed alcoves around the room were meant to mimic the light of hundreds of flickering candles. As I watched the shadows dance behind their glow, I could almost imagine the heat of them gently warming my skin.

"Great Goddess, I come into your presence as you requested," I said softly. Although I had looked upon the face of the Goddess Athena many times, her cunning grey eyes and the soft glow of her alabaster skin once again took my breath away. Her classic beauty was ageless and perfect. It was as if one of the marble statues from the Academy had come to life. Just as in all depictions of her image, her flaxen hair, the color of the soft sand on the beaches of Heliopolis, was tucked neatly away within her great, plumed helmet. Although she no longer needed her bronze battle armor (obsolete on Arcadia), she still wore her headdress with her flowing white peplos. The fabric of the peplos was created in the workshop of Hephaestus and it shimmered with golden figures, depicting the warriors of Greece flooding out of the belly of the great wooden horse and storming through the streets of Troy. As the Goddess moved the images on the peplos morphed from one scene into the next making it seem as though it had a will of its own. I always found myself mesmerized by display.

"Ardella, I have something I need to tell you," Athena said.

I felt her deep grey eyes on me, pulling my gaze upward. My empathy worked with mortals and Olympians alike, but today it told me nothing. Athena was hiding her feelings and may as well have been made of the same marble as the walls; therefore I could not even begin to guess what news she had to impart.

"Your brother has been ..." the Goddess began.

"Something has happened to Rafe?" I asked suddenly, unintentionally interrupting the Goddess in my concern for my twin brother.

"Yes," Athena replied, ignoring my outburst, "he has been... taken prisoner."

I was confused. "Who would kidnap my brother?" I asked.

"I did not say kidnapped, Ardella," Athena stated plainly, "Rafe was...he was...captured in battle."

For a few moments my mind could not process the words. The Olympian Gods had made a pact when they set out from Earth for their new home world. The pact forbad any one, God or mortal, from making war on another. The punishment for anyone breaking the Great Olympian Law was the death of the offender and the destruction of the offender's entire sect. This meant the death of every member of that society, both the guilty and the innocent. Since that terrible punishment fell on the Artemis sect almost 1000 years ago, no one on Arcadia (mortal or immortal) had dared to make war. It was a harsh but effective deterrent.

"How can that be? There are no battles—no war on Arcadia. It is against the Great Olympian Law. Who could he have been fighting?" I wondered.

Athena sighed, but did not answer. Instead, as was her way, she allowed me, this poor mortal, time to work out the answer for myself. I felt my heart freeze in my chest as I realized the truth. "He was fighting Alexander," I whispered in horror. My brother was in the hands of our mortal enemy.

"Yes," Athena confirmed, regret thickening her voice, "He tried to solve the problem of the Son of Ares...but failed."

"Rafe made war against Metropolis?" This was incomprehensible to me.

"He stole metal automatons, the creations of Hephaestus,

and changed their purpose. He led them into battle against the Son of Ares' fortress. I think he believed that if he succeeded in killing Alexander, then the aggression of the followers of Hermes would stop." Her explanation was given in a serene, but self-righteous tone.

I should have been suspicious of her intimate knowledge of my brother's plans and motivations, but was too shocked to care. *"He could not be sure enough of the outcome to take such a radical action,"* the voice in my head suggested. My twin Rafe and I had often debated whether or not the death of Alexander would in fact change the dangerous path that Hermes' followers had chosen. Although my brother had firmly believed the chaos caused by the Son of Ares would end with his death, I had never agreed.

As an empath, I felt Athena's anger, even before she spoke. To my horror I realized that I had unintentionally verbalized my last thought, and the Goddess was not pleased.

"What do you mean?" the Goddess asked.

I had served Athena long enough to recognize that tone meant she was not really asking a question, but giving me the opportunity to alter what I had said to her point of view. The Goddess was, after all, an Olympian. Although Athena wished to be perceived as a caring ruler, here only to guide us with her great wisdom, as my mother had warned me long ago, the Goddess had very little patience with mortals. The consequences for free expression in Athena's presence could be dire. My heart froze as images of Mistress Rianna flooded into my mind.

Mistress Rianna had been a history professor at the Academy. Her enthusiasm was contagious, and Arcadian history had become my favorite subject. She had a similar influence on many of the young students at the Academy. As a child, I did not understand that in New Athens many considered her Socratic teaching methods to be unorthodox and dangerous. It was many years later, when Mistress Rianna was called before the Council of Athena on charges of heresy, that I came to understand the pattern of her life—she had been trying to teach the Athenian youth to think for themselves and question the world around them. Unfortunately, her success with her students had terrible consequences for her personally.

I had wanted to help:

"Let me defend you, Mistress Rianna. I have been studying the law. There is no precedent for these charges," I argued.

"I believe there is little that can be presented in the way of defense, Lady Ardella. I am in fact guilty of doing exactly what they are accusing me of."

"But teaching is not a crime."

"That is up to the Goddess to decide," she replied with a stoic calm my empathy told me she did not truly feel. "I would be pleased to take your legal research, but you must promise me you will not speak even a single word of support at the trial. I would not have anything unfortunate happen to you because of my choices."

Although I did not understand why she would make such a request, as with my mother's fear a long ago, Rianna's profound sense of terror convinced me to accede to her wishes.

It wasn't until the trial that I finally understood the nature of my teacher's trepidation. The young people Mistress Rianna had taught through the years filled the audience that day, but like me, they watched in silent despair as Minister Acastas presented evidence of Mistress Rianna's unorthodox teaching methods. He painted her as a villain, trying to cause the most vulnerable of our society to doubt the Goddess. We were a room full of grateful students who knew in our hearts that our beloved teacher had done nothing wrong, but fear kept us silent.

I allowed myself of moment of hope as Mistress Rianna rose to present her defense. But even as she began her carefully constructed argument, using two millennia of Athena's own words to prove her innocence, I felt the wrath of the Goddess. The white-hot anger and the searing wave of pain that ripped through Rianna's mind hit me simultaneously.

Rianna and I cried out in unison as the agony of the Goddess' ire overwhelmed all other senses. This pain was not just a punishment for an outspoken mortal, but an obliteration of the mind that dared to have the offending thoughts. Joined by the tenuous ties of my empathy, I was pulled into the deep well of fire that was consuming everything that had once been Mistress Rianna's mind, and I screamed. Just before I was lost to sweet oblivion, I saw it—Athena's cruel sneer of contempt. It was in that moment that I began to understood the true nature of the Gods of Arcadia and how insignificant we mortals really were.

"Ardella?" the Goddess called, tearing me from my painful remembrance into my very uncomfortable present, "Do you have nothing to say?"

He could not be sure enough of the outcome to take such a radical action, the voice in my head screamed again. *How does one take back what has already been voiced?* "Forgive me. I am upset by the news of my brother. I did not mean to speak aloud," I offered weakly, but the Goddess was not in the mood to be placated.

"But you did speak aloud, Ardella. Explain yourself," Athena commanded.

I knew that this was my chance to adapt my words to fit the pleasure of the Goddess' mood. Perhaps explain in such a way as to not offend the Olympian. But for some reason I will never understand, that is not what I did. Instead, I told her the truth.

"Great Goddess, my brother Rafe and I often discussed Alexander. The Son of Ares may have started the Hermes sect on the aggressive path they have chosen, but nothing would be served by the death of one man."

"Did you not understand your role in the original search for the Son of Ares? Your gift was meant to save us from the evil nature of one man and his unfortunate influence on the less desirable elements of Arcadia."

"But the damage is already done," I offered boldly. "Pandora's box is empty, Great Goddess. I cannot imagine my brother would take the unthinkable risk of engaging in..."

The Goddess cut my explanation short. "Perhaps your brother felt the risk was worth taking," she interjected tersely. The little patience the Goddess had shown at my display of free will rapidly depleted. "Without Alexander the problem might not disappear, Ardella, but it could certainly be solved more easily. Don't you agree?"

Not really, I thought, but I knew from four years at the Academy and another ten years of serving the Goddess that her patience only went so far. Athena could be wise and patient, but she was still an Olympian who could kill even her favorite with a single thought.

"Of course," I murmured and lowered my head. Although so many words bubbled up from the depths of my tortured mind, I held my lips tightly shut so none of them could escape to further offend the Goddess. The moments stretched into an awkward silence and in that strange calm, I felt Athena's anger start to melt.

"You are quiet, my child," the Goddess finally whispered.

"Forgive me, Athena," I said. This time I looked directly into her grey eyes and saw they were actually filled with concern. It was in that moment that I realized I could feel her emotions. She was sad and upset, just as I was. Encouraged by this, I shared my burden with her. "It's just that Rafe...the Son of Ares will kill him for attacking Metropolis, won't he?"

"That is very likely," Athena said. There was genuine regret in her voice.

"Can't we help him?" I whispered.

"Why should we help him?" Athena replied, suddenly indifferent.

"Because..." I started to reply and realized I had no logical arguments to offer.

"Because he is your brother?" Athena suggested.

"Yes, I suppose. It just seems unfair. Even though he was exiled from New Athens, he fought harder than anyone to stop Alexander and the Hermians. Even this action was for our sake. It seems wrong just to abandon him."

"I appreciate all your brother has done for our cause, Ardella, but that does not mean that I can intervene on his behalf."

"So we just allow him to die? We sit back and do nothing?"

"Nothing is all I am allowed to do, child. "The Great Law binds all Olympians. If I try to help your brother, then it would seem as if I sent him to attack the Son of Ares. You wouldn't want that to happen, would you?"

"No, of course not, but he is an exile from New Athens. No one can hold you responsible for his actions."

"It is his status as an exile that allowed him to attack Metropolis without violating the Great Law."

"A clever way to twist the law to his advantage," I offered quietly, my mind starting to become suspicious of the Goddess' knowledge. *I wonder where he got the idea*?

"True. His cunning rivals even that of the Son of Ares. They are quite a pair," Athena offered with open admiration. "Rafe was able to act, because he acted alone, so now he must now face the consequences alone."

"That is a cruel reward. Rafe acts when even an Olympian could not and for his efforts he is forsaken."

"He failed, Ardella. The price of failure is sometimes death." Her tone was a mixture of cynicism and irritation. She was angry with my brother for failing. With sudden clarity I knew the Goddess of wisdom had put this insane idea into my brother's head. And now she was going to let him die without saying a word in his defense.

My anger exploded. I forgot in that moment where I was standing and to whom I was speaking. It nearly cost me my life. "You sent him. You put the idea into his head so he would do what you yourself could not."

A deadly silence filled the air all around us.

"And if I did?" Athena asked.

I sensed her annoyance, but would not relent. "Then you must save him. Please, Athena! If Alexander kills him, you're as guilty as ..."

"You overstep yourself, MORTAL!" Athena's voice was hard, but it was the tempest of her displeasure washing over me that trapped the words in my throat. I quaked involuntarily at this sudden contact with the full intensity of an Olympian's rage. It was just as I had felt on the day of Mistress Rianna's trial, but this time her anger was directed at me, not just reflected from another's mind. My head felt as though it was caught in the deadly embrace of a raging inferno. I crumbled to the floor.

"Mercy," I managed to choke out despite the intense pain that filled my head. White-hot Olympian rage engulfed me. My Academy trained mind could not help but appreciate the irony that in trying to save my brother, I might actually die before him, but all too soon, I could think of nothing but the pain. My mind teetered on the brink of oblivion and then the unthinkable happened.

Effortlessly, the Goddess shielded me from her emotions. Between one heartbeat and the next, the intense fire of her Olympian rage was gone. I took a deep breath as the pain faded.

"Thank you," I managed to whisper, although I was unable to find enough energy to lift my head.

There was a long moment of silence before Athena spoke. "I forget sometimes that you can feel as I do, Ardella," Athena offered repentantly. "I should have been more careful."

"The fault is mine, Great Goddess, for angering you," I said, finally able to raise my eyes to meet hers. For a moment it seemed as though they glistened with unshed tears, but I knew that was impossible.

"I understand, my child. We both care for Rafe," she replied. Her motherly, sympathetic tone touched my troubled heart.

"His exile from New Athens has always distressed me, but to know that he might die," I confessed.

Athena stared at me with her unfathomable grey eyes and spoke her next words very carefully, "Understand this clearly, Ardella. I care for your brother, even as you do, but *I* cannot do anything to intervene."

Finally, her words reach my simple, mortal mind. *I understand where she's been trying to guide me,* I thought. "But I can. I can go ..." I said. My heart suddenly filled with hope.

"Stop, Ardella." She motioned for silence, "Do not tell me what you plan to do."

I looked up into the face of the Goddess. Her features were those of a woman not much older than me, but her eyes were ancient. They had seen the fall of ancient Troy; experienced the golden age of the original Athens; witnessed the rise of the Roman Empire; was stirred by the Renaissance; wept at the carnage of four world wars; and observed the refugees of Earth flee to Arcadia over 2000 years ago. Despite everything she had seen and done, the Goddess Athena was not omnipotent. She was trapped, just as we humble mortals, by the Great Law of the Olympians. For just a moment it seemed we were not so different after all.

"That way you are not responsible," I said. I was beginning to understand what Athena wanted me to do - what she could not. She could not help Rafe directly, but she would not be unhappy if I were to take the necessary steps to free my twin. "Just like you were not responsible for Rafe's attack."

"The Great Law of the Olympians is a delicate balance, Ardella," she replied seriously. "If I openly break it, even when justified, I called down the wrath of the all the other Olympians not only upon me, but upon all my followers. Never forget that Alexander's great Metropolis is built on the bones of my sister Artemis' children. I will never allow anyone to endanger my sect."

"So you must find others to do what you cannot."

"Unfortunately, that is the path I must walk."

"Surely it would be more efficient to control the actions of those around you rather than constantly trying to manipulate their footsteps," I thought, but dare not say aloud. Ironically Athena seemed to be having a very similar thought.

"Every person on Arcadia has free will. It is one of our gifts to mankind. I can try to guide my followers, but they must make the decisions for themselves." She appeared calm but as an empath I could feel the strong resentment underlying her words. Her strange emotional response seemed to suggest her words were a lie.

For the first time in my life I wondered if there was something about the free will of mankind that even the Olympians could not violate.

Chapter 2

The sunlight gleamed off the metal skin of the automatons as they marched menacingly across the plain of Artemis toward the unsuspecting city of Metropolis.

**Denarian Strom of the Academy of Metropolis
Two thousand, six hundred and ninty-three years *Ab Terra Condita***

I COULD SEE the stone walls of Metropolis long before I reached them. They towered high into the horizon, obstructing the distant afternoon sun, and stretched through the rolling hills of what was once the Great Forest of Artemis. I had known that Metropolis rivaled even New Athens in size, but until that moment I did not truly comprehend its magnitude. If the scale of Metropolis had not been terrifying enough, I could not help but notice the carnage of human and mechanical bodies still strewn across the plain that lay just this side of the great iron gates. Metal heads and limbs had been ripped from their torsos, their wounds spilling wires instead of blood. The men of Metropolis had already begun stripping the metal soldiers of any useful components.

The humans on the other hand, while their bodies lay in less gruesome forms of disrepair, were what truly shook me to the core. I had never in my life seen multiple corpses. I was not unfamiliar with death, but it had always been someone elderly or ill. On one occasion I had witnessed a tragic accident that had killed two students at the Academy, but before me was a horrifying scene made even more so because it was intentionally inflicted and totally unnecessary. Most of the dead were already being hauled away to a massive funeral pyre that polluted the air with its painfully foul odor.

My mind recalled the battle scene I had witnessed on Athena's peplos. *Was this how that battle ended? Am I so naïve that I've never even contemplated the aftermath?* Death and destruction were part of war. I had studied the history of Earth warfare more closely than almost any mortal on Arcadia and yet, I was horrified by the gruesome scene. When I recalled that my own twin brother had been the cause of the massacre I saw before me, a new wave of revulsion washed over me. I buried it, pretending to watch calmly as the men of Metropolis went about their cheerless task.

No one stopped my progress across the field of the recent battle; no one asked who dared to enter the gates of the city or stood to oppose my climb to the citadel. It almost seemed as if they were expecting me. I passed through the gates and took my time up the incline to the city's center, Alexander's stronghold. As I walked, my gaze lingered on the astounding sites that met my eyes the further I advanced. At first glance, Metropolis reminded me of virtually every other sect I had visited – which considering its reputation, surprised me. The citizens went about their work, occasionally pausing to whisper and stare at the stranger. I soon realized that each captive sect had been divided into a "ring" of the circular city, their cultures quickly taking hold inside their new "home."

Having been soothed by this attempt at normality I was immediately startled to find that the innermost ring, centered around Alexander's citadel, was a mixture of cultures; followers of Demeter, Aphrodite, Apollo, and Hermes all living together. Considering the jealous nature of the Olympians, plurality such as this did not exist anywhere else on Arcadia. It was striking. Their homes were side by side, the buildings a hodgepodge of architectures. Their children played with one another in the streets as if it were natural for the daughters of Demeter to mingle with the sons of Apollo or the children of Aphrodite to play with the heirs of Athena.

Before I knew it, I stood at the steps of the citadel of Metropolis. I had reached the heart of the enemy stronghold. A quiver of terror stole up my spine as I contemplated the large cyclopean stones of the enemy's fortress. I was so small and insignificant standing beside the enormous edifice. I was one mortal against the might of the Son of Ares and his empire. The urge to flee gripped me and I had to force myself to stand firm. *I've come too far to turn back now,* I thought.

My long white cape billowed in the gusting wind as I entered the Great Hall of Metropolis. The fabric danced like the sails of one of the great naval vessels that long ago roamed the seas of ancient Earth. Although I had no honor guards with me, the crowd in the throne room cleared a path for me, as they had in the streets of the city, without a single word being spoken. Conversation stopped. Everyone peered at me from the edges of the room as they moved in silence to the small wooden benches. Above their heads were oval, glassless windows cut out of the stone walls, meant to let light and air into the throne room. They were arranged in pairs, which disturbed me. It was almost as if I was surrounded by many giant pairs of glowing yellow eyes—Olympian eyes. The irony was not lost on me; I had little doubt there were indeed Olympian's watching the mortal melodrama unfold.

At the far wall sat Alexander. His throne was ornate to be sure but it was no match for the one on the step above him. The top of the dais was consumed by what was surely the seat of Hermes, since it was wrought in solid gold and twice the size that any normal human would need. Behind the throne, a colorful tapestry took up the entire wall. I examined the tapestry briefly, noting that the winged Hermes overlooked a slightly older version of Metropolis, which showed no signs of the now under construction outer ring.

My eyes drifted downward to the other empty chair on the dais. It was the only feminine aspect of the entire scene. The wood was carved with ornate painted flowers that were so lifelike that from a distance one might think them real. *This must be the chair for Hermes' consort*, I realized. *How odd that there was a chair left for a woman who had died almost 75 years ago.* I wondered briefly: *Is Hermes different from his siblings? Is he able to understand the emotion we mortals called love?* My mind shuttered at the possibility and admitted it was more likely Olympian obliviousness. The perception of time for immortals was different and the 75-year gesture was really only a few moments to a God.

I moved carefully across the uneven paving stones, trying to exude a tranquil confidence that I did not feel. I did not allow my steps to slow until I stood before the dais. It had been years since I had seen him. Despite all the time and all of the reports of his actions over the past decade, in my mind Alexander had remained who he had once been, Lysander—the frightened young man that I had known so long ago.

The man cloaked in black before me was brooding and fearsome. His warm brown hair, set over cool blue eyes and fair features, did not lighten his appearance. The thin mustache and hooded gaze gave his face a sinister quality. His strong muscular shoulders carried the black and golden cloth that declared him the leader of the Hermians. Even without the symbols woven into his clothes, his confidant expression and arrogant stare would have made it easy to recognize him as the Son of Ares. Unfortunately, he did not remind me at all of the boy I had known in New Athens and the memory I had carried all these years was at last shattered into oblivion.

"Welcome to Metropolis, Lady Ardella. You are either very foolish or very courageous to enter my domain all alone." Alexander's voice was velvet confidence. However, I could sense only a slight twinge of suspicion because he seemed to be hiding his emotions from me (something I thought only the Olympians could do). "To what do we owe this unexpected visit?"

Despite the fear that blossomed in my chest, I made myself speak the words I had prepared. "You were not expecting me? You hold my twin brother captive. You didn't think I would come to his aide?" I did my best to match his tone, but I was not as confident as I would have liked.

"Your brother attacked Metropolis," he replied in a brisk, businesslike manner. "I am well within my rights to hold him captive. I am surprised the Athena sect sent you to plead on his behalf."

"I am not here as a member of the Athena sect or the Goddess' inner Council, but as the sister of your prisoner," I clarified. I tried to sound humble yet authoritative. I was by nature a self-confidant person. However, I couldn't help but wonder if others obeyed my orders simply because of my status as the Daughter of Athena. *Did I really have the gift to sway others to my cause?* I needed to be very persuasive, if I had any hope of saving my brother.

"So, Athena agrees it is within my rights to execute Rafe for breaking the Great Law of the Olympians?" he inquired. He knew I had to admit the truth or risk the followers of Athena.

"Athena understands Rafe has committed a transgression against the Olympian code. She does not condone his actions," I admitted with some trepidation.

Alexander smiled triumphantly.

I quickly added, "Perhaps you should turn him over to the Olympians for justice?"

I resisted the urge to scowl at him. And despite his best attempt to conceal his own feelings, I was hit by a powerful wave of hate at the mention of the Gods of Arcadia.

"I don't think I would find justice there. I am not sure that your brother's actions did not in fact have the unspoken blessing of some of the Gods of Arcadia." His sarcastic tone betrayed only a fraction of the frustration I felt as it seeped from beneath his tough emotional armor.

I knew from my recent conversation with Athena that the Olympians were quite adept at finding loopholes in the Great Law. *That must be the source of the frustration.* I bore no sympathy for him however; *had he not done the same with his raids on other sects?* "The Olympians had nothing to do with the attack on Metropolis. I believe my brother's actions were motivated by something of a more personal nature."

"Personal?" Alexander scoffed.

"Rafe was trying to capture you. He has been blamed all these years for your escape from New Athens and your reign of chaos for the last decade," I suggested, employing one of the many lines of reasoning I had rehearsed on my journey from New Athens to Metropolis.

"His hatred of me is no excuse for breaking the Great Law of the Olympians," he retorted.

"I believe his hatred of you clouded his judgment. His attack was not on Metropolis and the followers of Hermes...it was on you." I forced myself to stay calm even as the emotions of the crowd surged around me and filled my being. "That does not violate the Great Olympian Law. Attempted murder is not the same as making war, just as bullying and stealing from your neighbors is not making war." I managed to complete this rehearsed argument despite the now uncomfortable atmosphere in the citadel. The anger I felt from the crowd clearly indicated they did not appreciate this belittling of the attack that had killed so many, especially from an outsider.

Alexander, who shared his people's feelings, rose from his throne, his limbs shaking. He made no attempt to hide his rage, which poured off of him in waves and threated to drive me to my knees.

"Tell that to the twenty-two men who were killed as well as all who were wounded before your brother and his mechanical soldiers were stopped," he retorted. "You may use that argument to justify the assassins you sent to kill me, but that won't work in this case. No matter who his target was; Rafe is responsible for the deaths of 22 citizens of Metropolis."

The anger that accompanied those final words caused me to lower my head in pain. I thought I was going to faint and whispered, "Your anger is…" I tried to explain as my hands instinctively rubbed my temples to try to stop the force threatening to burst my head from within.

"Justified!" he said forcefully, although I felt his anger lessening. He was blocking his rage just as Athena had done earlier to protect me.

Did he realize his intense anger was hurting me? I wondered. *That's impossible. He's the Son of Ares, so my discomfort would have no effect on him.* I took a deep breath and lifted my gaze to meet his. "Forgive me, Stratagos," I said with all humility. "I do not belittle the tragedy of so much death. I was horrified as I walk across the plain of Artemis, but motivation is relevant, otherwise your justice is actually just revenge."

"You may call it revenge or justice. It doesn't matter to me, as long as your brother pays for his crimes," Alexander proclaimed to a roar of approval from the crowd around the dais.

"Are you sure you hold the high moral ground, Alexander? You and your people tread dangerously close to breaking the Great Law of the Olympians yourselves. It seems rather hypocritical to play the innocent now. How many have been killed during your raids upon other sects? At the massacre of Argos alone..."

"Enough!" he bellowed, although it was the strong wave of sorrow that hit me, which stopped my words.

I had expected anger, *but why did the Son of Ares feel regret over the massacre of Argos?* I wondered.

"This is not a debate. We were discussing your brother's crime, Lady Ardella." Alexander sat back down, his voice and his display of emotion now tightly controlled. "He is my prisoner, and will remain in a cell awaiting his fate no matter what arguments you employ."

I was desperate. I kneeled at his feet and sent a silent prayer to Great Athena that my plan would work. This was not my best idea, but it seemed to be the only choice left to me. "Is there nothing I can say to persuade you to show mercy?" I whispered.

"You are clever, Ardella, but I doubt even you can alter your brother's fate now."

I rose slowly and let him know with my gaze that I challenged his right to determine my sibling's fate. I would take more desperate actions. "May I share a story with your court?"

"Can I stop you?" Alexander scoffed and those near the dais laughed at his comment.

I didn't acknowledge his insult, but instead began my story. "There was a young boy named Lysander who lived in New Athens," I began. I drew upon my theatrical training at the

Academy to addresses them. The art of storytelling had long been practiced among the followers of Athena and I had proven to be an excellent student. I set out to win over the crowd and thus influence the Son of Ares. "Lysander was smart and ambitious, but sadly, he found himself born into the servant class. Despite his thirst for knowledge and his natural gifts, he was not allowed to reach above his station or to attend the Academy. He tried in vain to hide the anger and frustration he felt at the unfair limitations on his future."

"A sad, but unremarkable story," Alexander quipped. He gave no indication that he was the boy of whom I spoke.

I could feel the emotions of the people in the hall. As I spoke, their attitudes turned in support of the young boy in my story and by association me. It was the effect I was trying to achieve and so I continued the story as if Alexander hadn't interrupted me.

"The boy Lysander never dreamed that his circumstances could become worse, but they did. One night guards came to the home he shared with his mother and sister and took him away. He fought them, but he could not win. He found himself in a locked room in the Tower of Athena."

Alexander interrupted me, "If you think these people are unaware of who and what I am, then you are mistaken, Lady Ardella. You tell a tale they already know." While his voice contained a hint of annoyance, he was doing an excellent job of masking what he was feeling from my empathy. I could tell by the emotions of those in the room, however, that there was some truth to what he said. Nevertheless, I knew I could reveal aspects of the tale as yet unknown to anyone but Lysander and myself. I needed to shock them to confuse their emotions and turn the tide in my favor.

"Do they know it all?" I asked and then continued where I left off before he could respond, "Lysander soon learned that the

Council of Athena believed he was the Son of Ares who appeared once each century to cause chaos on Arcadia. He became the center of a debate in New Athens: should he live or die? Should he be condemned for crimes he had yet to commit?

"This is a touching story, but I don't see what it has to do with our current situation," he replied dismissively.

"Are you sure you cannot see the connection? Not so long ago, Lysander, you were the prisoner awaiting your fate in a lonely tower cell. Surely you of all people can feel empathy for my brother?"

This time his anger came through loud and clear. "You dare to compare my imprisonment for being born the Son of Ares with your brother's merciful incarceration pending sentencing for his unforgivable crimes? He is lucky to still be among the living after slaughtering so many of our brave sons."

No! With that outburst I felt the crowd transform—their anger and resentment at my presence renewed by his words. In a voice my rhetoric master would have said was far too whiny, I offered, "I did not mean your crimes were equivalent, but that you might feel empathy for a fellow prisoner condemned to death."

"You are the one with the gift of empathy, Ardella. Even when I went by the name Lysander, I never had your appreciation for the feeling of others."

Again, those nearest the dais laughed at his comment. I reminded myself that I was speaking to Alexander—the harsh and seasoned Son of Ares. It was not going to be possible to play on his pity – or the mercy of the citizens of Metropolis.

"A life for a life then," I tried a new strategy, "Rafe once helped save your life now you can save his."

Alexander laughed. "Have you chosen to rewrite history, Ardella? Don't forget young Lysander was there as well." He leaned forward in his chair and whispered conspiratorially, "You and I both know that Rafe was not the one who released me from my imprisonment in New Athens all those years ago." His gesture suggested his words were only for me, but his voice echoed through the room.

I felt the shock and curiosity of the crowd, some of whom were followers of Athena and all too familiar with very public trial and exile of my twin. I had kept the truth a secret for over a decade. *What would happen if I said the words aloud?*

"I owe Rafe nothing," he finished clearly and loud enough for all to understand that my twin was innocent of at least one of the crimes for which he had been accused.

I had to take a deep breath to gather my courage for what I had to say next. "But you would agree that you owe the person who released you? You owe that person your life?"

"I do not currently hold that person's life in my hands. I do not see how I could repay such a debt," Alexander smiled knowingly at me – certain I would never reveal the truth.

My mind was racing. The crowd's growing anxiety and tenor only added to my distress and began to encroach upon my sanity. I had rehearsed many different tactics in my battle of words with Alexander. I thought I had covered all the possible directions this conversation could go and had found a way to win the debate regardless. This turn of the events, however, was not one I had considered. I was rushing headlong toward a cliff. If I allowed myself to go over the edge, my future would be forever altered. I could never go back.

Now that the moment had arrived, I wondered, *Can I actually do it?* I wasn't sure I was that strong. I had let my brother accept the blame and live in exile for a crime I knew that he did not commit, while I lived a life of privilege as a member of the Council of Athena. *If I had been stronger, that would never have happened.* Suddenly I knew this was what I had to do.

"I can verify what you say is true. It was not Rafe who helped you escape from New Athens. There was no reason for him to have been exiled. I was the one who released you all those years ago!" My proclamation had a deafening effect. I sensed the shock everyone in the room felt, causing the words of explanation, which I had held inside for so long, to just spill from my lips. "I released you because I felt pity for your plight. I could not see allowing an innocent boy to be killed for crimes that he might someday commit. I did not think before I acted and then I was too much of a coward to speak up after I realized my mistake. I allowed my brother to be punished for a crime I knew he did not commit, because I did not want to suffer the consequences of my actions."

I heard the murmur of surprise surge through the crowd, and then I felt the tension of the moment explode, filling the room with its unseen energy. I wondered how long it would be before all of Arcadia learned that the leader of the resistance against the Son of Ares was also its greatest traitor.

Relief at my long overdue confession, and the shock on Alexander's face, who thought he had won the day by calling my bluff, made me giddy. Alexander realized this was not going his way, and I could feel the anxiety bubbling up in his chest. He was not sure how this debate was going to end, and it made him nervous.

When Alexander did not speak I decided to press my advantage, "So you admit that I am the one who saved you in New Athens and that you owe me your life."

"Yes, you were the one to release me," he agreed reluctantly.

"And...?" I prompted.

"I grant that I owe you my life, but again I don't hold your life in my hands, so this argument is pointless."

"A life for a life!" I exclaimed. I knew this was a dangerous path to tread, but I was unwilling to relent after having come so far, "You owe me your life. I owe my brother for ruining his life. Allow me to trade myself for Rafe and both our debts are paid."

"Do you have any idea what you are saying? This is not a game Ardella. If I allow you to take Rafe's place, you condemn the Athena sect..."

"No!" I interrupted. I had to make him understand or everything up to this moment would be pointless. "Rafe was an individual, an exile, not a representative of any Olympian or their sect. If I had taken responsibility for my actions so long ago—I would have been the exile. When I take his place I do so as an individual without a home or the protection of an Olympian."

"Again you are hiding behind your brother. You are saying because he was an exile, we are to assume his attack on Metropolis was not sanctioned by the Olympians. You expect me to believe Athena did not know of his plans?"

"I have served Athena for almost a decade now and I know for certain that she would never allow anyone to commit an act that would put her followers in danger," I declared.

Alexander's eyebrows arched in doubt. "So now you put words into the Goddess' mouth?"

"Those were her very words to me just before I left New Athens," I answered, truthfully. I saw his look of surprise at this revelation.

"Nevertheless Rafe did attack my people and his punishment may well be death. Are you willing to die in your brother's place?"

I paused at his words just as he intended. I did not want to die, but I could not allow my brother to die. Just as Alexander owed me his life, I owed my brother. If I had to die to save him—so be it.

"I will accept the consequences for Rafe's actions," I agreed. If the roar of voices that filled the citadel were a single note, then the tide of raw emotions that swept through the hall at my answer was a minor chord played full volume. I lowered my head at the pain and closed my eyes against the looming tears. My head was in agony and the world was spiraling out of control.

"You don't have to do this," a warm, comforting voice whispered. It sounded like Lysander. They were exactly the words I wanted to hear, but they were too late. As I looked up to see pity in the eyes of my nemesis, I knew I could not turn back. This was my fate.

In a clear and melodic tone that carried throughout the noisy hall, I symbolically jumped off the cliff. "I call upon the Olympians to judge me. I call upon Athena to show all of Arcadia that I should be punished and my brother set free!"

Although I had not told Athena what I planned to do, I knew the Goddess would be with me in Alexander's citadel. I counted upon her curiosity and her desire to see my manipulation of the Son of Ares to gain my brother's freedom. I hoped she would send a sign, or perhaps make the sky rumble to show my words were true. It was in that moment I learned that I did not know the Goddess Athena as well as I thought.

A bolt of lightning suddenly split the air with its primal power, shattering the roof of the citadel above the dais. As I watched the huge stone shards move closer, the moment froze in my mind. My certainty that this plan to gain Rafe's freedom had been all my own idea crumbled as I realized that although Athena couldn't have known that I would ask for a sign, she must have suspected. She must have wanted me to call upon her. She manipulated me, just as she had my brother. And now she was using my desperate gesture to her advantage. *She didn't send me here to save Rafe, she sent me here to bring an end to Alexander.*

The lightning bolt to the roof would not only kill me, but everyone around me—including the Son of Ares. My brother had failed, but now I would, by my own actions, finish what he had started.

"Ardella," Alexander cried as he wrapped his arms around me, throwing me backwards. Together we rolled down the stairs of the dais and I felt the concussive blast shoot through my body as the stone roof hit the top of the platform. I heard screams of horror and pain, but realized none were my own.

My body was entwined with my enemy and entombed between the stone of the ceiling and that of the floor. In that total darkness that surrounded us, I heard Lysander whisper, "Are you alright?"

Suddenly I felt like laughing. "I am still alive," I replied. Despite the best laid plans of the Goddess of Wisdom, the Son of Ares and the Daughter of Athena were both still in the land of the living.

Chapter 3

One cannot predict the future – only see one of the many paths our lives may follow. The reality of premonition is that our very knowledge of the future changes it.

Creusa, 12th Pythia of Apollo
512 years *Ab Terra Condita*

I SAT FOR a long time on one of the benches near the doors of the citadel without moving. The cool, hard surface was a stark contrast to my overheated limbs. I was free and yet could not quite believe the truth. It had felt like an eternity that I had been trapped within the darkness of that the stone cocoon with my nemesis. Thick, stale air formed a haze around me. It required all of my energy just to breathe. During those agonizing hours, I found comfort from the hand holding mine in the darkness—the hand of the Son of Ares. When the first ray of light appeared as the rescuers removed the rubble that had trapped us—it was the most incredible sight I had ever seen.

Although I had survived Athena's attempt on my life, I could not help but feel the evaporating shock and sadness of the less fortunate who lay under the rubble of the collapsed roof. *More deaths to be laid at the Goddess' feet*, I thought, *or perhaps this time they should be placed at mine.* Was my naivety the cause of this suffering? My head pounded not only from my injuries, but also from the raw emotions all around me. I wasn't sure how much longer I could stand the anguish.

"That is my responsibility, not the Council's," I heard Alexander bellow.

"I doubt Hermes and the other Council members will agree," a tall, thin man in the grey robes of the Hermian Council replied. Suddenly his gaze fell on me. "What is she still doing here?" he asked scowling.

"Lady Ardella is none of your concern, Councilor Peryn," Alexander contended.

"If I were Strategos, she would be in a cell next to her brother."

Alexander's sudden movement took both Councilor Peryn and I by surprise. Peryn's expression changed from anger to fear as Alexander seized the front of his robes and shoved him against the ruined wall of the citadel. "I did not seek your opinion, Councilor. I am Strategos—chosen by Hermes himself to lead. I suggest you remember that."

"I meant no offense...Strategos," Councilor Peryn managed to choke out, despite the intense pressure of Alexander's fist against his windpipe.

Alexander released the counselor, leaned toward him and in a deadly calm voice said, "Your Strategos forgives your momentary lapse in judgment, but remember I am also the Son of Ares. The God of War is not so forgiving."

The unfortunate Councilor staggered away with no further comment.

Without even a glance my direction Alexander returned

to what he had been doing. I briefly wondered. *Had he been defending me or responding to a challenge to his authority?* I decided it didn't really matter. Since the Strategos' emotions were carefully shielded from me, I began to be more and more aware of the citizens of Metropolis all around me. I found myself watching in fascination as Alexander coordinated the rescue efforts. His orders were obeyed without question. Rather than the fear and resentment that I had expected, I could feel that his authoritative attitude gave those around him strength and hope.

My mind reeled at the inverted twist that my reality had taken. My beloved twin brother had murdered innocent people, while my patron Goddess had taken additional lives, intending to include me and the Son of Ares in the body count. To make the absurd scene even more ludicrous I now watched as my sworn enemy played the hero of Metropolis.

"This is wrong," I heard Athena whisper in my head. This startled me. It wasn't that I never experienced the Goddess' telepathy before, but up until now it had always been when I was in her presence. I had never even suspected she could communicate at such a great distance. Again the awesome power of the Olympians terrified me.

"What is wrong?" I asked softly.

"Do not speak aloud. They will hear you," the Goddess chastised me, causing my already aching head additional agony. *"Think your words and I will hear them,"* she instructed.

"*What is wrong*?" I asked again, but this time without vocalizing the thought.

"He lives," she hissed - just a hint of her frustration travelling with her words.

"*As do I*," I replied softly. "*Your lightning was not very accurate,*" my inner voice added sarcastically.

"Don't be impertinent." Athena barked.

Terror stole the air from my lungs.

"You heard that?" Fear blossomed in my chest as I realized the implication. *"Athena, I didn't mean to send the second thought to you,"* I said warily.

"Because you are so far away, Ardella, I must maintain a foothold in your mind to communicate. Therefore I hear everything," she explained.

"Then you can actually read my thoughts—all my thoughts?" I asked terrified. I took a deep breath as my mother's advice came flooding into my head, *"You must learn to control your words in the presence of the Goddess."* Words I could control, but no one could control their thoughts!

"Why would your mother give you such advice, my child? There is no need for you to fear. The lightning was not intended for you."

"Even if I was not the target, you could have killed me along with Alexander."

"I couldn't aim it directly at him. I had to..." she started to reply and then stopped abruptly mid-thought.

Was that actually a twinge of guilt I felt from her? I wondered. *"You had to make it look like you were trying to punish me, and only killed the Son of Ares by accident,"* I finished for her. I felt a tremor of panic shake my limbs as I realized in my exhausted and highly emotional state I had no hope of controlling my thoughts and feelings. Before this conversation was over, the Goddess was going to be offended by my thoughts and there was a good chance I was going to die.

"I had a chance to eliminate the Son of Ares. You must understand why I had to do it?" The Goddess said serenely.

"Unfortunately I am beginning to understand your true motivations all too well, Great Goddess..." the thought escaped before I could stop it.

"*And disapprove,*" Athena scoffed. "*I cannot recall the last time a mortal dared to express disappointment in my actions.*"

I tried in vain to banish the anger and fear from my mind. My only hope for survival was to tell her the truth. "*Forgive me, Great Goddess. I did not express disapproval; I only thought it.*"

"*I fail to see the difference,*" Athena retorted.

"*I am but a weak mortal. I am always careful not to offend you with my words, but you are inside my head. We mortals cannot control the way we feel or silence the stray thoughts that pop into our minds.*"

"*So all these years you have only said what you believed I wanted to hear?*" she asked.

I was certain I heard a hint of disappointment in her tone, which made me feel guilty; a feeling that surprised me. Despite everything that had happened today, my first impulse was not to disappoint this powerful Olympian.

I replied carefully, "*No, Athena, please do not think that.*" Apprehension wove its delicate web within my heart. "*Each time I have expressed support for your words and actions, I was being truthful.*"

"*And when my words and actions displease your mortal sensibilities?*" she asked.

"*I remain silent,*" I started to explain diplomatically until my subconscious decided to finish the thought for me "*as do all your followers who wish to live.*" I winced as I anticipated Athena's displeasure. I tried to get my wandering thoughts under control, "*We wish to please you, great Athena. We mortals understand that sometimes the words and actions of an Olympian are beyond our comprehension.*"

"*So you understand my action in this case, but do not approve,*" she concluded.

"*Since your action was meant to kill me, no!*" my sarcastic inner voice snorted. I winced and then added more carefully, *"Like most mortals—I want to live."*

"Even if your sacrifice would have meant the end of the Son of Ares?"

"Why did it have to be my sacrifice?" I asked as the pain of her betrayal squeezed my heart. I fought back the tears as I ached for this indifferent, immortal being to recognize that her actions had hurt me. *"Your crusade to bring about the destruction of the Son of Ares is more important than anything or anyone—even one who has served you faithfully all her life. Even one you call a daughter."*

I sensed not even a twinge of remorse from the Goddess I had served for almost a decade. Only her righteous ire travelled the tenuous link across Arcadia, *"You mortals are too limited to see the greater picture. You are too tiny to see your role in order of things."*

I was nothing to this Olympian; nothing but a tool. Caught up in the torrent of this betrayal I could not control my resentment. *"I understand my role in the order of things all too well. I was just a means to an end for you—just a pawn to live or die for your amusement."*

There was a long pause. I wondered for a moment if the Goddess was still in my mind.

"Apparently you can hear my inner thoughts as well. That is... unexpected. You know that you are more than a pawn, Ardella. You are my daughter. I care for you as much as I can care for any mortal," Athena replied softly.

Instead of soothing my troubled mind, her attempt to placate me had the opposite effect. I felt the hot flush of anger surge through my soul and I had no chance to filter my next thought. *"You are an Olympian and incapable of understanding love. You don't care for me or my brother."*

"Watch yourself, Ardella," Athena warned.

"Please, Athena, you must understand I cannot control the stray thoughts that enter my head," I implored, but my inner voice had to add, *"Why should I fear you? You have already tried to kill me once today and failed."*

"Again you overstep yourself, mortal!" Athena bellowed in my head. I felt her Olympian anger explode in my mind. Unexpectedly, the distance muted its intensity. It was not pleasant, but it was not deadly either. I felt her surprise even as I a felt my own. Neither of us could believe that the hot white pain was not tearing through my mind. I felt a sudden rush of relief and then freedom.

Freedom—in that one simple emotion I found the strength for defiance. It was something I had never dreamed I was capable of; I suspect neither had Athena.

"While I am being honest with you, Great Goddess, I would like to tell you that I don't appreciate being manipulated."

"You don't appreciate?" she scoffed.

"You didn't send me to Metropolis to rescue Rafe. You sent me here so you could kill Alexander. Just as you sent Rafe to his doom before me."

"Ardella!" she hissed.

"If you wanted the Son of Ares dead, you should have killed him yourself. Oh I forgot – you can't kill him, can you? The Olympians are as trapped by the Great as we puny mortals," I scoffed.

Athena's surprise quickly gave way to irritation and she snapped, *"You are a fool, Ardella. You could never have saved your brother. You sacrificed yourself for nothing. There is no pity in Alexander."*

Her taunt stole all my righteous anger. Suddenly I saw the situation from her perspective and suspected that she was right. I was not only a pawn, but stupid one as well. I came to Metropolis because I wanted to believe I could save my twin brother by matching wits with the Son of Ares. It was a foolish belief. Despair threatened to crush my chest as I struggled to breathe. I felt the Goddess' satisfaction that her words had managed to inflict the pain her distant emotions could not. Even without the stress of this conversation, my head was pounding in agony. Despite my exhaustion, I managed to tap a reserve of strength I didn't know I possessed. I would not give up just because the Athena decreed it was impossible.

"You are wrong, Athena. I will save Rafe." My whole body trembled as I rose, although whether from the physical or emotional strain I could not be sure. I could not change the fact that Athena had tricked me, but I was going to free my brother. My feet carried me toward Alexander with one purpose in my heart and mind.

As I approached Alexander, I whispered, "I must speak with you."

"I am busy, Lady Ardella. Perhaps later," he replied.

I was not in the right frame of mind to be dismissed after everything that I had been through. "I need to speak with you, NOW," I insisted.

I saw his head tilt and amusement fill his eyes at my imperious tone.

"Indeed," he said, turning toward me speculatively.

Good. I have his attention. "I wish to discuss my brother."

I felt the lance of irritation strike Alexander's chest, "I am through talking about your brother. Thanks to him and your cursed Goddess, I have a great deal of work to do," he said turning back to the rescue operations.

"Lysander, you promised his life for..." I insisted. I reached out and touched his arm.

This time, the raging inferno of anger and frustration came pouring from his body. He spun around wildly and yanked me against his chest. "My name is Alexander," he bellowed as he forced me to look up at him. "And I promised you nothing."

I felt the tears bubbling to the surface but I forced them away. I had not let Athena make me cry, and I wasn't about to let the Son of Ares bring me to tears.

"I didn't mean..." I began.

But he continued as if he had not heard me. "You are in no position to ask anything. You came here seeking a life for a life. Well, I just saved your life. As far as I am concerned, we are even," he hissed. When my eyes widened, he scoffed, "It hasn't even occur to you that you are alive because of me.

I'd been there and knew what had transpired. *So why did his words surprise me? By the Goddess—the Son of Ares had saved me from Athena.*

"I know you saved me. I was there when you..." I stammered, and then stopped and took a deep breath. "I just need to talk to you," I murmured softly as one rebel tear managed to escape down my cheek.

There was a long silence as the air around us grew still. The roar of his laughter broke the strange spell and caused my heart to sink. "You're not in the Tower of Athena anymore, my lady. No one here has to jump to do your bidding," he replied contemptuously as he pushed me away from his chest.

"You are a most unreasonable man," I mumbled.

Again his haughty laughter filled my ears. "What do you expect, Ardella? I am the Son of Ares," he said, and then turned back to the rescue efforts.

"*You are a fool, Ardella. You could never have saved your brother. You threw your life away for nothing,*" Athena taunted in my head.

"*I have come too far to give up on Rafe,*" I replied.

I chased after Alexander. Frustration welled up in my throat just as I reached him. "I won't let you kill my brother," I said firmly, striking is back with my fist.

He turned and the cruel smile on his face burned the last of my defiance to ash. "Your Goddess just did her worst and failed. How did you plan to stop me?"

The chaos and stress of the last few days finally took their toll on my weary soul. The cold wave of reality hit me like a tidal wave. *I can't fix this; my brother is going to die*, I thought.

This time my eyes brimmed with tears that I could not stop. Despair took control. "Please," I croaked. Like when I was a little girl scared of going to the Academy, the floodgates burst open and tears rolled down my cheeks, leaving me unable to form coherent words.

"By the Goddess, Ardella. Don't do that," Alexander groaned as his arms went around me and pulled me into his warm, comforting chest. The hours in the darkness had taught me to crave the comfort my nemesis offered, I allowed myself to be held in his arms and draw upon his strength. I forgot where I was and who I was as the Son of Ares pulled the sorrow from my chest like slivers of metal drawn by a magnet. Slowly, my sobs ceased, but still I did not move from his embrace.

This time there was no laughter in his voice when he spoke, "I am too tired to deal with this right now. Please, Ardella, go back to your escort. Return tomorrow and I promise, we will talk about your brother."

Pressed together as we were I could feel his compassion and concern seeping from his body into mine. His words were not a lie. *Is this real? Is it possible that the Son of Ares can show me compassion, when my own Goddess would have seen me dead?* A tiny seed of hope was born in that moment, and it was that fragile promise that loosened my tongue and made me tell him the truth. "I have nowhere to go," I managed to whisper.

"I know you want to save your brother, but nothing can be

accomplished tonight. Go back to your escort."

"You don't understand," I said softly. "I sent my escort away before I entered Metropolis."

"Why would you send them away? How did you plan to return to...?" he asked confused. Suddenly the concern and compassion were washed away by a strong burst of anger. The Son of Ares was furious. His grip on my arms tightened, although I doubt he realized what he was doing.

"Were you afraid I would harm your escort?" he demanded, "Or did you believe that I would imprison or kill you upon entering Metropolis?"

I took a deep breath and tried to decide how to respond. "You are the Son of Ares. I didn't know what to expect." I could not comprehend why he was so angry about my precautions. He was my mortal enemy. Therefore, my concerns were reasonable under those circumstances. But I knew from his emotional reaction that Alexander was deeply offended by my assumptions.

"Ardella of New Athens didn't know what to expect? But you are the great expert on the Son of Ares. You tell everyone on Arcadia what a vile monster I am," he hissed.

"What are you talking about?" I asked, confused. I felt his anger give way to an even more intense emotion: pain.

"Don't pretend you are not the bane of my existence, Ardella," he still sounded angry, but as he stared down at me, I saw the agony in his eyes. "I know you are the source of all the tales that make the citizens of Arcadia fear and hate me."

"You think that I make the citizens of Arcadia fear and hate you? You are the Son of Ares. The sole purpose of your existence is to create chaos."

"Listen to yourself, Ardella. Do you really believe that my purpose is to create chaos?"

"Your reign of terror across Arcadia is the cause of the

remorse I have lived with every day since I let you escape from New Athens."

"You're a hypocrite. You live safely in your Tower in New Athens. You have no idea what your campaign of fear has done," he grumbled. Now that all his barriers were down, I knew that he truly believed that what he said was the truth. But I still could not fathom how he could blame me for his ruthless behavior?

"This is absurd," I started to point out, but Alexander cut me off.

"Do you realize that people believe what you say about me? Men and women I have never met fear me—they hate me because the great and wise Lady Ardella told them they should."

I started to reply but the hurt on his face froze the words on my lips.

"I have never killed a man except in self-defense, but somehow I am considered some sort of monster. Your precious, murdering brother, on the other hand, is a hero—all because Ardella says that it is so."

The image of the bodies strewn across the plain of Artemis flashed through my mind and guilt stole into my heart. *Could he be right? No. No, he is trying to confuse the issue—he is trying to confuse me.* "You are the Son of Ares. I didn't make that up," I replied.

"But you defined what it meant to be the Son of Ares. You once looked at me and saw an innocent boy. You helped me to escape New Athens, because you believed in me. What changed?" The anger in his voice was gone, and I could feel the sorrow behind his question.

"You changed. You responded to my act of mercy with betrayal. You took control of the Hermians and turned them into raiders. You harassed your neighbors and took what was not yours. You used the threat of violence to frighten all of Arcadia into submission. You became a monster - a monster that I was responsible for unleashing onto the world."

"If I am the monster you say I am, then why are you still in the land of the living? Ardella of New Athens, my sworn enemy, delivers herself into my hands. Did I beat you, imprison you, or torture you? No, instead, I protected you from the wrath of your own Goddess." His forthright anger was back and it flowed all around us.

"One act of mercy does not change a lifetime of..."

"You think this is my first act of mercy? Do you want to know why your brother's head is not on a pike at our front gates? After the battle he lay at my feet unconscious and helpless. All it would have taken was one swing of my sword. After all the men he had killed, it was what he deserved."

Although he did not finish the thought, his emotions revealed the truth. "You couldn't kill a defenseless man," I finished. My epiphany surprised us both.

Alexander looked deep into my eyes. The anger was gone; all I saw was the depth of his pain. "Explain again how that makes me a monster?"

My shame sucked all the air from my lungs and a rosy blush stole over my face. There was a heart within the Son of Ares that was as vulnerable as any mortal. *Perhaps he's not as evil as I thought—just as I'm not as good as I wanted everyone to believe*, I reasoned. "I owe you my life and my brother's life," I said softly. Tendrils of weariness crept into my soul.

He did not reply. There was nothing to say. Slowly Alexander released his hold. As he turned back to the other rescuers, who had gotten very quiet during our exchange, I felt his intense emotions begin to melt away like snow on a sunny day. *No, Alexander is not a monster; he is simply human.*

"Kern, find some place for our guest. I don't have the time or the patience to deal with her tantrums at the moment," he ordered one of the rescue workers standing nearby. Although his words and his attitude suggested to those around him that he was still angry, I knew the truth: he was too weary to hold onto his anger.

"Of course, Strategos," the man replied as he moved with purpose toward me. "This way, my Lady."

I looked back toward the Son of Ares and wanted to say more, but his face was turned away from me.

As I watched Alexander resume the rescue effort, I was overcome with a strange desire. I knew I had to ask for forgiveness. I whispered, "I was wrong. You are not a monster."

Alexander did not move or reply. I wasn't even sure if he heard me.

Resigned and exhausted, I followed Kern.

Chapter 4

Mortals are the strangest of creatures. They struggle against their fate; they love when it is not in their best interest; and they cannot see the obvious before their very eyes.

The Goddess Athena
476 years *Ab Terra Condita*

KERN LED ME to the tower room in silence. "Remain here," he instructed. He placed a small candle on the table and left without saying a word. The sound of the door clicking shut startled me. I felt my heart flutter. By the light of that single candle I examined my surroundings. My cell was stark with a small bed, a chest and the table and chairs. Opposite the door, an archway led to a small balcony, presumably to allow fresh air and light into the otherwise windowless room. Tonight it admitted only a thick, black darkness and the mournful cries of citizens of Metropolis. *Perhaps I should be wailing in the night, as well.* I thought. *I'm a prisoner of the Son of Ares with no idea what my future might hold.* I was alone and abandoned in this strange new world.

Suddenly, a burst of wind tore through the room,

extinguishing the candle. The only ray of light and hope was suddenly gone and I felt like a child again, frightened of the dark. I tried to take a deep, calming breath and found that I could not draw air into my aching lungs. The sensation of suffocation only added to my rising panic.

"Why?" I murmured to the lonely room. "How can I fail at this? How can I let my brother die?"

"Failure is a part of being human, Ardella," a voice whispered in the dark. It took a moment for to realize that the sound came from my own mind. It was a voice I recognized.

"Athena?"

"I am here, my child. I am always with you. You are not alone." The Goddess' tone was comforting and confident. Instead of panicking that she was once again in my mind, I was soothed by her voice. I tried to remember her betrayal, and my own anger, but I was too frightened. I was too glad not to be alone in the dark.

"Help me, Great Goddess. I must save Rafe," I pleaded.

"What would you have me do, child? I am in New Athens. You are the one in Metropolis with your brother."

"You are an Olympian. Help me, please."

"Give yourself to me, child, and I will do what must be done," Athena promised.

"I don't understand?" I replied.

"Open yourself to me, Ardella. Let me into your mind," the Goddess demanded.

"But you are in my mind. I can hear your words all the way across Arcadia," I babbled, unable to comprehend her instructions.

"Let me have your mind, Ardella. Let me see what you see. Hear what you hear. I will give you the power of the Olympians, so that you can save your brother," her voice instructed.

"You can do such a thing from all the way across Arcadia?" I marveled.

"How can you doubt my power? You are my child—a living embodiment of Olympian supremacy. I can do anything. Surrender your will to me," she replied. Her sudden concern for my plight and her strange burst of satisfaction should have alarmed me, but my desire to save my brother was too great.

I did as she commanded and the world spun into darkness.

⁂

"Killing me with my own dagger is rather droll, don't you think," Alexander's voice penetrated the darkness in my mind, yet it met only confusion.

"What?" I murmured as I slowly opened my eyes. Many things assailed me as all my senses collected data from the world around me simultaneously. I felt his hard body pressed against me as I straddled his chest. I smelled the manly scents of wood and leather in the room. I heard Alexander's heart beating frantically. I saw the dagger my hand held against his throat. I felt his desperation and fear seep beneath the ice walls of his Herculean control. Despite this multitude of information I had no clear answers to the questions burning in my mind: *How did I get here? What was I doing*?

Suddenly, the strange conversation in the dark tower room flooded back to me. Athena had done this to me. *How could she?* I had been tricked again. She had taken my body not to help Rafe but to kill Alexander.

"*You did tell me that next time I should kill him myself?*" Athena taunted. I ignored her.

"Threatening my life is not one of your better plans, Ardella," Alexander said in a calm, logical voice that drew me back to the present problem. "Killing me will not free your brother," he added.

His words brought me hope and an irrational idea. *Perhaps I can thwart Athena and free my brother, too.* "I will not harm you. I will trade Rafe's life for your own." I offered with a confidence I did not actually feel.

"Although I am quite enjoying the sensation of you astride me, it does make it difficult to issue commands to my guards with a dagger at my throat." he sneered.

By the Goddess, this just might work. "Give me your word that you will free my brother and I will release you," I replied.

"You would take the word of the Son of Ares?" he asked.

I was not amused by the mockery in his tone. "I will know if you lie."

"And if your gift tells you that I will never free Rafe, will you kill me?"

"I would do anything to save my brother."

"Then take your dagger from my throat and I will order my men to release your brother from him cell," Alexander said in firm and believable tone.

My empathy told me he was lying.

"*He will not release Rafe,*" Athena's voice echoed through my dazed mind. "*Kill him.*"

"No!" I hissed aloud, "If you wanted him dead, you should have killed him while you were still in control."

I felt the Goddess' surge of frustration through our tenuous mental link and her feral curse, "*I tried.*"

"Ardella?" Alexander questioned.

I heard the confusion in his voice and felt the rising bloom of curiosity crowd out the lingering fear in his mind. He knew something was wrong.

"*Kill him, Ardella, or he will kill you,*" Athena commanded.

"No! You are no longer in control!" I cried as I lifted the dagger from his throat and held it suspended above his chest like a viperous snake ready to strike.

Suddenly Alexander's feeling of fear was back, but what I saw understanding in his eyes. He knew the truth. "She can't make you do this," he whispered.

"*Kill him*," Athena once again demanded.

I felt my control slipping. In my exhausted state I was no match for the will of an Olympian, but I had no intention of being her pawn. Instead I plunged the dagger into the pillow next to the Son of Ares' head.

Almost before I could remove my hand from the abhorrent weapon, I found myself rolled over and my body pinned beneath Alexander. "What were you thinking? I could have you executed for turning a dagger on me," Alexander growled.

"I didn't mean... I didn't know..." I tried to explain, but could not find the words, because I could barely believe what Athena had done myself.

"You didn't know that an Olympian could possess a mortal, or that Athena would once again use you to try to kill me?" he offered, coldly.

"I am a fool," I managed to whisper.

"By the Goddess, Ardella. What am I going to do with you?" he replied.

I struggled to reply—to plead for my life, but between his weight making it hard to breathe and the trauma of the Goddess' possession, my head felt ready to explode. This time the emotional typhoon was too much and I was lost to oblivion.

Chapter 5

The future is like a path that twists and bends. Sometimes it lies out of sight yet is just what we expect; other times it seems so clear, but is nothing that we could ever have imagined.

Titannia, 13th Queen of the Amazons
677 years *Ab Terra Condita*

I AWOKE IN my tower room. The morning sunlight danced in from the balcony and revealed what the shadows of the previous night had not. I was in a guest chamber, not a prison cell. In fact, I soon discovered that the door was not even locked. I laughed. That didn't seem to matter, since I had nowhere to go.

Although Kern had appeared mid-morning with food and wine, I didn't see Alexander again until late that afternoon. I was standing at the balcony drinking in the sunlight when I felt his approach. Alexander's intense satisfaction and pride preceded him into the room. Multiple brushes with death had apparently intensified his pleasure at being alive. Despite the bleak outlook for my future, his mood was contagious and I had to fight off a smile. *How did he do that to me? Actually, he was always able to do that to me.* I suddenly had a memory of a frightened fourteen-year-old girl from over a decade ago:

"You are being unreasonable, Ardella. Your judgment is clouded where Lysander is concerned," Rafe said from across the table where we were sharing a quiet meal.

"You think it is right to condemn a boy not much older than us because of who his father is?" I replied reaching for the basket of bread.

"I didn't say I agreed with the Council's position, but they are the governing body of New Athens—chosen by Athena herself. It is their right to pass judgment on whomever they please."

"They are passing judgment for crimes Lysander may never even commit," I argued tearing off a piece of bread.

"They are trying to keep him from creating the chaos that former Sons of Ares have brought to our ancestors," my twin replied.

"He is not evil, Rafe. I can feel his pain and confusion. This is not fair."

"You must learn to control your gift, Ardella. You are letting another person's emotions influence your reasoning."

"Why must there be such a chasm between our emotions and our logic? They are both properties of the mind and both have a role to play in our thoughts and deeds."

"That is a very unAthenian point of view," he scoffed. "I would be careful who you say such things to. Your notions would not be widely accepted among the Council of Athena."

"I dread spending the rest of my life being careful about what I say and to whom I say it. Being a member of the Council of Athena is not so much an honor as a burden," I complained.

Anger shot through Rafe's mind, like a white-hot dagger, surprising me with its intensity.

"You are the chosen one of Athena, her precious empathy, with a seat on the ruling Council at the age of fourteen. How dare *you complain that this great honor is a burden! Do you know how many people envy your life? Do you know what I would give to..."* he suddenly broke off and stormed from the room his jealousy trailing behind him like a mantel.

"I hope you will be comfortable in the tower," Alexander said, startling me from my memory. "Although small, it has one of the best views of the city."

"Thank you. It is..." I faltered. I never expected to need a room in Alexander's citadel. *How does one discuss such mundane matters as accommodations when the life you knew has come to an end?* "It is very nice," I finally managed.

"I am glad you like it, Lady Ardella," he said. He strode across the room, leaned on one side of the archway and stared out at Metropolis. "I miss this view," he said quietly.

"This was your room?" I mused more than a little startled.

"For almost three years, until the duties of Strategos required larger living quarters." He smiled at me and my heart was suddenly filled with guilt. *I had tried to kill him and yet I am being treated like an honored guest.*

"About what happened last night...with Athena. I want to..." I said cautiously, trying to approach the subject that had worried me since I awoke this morning.

"It is best forgotten," Alexander said.

"Forgotten, then you are not going to..." I murmured, but stopped myself, when I realized I was about to suggest I deserved some sort of punishment for my actions.

"Punish you for being an Olympian pawn?" he anticipated my thought and laughed. "Even I am not that much of a monster."

"I know you are not a monster," I whispered.

I felt his surprise. I realized he hadn't heard my admission last night. I felt a wave of relief wash over me and I wondered that an apology to the Son of Ares could stir such an emotion.

"No one knows it happened except you and I," Alexander suggested.

"And Athena. I should never have let her..." I started to explain and then stopped when the words did not seem to come.

"You should not have let her what?" Alexander asked.

"I let her manipulate me—again. I gave ten years of my life in her service, only to become nothing more than a means to an end, not once but twice in the same day is..." I couldn't find a word that would express the pain of betrayal and loss I felt.

"Can you keep her from controlling you?" he asked, obviously concerned.

"I was exhausted and soul sick last night. She played on my fear."

"And your desire to free Rafe?" he speculated.

I nodded.

"Perhaps the question I should ask is will you keep Athena from possessing you in the future?"

I was quiet for a moment, but finally responded, "I will try."

"You will have to do better than that," he retorted.

He sounds just like my mother.

When I didn't respond, he continued, "Just remember that if you had succeeded in killing me last night, you and your brother would both be dead right now. The people of Metropolis would have torn you apart."

"I am not sure that the life or death of her pawn was ever a concern for the Goddess," I replied.

"You are certainly calm about all of this," Alexander observed.

"So are you."

"Yes, but I have been through this before. Athena has tried to kill me so many times I've lost count."

I had no idea how to reply to such a comment, so I said nothing.

Alexander continued, "Now I remember my reaction the first time you sent an Amazon assassin."

"Please do not go there, Lysander," I begged.

He frowned at the name, but made no comment. "As you wish, my Lady," he said with a quick bow. "I have been thinking about the matter of your escort. After your confession yesterday, I doubt they would have waited for you anyway. It seems like you will be staying in Metropolis. Perhaps it is fate. You may consider yourself my guest, Ardella."

"Guest?" I repeated.

"Remember—I have decided not to be a monster today."

"That is not funny."

"Nothing about this situation is particularly funny, my lady."

"Why would you want me to remain in Metropolis?"

"Because it is where you belong. Metropolis is the haven for misfits, outcasts and exiles. You seem to be one of us now."

"You expect me to believe you are welcoming me, when I tried to kill you?"

"Surely your gift tells you I harbor no hostility towards you," he said.

He sounded sincere. It was true that I had been reading his emotions since before he had entered the room and had felt no animosity—hidden or otherwise. Nevertheless, I was cautious. Alexander and I had been enemies for too long. I had watched in horror over the years as he became more and more aggressive towards his neighbors. I had openly and vehemently opposed him from New Athens and had worked for years to bring an end to his reign in Metropolis. Despite my gratitude to him for saving my life, I still held distrust for my enemy. Distrust that only yesterday I could feel he returned in kind.

Why is he different this morning? Does he truly mean me no harm or has the cunning Son of Ares found a way to project false emotions for the benefit of my empathy? "What if I told you that I no longer have the gift of empathy, so you will have to reassure me with your actions," I goaded.

"I would say that is a very clever way to ask what my plans are for my new guest." He grinned, and softly added, "But I must admit that I cannot imagine you without your gift of empathy." Suddenly, his smile transformed into a smirk, and I began to suspect that he knew exactly how his mood influenced mine. *Hadn't his emotions lead me to free him all those years ago.* I reasoned. *No!* I was tired of being manipulated by Athena's gift.

"My empathy," I snapped, "made me a naïve fool who could be manipulated by the feelings of another. I have had to live with that mistake every day since."

I saw him wince at my words and felt a genuine pang of regret enter his heart.

Again his emotions softened me towards him, but this time I fought back. "Should I be grateful that you regret what you did to me all those years ago?" I scoffed. I had once felt sympathy for a frightened young man named Lysander, but I could not allow that to color my perception. I had to accept the idea that the difficult stranger before me was that scared boy all grown up. Lysander was gone.

"I had forgotten how much I hate that little mind reading trick of yours, Ardella." he sighed. His cheery mood was beginning to fade.

"I am not telepathic," I corrected automatically. "I can read emotions, not the thoughts behind them."

"But your empathy tells you when someone is lying?"

"Usually."

"Then tell me if I am lying when I say that I mean you no

harm and that you are welcome here in Metropolis," he offered. He took my hand and looked into my eyes. The air between us grew still and I knew he was telling the truth.

No. He's the Son of Ares. This has to be a trick. "My empathy does not work that way," I retorted. I pulled away from him and moved to the far side of the table—as if distance would make it easier to resist the call of his emotions.

"Oh doesn't it," he scoffed. I heard his irritation even as I felt its emotional counterpart slap me in the face. "You are Athena's human lie detector. I should know. I had enough of your peering into my soul the first time," he said, sarcastically.

This time it was me who felt the twinge of remorse. I suddenly recalled the first time we met and the way my gift had forced his identity into the light:

I walked solemnly before the three young men trying to look serious and intimidating, which wasn't an easy task considering at fourteen I was actually younger that any of them. Ever since I had manifested the gift of empathy a few months earlier I had been on the search with members of the inner Council of Athena looking for the latest incarnation of the Son of Ares.

Like most of the people who I had already interviewed, I could sense their fear and confusion. The intense emotions in the room were starting to make my own head pound. I just wanted to get this interview over with and then I could rest for a while.

I spoke to the first boy. His red hair and green eyes were unusual in New Athens. His fear was the strongest of the three. I didn't see how he could be the one we were searching for, but I knew I was expected to make sure.

"What is your name?" I asked.

"Tannis," he said nervously.

"What is your purpose in the sect of Athena?" I continued.

"I am a gardener in the Grove of the Dryads," he said his head slightly bowed and his gazed focused on the ground.

Despite his humble demeanor, I could feel the little burst of pride with his answer. I could not help but smile at his obvious enthusiasm for his work. "I sense that you are happy with the path that the Goddess has chosen for you."

His eyes lit up. "I love plants and growing things. It is a joy to tend another living thing and watch it thrive. I often envy the followers of Demeter who can actually use their gift to influence the growth of plants."

"Yes, would have been enough, Tannis," the boy next to him said drolly.

I looked at the interloper, seeing him for the first time. He was a little older than the other two boys and obviously stronger—at least the muscles pushing at the seams of his gardener's shirt seemed to suggest that. Most striking was his silky brown hair, pulled back for convenience by a simple cord. Although most young men in New Athens would have cropped it short, he had chosen to flout tradition. I had no doubt that unbound it would flow well past his shoulders.

"What is your name?" I asked.

"Why don't you tell me? You are the one who can read minds," he retorted, sarcastically. This was unexpected and his belligerent behavior was not something I had experienced before.

"I cannot read minds, just emotions," I assured him.

"But you can tell when someone is lying to you."

"Usually. That is what makes me so valuable in this search."

"What are you searching for?" he asked curiously.

"Not what, but who. The Goddess wishes me to seek out someone for her," I informed him. Suddenly I realized I still didn't know his name. "What is your name?" I asked quietly.

"Lucus," he said without hesitation. The sudden wave of

shock from the other two boys told me that this young man was lying. Surprisingly, his emotions had been calm and certain. I was not sure I would have recognized his lie if we had been alone.

"What is your name?" I asked again, making it clear to all that I knew he had not been truthful.

"I told you my name is..." he began calmly.

"By the Goddess, Lysander, stop this!" Tannis snapped at his companion. "I don't understand what the Goddess thinks we have done wrong, but treating her chosen one with such disrespect cannot be helping our situation. You could lose your position."

"Do you think I am concerned about losing my job? I hate that stupid park and I will go crazy if I am expected to spend the rest of my life digging in the dirt and sprinkling the flowers with water."

"But care of the parks and groves in New Athens is important for the well-being of our society. Without us the others ..."

"Without us the others would have to tend their own plants, water their own gardens, pick up their own trash and take care of themselves. We are part of the servant class that makes society better—better for everyone but us."

I felt Lysander's pain and frustration as he spoke these words. His heart ached to have what could not be his. I shuddered at the echo of his grief, stronger even that his indignant anger.

"What do you want, Lysander?" I asked.

He looked at me with intensity in his eyes that startled me. "Respect. Opportunity," he answered with a conviction I felt reflected in his heart, "I want to become more than I am now. I have a destiny."

"How do you know you have a destiny, Lysander?"

"I can feel it. There is something inside me that drives me to be something more—something greater. I can't explain it. I just know that I am not supposed to be a gardener, even if that is what Athena believes I should do."

My heart skipped a beat at his words. My young mind

feared the Goddess' reaction to his outburst, but it also admired his courage to speak so freely. I found something compelling about his passion. I wondered if the Goddess would appreciate his conviction and allow him to live his dream. I should have known the answer to that question.

"He is the one," Counselor Tressa said from the shadows. Nothing at that moment could have been more shocking than that pronouncement. Two adult members of the Council always observed my interviews, but this was the first time either had spoken. I felt Counselor Tressa's sudden rush of relief and then her intense hatred. I know I cannot read minds, but something about the Councilwoman's satisfied grin told me that if Lysander were indeed the Son of Ares then his life was in great danger.

"Ardella," I heard a voice call. I looked up at Alexander and realized from the look on his face that he must have said my name more than once. "Where did you go?"

I saw no point in denying the truth, "I was thinking about the first time we met."

"Oh," he whispered. Since he didn't change the subject and I could feel his curiosity, I decided to chance a conversation long overdue.

"Do you ever wish that the search never happened and that you were back in the Grove of the Dryads with Tannis and Corin?" I asked.

"Never," he said curtly. The same intensity of purpose that I had felt all those years ago came roaring to life within him. But then his eyes became introspective and he added wistfully, "I do sometimes wonder what happened to them. I can almost picture Tannis and Corin tending the trees and flowerbeds together."

"Corin still works in the Grove of the Dryads, but Tannis seems to have picked up some of your bad habits," I told him casually. "He decided he wanted more out of life than one simple garden could offer."

"I don't believe you," he retorted. His concern for his friend's fate had bled through his casual tone. "Tannis was passionate about living things. He loved horticulture."

"I know," I smiled, reflecting on my long friendship with Tannis. "That is what makes him such a good teacher. The Academy even sent him to study the growing techniques of the Demeter sect. I have never seen anyone happier or more excited about anything in my entire life."

"Stop!" Alexander snapped. He was suddenly irritated. His tone had turned mocking, "I think that is enough about the past. Perhaps we should concentrate on the here and now." Although he sounded angry, it was the tiny bud of agony in his chest that ended any further discussion.

"Perhaps that is for the best," I agreed. All traces of his cheerful mood were gone. I looked into the dark, brooding vestige of the Son of Ares, reminding myself that the young Lysander no longer existed.

He looked out onto the park below and sighed. "I believe you wanted to know what I planned to do with you?" he muttered. Suddenly his mood turned playful again and I marveled at his control over his emotions. Thankfully my empathy told me his next words were teasing, rather than condemning. "You arrive in Metropolis, bringing your Goddess' lightning bolts with you. Your Goddess is determined to kill me."

"I think the Goddess was aiming at me," I quipped.

"I don't," he replied. One look at my face must have given away that his thoughts about Athena's motives were all too true. "At least I know you weren't in on it intentionally," he mused.

"Have you suddenly become a telepath?" I replied grinning at his comment.

"No. But I saw the look on your face when you realized Athena had thrown the lightning bolt and the ceiling was coming down on both of us."

That memory sobered me. "I knew that there were no guarantees when I walked into your citadel," I reminded him.

Suddenly his emotions were serious as well. "You were willing to risk everything to save your brother?" he asked. There was just a hint of envy in his voice.

I found myself wondering if anyone would risk everything for him. *Why should I concern myself with such things?* "Yes, and I would do it again," I snapped more harshly than I had intended, but quickly added, "Only this time I would tell the truth sooner and prevent Rafe's exile."

Alexander chuckled, "Don't assume that being an exile is the end of the world. Being cut off from one's former life gives you the opportunity to reinvent yourself. You can do or be anything when you have no ties and nothing to lose or regret."

"Are we still talking about Rafe or are we talking about your exile from New Athens?"

"I will admit I have fared better than your brother. When I left I knew I could never go back and it broke the bonds cleanly. I am not sure Athena truly ever let your brother walk away. Even if she didn't order your brother to attack Metropolis, she drove him to it." His assessment of the situation was dangerously close to the truth and not good for either my brother or the Athena sect, so I carefully diverted the subject.

"What are your plans for my brother?"

"Besides executing him for the attack on Metropolis?" he mocked.

My frown deepened. "Lysander, I am serious. I understand you must uphold a certain reputation for ruthlessness, but Rafe's death won't bring back your people or…" Alexander's sudden movement stopped me short. Once again his strong arms reached out to yank me toward him in a cruel mockery of an embrace, but there was no softness or affection in his touch, nor was there anger. Now in physical contact with Alexander, I could feel the frustration.

"Let's get one thing straight, Ardella. I am not the simple, frightened boy you knew as Lysander. I am the Son of Ares and my name is Alexander. Say it, Ardella. Say my name."

"Alexander," I gasped as his hands dug painfully into my arms. "That hurts," I whispered.

I felt his rush of remorse, although he said nothing as he released me. The silence loomed between us until I found the courage to ask, "Please, Alexander. There is no one here but you and I. Be honest with me. Surely it won't matter who pays for the attack on Metropolis? Let me take his place."

"Even if I allow you to take Rafe's place and set him free, there are a number of families in Metropolis who lost love ones in his attacked that would likely kill him before he could reach the gates of the city."

"Then protect him until he leaves Metropolis," I pleaded.

He shook his head. "I can't think of anyone in Metropolis I could trust with that task. Besides, where do you suggest I send him? He is an exile that no sect will have for fear of being associated with his crimes. For your brother, inside his cell is the safest place in all of Arcadia. "

"I did not come all this way to have my brother spend the rest of his life in a cell in Metropolis."

"You are a stubborn woman," he mused.

"I am also relentless," I added.

He laughed. "That you are," he whispered in a soft tone I had never heard him use before. For a moment his eyes caught mine and I was lost in their deep brown depths. I felt my body lean toward him of its own volition. Then he suddenly stepped back and announced, "I am very busy. I'm afraid I have important work waiting for me, so..."

His words struck me hard, but I managed to reply, "We are discussing the fate of my brother."

"And your future in Metropolis."

"My fate as well. You cannot just leave in the middle of the discussion."

"That is where you are wrong. I have waited ten years to finally have the upper hand with you, Ardella. I am going to savor every moment."

"Alexander! This is not a game!" I cried in frustration.

"You only say that, because you are losing. It has been fun. Goodbye, my lady," he chortled.

I watched in frustration as he strode across my tower room toward the exit. He was right. I had played every card in my hand, and I was no closer to freeing my brother than I had been standing in the Tower of Athena.

Just as he opened the door to leave, he peered over his shoulder and added, "Oh, I almost forgot. You will have a chance to present your case. Hermes and the Council have decided to meet with you and your brother to determine what should be done. If by chance Hermes does grant your brother his freedom, then everyone in Metropolis will have to allow him to go."

"Oh," I gasped as a shiver of hope travelled through me. It was exactly the opportunity I hoped for. It was wonderful. "You could have mentioned that when you first came in," I muttered.

"What would have been the fun in that?" he replied with a wink, and then he was gone. All that was left in the doorway was the echo of his amusement. I saw red.

My frustration exploded like the eruption of ancient Vesuvius. In the next moment the mug from my lunch tray slammed against the door, shattering into hundreds of satisfying shards.

This was a matter of life and death for my twin, and the Son of Ares was treating it like a game. *Maybe he is a monster after all.*

The fury evoked a memory from long ago—one I had tried hard over the years not to think about. The original reason I had come to regret releasing the Son of Ares:

"Hurry, this way," I whispered as we entered the Grove of the Dryads. This was the location I had agreed to meet the young Hermian woman who was to take Lysander away from New Athens to safety.

"What are we doing here?" Lysander asked. Although he had followed me from the cell a few minutes earlier without question, I could feel his doubt and concern.

"A follower of Hermes has agreed to meet us here and take you back to her caravan. They are departing in the morning. You should be safe with the Hermians. They do not know who you are and take in strangers all the time," I told him.

"Why are you helping me?" he asked.

"I do not want them to hurt you," I replied.

"Are you coming with me?" Lysander asked.

"No. New Athens is my home."

"Until a few days ago I thought it was my home as well. It is cruel how fast the fates can turn your life upside down," he said bitterly.

I could not help it. At his words my need to comfort him was overwhelming. I moved closer. "I am sorry for my part in all of this," I whispered "When Athena asked me to help locate the Son of Ares I had no idea the Council was planning to kill you."

"What did you think they would do when they found such a dangerous enemy? Did you even think about the consequences?"

I could feel his anger and frustration bubbling up and it

frightened me. "I am sorry," I managed to whisper as tears filled my eyes. I felt the softening in him as he pulled me gently into his arms.

"Forgive me, Ardella. I know how much you are risking helping me. I don't have your gift of empathy, but I have understood from the beginning you were innocent in all of this," he said. His hands soothed my back in an attempt to comfort me. It felt good to be in his arms and I let myself relax in his embrace.

"I want you to be safe. I know leaving is hard, but in the end it will be for the best."

"I will miss my mother and sister, but I think I will miss my life that might have been the most of all," he said. He pulled me closer and touched my lips with his. It was my first kiss. I allowed myself to enjoy the new sensation, unsure how to participate in what was happening. It was the first time I had felt another person's desire for me. It was a little frightening.

"Come with me Ardella," he said against my lips.

"You want me to come with you?" I whispered.

"Imagine what we could do. The Son of Ares and the Daughter of Athena would be unstoppable. Bring all that knowledge you found in Athena's archive. It is the legacy of our ancestors. Athena must fear what it can teach us, because she keeps it hidden away."

"Athena fears nothing. She is just trying to protect us from dangerous ideas."

"Knowledge is not hers to control. It belongs to mankind."

"Why do you think I still have all those horrible images?"

"I know that you always carry the crystal reader with you. Come with me and we can use it to reshape Arcadia," he said in a dark, seductive whisper.

"Do not say things like that, Lysander," I said and reluctantly pulled away. But his arms wouldn't let go and brought me back against his chest. I felt the sudden sadness in him even before he spoke.

"I'm sorry," he said. "I hoped it could be different." His lips once again met mine and I felt the telltale tingle of passion rise between us. I don't know if it was my inexperience or the intensity of the kiss, but it took a few moments for me to realize his hands, which had moved to caress my neck, were tightening and making it difficult to breathe.

"Lysander?" I gasped as darkness overtook me.

When I awoke later under the great oak in the Grove of the Dryads, I was alone. Lysander was gone with the Hermians and so was the crystal reader with all my research on ancient earth and its many wars. I had not only helped the Son of Ares escape, but I had given him the sword that he could use to conquer Arcadia.

Chapter 6

Dryads are mystical spirits the dwell within the ancient trees in sacred woods all over Arcadia. In my experience they are playful, mischievous, and totally unpredictable.

Tannis of New Athens
Two thousand, six hundred and forty-two years *Ab Terra Condita*

AS DUSK CREPT across darkening sky, I sat beneath one of the great oak trees that shaded the tomb of Artemis. I had noticed the aging marble edifice from my balcony and was inexplicably drawn to it. As I approached the miniature temple that enclosed the dormant body of the Goddess, I felt the faint vibration of her life force even through the layers of cold marble.

"Can you hear those of us in the world of the living from inside your tomb, great Artemis? Do you feel the passage of time?" I whispered. *I wish I could join you in your blissful sleep and like you leave all the problems of this world behind.*

I let the tears that I had been fighting all day begin to flow and released the pent up fear and frustration that threatened to overwhelm me. I had no one to talk to, no ally, in this strange new world. I had never felt more alone or hopeless and for the first time in my life I had no plan for the future.

"Why do you cry?" a faint voice asked. Startled to be caught indulging in self-pity by a stranger, I looked up but did not see anyone.

"Who is there?" I called softly toward the trees that shaded the tomb. They were the only place close enough to shelter the stranger and yet the voice hadn't seemed to come from that direction.

"Why do you cry?" the voice asked again. This time I knew the sound didn't come from the grove, but from inside my mind. I began to suspect I was not speaking to a mortal.

"Where are you?" I asked.

"Here," the voice said. I looked again at the grove and finally saw the glimmering form a woman emerging from one of the older original oaks. I had met such creatures before in New Athens. They were tree spirits called dryads and they communicated telepathically. Although not everyone could see with these ethereal creatures, I had always been sensitive to their presence.

"I see you, spirit. Are you one of the dryads of this grove?" I asked.

"I am a dryad?" the voice echoed. The tree spirit seemed confused and I could sense her fear, which reminded me of an elder with early stages of dementia. In hopes of helping her, I used my most soothing tone of voice. "That is what the spirits of the trees are called in the grove in New Athens," I explained.

"I am a dryad," the voice repeated and then paused. "Yes, I am a dryad. It has been so long since I had heard the word that I had forgotten."

"Are there other dryads in this grove?" I asked.

"No!" the spirit whispered sadly, "I am the only one left."

"Then you know how I feel, spirit. That is why I was crying.

I felt alone and sorry for myself."

"We are not alone anymore. This place is once more full of life," she said. Her eyes shined with hope.

"You mean the citizens of Metropolis?"

"They once again care for the tomb of the Goddess. They even plant new seedlings and add life to this lonely hill. They awoke me from my long slumber."

"How long were you sleeping?"

"I don't know. How long has my Goddess slept?"

"Almost a thousand years."

"So long?"

"I had no idea dryads lived that long. The ones I know in New Athens are only a few centuries old."

"So, you are a follower of Athena." She giggled like a young girl and the branches of the surrounding trees shivered in response. "I always found the followers of Athena to be so serious and stuffy. They do not like to frolic and play games like Artemis' children."

"I am afraid that Athena's children are still a little stuffy," I told her.

"Very little changes on Arcadia, even after a thousand years," the dryad mused.

There was a long pause and I realized the dryad was lost in the memory of a world long gone. She sighed. Suddenly remembering I was still there she asked, "What is your name, child?"

"My name is Ardella. What is your name, spirit?"

"My name is..." there was a silence. "It has been so long since I have spoken it. My name is..." her distress became more pronounced as she tried harder to remember. I could feel her panic rising and feared it might consume us both.

"Do not worry, spirit. You will remember," I offered.

She continued to search her memories, but it was to no avail.

"No. It is lost. It is gone," she bemoaned. "There is no one left alive who remembers my name. Great Artemis, I have no name!"

Again I felt the terror and confusion overwhelm the elderly spirit and I tried desperately to think of a way to calm her. "I could give you a new name," I offered.

"But it would not be my name," she moaned.

"Many mortals choose to take on a new name to mark a new phase of their life," I said, trying in vain to shake the dark visceral image of Alexander, which suddenly flooded my mind.

"You would give me a new name?" the dryad asked finally showing interest in the possibility.

"Certainly. Let me think." All at once it came to me. "My grandmother's name is Muriel. I think you should be Muriel, too."

She smiled. "Muriel. That is a good name. My name is Muriel."

I sighed with relief. "I am glad to meet you Muriel. I have always been very fond of dryads."

"You know other dryads. Is that why you can see me? I have tried many times to speak to the ones who tend the grove, but they cannot see me, so when they hear my voice they become frightened."

"It was my grandmother Muriel who introduced me to my first dryad when I was just a little girl. I don't know why, but I have always been able to see and hear your kind. I am sure there are others in Metropolis with this ability. Perhaps if I tell them you are here, they will come to speak to you as well."

"I would like that. I have been alone too long. I was waiting for something—something important, but I am no longer sure ..." Again Muriel's thoughts wondered off into an inner world of her own. The peaceful joy that filled her made my heart ache with envy.

"Good night, Muriel," I whispered as I left her to her memories and returned to my tower room. I felt less alone than I had only minutes earlier, and just a little hopeful. Muriel was a miracle. *Maybe there's hope for the future after all,* I thought.

Chapter 7

My children are wanderers and gypsies. They hunger for the view that lies beyond the horizon. I would have them no other way.

The God Hermes
3 years *Ab Terra Condita*

I LOOKED OUT over the park that was the center of Metropolis. Miniature waterfalls leaped down from concealed sources into the crystalline pool of the deepest cerulean. The original grove had been expanded into a well-orchestrated montage. Colorful shrubs placed strategically among the trees created an impression of barely contained chaos - much like Metropolis itself.

Even though I was still unsure of many things in Metropolis, I agreed with Alexander that my balcony must have one of the best views in the city. The ornamental grove planned around the tomb of Artemis was easily as impressive as anything in New Athens, Heliopolis or Amazonia. In fact many things in Metropolis were up to the standards of the other Olympian capitals. This was unexpected.

After all, the Hermians had been wandering nomads for 2000 years. They were gypsies with no ties to any one place. They traveled in small groups of caravan ships that had wandered far and wide across Arcadia. Occasionally, they would camp near the Olympian capitals to trade for needed goods. It was the wanderlust of these people that had led me to think of them as a safe place for Lysander. It never occurred to me that the Son of Ares would be able to influence the God Hermes and his followers in such a profound way. He unified all the tribes and transformed Gypsies into Raiders.

With the centralized castle-like fortress of Metropolis as their base, the Hermians used the massive caravan vehicles for raiding. A large group of armed raiders would suddenly arrive at an unsuspecting village or outpost and demand whatever they wanted as tribute to Hermes. If the villagers refused to freely give them what they demanded, then the armed men would wreak havoc on buildings and people until the citizens changed their minds. Occasionally, someone was hurt or even killed in the process, but that was rare.

Food, furniture, clothing, wine, and books were obtained for Metropolis in this manner. There were even some reports that people were abducted and forced into slavery in Alexander's Metropolis. Truthfully, what little I had seen of the city and its people didn't seem as oppressive as I had expected. I hadn't seen any chains or collars—nothing to indicate whether the reports of slavery were accurate.

I found myself wondering how much of what I thought I knew about Metropolis was true. *Could I have been that naive?* I reached out for a memory—any memory that would support my now crumbling picture of Alexander's city. The memory came to me like a dagger to my heart—Argos:

The solemn procession moved slowly toward the Grove of the Dryads. The twinkling candles carried by each person blended into a giant undulating creature that filled the streets of New Athens. I was captivated by the scene and felt compelled to join the vigil, but fear kept me on my balcony in the Tower of Athena. I was an empath after all and a multitude of this size in a highly emotional state was my worst nightmare.

As I watched the people and their lights converge on the Grove of the Dryads, I wished with all my soul to be with them. I needed to be with them to share our common grief at the tragedy of Argos. Although none of those who were killed by the raiders were Athenians, the followers of Athena demonstrated their solidarity with the Amazons and the Elusians who had been taken by the tragedy.

Mesmerized by the moving lights I allowed my mind to wander, and once again fixated on the originator of this disastrous event. One man was responsible for the escalating series of transgressions that had led to the massacre of Argos—the greatest loss of life on Arcadia in over 500 years. I would never forgive Alexander for his role in this calamity.

"Lady Ardella," I heard a soft female voice behind me query.

I turned to find a woman in her late twenties, dressed in the typical cotton garb of most of the citizens of Metropolis. Her dark hair and green eyes were striking. Although her demeanor was quiet and reserved, my empathy couldn't help but sense the strong, passionate core of this woman.

"Yes," I replied.

"Lady Ardella, the Strategos sent me to serve you," she stated matter-of-factly.

"Serve me?" I prompted.

"He said that..."

I saw the look of doubt on her face and felt the nervousness in her heart at how to answer my question. I decided she was likely grappling with the orders she had been given. "It's alright," I assured her. "What exactly did Lysander, I mean Alexander, tell you to do?"

"The Strategos said that you would be staying with us in Metropolis and that you were used to having servants to take care of your needs in the Tower of Athena."

I couldn't decide if I should be grateful or insulted by my enemy's assumption. "Is it normal for people in Metropolis to have servants?" I asked.

I saw her think about this for a moment and felt her calmly decide to be truthful. "No it is not our custom. Everyone here does for themselves. Only children and the elderly need caretakers," she informed me.

"Then I will live as everyone else does. I will admit I am used to servants surrounding me. I lived that way for so long because it was our tradition in New Athens. I hope that I will find I am capable of taking care of myself," I said.

I felt her sudden panic at my refusal of her offer.

"Lady Ardella, please reconsider. I can be useful to you. I can be a guide to Metropolis," she offered. "The city can be a difficult place for a newcomer."

I felt the desperation both in her voice and from the waves of panic pouring off of her. I could sense no malicious motives or intent to do me harm—only panic. I assumed this was because not fulfilling the task that Alexander asked of her put her at risk. Although refusing her help might annoy my nemesis to some degree, it might also get this woman in trouble with her ruler. I had no doubt that the feeling of panic meant Alexander was the type of ruler who expected to be obeyed no matter what and I found I was moved by her plight.

"I do feel a little lost in your city. Perhaps a guide would be appropriate," I replied. I felt her rush of relief and found myself smiling at the face I hoped would become my first human friend in Metropolis. "What is your name?"

"I am called Deidra," she said. "Is there anything I can get for you, my lady?"

My mind reeled at all the possibilities of that simple question. I wanted my life back; my Goddess' favor again; that my brother had never attacked Metropolis; that I had never found the Son of Ares. I forced myself to return to the practical needs that this woman offered to fulfill. Appreciating how rash and ill planned my bid for my brother's freedom had been I was humbled to have to ask for simple necessities.

"Well..." I hesitated. Now it was my turn to be at a loss for words.

"What do you need, my lady?" Deidra promoted, "I will do what I can to help you."

"Thank you, Deidra," I said and then took a long deep breath. "What I need is something else to wear. When I left New Athens, I didn't really stop to pack. Could you find me some water to bathe and might I borrow a change of clothing?"

I felt her shock at my simple request. I smiled at her. "I have surprised you?"

"Yes. I mean... no," she replied confused that I seemed to know what she was feeling. "I would be happy to get what you requested, my lady. Could I get you something to eat as well?"

"That would be wonderful," I replied. "Thank you."

"The Goddess provides," she whispered a traditional blessing of the Demeter sect and turned toward the door. I felt her marshal her courage as she turned to say, "You don't seem to be the spoiled and pampered woman that ..." she trailed off as she realized what she was saying.

"That Alexander told you I was," I finished for her.

"Forgive me for asking, my lady, how do you know so much about what I am thinking? Is it true that you can read minds?"

I laughed softly. "I am an empath. I can feel what those around me are feeling. I read emotions not thoughts."

"But you can tell when someone is lying?" I heard her repeat those familiar words.

"Alexander told you that," I said.

She nodded.

"It is true to a point. I can often feel the tension and panic one feels at telling a lie. Of course, with an expert liar like Alexander, my empathy is practically useless."

"Do you actually hate the Strategos, Lady Ardella?" she asked softly.

It was such a simple question, but a much more difficult answer. *Do I truly hate Alexander? I have been angry with him for so long and have felt guilt over what I had allowed him to do, but did I hate him?* Suddenly, it occurred to me that I felt no anger, fear or hatred from Deidra when she spoke of Alexander. "Don't you hate him for bringing you to Metropolis against your will?"

"I came to Metropolis of my own free will, my lady," Deidra replied without hesitation, but I felt a twinge of doubt prick her heart.

"Forgive me, but you don't look like a Hermian. I would have guessed you were a follower of Demeter," I told her.

"Before I came to Metropolis, I lived in the Elusian village of Pyrthia," she said, anxiously. I felt the fear shoot through her chest like an arrow.

My empathic senses told me her words were not entirely true. My suspicions were confirmed when she looked away from me as if scared that I would call her a liar. *If she wants to keep her origins a secret, what business is it of mine?* I thought.

"Why would any child of Mother Earth want to live in this stone fortress?" I asked.

"We have the park and the countryside around Metropolis. I can enjoy nature and worship Demeter anytime I wish," Deidra explained.

"Hermes tolerates the worship of another Olympian in his capital?"

"I had never thought about how Hermes might feel. Alexander is the one who allows the freedom to worship who we choose."

"Freedom to worship any Olympian you choose. That is impossible."

"The Stragetos says that Metropolis is a city-state based upon an ancient Earth kingdom called Greece. Our ancestors on Earth were allowed to choose who they worshiped and how they lived," she said.

I shook my head vehemently, "I am aware of our history, but I still don't believe it is possible. I have served the Goddess Athena all my life. In my experience, Olympians are not that tolerant."

"Before I came to Metropolis I would have agreed with you. You will see, my lady, that things in Metropolis are very different from the rest of Arcadia," Deidra stated with no small degree of pride.

I knew from her strong emotions that she believed what she said, but I still didn't see how that could be. "But if what you say is true, surely I would have heard of it," I insisted. My doubts about the accuracy of my knowledge about Metropolis came flooding back.

"Someone who spent her life in in the Tower of Athena would not know the common world of Arcadia," she stated.

I was a little shocked by her observation. I realized how

long it had been since anyone had spoken to me with such honesty. When I did not reply, I felt her anxiety begin to flower like a Hephaestian fire blossom and she whispered, "I did not mean to offend you, Lady Ardella."

"I am not offended, Deidra," I assured her. "I am glad you decided to be my guide. I think your honesty will serve me well. It is also beginning to look like I am going to need quite a few lessons about this place."

"What do you want to know?"

"Let's start with the notion of freedom to worship any Olympian."

"Most of the Olympian sects have followers within the walls of Metropolis," she said.

"I saw the evidence of that in the outer rings as I entered the city"

"We are allowed to build communities similar to the homes we left behind. We are allowed to worship any Olympian we chose. There is even a small group that has chosen to worship the Goddess sleeping in the park," Deidra said.

Metropolis was full of surprises, I thought. "There are worshippers of Artemis in Metropolis? There have been no followers of Artemis for almost a thousand years," I marveled.

"There are now," Deidra offered quietly.

I thought about the vibrations of life I had felt within the tomb and wondered if the Moon Goddess was aware of her new worshipers. I knew that the twin Olympians had been absent from day to day life in Arcadia for a millennium. *Imagine the consequences to Arcadia, if they were to awaken.* "I wonder how the children of Apollo feel about the worship of Artemis?"

"What do you mean?" she asked.

"It was the destruction of her followers by the other Olympians that caused the Goddess Artemis to fall into her eternal sleep. Although Apollo could not excuse the attack on the Amazons, he could not go on, knowing what had happened to his twin. I have seen the giant God Apollo standing in the harbor of Heliopolis. He is frozen in place for eternity just as his sister sleeps within her tomb," I informed her.

"You think it is possible that worshiping Artemis might wake her? And if she awakens, then so will Apollo?" Deidra asked in awe.

"I am beginning to think anything is possible," I replied. My mind drifted from Artemis to her sleeping twin in Heliopolis. . "Although I doubt it would be good for Heliopolis," I speculated. I could not help but imagine the terror of the corrupt leaders of Apollo's capital upon learning of this possibility. I knew that it had been a long time since the followers of Apollo had had any communication with their God. The royal family had been manipulating the selection of the Pythia for generations, fraudulently ruling in the name of Apollo. If he were to awaken there would be a reckoning. I was certain Prince Andros would do almost anything to avoid the wrath of the Olympian he and his ancestors had wronged.

"What else do you wish to know, my lady?" Deidra asked, drawing me from my contemplation.

I laughed softly. "I am not sure. I am supposed to be an expert on Alexander and Metropolis. I read reports from all over Arcadia and none of them every mentioned this pluralistic or tolerant society."

"Your reports were coming from the leaders of the Olympian sects. Why would they tell you that many of their common people were deserting to Metropolis?" Deidra stated, factually.

I was a little shaken by the truth of her observations. The need to understand filled my heart. "Deserting?" I asked.

"Most people in Metropolis who are not Hermians came

here because they were unhappy, unwanted or oppressed in their original sect."

"Alexander said that Metropolis is the haven for misfits, outcasts and exiles."

"Metropolis is a place of freedom and hope," she beamed.

"This is too much to take in all at once. I can't believe my knowledge of Metropolis was so inaccurate," I murmured. I massaged my temples; I suddenly felt quite drained.

"Would you like to meet the people of Metropolis for yourself? I could ask for permission to take you on a tour."

"Permission? I am free to worship as I please, but not to move around the city?"

"Metropolis is not as... civilized as New Athens. The Strategos said you are under his protection. I must honor that," Deidra explained.

"You have promoted yourself from my servant to my bodyguard," I countered.

"I only obey the Strategos," she continued. "He asked me to serve and protect you."

"You forgot to mention the protection part earlier."

"Forgive me. I have spent all my life among common people. This is all new to me," Deidra said.

"The common people," I mused, "that is Lysander... Alexander. He was a common gardener in New Athens."

Deidra paused, "Yes, that is why Metropolis is a place of hope for common people. If they are unhappy in their sect, they come here for a new start."

"Alexander is responsible for the tolerance in Metropolis?"

"Of course, he is the Strategos. There are some in the city who would follow him into the realms of Poseidon if he asked them to," she replied. I felt her pride and confidence from across the room. There was the answer to my earlier question about whether or not someone would sacrifice themselves for Alexander.

"You admire him," I suggested.

"I know what his reputation is beyond the walls of Metropolis. Before I came here, I heard the stories of his cruelty, too. I was terrified of this place," Deidra said.

A spark of guilt struck me as I realized Alexander's heated accusations might actually have some truth to them.

"And now you believe Alexander is some kind of hero?" I scoffed.

"I am not saying that Alexander is perfect, but the stories about the atrocities of Metropolis are not true."

I was allowing myself to fall under the spell of Deidra's words and forget all the truths I thought I knew about my enemy. I shook my head and retorted, "Are you trying to tell me that Alexander does not send his the Hermians out to raid the other sects and commit violence in his name?"

"No," she admitted, and then added, "but isn't the reason he raids other sects important?"

"I am afraid Alexander is influenced by the driving passion for conflict that is his father's nature. After all, he is the Son of Ares," I said.

"You make him sound like a monster that steals for his own pleasure."

I winced at her use of the word "monster," but managed to focus on our conversation. "So why raid and drive your followers closer and closer to the limits of Olympian patience? One day that behavior could mean the death of everyone in Metropolis."

"The raids are necessary for our survival," Deidra insisted.

I sensed a growing tide of frustration building inside her.

"Without supplies and resources Metropolis could not exist. This place is too important. It must survive," she continued.

Her words suddenly brought to mind the dreams and

ambitions of Lysander. The memory of him came flooding back.... How could I have forgotten?

"What do you want?" Lysander growled at me as I stood peering through the bars of his cell. I had known where he was being held for days and had only recently found the courage to come and see him myself.

"I came to see if you needed anything. Is there something you would like to eat or drink?" I offered politely. I tried to pretend he was simply a guest for whom I was being solicitous, but he would not allow me to assuage my guilt so easily.

"The guards are providing me with food and drink," he barked, "I don't think the plan is to execute me by starving me to death."

"There are no plans to execute you at the present time," I assured him.

"But in the future?" he asked. Waves of hopelessness crashed into my psyche. I didn't know what to say or how to express my regret.

"They are still debating your fate," I admitted, "They are just scared."

"Scared of a boy they keep locked in a cage?" he asked.

I knew he was falling back on sarcasm to cope with the fear and anger, which I could feel was threatening to consume him.

"They are scared of what you might do someday," I explained, "Your father is the God of war. They fear his influence will make you aggressive and dangerous."

"So, I am to be executed for crimes that I might commit someday?"

"War is a terrible thing," I said. I handed him my crystal reader. On it was displayed an image of a horrible destructive force called an atomic bomb used during an Earth war. "On ancient Earth war caused the unnecessary deaths of countless innocent people and destroyed entire cities and civilizations. The Olympians brought us to this planet to provide a better world for us. They only want to protect Arcadia from the evils of war."

"And my father Ares, isn't he an Olympian too?" Lysander asked.

"Ares is imprisoned somewhere within Mt. Olympus to keep his influence from affecting Arcadia."

"And just to be sure, there is the Olympian Law that forbids any sect from making war upon pain of oblivion to the offender and his entire sect."

"That is true," I replied.

"So what do they think one person can do to upset their perfect world?"

"I..."I began, but realized I had no answer for him. I looked into his eyes and could not help but feel branded by his accusation. Though I was one of Athena's chosen, I could not defend the reasoning of her Council or the Goddess herself. There was no rational reason to condemn this boy to death.

"You don't know, do you? Even with everything you have read about the evils of war," he said, indicating to the crystal reader, "you can't explain why they fear me, because you don't understand."

"No," I admitted, lowering my eyes.

For the first time since I had met him I felt satisfaction in his heart. "Ironically I understand why they fear me."

I looked up curiously; I was awed as his emotions changed from fear to determination.

"If this one mortal were given the chance, I would gladly upset their perfect world. I would take the knowledge that Athena hordes and share it with everyone on Arcadia. I would see Elusians use the gift of Demeter to grow crops not just in her sacred circles, but in every city. I would take from the royal house of Heliopolis who have too much and give it to those in need. I would see Amazons take husbands and the followers of Aphrodite create beauty for all. No one on my Arcadia would ever be told what they must be or not be, where they must live, who they may love, or what Olympian they may worship. No one would ever be told that because his father was a gardener then he too must be a gardener. No one would ever be told they are not good enough to go to the Academy, or be deprived of viewing the knowledge that is the birthright of all mankind."

He had been a boy who had been denied his dreams because of the traditions of Athenian society. I was beginning to understand that Metropolis was the world in which he wished he had grown up.

"You seem to know Alexander very well," I suggested, hoping to prompt her to tell me a little more about herself.

"I have known him for many years. My husband is one of his inner circle. Kern is devoted to the Strategos and I must admit I have come to have a great deal of respect for him as well."

"How is it that you came to be the one sent as my servant? It seems an unlikely task for the wife of one of his favorites."

"I am one of the only ones with time to spare for this. The task fell to me since I do not have children to fill my hours."

I heard the wistful sadness in her voice at this pronouncement, but that was nothing compared to the wave of sorrow that hit her like a sea storm ripping through fragile marshlands, leaving devastation in its wake. I had felt this ache before. This woman had lost a child—I was sure of it. "I am so sorry," I whispered without thinking.

Deidra looked at once startled and terrified. "I should go. I will return soon with your food and clothes," she said briskly, then she exited the Tower room as if the Furies themselves were chasing her.

I started to go after her to apologize, when a sudden wave of blue light struck me with such intensity that I fell to my knees. Every nerve ending tingled as the strange glow engulfed my body. Terror stole through my heart and I found myself unable to speak or move. Just as the hands of the Son of Ares had once twisted around my neck, I felt the touch of the blue flame squeeze tighter and tighter. This time it was Athena who choked me until the blackness came.

It was a dark, moonless night and I stood on my balcony in the Tower of Athena looking out over New Athens. From my vantage I could look across at the parks and towers of the city now deserted by the sleeping masses. I could see the twisting spiral of the Academy in the distance. The moonlight cast a ghostly pallor across the metal and marble landscape, and suddenly an uncontrollable fear tore through my chest. It was then that I heard the cries of pain and saw that flames engulfed the far side of the city. The flickering light of the fire slithered through the darkened landscape like an Arcadian viper seeking its next unwary victim.

"Why, Ardella? Why did you do this to us?" I heard voices call from the burning streets of New Athens. I tried to respond that I did not do this, that I would not do anything to hurt Athena's people, but my voice was frozen.

Suddenly the Goddess herself stood beside me. "Tell them this is not my fault," I tried to beg of the Goddess. Again my voice produced no sound, but Athena knew what was in my heart.

"I will feel the pain of your absence, Ardella. I wish that you could return to my side, but that is not possible. Your actions both past and present would harm New Athens. Remember that your sacrifice protects my children from this terrible fate," Athena said solemnly and then disappeared from view.

My mind rebelled at this cruel fate. I had not harmed New

Athens—only angered the Goddess. I did not transgress the Great Law of the Olympians. My only crime was being young and naïve. There was still so much I wanted to do in New Athens—it was the only home I had ever thought to know.

I looked back out over the blazing edifices and cried as I witnessed the world I had lost.

I awoke suddenly from the vision, no doubt a message from Athena. I knew that I had been exiled. I was not surprised by this outcome, but I was surprised by my reaction to it. My heart was heavy and my soul felt lost. I curled up on the cold stone floor where I lay, and felt the tears rolling down my cheeks.

Chapter 8

The sweet songs of my children brighten my heart and fill my days with joy. The priestesses of my temple are my family even more than my Olympian brothers and sisters.

The Goddess Aphrodite
229 years *Ab Terra Condita*

LATER THAT DAY, dressed in my new metropolitan clothing, I left the citadel and entered the outer rings and cobbled streets of the city. The buildings and foliage I passed interlaced into a soft mosaic of browns and greens that gave the city a warmth and charm. Again it was not what I expected of Metropolis. It was not the bleak stone edifice filled with dirty, unhappy people that I had imagined. In fact, I could feel that most of the people in Metropolis were happy to be here.

Deidra walked beside me, often greeting people as we passed by. Having felt her pain at her lack of children, I soon realized that she had poured her strong maternal drives into helping others. It was apparent from the words and emotions of those around us that Deidra was well liked among the citizens of

Metropolis whose needs and concerns she made her own.

It said something about the emerging population of Metropolis that only a few of the people we met felt even a little curiosity about the newcomer with Deidra. I was glad. Thanks to Deidra's presence, most of the feelings of the people around us were skewed to the positive spectrum. I was certain that if they knew who I was, or worse, who my brother was, I would have received a very different reception, and the emotional cost could be devastating.

In New Athens I had never been able to walk the streets in anonymity as I did here. Just a few hours ago I had been weeping over the realization that I had truly left my old life behind. *Now, perhaps, Metropolis will be part of my future.* The further we walked the more I began to feel excitement about my surroundings. I was able to study the people and buildings that we passed without my stares being noticed or considered rude. I was just another newcomer to the city. There were no expectations or responsibilities. For the first time in my life I was completely unrestricted.

The people of Metropolis were not so different from those of New Athens, except in one respect. They seemed to possess an air of self-confidence and self-importance on a personal level rather than as a society. In New Athens everyone knew their function and went about the day to day activities of life in a calm and dignified manner. In Metropolis each person performed their duties with a fervor I rarely saw in New Athens—the exception being Tannis and his love of gardening.

The stones used to build the walls of the houses and shops were smaller than the cyclopean stones used in the walls of Metropolis. I suspected from their irregular shape they were the shards created during the building of the outer walls. The floors were dirt or wood, the windows had no glass, only shutters, and the roofs were flat sheets of a metal Deidra said was called tin. Although the glass and metal towers of New Athens with their spacious architecture would be considered superior by most standards, I found the simple homes of the citizens of Metropolis refreshing.

Several of the people we met greeted me, but most spoke only to Deidra, with one exception, a tall, athletic brunette who approached me while Deidra was involved in conversation with a group from the Demeter sect.

"Lady Ardella."

I turned toward the voice surprised that anyone knew my name. "Do I know you?"

"My name is Kendra. I just wanted to tell you that I am a friend. If you ever need anything, I work in the Medusa tavern near the outer wall."

"That is kind of you."

"I just wanted to make sure you knew that you are not alone in Metropolis. There are other friends who you may call upon," she said with a curt nod. I felt her strong sense of determination and suspected I had just met one of Queen Lyessa's Amazon spies.

"Thank you. That is good to know," I turned to reply, but the woman had melted back into the crowd of strangers like a ghostly messenger from the lands of Hades. I took a deep breath and looked over at Deidra, but she was still deep in conversation and had not noticed the encounter. I moved toward the group Deidra was speaking to, but was stopped short by a sudden burst of intense terror that shot through me like an arrow.

Deidra noticed my discomfort immediately. "What is it, my lady?" she asked and moved to my side.

"I am not sure. Someone nearby is terrified…" but my words were cut off by a woman's scream behind us. We turned to see an enormous bellowing giant dragging a struggling blonde woman by the hair. I felt Deidra's fury as she rushed toward the harrowing scene.

"Let her go, Davin!" she demanded. Her quiet strength clearly relayed her displeasure even for those without the gift of empathy.

"Stay out of this, Dee," the woman pleaded; her terror intensified to levels that threaten to knock me to the ground.

"You heard her, Dee," Davin scoffed. "It is my right as her provider to complain about her housekeeping skills."

"If you beat her senseless, Davin, then who will cook for you? Are you planning to go hungry tonight just to teach her a lesson?" Deidra countered.

The large, brutal raider sneered at the remark, but was silent as if truly contemplating his choices. "I don't know why I even bother to keep you," he laughed cruelly and gave her hair one last wrench before he dropped her trembling form to the ground. "I expect dinner to be ready and waiting when I get home or you and your two brats can find another place to live."

"Of course, Davin. I'll make lamb stew tonight; it's your favorite," the woman said in a sweet voice that gave not even a hint that the man she was offering to cook for was the violent lunatic who had been brutalizing her.

He scoffed and turned away from her. He looked over at Deidra with contempt. I could feel his intense anger at her interference and suspected she was in danger.

"He is very angry," I whispered to Deidra as he moved toward us like a raging bull.

"Good," she said as his approach picked up momentum. She stepped away from me and took up a defensive stance. A stance I had seen used before—in Amazonia. That is why I had sensed hesitation in her answers yesterday. Deidra wasn't an Elyusian; she was an Amazon.

No wonder she had lied about her origin, I thought. Deserting the Amazon nation was a death sentence. She would never admit her heritage to a stranger. Armed with this latest insight about my guide, I was not surprised to see the giant fly through the air and land with a loud thud on the hard packed earth. Deidra was a defiantly Amazon warrior and a good one at that.

"How dare you..." he growled, red faced. I felt his embarrassment mix with his anger and knew that he was even more dangerous than before.

"You attacked me, Davin. You know that everyone in Metropolis has the right to defend themselves. I didn't dare anything. If you continue to attack me, I will fight you and I will win. Do you really want that?"

"I'll get you for this," he snarled, but made no move toward her. Actually, I could feel fear building in his gut and I suspected his attitude was a bluff.

"While we are issuing threats, Davin, let me make one thing clear. If I ever see bruises on my friend Kaylee again, you will regret it. Ask around about what I do to men who mistreat women in Metropolis."

To my surprise, I felt a wave of abject terror shoot through Argus. I wondered what Deidra had done in the past to warrant such a reaction from this giant brute. His fear won out and his bellowing was all bravado. "I'm not worried about some slut who thinks she is some kinda warrior," he muttered. I felt Deidra's disappointment as Davin stood up and huffed off. I suspected she had been looking forward to the fight.

In contrast to Deidra's disappointment, I could feel a wave of relief wash away Kaylee's fear as Davin walked away scowling.

"Are you alright?" Deidra asked and knelt beside the woman. I could feel her concern mixed with anger and frustration. I suspected this was not the first time Davin had lost his temper.

"Thank you for stopping him, Dee."

"Why do you let him do this again and again?" Deidra asked. Her voice was tinged with frustration.

"You know why, Dee. I need a provider. Davin is the only one who will have us."

"Leave him, Kaylee. You know Kern and I would not mind providing for you until you can find a more permanent solution."

"That is sweet, Deidra. But it is not just about me. I have to think of the boys. Davin is a good provider... besides, he isn't like this all the time—just when he drinks."

"I wish there was something I could do to help," Deidra offered.

"I wish the boys' father stilled lived to care for his children, but I will do what I must to survive."

"We lost many good people that winter," Deidra said.

I felt the horrible wave of sorrow tear through her again, and wondered if it had something to do with her lost child. Despite her inner pain her outward countenance was cool and reserve.

"That is why I stay with Davin. My sons must be well fed and healthy, so they don't get sick like their father."

"If you ever need me, I will ..." Deidra started to assure her.

"I know you want to help, but Dee this is my problem. Rork and I left New Corinth because we didn't want the children to suffer just for being born as they were. They didn't meet the standard of perfection for followers of Aphrodite and would have been sent to living death in the mines. I will endure whatever I must to make sure they have a future," she said ardently.

"I know," Deidra replied. She watched her friend depart and I knew she was still filled with a mixture of frustration and sorrow.

Perhaps Metropolis was the haven for the misfits, outcasts and exiles of Arcadia, but what I had just witnessed proved that it was far from perfect.

"Your fighting skills are impressive," I said, softly, in an attempt to end the strange silence that had formed upon Kaylee's departure.

Deidra startled expression and the waves of guilt again confirmed my suspicions about her true origins. "I learned from the best," she replied. "I had an Amazon teacher."

I smiled at her clever answer, which explained her skills without giving away her true origin.

"Then we have something in common. I was taught to fight by an Amazon as well, although I will never come close to your skill level."

"It is simply a matter of practice. There is a group of women who train in the park every morning at dawn. You are always welcome to join us."

"Thank you. Lyessa always said I needed to practice more."

"Lyessa," Deidra gasped in amazement. "As in Queen Lyessa?"

"All my lessons were before Lyessa took the crown—back when her mother Breanna was still queen."

"How did you come to be taught by an Amazon princess?"

"She is one of my oldest friends. We met when we were teenagers. Because of our positions in society, we both found ourselves overprotected and isolated from others our age. We found in each other a lonely, kindred spirit and have been friends ever since."

"I had no idea," Deidra replied. Her comments were casual, but I felt the strong tide of excitement flood her heart. *Why should it matter to her if I am friends with Queen Lyessa of the Amazons?*

"Perhaps we should get back to your tour," she suggested.

Our journey through the city continued and I lost track of the new names and faces. After our encounter with Kaylee, I became more aware of the dirty, haunted faces of some of the less fortunate citizens of Metropolis. I saw beggars and homeless children wandering the streets and could feel their desperation. Although many felt pity for these lost souls, they turned away from them. I felt Deidra's distress at their misery, but even she felt powerless to save them.

I spent so much time looking at the people of the city that I did not pay attention to our surroundings. I was surprised when we stopped at one house at the end of long row. They were so similar and didn't seem to have any distinguishing marks I could see to identify which families dwelled within.

"I need to check in on Hazell. She is eight months pregnant with her third child. I want to see if she needs help with anything," Deidra said as she knocked on the door.

A pale round woman answered and I could hear the curious voices of two toddlers in the background "Mommy, who is it? Mommy, did they come to see us?" She smiled at Deidra, but her emotions were weariness and fear.

"Good morning, Hazell."

"Good morning, Deidra."

"I wanted to stop by to see how you are doing!"

"Did Kern ask you to check on his brother's wife?"

"Actually, Draenon spoke to me before he left for the raid. He knew the end of your pregnancy would be a difficult time and he hated leaving you to care for the other children by yourself," Deidra said.

"He had to go on the raid. We need the supplies, especially with another mouth to feed."

"Draenon and Kern are good providers. I know how much my brother-in-law cherishes you and the children. I promised to make sure you were doing well and see if there was anything I could do to help."

"I appreciate your concern. The children and I are doing

fine. I can't think of anything we need at the moment," Hazell replied.

Deidra looked over at me and I shook my head. Although the young mother was putting up a brave front for her sister-in-law's benefit, she was exhausted and frightened. Deidra smiled at me, knowingly. I suspected that she already recognized this woman's mental state.

"Would you mind if we took the children to the park for a little while? It is such a beautiful day and it will do them good to run and play outside," Deidra asked her sister-in-law.

The excitement at the offer of a few hours of peace and quiet to rest was obvious even to a non-empath. She quickly led us into her home. The children came running up to Deidra clearly excited to see their aunt again.

"Would you two like to go to the park?" Deidra asked.

The children's affirmative chorus surprised none of us and we were quickly dressing the Lissette and Sinon in their capes and helping them tie on their shoes. Within minutes we were headed back up to the citadel.

"Are we going to the grove of Artemis?" I asked as I realized the direction we were headed.

"Yes," Deidra said.

"Alexander allows his favorites to use the Grove as a public park." I was astonished.

"Alexander allows everyone in Metropolis to use the grove of Artemis. It is a public park," Deidra replied. Again her pride was obvious.

My enemy surprised me once again. The more I learned about Metropolis, the more I wondered how much of my information had been questionable. I didn't suddenly believe Alexander was innocent, but perhaps he was not as guilty as I had once thought.

The energy of small children is amazing. I was exhausted from just watching Lissette and Sinon chase each other up and down the paths of the park. It seemed the two children (and the other dozen or so we had encountered in the park) had run through every corner of the greenery with one very noticeable exception. Everyone seemed to avoid the tiny central grove around the tomb of Artemis.

"Deidra, is there are reason everyone seems to be avoiding the tomb of Artemis? It is the central point of the park and yet I have seen no one approach it in the entire time we have been here?"

"Most stay away out of respect for the Goddess," she said. Her emotions were jumbled and fearful.

"And the others?" I prompted.

"It is strange how you can do that," she said. She was clearly troubled by her inability to tell even white lies to me.

"I am sorry, Deidra, I didn't mean to make you uncomfortable. I was just curious," I said.

"You are correct that people avoid the tomb of Artemis. Many say they have heard a woman's voice call to them, but there is no one there. Some say its Artemis. Others say it is a ghost and the grove is haunted," Deidra explained.

While I could feel her skepticism, I could not stop the wide grin that spread across my face. "I think I know why people have heard a woman's voice. If you will come with me to the grove, I will show you," I offered.

Although she showed no outward sign on her face, I felt her sudden doubt at my pronouncement. "I'm not sure…" she said.

"I actually know something about Metropolis that you don't. Don't you want to find out what it is?" I teased.

She shook her head, and rose to follow me.

We walked slowly toward the tomb and the grove. When the children realized where we were headed they came running headlong behind us. I realized that several other groups of children were also tempted to join us, but were being held back by the adults who watched over them.

"Are you sure about this, Lady Ardella?" Deidra asked as we stopped in front of the tomb.

"Muriel," I called toward the grove, "Can you hear me? It is your friend Ardella. I have come to visit you. I even brought new people for you to meet."

For a long moment there was silence and I felt more doubt begin to creep into Deidra's mind.

"Muriel," I called again.

"Ardella, the follower of Athena," I heard the dryad say in my mind. I knew that Deidra and the children heard her, too as I felt their surprise.

"Where are you, Muriel?" I asked.

The fluttering form of the dryad greeted me as she separated from the great oak that she called home. Her ethereal form seemed to float towards us.

"It's a pretty lady," Sinon muttered.

"A very pretty lady," Lissette agreed.

"Muriel is a dryad," I told the children. "They are spirits that live in trees in the groves all around Arcadia."

"They can see me?" Muriel asked delighted.

"What is going on, Ardella? Who are you and the children talking to?" Deidra asked, confused.

The happy dryad ignored the startled Deidra and her question and floated toward the children. "They are talking to me. The children can see me. After all this time it is a wonderful to be heard and seen," Muriel babbled.

I decided to intervene. "Muriel is a dryad, Deidra," I explained. "Although many adults cannot see them, apparently children can."

"But you can see her?" Deidra asked.

"Yes, but I think that is because my grandmother introduced me to a dryad in New Athens when I was just a child. It made me sensitive to their presence. I know a few other adults who can see them as well," I explained.

"And this dryad has been here in the park all along?" Deidra asked.

"Muriel was here long before Metropolis. She was sleeping. She said it was people working on the park that woke her. She has been trying to communicate, but until now no one could see her," I said.

"I can't believe that there is an ancient woodland spirit that has been living here in the grove all this time."

"That is why you can't see me," Muriel offered, sagely and everyone laughed.

Chapter 9

My love is like bird soaring on the wind. It is strong and true when it can move freely among the clouds, but lock it in a cage and it will wither and die.

**Sarriah, poet laureate of the Apollo sect
One thousand, eight hundred and fifty-three years Ab Terra Condita**

I KNEW ALEXANDER was coming up the stairs to my chamber even before he arrived. I was filled with a sudden wave of nervousness and my heart pounded. Everything I had learned about the Son of Ares and his unusual city had been a revelation to me, and chipped away at the armor of wariness I had donned as I approached Metropolis.

"Lady Ardella," he whispered from the doorway.

I stood with my back him, looking out at the grove of Artemis. "Come in, Strategos."

"How are you doing this morning?" His tone was jovial.

"My mood is nowhere near as good as yours," I scoffed.

An invisible wall suddenly arose between us. His ability to

create a defensive cloak against my empathic powers still awed me.

"Did you enjoy your time in the park?" he asked. His authoritative tone intended to remind me that Deidra reported to him.

"Deidra's niece and nephew are adorable and very energetic. I think they had a wonderful time," I replied.

"And their mother had a few hours of peace. Her husband is worried about her health," Alexander added.

"Perhaps it would be better if he were here looking after his wife rather than off raiding in some distant village," I retorted.

"Raiding is a necessity of life in Metropolis. Every family needs supplies to stave off hunger and the elements. Those provisions are gained through raiding. Surely you don't want Lissette and Sinon to starve because you look down on how their father provides for his family?"

"Do not put words in my mouth, Alexander," I huffed. "Of course I do not want anyone to starve, but there are other ways to provide for a family. There is farming, herding or even trade." Goading Alexander into this debate was not really about Deidre and her family; it was born out of a twisted need to fight my growing admiration for my enemy. I wanted him to defend his bloody ways and remind me why I had spent the last few years of my life working to defeat him. I should have known that he would not cooperate.

"We actually have a thriving merchant class who use the barter system to move goods obtained on raids and trade them to the people who need them. They are the older men who cannot physically participate in raids anymore. However, they can still provide a valuable service to the city, which helps bring food and clothing to their families," he said. My empathic gift told me he took great pride in his people's resilience. I was not going to let his feelings influence mine today.

"Your perfect society is balanced upon a shaky foundation, Alexander," I insisted. "You teach your men to take what they want from others through intimidation and threats of violence and then expect them to behave as civilized members of your society."

His silence and the burst of trepidation in his heart told me that I had hit upon a truth he would rather not face.

"How often do they turn that violence upon each other or their own families?" I pressed. I could not help but think of the woman I saw yesterday—the one who would have been beaten by the man who was supposed to provide for her, if Deidra hadn't interfered.

He had the good grace to look uncomfortable with my comment. "No system is perfect, Ardella." His demeanor remained calm, although regret bled through his emotional armor. "I will admit crime and violence in Metropolis is higher than in other sects on Arcadia, but that is a small price to pay for no Olympian menacing our freedom of choice."

"Are you saying that Hermes is not the patron God of Metropolis; that he doesn't rule here?" I asked. *Maybe he will reveal what kind of a deal he has made with Hermes to justify freedom of worship in Metropolis.*

"Hermes is the patron of Metropolis and it is by his grace that its citizens are allowed the freedom to live here and worship any Olympian they wish," Alexander said.

"Unconditionally?" I pressed.

"Nothing comes without a price, Ardella. All citizens of Metropolis must show Hermes the respect and honor due an Olympian. And, they must pay the necessary taxes for the upkeep of the city and its defenses. In exchange they may live as they please; worship whom they please; marry whom they please. It is a fair exchange."

"You do seem to have convinced people from all over Arcadia that their lives would be better in Metropolis. I wonder how many are disappointed with the harsh realities once they arrive?" I argued.

"Unlike other sects of Arcadia, anyone who is unhappy with their life here is free to leave. Very few choose to return to their former sects, despite the struggles to survive in Metropolis. That should tell you something about the value they place on the freedom," he replied with growing sense of passion I could recognize even without my empathy.

"It seems too good to be true, Alexander," I suggested.

"If you don't believe me, surely you believe the citizens of Metropolis," he scoffed. "You saw my city for yourself yesterday."

"One guided tour of Metropolis will not suddenly change my opinion, but..."

"But?"

"I will admit I had no idea you had created such a society. Most of the reports I received were about the raids and how you terrorized those who were forced to join your cause."

"Forced to join," he said laughing, "I will admit early on to recruiting people with skills that we desperately needed, but once they served their purpose they were free to return home - some did, some didn't."

"Is that your excuse for kidnapping Apollo's healers?" I asked.

"It was necessary. We had no hospital; no journeyman sent from Heliopolis. However, once those men taught us the basic skills of medicine, I gave them the opportunity to return. Only one chose to leave. Most of the others are still here and have married women of Metropolis. Our hospital rivals those that can be found in any Olympian capital outside Heliopolis. I would be happy to show it to you," he said.

I hated how my heart sped up at the prospect of touring a facility forbidden to me in New Athens. I was irritated with myself for letting him tempt me and replied, "We will see."

He laughed at my reluctance, but continued, "I heard you were forbidden to enter the hospital in New Athens."

How does he know that? I wondered.

"There are no limitations here. You will be impressed with our healers and their dedication to Metropolis. This is their home now," he boasted.

"Did it ever occur to you that once you had forced the men of Heliopolis to share the secrets of Apollo's healing with outsiders they were too scared of punishment to return home?" I was determined to contradict him.

"Why should they be punished for sharing knowledge with others who want to learn?" I had hit a nerve; he was irritated. He began to rant, "Why should the followers of Demeter be too scared to make food grow on the hillsides around Metropolis. Why would they object to putting an end to the need to steal our food from their brothers and sisters in Elyusia? Why do Athena's followers refuse to share the knowledge of the Academy with their fellow citizens to improve life for everyone?"

"The Olympians set up our world to be a delicate balance. Each sect provides a vital service required by all of Arcadia for survival. It drives the trade between the sects. Without this secrecy a sect might lose their advantage and harm their society. It has always been that way," I suggested.

"Has it always been this way...or is that just an Olympians deception?"

"You aren't wise to speak such things aloud," I whispered. I was too used to life in the Tower of Athena to respond any other way.

"That is the wisdom of New Athens, Heliopolis or Amazonia,

but it is not the way things are done in Metropolis," he pronounced. The anger and frustration he could no longer suppress burst through his emotional armor.

"I say the Olympians are liars who have manipulated mankind for over two thousand years. We should be free to live as we please! We don't need Olympians telling us what to do!"

His last words echoed off the walls, causing me to cringe. It was several moments before I realized I had been holding my breath in anticipation of the Olympian's wrath. But nothing happened. There was no lighting, no roar of thunder, no voice reprimanding Alexander for his heresy. There was only silence.

For as long as I could remember, I had been skeptical about the true nature of the Olympians and their control over Arcadia. My mother's warning, however, had ruled by tongue for over a decade. I had lived in awe and fear of the Goddess my whole life. Now I found myself envying my rival's fearless attitude.

"Is it because you are the Son of Ares that you do not fear the Olympians?" I asked.

"It is because I am the Son of Ares that I am driven to bring change to Arcadia."

"To cause the chaos that the Olympians fear?"

"The Olympians do fear me, don't they?" he chortled.

I felt rays of intense satisfaction lighten up the dark corners of his mind. *He enjoys irritating the Olympians*, I observed. I thought about Athena's reaction to Alexander over the years and found myself fighting the urge to smile as well.

"You have always believed you had a purpose in life—a destiny," I said, recalling things he had said as a prisoner in New Athens.

"And you don't believe that your life has a destiny?" he asked.

I had often wondered that myself, but had come to the

conclusion it wasn't so. "If I have a destiny then it seems to be interwoven with yours. Athena gave me the gift of empathy to discover your identity. My own compassion allowed you to escape from New Athens. My life's work has revolved around trying to stop you and make up for that mistake."

"Is that how you remember it? That releasing me was a mistake? You believe I manipulated you?" The tone in his voice was unfamiliar and haunting. It beckoned for the truth.

"Whether you did it intentionally or not, Alexander, I could feel your fear and frustration. I made my decision to help you based upon those emotions and my reactions to them. My brother and I have been paying for that one choice for over a decade," I replied in an even tone.

"No matter what the motivation, the choice to act always rests with the individual. Actions have consequences. If we take action, we must accept whatever comes," he said.

"Is that why you refuse to let my brother go?" I asked.

"I told you before: you and Rafe must face Hermes and the Council. I do not have the authority to release him."

"You are the Strategos of Metropolis." I was irritated. "You expect me to believe you cannot order the release of my brother?"

"For that you will have to appeal to Hermes. Perhaps he will show mercy for a beautiful woman." He smiled.

"And when am I to meet with Hermes?" I asked.

"After you run a small errand for Metropolis," he said.

I looked into his eyes for any signs of what game he was playing, but instead saw a look of nervous anticipation. *He really does need me to do something for him.* I was shocked. "You want me to run an errand for you…for the chance to speak to Hermes on my brother's behalf, but with no guarantees of his freedom?" I asked, incredulously.

"Something like that," he said. Although he was smiling, I

could not sense his true feelings. *Is he being serious or is this was some sort of cruel joke,* I wondered. "What exactly do you want me to do?" I asked.

"I want to send you on a mission," he said.

"What kind of a mission?"

"I need your diplomatic skills, Ardella. They are rare in Metropolis and I find I need ... an ambassador. I want you to negotiate a treaty," he admitted.

"You want me to negotiate a treaty between the Hermians and another sect?" I asked. The entire situation was preposterous. We were adversaries. Just because I was trapped in Metropolis while I was trying to free my brother did not mean I would change sides in this struggle. *Why would he make such an absurd suggestion?*

"You just have to deliver my proposal for a peace treaty. Nothing more," he explained.

"A peace treaty with whom?"

"Hera and the Amazons," he said without hesitation.

My heart froze in my chest. By the Goddess! He is playing some sort of cruel game. Deidra told him about Lyessa and now he wants to use my friendship with Queen of the Amazons to his advantage. A long forgotten conversation was stirred by his request:

"You have got to be kidding," I replied.

The tall and beautiful queen of the Amazons only laughed. It was late afternoon and the intense rays of the sun brought out streaks of red in her light auburn hair, which fell into soft waves around her face. I again found myself envying Lyessa her lustrous hair as I tuck a wayward strand of my bland, brown hair back into the bun I always wore.

"Rafe said you would be shocked by the suggestion," Lyessa

said.

"You discussed this plan with my brother?" I asked.

"We spent hours arguing whether or not it would work when he was last here."

"I didn't realize you allowed male guests in Amazonia," I laughed.

"Your brother is a rare exception," Lyessa replied casually, but the strange fluttering in her chest made me wonder if there might be something more between them than just planning Alexander's downfall.

"I know Rafe believes that removing Alexander from power will end the aggression of the Hermians, but I am not so sure. Sending an assassin is a radical and dangerous step," I argued.

"We have to find a way to stop the raids, Ardella."

"But what if the other Olympians see the assassination as an act of war? Can we risk taking the life of the leader of another sect?" I cautioned.

"Alexander and the Hermians are becoming more and more of a threat. My reports say that he has finished a second cyclopean wall around Metropolis. They are stealing more and more every day. Are you saying that the death of one man is not justified, if it saves so many others from the horrors of these raids?"

"I don't know. I hate to resort to violence. It makes us no better than him," I responded.

"Ardella, I have always admired your passion for stopping the Son of Ares, but your empathy for others keeps you from seeing what must be done."

"I cannot be anything except what I am, Lyessa," I reminded her.

"I know, my friend. I didn't say there was anything wrong with your empathy. You are a compassionate and generous person. What you have to realize is that those are not the qualities needed to make this decision."

"You are the warrior."

"Do you trust me?"

"Of course."

"Then trust me. We need to send an Amazon assassin to rid us of the Son of Ares once and for all."

"I will not do it. You want to use me to manipulate the Amazons," I replied angrily returning to the present.

"I am not trying to manipulate anyone, Ardella," Alexander assured me.

"You expect me to believe the Son of Ares wants a peace treaty? What would the God of War have say about that?"

"Fortunately Ares does not manipulate my life the way Athena seems to manipulate yours," he snapped.

"Just because you do not do everything Ares tells you to, does not mean his words have no effect on you. Olympians are wily ..."

"I don't hear the voice of Ares in my head," he interrupted me.

I just stared for a moment dumbfounded. "Really?" I managed to gasp. I still could not believe I had heard correctly. One of the results of being touched by an Olympian was the ability to communicate telepathically with our sire. I had never met any child of a God who did not hear them in their mind's eye—whether they wanted to or not. Perhaps the Son of Ares was somehow different.

"I have never heard his voice. Ares does not direct my actions," he repeated.

"He has never spoken to you?" I questioned. b"But everything you have done?"

"Ares gave me the drive to change the world, but every idea

and every decision has been mine alone."

"Stealing the crystal reader, taking control of the Hermians, the raids, everything you have accomplished in Metropolis..."

"...was all me," he said.

Great Goddess! He could not only keep me from reading his emotions, but he could keep an Olympian as powerful as Ares from getting into his head. I was stunned. *Someday I had to learn his secret.* I would give anything to ensure that Athena could never again intrude upon my thoughts.

I shook my head and forced myself to return to the original argument. "That still does not explain why you need me to propose a peace treaty."

"Please, I need you to trust me. I will prove to you my words are true." With a great deal of determination I could feel Alexander open up the wall and allow his feeling full reign. I felt everything he felt.

"I want to make peace with Queen Lyessa and the Amazons. I have no ulterior motives nor do I intend this treaty as a trick to harm the followers of Hera," he said.

Although a voice far back in my head whispered that he was a talented liar and that this was a trick, my heart would not listen. I knew in that moment he was telling the truth. His need and desperation were too clear to misinterpret.

"Why do you want peace with the Amazons?" I asked, cautiously.

"Maybe so they will stop sending assassins to kill me," he retorted, but his emotions told me there was more to it than that.

"And..." I prompted.

He sighed. "I don't want what happened at Argos to be repeated."

As he spoke, I sensed the steady trickle of sorrow drown out his desperation. Alexander knew something I didn't about that massacre and it haunted his soul.

The massacre of Argos has troubled me ever since it happened. After years of raiding with only a handful of casualties, suddenly a dozen people, including several Amazons, had been slaughtered by a raiding party in the small village of Argos. No one had been able to give me the details or an explanation of exactly what had happened. Although I was beginning to suspect I didn't really want to know the whole truth, I had to ask.

"What did happen at Argos, Alexander?"

"Human nature happened," he replied, turning toward me.

I saw his head fall as he admitted his role in the tragedy. "I miscalculated. Argos had always been a simple raid without much resistance, so I made that Rennin's first command. I didn't stop to think about the fact that most of his men were also inexperienced. If I had known there would be a problem, I would have sent more seasoned men. Perhaps they wouldn't have acted so rashly."

"So you did not order the men to...?" I tried to ask, but couldn't bring myself to finish my question. I felt the sorrow and pain pouring out of him as if there were a gaping hole in his chest. I knew in that moment that Alexander could not have ordered the deaths of the villagers of Argos. My failure to complete the accusation encouraged him to continue.

"I sent the men on a raid just like a hundred times before. The incident was a horrible accident," he explained.

"I still don't understand why the raiders killed that day."

"That day, the villagers decided to resist the raid. From what I understand, they were supported by several well-armed Amazons. Rennin and his men panicked. At the inquiry they stated they had feared for their lives and killed in self-defense. As I wasn't there, I cannot be sure if they were telling the truth or if they simply killed in the heat of the moment."

I was stunned and felt the growing shame spread through

my soul as I realize that I knew more about the massacre of Argos than I had first suspected.

"I don't know why the Amazons were doing there that day," Alexander continued, "but if I had sent different men, perhaps things wouldn't have turned out as they did."

For the second time in my life I had to face the horror that my actions had had unanticipated consequences:

"You asked me to come up with another idea, old friend. Why are you so reluctant?" I had asked the Amazon queen.

"It is too sneaky and indirect for my warrior's instincts," Lyessa replied.

"Odd that you use the word 'sneaky'; that is what Rafe said too," I laughed. I saw her blush and knew from her reaction that my brother and I were again working at cross purposes.

"I still think a more direct attack on Metropolis has a better chance of success," Lyessa said.

"The assassin I agreed to let you send failed. So did the next three you and Rafe sent behind my back," I said.

Although I felt her sudden unease with my words, her face betrayed no guilt. "Ardella," she began, but I cut her off. I had planned this argument out in my head and had no intention of getting side tracked into another issue.

"Your direct approach is not working. Give my idea a chance," I continued.

"You want me to send out Amazons to the Ellusian villages to try to encourage them to resist the raids?" Lyessa asked.

"The raiders are over confident, especially with the Elusians. They meet little resistance and take whatever they want unchallenged," I explained.

"Because they challenge unarmed farmers and craftsmen," the Queen of the Amazons interrupted.

"What do you think will happen if they find themselves trying to intimidate fully trained and armed Amazons?" For the first time I saw a spark of awareness in her eyes, and knew the argument was won.

As the realization of my role in the massacre of Argos dawned, I felt my stomach lurch and my hands began to tremble. This time I was the one who had set pawns in motion without a thought for the possible consequences.

"I am so sorry. I never imagined," I murmured, suddenly falling to my knees.

"Ardella, what's wrong?" Alexander knelt beside me. I could feel his concern for me overriding his sorrow.

"I know what the Amazons were doing there," I managed to whisper.

Although I felt his curiosity aroused, it was Alexander's silence that urged me to continue.

"I told Queen Lyessa..."

My words stopped abruptly as I felt rage begin to pour out of Alexander. I could not seem to stop trembling. *What am I doing? This man is the Son of Ares.* I had felt his anger directed towards Rafe and his attack on Metropolis. *What will he do to me once he learns the truth about Argos?*

Alexander reached out and took my hand in his. "Tell me the rest, Ardella. I need to know what happened," he said, echoing my own longing of minutes before.

But now that I knew the truth, I wish I didn't understand. Besides I didn't think my empathy could withstand the hatred of a man as passionate as Alexander.

"Please, Ardella," Alexander urged.

"Your anger ..." I moaned.

"I realize you can feel my anger. I am trying to keep it in

check, but ..."

I looked up into his eyes and saw the realization dawn.

"Ardella, you have no cause to fear my anger. It is not directed at you, I swear. I am angry at the situation...at myself for letting it happen," Alexander said with such passion I could not help but believe him.

I shook my head. "I'm not sure I can ..."

"Please! I swear by Athena and Ares that I won't hurt you, no matter what you tell me. I have to know the truth, Ardella. It is the only way to keep it from happening again," he pleaded.

I felt his desperation. I felt his driving need to know why Argos had happened. The same need I had had. Even if the answer was painful for us both—it was preferable to the doubt. That thought finally loosened my tongue.

"I told Lyessa that if her Amazons helped the villagers stand-up for themselves and refuse to hand over the grain, the raiders would back down. The Amazons were there at my suggestion to help the people of Argos say 'no' and intimidate your men into running away."

"But instead of running away my men resorted to violence and killed people in the process," he murmured.

I had no doubt now that the rage I felt in him was self-directed. My empathy meant I could feel what he felt, and I found myself longing to comfort him.

"It was not your fault," I said without thinking. *Why am I consoling the Son of Ares over his regret that his raiders killed innocent people?*

"I didn't know the Queen of the Amazons was taking strategic advice from you or perhaps I would have acted differently," he said.

"Lyessa and I spent much of our time together trying to figure out a way to stop your raids. For too long they have disrupted life in Arcadia, causing everyone to live in fear," I said, suddenly feeling the need to defend my actions.

"Fear of sharing a little of their bounty?" he grumbled.

"Fear of being attacked and robbed by their neighbors. Is it so unreasonable to want to live without being raided?" I argued.

"No," he said, "But without the raids the people of Metropolis starve. Come up with another way my people can survive and I will willingly stop the raids."

In my heart I knew he was right, and I had no answer for him.

The palpable truth of his last words floated in the air between us like one of the furies of ancient mythology and we lapsed into an uneasy silence.

"That might take a miracle." I finally whispered.

"Indeed and no Olympian, including Hermes, is likely to undertake the task."

"Hermes wants you to raid?"

"I think he allows us to do it to irritate the other Olympians. It is all a game to them. Unfortunately, for the everyday man in Metropolis it is not a game, but a means of survival," he admitted.

"I never thought about the problem from Metropolis' perspective. Perhaps if I had taken a more holistic view of the issue, it would have occurred to me to seek a solution for all sects on Arcadia."

"So Lady Ardella of New Athens is not perfect after all?" Alexander scoffed.

"Really?" I retorted lightly, having become used to his sarcasm. The wave of frustration that suddenly punched me between the eyes was my first indication that there was more to this comment than our usual bantering.

"I am so tired of trying to match wits with the great Lady Ardella of New Athens. Every step I take as a leader of Metropolis

I must measure my actions against how you will view it and how you will respond. I am through playing this game. You win, Ardella. Does that satisfy you? YOU WIN!"

He sounded so pitiful and sincere in his admission of defeat that I wanted to feel sorry for him, at least until the reality of the situation came flooding back. I found some irritation of my own as I scoffed, "Since my brother is imprisoned somewhere in your city and I am a permanent guest here because I have nowhere else to go, I cannot see why you are admitting defeat or why you are so angry with me."

"I'm not angry with you. I'm angry because..." Alexander began. He suddenly slammed his fist into the wall.

Although startled, I felt his anger really wasn't directed at me, and that gave me the courage to touch is shoulder and ask, "Why are you angry, Alexander?"

"I am angry because I am trapped in a cage of my own creation and don't see a way out. You and I both know that I cannot continue raiding forever and yet I have no other means to support Metropolis and all the people who have come here counting on my promise of freedom."

"Raiding was working fine up until Argos," I admitted. "Lyessa and I were just trying to stop your people's aggression and we pushed you the wrong way."

"Argos was one step too far. It is what I had been trying to avoid since the beginning. That one mistake became a blood bath that escalated the violence. From the moment I learned of it, I feared what Argos would drive the other Olympians to do. I know your brother would never have attacked Metropolis, if it hadn't been for what my men did in Argos. Nor would the other Olympians have stood by and let him do it."

"Now there have been deaths on both sides, ..."

"I am scared of what could happen next," he admitted. That

is why I have to at least try to work out some of our differences peacefully with the Amazons." He sighed. "I can't do it without your help, Ardella."

"Considering my confession about helping you escape New Athens, I am not sure I am the right person to…"

"You are perhaps the only person Lyessa will listen to. Deidra said you two have been friends for years," Alexander encouraged.

"She said that?"

His eyes widen and he offered quietly, "Don't be mad at her. She was trying to help. She understands the Amazon issue better than most."

"She would—considering her background," I replied.

"I didn't mean that Deidra had special knowledge of Amazons…only that she…"

I felt the panic squeeze his heart and suspected that he not only knew Deidra was an Amazon, but he understood the terrible penalty if she were found out.

"Alexander, I understand Amazonian law. I would never say anything that could harm her," I assured him with a smile.

For a long moment his gaze searched mine. He sighed again. "No you wouldn't, would you," he whispered. "You may not believe it, but neither would I."

"I can feel what you feel, Alexander. I believe you."

"Then can you believe I want to help the citizens of Metropolis?" Alexander asked.

"Of course, but the Amazons may not…"

"It is not just Metropolis. You will also be helping the Amazons. The violence between our two sects is escalating, and if we don't stop it, we could lose everything. The Law of the Olympians looms over both our heads and we must find a way to get out from under its shadow. Please, Ardella, just deliver my offer?" he pleaded.

I stared at him as if considering my options, but I already knew my answer. I was, after all, an expert on the Great Law of the Olympians. I had long understood what a precarious edge Alexander walked with his raids.

I smiled as I remembered a day long gone that I had stood up for what I believed and won:

"Order! Order! This is the Council chambers of Athena, and such outbursts will not be tolerated!" Elder Councilor Gagarin demanded over the murmurs of the assembled throng. I was left with the conclusion that the Athenian Council and those gathered to witness the deliberations did not agree with my point of view. I gripped my hands tightly together to try to prevent their trembling. It had taken all my courage to speak the truth.

"Perhaps we misunderstood. Did the Lady Ardella actually suggest that the Hermians have not broken the Great Olympian Law by their attacks on the villages of Demeter and Apollo?" Minister Tressa said with an eerie imitation of Athena's own condescending tone.

"The actions are reprehensible, but I do not believe they violate the Great Olympian Law," I stated in a calm tone that belayed the continued trembling of my hands.

"Your opinion has no bearing on the law," Minister Tressa scoffed.

"It is not an opinion. Read the law for yourself, Minister," I suggested, indicating the worn parchment scroll on the table.

"You took it upon yourself to remove a sacred scroll from Athena's archives?" Minister Tressa scolded.

"How could I decide upon the validity of the crime without reading the law for myself?" I replied. Why did she find it odd? "Have you read the words recently Minister Tressa?"

"Do not presume ..." Minister Tressa began, but was interrupted by Elder Councilor Gagarin's deep alto voice.

"Perhaps we should all hear the words of the Great Olympian Law, Tressa," the older woman suggested.

"Please, Minister Tressa, I think a reading of the document is appropriate before we reach a verdict on the matter."Councilor Loriana said softly and the other members of the Council nodded their heads in agreement.

"As you will," Minister Tressa hissed and reached for the ancient parchment. Her voice, a melodious soprano polished to perfection from years of public speaking, held the room memorized as she intoned the words of the ancient law:

> The fires of war shall not touch our new domain.
> Nor shall the soil of Arcadia be cursed by blood's dark stain.
> The ways of Ares are banned from this sacred sphere.
> Neither priest nor temple to war shall be tolerated here.
>
> Neither Olympian nor mortal shall cry out for war.
> The battlefields of ancient Earth shall be no more.
>
> Your neighbor is father and mother, sister and brother.
> Therefore let no sect take up arms against another.
> Death to the transgressor and all will be lost.
> Death to their entire sect, the horrible cost.

"So we have heard the law. I do not see how that changes the facts of the Hermians' transgression," Minister Tressa stated coldly.

"The law says: 'let no sect take up arms against another,'" I stated.

"So?"

"The Hermians did not take up arms. They do not take up

swords and attack. They intimidate and harass their neighbors and come to steal in the middle of the night, but they do not, in fact, make war. They are thieves and bullies, but that does not violate the Great Olympian Law."

"You presume to interpret the Great Law for this Council? Just how old are you?" Minister Tressa scoffed.

"You are well aware of the fact that I celebrated my seventeenth birthday just last week."

"And with your vast multitude of experience..."

"I concede you are more experienced than I. How could you not be? You have served on this Council for more years than I have been alive. Nevertheless, our ages do not change the fact that on this particular question I am right ... and you are wrong."

The room again erupted into a wild uproar. From her alcove at the end of the chamber Athena's soft laughter could be heard despite the din. As each of her followers became of aware of their Goddess' reaction the room grew silent.

"The child has a valid argument, Tressa, and a highly intelligent mind. You would do well to listen to her," Athena advised.

"Forgive me, Great Goddess. I didn't realize that you agreed with Lady Ardella's opinion?" Although Minister Tressa spoke solicitously, I could feel her resentment at what she felt was a betrayal.

"Lady Ardella managed to do what it seems none of her elders could. She looked at the issue objectively. She was not influenced by anger or a need for revenge. She simply sought the truth. I am proud to call her my daughter."

I looked up into Alexander's face and realized he was waiting patiently for me to finish thinking and give him an answer. I could feel anxiety challenge the hope in his heart. Even if I knew I would soon be going to Amazonia, I decided after all he had put me through in past few days, he deserved at least a few hours of torment.

"I'll get back to you," I said, smiling. "Right now I am too busy to decide."

Chapter 10

Stella meaning star – twinkling brightly in the night. So near and yet so far with its ever shining light. Someday time may take it without concern or care. That star shall live forever – for I have known it was there.

Andrea the Lesser (Apollo sect)
One hundred and thirteen years Ab Terra Condita

SEVERAL HOURS AFTER Alexander became speechless and stormed from my tower, I sat on the balcony watching the activity in the park below. From this vantage I could observe the citizens of Metropolis. And while I could not eavesdrop on their conversations, their positive emotions, such as joy and happiness, floated up to tantalize my senses. I was thoroughly enjoying a relaxing afternoon.

"You are not really going to speak to the Amazons are you?" an annoying whine in my head asked, spoiling my good mood.

"Leave me alone," I retorted.

Athena was not so easily dissuaded. *"Don't be difficult, Ardella. The Son of Ares is trying to manipulate you."*

"Really?"

"He is tricking you into helping him with the Amazons by vague promises. He is lying to get what he wants."

I had to laugh at the hypocrisy. "Just like you lied about wanting to help me free Rafe, to gain possession of my body and try to kill the Son of Ares?"

"It is not the same at all. If you had let me kill Alexander then you are Rafe would..."

"We would be dead – killed by the citizens of Metropolis."

"You don't know that would have been the outcome," the Goddess argued.

"You did not care if Rafe and I died as long as the Son of Ares was dead too."

"You are too limited to understand the mind of an immortal."

"I believe I am coming to understand. You think because you are an Olympian, you have the right to manipulate mortals as if we were your personal playthings," I informed her dryly. It was strange to speak so frankly to the Goddess; now that I was not longer concerned with the repercussions of my words.

"Not toys, Ardella, but not equals. Every mortal in New Athens is mine to cherish, manipulate or destroy if I wish."

"How fortunate that I am no longer in New Athens and no longer yours to control."

"You will always be mine, Ardella. You are my daughter," Athena reminded me – her irritation traveling the link along with her words.

"I am not your daughter. You did not give me life. My biological parents did that. You cannot love like a parent loves. It is a weakness of the Olympians."

"I made you what you are."

"You simply touched me and manipulated my DNA to turn me into your human lie detector. All part of your quest to find and destroy the Son of Ares."

"You are a child of an Olympian whether you wish to be or not. I made you more than human by gifting you with empathy and you will always be mine."

"Then take back your gift. I don't want it ... or you."

I felt her rage surge through our mental link, but dulled by the distance it caused me no pain.

"*That is never going to happen, Ardella*," she snapped.

I felt her indecision and a touch of trepidation, *"I won't take back your gift."*

"You mean you cannot take back my gift," I taunted.

The silence loomed over us like the harpies that had once plagued poor Phineas. *I was right.* I had stumbled upon a truth the Olympians didn't want mankind to know. I felt Athena's anger and frustration building.

"*Ardella*," she warned.

"You can bestow gifts, but you cannot take them back. Can you? Olympians have weaknesses just as we mortals do. Like Apollo's gift of prophesy for Cassandra or the golden touch that Dionysus gave Midas, once an Olympian bestows a gift it is irrevocable."

"*You speak of the myths of ancient Earth, not the reality of Arcadia.*"

"They are one and the same. What about the gift of free will?"

"What about it?"

"My mother taught me that free will is the Olympian's gift to mankind; a gift that we have established the Olympians cannot take back."

"*So you are free to choose your own path—even if it leads to your doom.*"

"So I am free to do as I wish. I may choose to stay in

Metropolis. I may choose to seek help from others to free my brother. I may even choose to speak to the Amazons and help the Son of Ares."

I will never know what Athena might have replied.

"Lady Ardella," Deidra's voice echoed from outside the door of my tiny tower chamber. My link with Athena suddenly severed, I found my hands trembling. *Did I just say those things to Athena? I felt like a new person. Something about having nothing left to lose was changing me and my attitude toward the Olympians.*

"Please come in," I said, opening the door.

"I have dinner for you," Deidra informed me as she carried in a covered tray. I noticed her usual cotton dress had been replaced by a soft linen gown of emerald green that accentuated her dark hair and green eyes.

"That is a very beautiful dress, Deidra."

"Thank you."

"Is there a special occasion I should know about?" I asked playfully.

Deidra blushed and I felt the soft tingle of excitement steal up her spine. "Tonight is the Bonfire of Demeter," she offered as she placed the tray on the table by the balcony. I knew from my books that the followers of Demeter built a bonfire in honor of their Goddess on the first full moon of each month. Her worshipers then sang and danced around the bonfire until the wee hours of the morning.

"I have heard of the Bonfire of Demeter, but I have never seen one before."

"You will be able to see the one tonight. Look to the east just outside the wall. You can't miss the glow of the Bonfire, unless you would like to come with Kern and I, and see it up close?"

"Although I am not sure I want to be a follower of Athena anymore, I am not ready to consider worshipping another

Olympian so soon."

"Our Bonfire is as much about celebrating life as worshiping Demeter. It is regularly attended by followers of Hermes, Apollo, Dionysus and even Athena."

"Really?"

"Why don't you come and see for yourself?" she laughed.

"I am not sure," I hesitated. Because of my gift, I had difficulty being in crowds.

"You can watch from your balcony and if you change your mind, you should be able to find your way."

"That sounds perfect. You are very kind, Deidra. I really appreciate you and Kern providing for me."

"Providing for you?"

"I hope I have not put too much of a strain on your resources."

"Our resources?"

"From the raids. I hope it is not too much of a burden. Perhaps I could help with cooking or find some other way to repay you."

"You are not a burden, Ardella. I simply bring you the meals and the clothing. Kern and I are not your providers."

"Oh?"

"Every meal, everything you have requested—including the dress you are wearing— came from him."

"Him?" I asked as twinge of concern seeping into my mind.

"The Strategos. Alexander is your provider."

"Oh dear. I didn't realize." A strange mixture of concern and excitement churned the butterflies in my stomach and made my breath catch in my throat. "I'm not sure that is such a good idea."

"There is no reason to be concerned. Alexander is well off. Providing for you will not be a strain for him."

"But what about his expectations as my provider?"

"What do you mean?"

"Your friend Kaylee. That horrible man is her provider. That seems to give him control over her. He treated her as if she were..."

"It is not always like that," Deidra quickly assured me. "It depends on the man. Most providers are husbands and fathers who raid to take care of their family. For men like Davin raiding gives them a sense of power. They raid for the thrill of it and don't really care about the ones they provide for."

"And it is acceptable for him to treat her the way he does, because he provides for her and her sons?"

"Unfortunately the freedom of Metropolis means everyone controls their own behavior. We don't have 2000 years of traditions and taboos to protect our society from human nature."

"So you have no laws in Metropolis?"

"We have laws, but not many. There are really only three offenses for which a citizen can be punished by the state. Murder, rape, and disobeying a direct command from the Strategos."

"So I am supposed to obey him because he is my provider and because he is the Strategos."

"It's not so bad. Alexander provides for many newcomers to Metropolis."

"Of course. The Son of Ares is a great humanitarian."

"The Strategos is hard when he has to be, but he is fair. He is the foundation upon which Metropolis is built. You need not worry about Alexander, except..."

"Except?"

I felt concern battle with reluctance in Deidra's breast. I felt the sharp thrust of determination before she said, "Keep in mind that you have not seen the Strategos at his best. Recently he has been acting a little strange," she admitted.

"Strange?"

"I..." The odd expression on her face told me as clearly as her feelings of uncertainty that she wanted to ask something difficult.

"What is bothering you?" I encouraged. I felt the tug-of-war between her heart and mind and knew the moment her heart won.

"Can your empathy affect other people's emotions?"

"Affect other people's emotion? No. I don't think so," I replied.

"I thought it might explain his behavior."

I raised one eyebrow, but had no idea what to say to such a comment.

"Alexander is always reserved and in control of his emotions," Deidra explained. "His ability to remain calm and focused in a crisis is legendary in Metropolis. Even when the metal men attached our walls, he was fearless in the wake of certain death. For the past few days, however, he has been either unreasonably angry or unexplainably giddy. It has many of us worried."

"I have never heard of my empathy having that kind of effect on a person."

"I just wondered. Forgive me. I am asking you questions while your food gets cold."

"I am famished. What have you brought me today?"

"Medusa pie."

My brow wrinkled as my lips formed a faint smile. "I have always loved the legend of Perseus, but please tell me that a medusa in this case is a local flora or fauna you cooked for me."

Deidra laughed. "I am afraid I didn't cook tonight's dinner," she admitted. "The Medusa Tavern makes the pie. It has venison, carrots and potatoes all baked in delicious brown gravy. I have never been able to get the cook to share his secret."

"Medusa Tavern—Medusa pie. I feel much better about the prospects for dinner," I chuckled.

"You are in for a treat, Lady Ardella, which is why I obtained two Medusa pies—one for each of us."

"So now the Strategos is providing for us both?"

"It seemed a reasonable payment for my services recently."

⁓

Later that night, as the wind rustled through the trees of the park and the soft calls of nocturnal creatures filled the night with their soothing songs, I found myself standing uncertain at the base of my tower. As Deidra had promised, the glow to the east filled the night sky, almost overshadowing the brightness of the full moon. The sound of music and laughter drifted on the breeze welcoming me, but still I hesitated.

"Lady Ardella?" a woman's voice asked softly.

I turned to find a familiar brunette staring at me curiously.

"Kendra." I smiled at the woman I suspected was an Amazon spy.

"What are you doing out here?" Kendra asked.

"Hesitating," I responded with a chuckle.

"The Bonfire?"

"Deidra invited me to attend, but ..."

"Your gift of empathy must make it hard to be in crowds."

Her insight into my plight encouraged me to share my burden. "Still I wish I could see it," I whispered.

"I think I have the answer. Follow me," she said and held out her hand. I felt her strength and determination more strongly as our skin touched and she lead me across the Grove of Artemis to the cyclopean wall at the far side. Behind a small copse of trees were narrow stone steps that led up the side of the wall. From the top of the wall I had a perfect view of the bonfire and the dancers without the bombardment of their emotions overpowering me.

"It is perfect. Thank you."

"I am glad I could help," she said, smiling. "I should get to the Bonfire. It is expected of a follower of Demeter," she said with a wink.

"Of course," I laughed.

"Who knows—I might even conceive a girl child to take home with me after all this is over."

"Conceive a child?" I asked, startled.

"You don't think all they do is dance around the Bonfire, do you?"

"That part was not in any of my books!"

"I can't imagine it would be," she laughed, and returned soundlessly down the stone steps.

Her grace and stealth from years of Amazon training shone like a beacon in the night. I thought about Deidra and her fighting skill and wondered that no one had suspected the true origin of either of these two women. Then it hit me: *Neither Kendra and Deidra seemed to suspect the other is an Amazon. Humans could be blind to what was before their very eyes.*

Chapter 11

You can never have too many friends and family. They will give you strength in your time of need and make the joyous days even brighter. Keep them close and treat them well.
You cannot live without them.

Rachella, high-Councilor of the Athena sect
One thousand, four hundred and twenty-two years Ab Terra Condita

THE CONVERSATION THAT took place before I entered the citadel was recorded by the court secretary and is part of the archives of Metropolis. It reads:

Alexander: Welcome home, Draenen. It seems Athena's followers have been generous.

Draenon: The villages of Wrenn and Vidalia did seem to have more to share than usual.

Two raiders carried in a trunk.

Draenon: Your share, Strategos.

The strategos bent to inspect the items in the trunk: a beautifully woven bolt of cloth, an intricately carved dagger, several packets of rare herbs and spices, and a few books. He smiled when his eyes fell upon a small wooden cup in one corner of the chest. He lifted it up and handed it back to Draenon.

Alexnader: Let's call this a gift.

Draenon: Strategos?

Alexander: A gift for your new son.

Draenon: My son!

Alexander: Born only a few hours ago.

Draenon: And his mother?

Alexander: Deidra says Hazell and the baby are doing well. They are resting comfortably in your home.

Draenon: Thank you, Strategos.

Alexander: I was ordered to send you to see your new son as soon as you returned.

Draenon: Who would dare to give an order to the Strategos of Metropolis?

Alexander: That would be your lovely wife, Hazell. According to Deidra she was not pleased with having had to endure childbirth alone. Please hurry home and appease her for both our sakes.

Draenon laughed.

Draenon: I will try, Strategos, but first I have one more item from our raid that you should be aware of.

Three cloaked figures stepped forward.

Draenon: These three were waiting for us in Wrenn. They asked us to bring them here to Metropolis for an audience with you, Strategos.

Kern pulled his sword.

Kern: Are you a fool, little brother? How dare you bring three potential assassins into the presence of our Strategos?

Draeonon: I made sure they were unarmed, and had them watched at all times. They never appeared to be dangerous.

Kern: Speak strangers, who are you and what do you want with the Strategos of Metropolis?

The tallest of the strangers stepped forward and removed his hood.

Alexander: Tannis

TannisLysander or should I call you Alexander?"

Alexander: You, my old friend may call me whatever you wish. It is good to see you.

The strategos stood, crossed to the man, and offered his hand. Tannis hesitated but accepted the gesture of friendship.

Tannis: I never thought I would lay eyes upon the man who I had once called my friend, Lysander. However, I was approached by someone who needed an introduction to the Strategos of Metropolis. I agreed to accompany her here.

The shortest of the cloaked strangers stepped forward. She removed her hood. Her hair was streaked with gray, yet her face had a vitality and strength of a woman much younger.

Tannis: This is Lucinda, the mother of Rafe and Ardella.

Lucinda: You are the man who holds my children?

Alexander: I am.

The Strategos smiled.

Lucinda: I would like to know by whose authority you imprison my children?

The Strategos stopped smiling.

Alexander: Rafe is held by the authority of Hermes for crimes committed against his capital city of Metropolis.

Lucinda: And Ardella?

Alexander: Ardella is here of her own free will.

Lucinda: Then I ask you to allow me to see them, NOW!

Kern: Now I think I understand where the daughter gets her fire.

Alexander: They do share a certain audacity.

Peryn Strategos, you cannot allow this Athenian woman access to the prisoner or his sister. She has no right to ...

The Strategos cut him off.

Alexander: Councilor Peryn, how long have you been under the delusion that the Strategos of Metropolis was yours to command?

Peryn: Your pardon, I did not mean...

Alexander: This is not the first time you have presumed to dictate what I should or should not do about the Lady Ardella. I remind you that I am the chosen leader of Metropolis and will do what I deem best. Your thoughts and opinions are neither wanted nor required. You are dismissed.

Peryn: Strategos, I only meant that..."

Alexander: Councilor Peryn, leave the citadel at once or I will have Kern remove you by force."

Councilor Peryn's face grew red, but he obeyed the command.

Lucinda: Does that mean you will allow me to speak to my children?

Alexander: I guess we should send for Ardella. Where is your wife, Kern? I have no doubt Deidra would know where to find Ardella.

Kern: Anticipating your instructions, Strategos, she already set out to find her. Ardella should be here any minute.

Alexander: Your wife is efficient as ever. She is an asset to me and to Metropolis.

Kern: I agree, Strategos.

Alexander: Meanwhile it must have been a long journey, Lady Lucinda, may we get your something to eat or drink?

Lucinda: This is not a social call, Son of Ares. I do not want anything from you.

Alexander: Except your children. I suggest you remember that before you speak again, Lady Lucinda.

The daughter, Ardella, appeared with Deidra at the doorway of the citadel.

I will tell the rest, as I was there as witness.

"Mother," I shouted as I rushed across the floor of the great hall into the welcoming arms of my childhood. For a few moments I felt the safety and love of a mother's embrace wipe away all the aches and pains of adulthood, until she broke the spell with her first words.

"What did you think you were doing?" she asked in the I-am-disappointed-in-you-voice of my childhood.

I had asked myself that same question several times over the past few days. I finally knew the answer. "Following my heart instead of my head," I replied.

"As usual," my mother laughed. She released me from her embrace and carefully inspected me to insure that I was indeed unharmed.

"I am sorry if I disappointed you, Mother," I said.

"You came to Metropolis to save your brother's life. How can any mother be disappointed in that?"

"But I failed. He is still a captive here and still in danger of being executed," I blurted out. I realized from her shocked expression that she had not known before.

Suddenly her eyes were full of anger and she turned toward Alexander, "Why do you keep my daughter here if you have no intention of releasing her brother?"

"Rafe will have a chance to speak before Hermes and his Council at the end our mourning period for the dead. It is Hermes who will decide your son's fate. The only promise I have made to your daughter is that if she remains here in Metropolis, she may speak in defense of her brother."

Liar, I wanted to scream at him, but I knew it was a moot point now.

I looked over and for the first time saw Tannis standing behind my mother. "This explains a lot. Tannis, I asked you tell my mother I had gone to Metropolis to try to free Rafe, not bring her here," I said, teasing my old friend.

"Forgive me, Ardella, but your mother is the only person in Arcadia more stubborn than you. I had no choice. If I hadn't agreed to help her, then she would have set out for Metropolis on her own," Tannis replied.

"Since I have never been able to win an argument with my mother, I cannot really blame you," I laughed.

"You two can stop talking about me as if I am not here. It doesn't matter how I came to Metropolis. Now that I am here and can see for myself that Ardella is safe and well. I give you thanks for that, Strategos."

"Your thanks are unnecessary, Lady Lucinda. I have no reason to harm your daughter." Alexander's voice was tinged with ire, but his defensive wall was up and I felt none of his emotions.

"But you do have reason to harm my son," Lucinda replied. She was no longer contrite, but terrified.

"Rafe led an army against Metropolis. He broke the Great Law of the Olympians. Too many men died defending this city to allow your son to go unpunished," he replied, his voice void of emotion.

"Even a condemned man should be allowed a little comfort. May I speak to my son?" Lucinda asked.

"Certainly, but a guard will be present during your visit to make sure you don't try to give him tools or information he could use to escape."

"Agreed. So where might I find my son?"

"Kern will you take Lady Lucinda to Rafe's cell?" Alexander commanded.

I hoped I might finally learn where in Metropolis Rafe was being imprisoned, but no location was revealed in the exchange. *Of course one of his inner-circle would know where to go without being told*, I realized.

"I will see you soon, Mother," I called as she turned to go

with Kern. It was then that I noticed Kendra. She slipped out just after Kern and my mother. *By the Goddess, please let her be an Amazon spy and please let her be following them to learn the location of my brother.*

"Lady Ardella," Tannis said behind me, "There was one other person who asked me to bring him to Metropolis to see you."

The third cloaked figure removed his hood. I recognized the familiar face and gasped. "Teldar," I said. I could not believe that he would come all this way.

"Ardella," he said. He moved towards me, "Are you unharmed? Has anyone mistreated you?"

"No one here has mistreated Lady Ardella," Alexander spoke from the newly erected dais in the now roofless citadel. Despite his wall I could feel his irritation at this affront. "Who exactly are you, stranger?"

"Alexan...Strategos, may I present Teldar. He is the Headmaster of the Academy ... and my betrothed," I said.

Teldar's and Alexander's mutual annoyance struck me simultaneously.

∽

"Sorry," I said, sitting down beside Teldar under the ancient oak of the Grove of the Dryads. I looked over at the remains of the picnic lunch that he had obviously already eaten. *"I guess you could not wait for me?"* I observed.

"You are over an hour late, my dear. I have a Latin class in fifteen minutes."

"I found a fascinating new book in the archives and I guess ..."

"...you lost track of time," he said finishing my most common excuse.

"I guess this isn't the first time ..."

"Please, Ardella. Your fascination with the written word would drive even the most patient man to..."

"And what did you do while waiting for me to arrive?" I laughed.

"Besides have my lunch alone?" he scolded and then laughed too. "I had a book to read."

"I love you, Teldar."

"But not more than your books!"

Chapter 12

A beautiful woman is like a glass of fine wine. They should both be savored and appreciated for the pleasure they bring.

**Lord Hubert of the Dionysus sect
Seven hundred and thirty-two years Ab Terra Condita**

A FEW MINUTES later I stood beside Teldar on the balcony of my tower room. As we looked out over the great mall at the grove of Artemis, I could feel his excitement and wonder.

"Is that truly the tomb of Artemis?" he asked.

I don't think he knew he'd spoken his wonderment aloud. Still, I chose to answer his question, mostly to break the strange silence that had fallen between us. "It is strange how the real tomb far surpasses all the descriptions I had ever read about it," I commented.

"Was the grove here before or did he add it?" Teldar asked.

"There was a small grove beside the tomb, but Alexander added more trees and designed the park that surrounds it now."

"It would seem that Alexander's gardening skills are almost

as impressive as Tannis'," he said.

"They once worked together in the Grove of the Dryads in New Athens."

"So Tannis told me on the journey here. He told me many things about a young man named Lysander who turned out to be the Son of Ares. Strange that in all the time we spent together you never mentioned that you actually knew him," Teldar said, finally getting to the heart of what was bothering him.

"Lysander left New Athens long before we met. We often spoke of Alexander. I guess I forgot that you did not know his history." I knew it was a weak excuse.

"It doesn't really matter, I suppose. It is the present that we must deal with," he said.

I felt the hurt he would not give voice to, but I chose not to insult our long-time relationship by referring to his emotions, so I changed the subject. "I am sorry I left so abruptly without saying farewell," I apologized.

"Or telling me what you planned to do," he added. His emotions turned from hurt to irritation.

"I think I was afraid you would try to stop me," I admitted.

"You think I would have tried to stop you from helping your brother?" he asked.

"No. I was afraid you would try to stop me from..." I paused unsure of how to explain something I didn't quite understand myself.

"...giving up your future in New Athens," he supplied.

"From risking so much to free Rafe," I clarified.

"I might have pointed out that the solution you had planned was likely to cost you a great deal more than you gained."

"And you would have been right. You might even have talked me out of it," I admitted.

"Would that have been so bad?" His voice held only a sliver

of the hurt and anger that I could feel multiplied a hundred fold within his chest. I felt tears spring to my eyes at his pain.

"I do not know," I admitted. "If I had stood by and done nothing while Alexander executed my brother I would not have been able to live with myself."

My confession seemed to soften his stance. "Were you really the one who released the Son of Ares?"

"So bad news really does travel fast," I scoffed. "Yes. I was young and naïve. I had no idea what that decision would cost Arcadia. On top of everything else, my choice ruined Rafe's life."

"Is Rafe really why you are here?" His gaze met mine and a tremor of regret shook my body. For a moment the question hung in the air between us, but I could not bear the weight of the answer.

I looked away and blinked at the tears in my eyes. "The reality is that I am here."

"So where does that leave us, Ardella?" Teldar asked quietly.

"Have I been officially exiled by the Council of Athena?"

"Athena herself announced it to the people. You are an exile, just like Rafe."

"Do they have plans to revoke Rafe's exile based upon my confession?" I asked, hopefully.

"No. He broke the Great Olympian Law when he attacked Metropolis and they don't want New Athens to be associated with his crimes," Teldar replied.

"So everything I gave up was in vain. I was too late to make a difference. I will never see my home again and neither will Rafe."

"I'm sorry," he offered calmly, but I could feel his tension.

"So our engagement is nullified with my exile," I stated, plainly.

"Yes, unless I join you here in Metropolis."

"No! You cannot give up the Academy. It is your life. Your world is New Athens."

"I always thought New Athens was your world as well, Ardella. It was one of the things we had in common," he said.

"I think the greatest thing we had in common was our love of books."

"That is not unusual in New Athens. We are not the only couple who spent hours in the Grove of the Dryads reading and talking."

"Yes, but we are both a little obsessive about our books. I recall your students teasing you for always giving me books as gifts. They never understood that I loved them as much as you did."

"I'm afraid I have done it again," he said pointing to the three crates that he had brought with him. "I was only allowed a few hours to pack up your possessions. I am afraid there are more books than clothes or luxuries."

I threw my arms around him, "You brought me my library," I exclaimed.

"All of it, including a few books that I think might have been on loan from the archives of Athena," he said with a grin.

"I love you," I bubbled.

Teldar and I were extremely well suited. It is little wonder that the personality profiles, required by all young adults considering marriage in New Athens, paired us up. For many years I had felt guilty about what had happened to Rafe, but more than that, I had missed his companionship. Being twins, we were very close growing up. When Teldar came into my life he filled the void Rafe's absence had created. He has been so easy to fall in love with.

"I know you love me," Teldar said

His voice brought me out of my reverie.

"In the world of New Athens we were the perfect match," he said.

The certainty in his voice drove home just what I had given up, and what a fool I was to have not appreciated him more.

"I am sorry I made this decision without telling you. It was wrong of me," I admitted.

"You told your mother that you followed your heart not your head."

"That does not mean ... I wanted the life we planned together," I offered, but even to my ears, the words sounded inadequate.

"Our future wasn't important enough to stop you from leaving because you were still consumed by your past," he said. I had a strange feeling that he was referring as much to Lysander as Rafe.

It wasn't unfair of him to question my devotion. After all, if I had truly loved him with all my heart, nothing would have compelled me leave New Athens—not even Rafe. I had barely spared a thought for Teldar when I chose to leave.

"I am sorry."

"It least now I understand why I never truly had your heart. Even when I held you in my arms I knew that I only had part of you. I always thought it was because you were the Daughter of Athena, but now I am not so sure."

"I cannot imagine what you are talking about."

"Really? You may be the empath, Ardella, but I can clearly see a light in you that was not there before. You may not have sorted out all your feelings for him, yet, but they are there nonetheless."

"Feelings? For whom?" Suddenly a familiar face flashed before my eyes. "For Alexander? I do not have feelings for the Son of Ares." Even as I spoke the words, I knew they were a lie.

"The Son of Ares would seem to be the perfect match for the Daughter of Athena."

"Teldar," I whispered as my hand gently touched his cheek.

"You have given up a great deal for Rafe. Perhaps you have gained something as well. Don't waste second chances," he said. His lips softly brushed my palm.

"Goodbye, Teldar."

"Goodbye, Ardella."

~

"I can't believe he just left. I don't think I would have given you up quite so easily," Alexander mused from my open doorway.

Only a few minutes ago my betrothed and I had said farewell and I was not in the mood for our usual banter. "Please, Alexander. I cannot do this, now."

There was a long pause. "I'm sorry, Ardella. I should have turned you away from Metropolis rather than allow you to debate for your brother's life. I let my desire to match wits with the great Ardella of New Athens influence my judgment.

"Are you saying you feel guilty?"

"Perhaps. You lost your place on the Council, the favor of your Goddess, your home, your…"

"…betrothed? I am not sure he was ever mine to lose. Like most couples we were matched based upon our similar personality and interests," I said. This confirmation was for my benefit, not his.

"Didn't you love him?" Alexander whispered.

"It is hard not to love someone you are so comfortable spending time with. It was contentment more than passion."

"That is not unusual in marriages in New Athens," Alexander said.

I nodded. I imagined my life in New Athens with Teldar, but suddenly it was Alexander's face I saw.

"I just realized something. If the Academy had not been forbidden to you, then you might have become who he is now," I said.

"Who?"

"Teldar."

"What do you mean?"

"Teldar has a passion for knowledge and learning. His ambition is to know all there is to know and then expand the knowledge base of Arcadia through the institution of the Academy. He is the perfect Headmaster."

"You picture me as Headmaster of the Academy?" Alexander asked.

I smiled at the pride in his voice, but replied cautiously, "Perhaps."

"You actually believe I have a passion for knowledge?" His voice rang with doubt that my gift told me also filled his heart. *I wondered why I wanted to change that.*

"Look what you have done in Metropolis," I said, encouraging him to see himself as I was beginning to see him.

Again his passionate nature took me by surprise. "Knowledge is important, Ardella, but Metropolis is the application of that knowledge to improve the world as we know it."

"That sounds like a concept from ancient Earth," I offered.

"It is. Leonardo DaVinci believed it is not enough to know; it is more important what a person does with that knowledge." He saw the astonishment flash across my face. He laughed. "Your crystal reader contained a very complete history of ancient Earth—not just the wars."

"Really?"

"Knowledge is power. Athena knows that. So does Ares. My father's drive makes me want to use what I learn to change things," he said.

I felt the heat of his passion surge and fill the air all around us with its energy. I suddenly realized he had no doubts about his destiny or his role in the world of Arcadia. I was more certain than ever that it was driving force of his ambition that had brought about Metropolis.

"Perhaps it is just as well you were not able to attend the Academy. Arcadia has benefited greatly from your need to change our world," I admitted.

"Does this mean I am not the enemy anymore?" he said, moving closer.

"I am not sure of anything anymore."

"You look so sad. Tell me what I can do to help," he whispered.

The air between us crackled and my face flushed. I not only heard the words, I also felt the genuine concern behind them. I recalled the young man who I had felt so strongly about that I had risked everything to free him. Teldar's words: *Don't waste second chances*, echoed through my head. In that moment, I knew precisely what I wanted, but could I actually say the words?

Just when I thought I didn't have the courage to voice my desire, I heard myself say, "Hold me, just for a little while. I do not want to be alone. I ..."

I never finished the thought...his arms encircled me. I felt his joy and contentment as his skin touched mine. It was such a pleasant feeling. My need for his strength after all that had happened over the past few days overwhelmed me. This was where I wanted to be.

I felt a change in the intensity of his emotions just before his lips touched mine. It was glorious. His arms felt warm and safe and his lips offered comfort and hope. For that brief moment mistakes of the past and the problems of the future didn't matter, there was only the honest simple happiness of the present.

I am not sure how long that kiss lasted, but as it ended, I felt him pull away from me both physically and emotionally.

"I'm sorry, Lady Ardella," he said. He returned to the decorum of his position. "I didn't come here to take advantage of your grief."

"I know that, Alexander," I said. "Remember I felt what you felt as you kissed me."

I felt his relief wash across both of us. He smiled and let his guard down once again. "I think that is the first time I am glad that you can read my emotions. I want you to…"

The sudden knock on the door startled both of us. I pulled away from his arms and turned to face the door. "Come in," I called.

A familiar red-headed figure entered. "Ardella, I came to talk to you about...." He froze when he saw Alexander. "Is now a good time?"

"Certainly, Tannis. We need to talk. Alexander was just leaving," I assured him.

Although I felt Alexander's impatience at my dismissal, he allowed reason to prevail and headed to the door. "Goodnight, Ardella." His rich baritone voice seem to touch my skin even as the words fell upon my ears.

As he turned away and walk toward the door, I had this sudden urge to go after him and continue our first civil conversation. When we weren't arguing he was quite pleasant…and the kiss…. I forced the image from my head to regain my composure.

I turned to Tannis, hugged my old friend, and said, "Thank you for bringing Teldar and my mother to Metropolis. I realize how much trouble you went to on my behalf."

"I know how much I owe you, Ardella. This is a very small token on my part," he replied.

"You don't owe me anything, Tannis," I assured him. I knew he was speaking of my support for his travel to the fields of Demeter and his subsequent post as a professor at the Academy, but I had done those things for a friend.

"That is not true. You encouraged me and petitioned for me before the Council," Tannis said, "I would not be where I am today without you."

"I have never seen anyone more passionate about horticulture than you, Tannis. You deserve the life you have created for yourself in New Athens. You are living proof that knowledge should be available for everyone in our society." I felt unease and worry welling up inside him even though he spoke not a word.

"What is it?" I asked concerned.

"Lysander said..." he began but he stopped himself. "It doesn't matter."

"What is it, my friend?"

"Lysander suggested you helped me out of guilt."

"Because I could not help him," I supplied. I found myself irritated at the truth of those words and the obvious hurt it had caused an old friend.

"Is he right?" he asked.

I felt his genuine desire to know the truth, so I gave it to him. "Maybe a little—at first, but you quickly became my friend and I continued helping for that reason and that reason alone."

"I shouldn't have even asked such a question."

"Tannis, very few people are comfortable enough around me to truly become my friend. You have never held my empathy against me. I have always treasured our friendship. Does it really matter how it started?"

"I'm sorry, Ardella. I didn't mean to offend you. I guess I just let what Lysander said influence me."

"No offence taken. Do not let it bother you. Alexander is very good at making people second-guess themselves—even me."

"Teldar says we will head back soon. Alexander has offered us a ride in a caravan ship leaving for one of the outer villages of New Athens."

"Is he making you go on one of his raids?" I quipped.

"As far as I know I am just a passenger, but is there anything you want me to pick up for you while I am there?" he said, playing along.

My new friend's image flashed before me. The joke suddenly became earnest. "Can you send back some honeysuckle cuttings? There are no honeysuckle plants in Metropolis."

"Why do you need honeysuckle?" he queried.

"It is not for me, Tannis. It is for Muriel."

"Muriel?"

"You know how much dryads love honeysuckle!" I smiled and added, "Would you like to meet the 1000 year old dryad that lives in the grove of Artemis?"

⁓

I saw Kendra near the grove of Artemis as I passed by with Tannis on our way back to the tower. The subtle movement of her head told me not to acknowledge her. More than ever I was sure she was an Amazon spy, and I was overwhelmed by the desire to speak with her about where Rafe was being held and what could be done to help him.

I managed to make it back to my tower room and politely dismiss Tannis. I waited only long enough for Tannis to be well gone and then slowly opened the door and hurried down the steps back to the grove praying that Kendra was still there. She wasn't.

I sighed and returned to the tower, and ran into her as she came down the stairs of my tower. "Kendra," I gasped. "I was just looking for you."

"I think it best if we speak in private, Lady Ardella" she said.

I led the way back to my room and quietly shut the door. "I saw you leave the citadel shortly after Kern escorted my mother to see Rafe. I hope that means you know where Alexander is keeping my brother."

"I already knew where your brother was being held. It is fairly common knowledge in Metropolis," she offered.

"Is it well guarded?" I asked.

"Do you plan to help him escape from Metropolis? I thought you were going to plead his case before Hermes and the Council," she said.

"I will present the best defense I can before the Hermian Council. I just want to be ready in case my plea fails. I will not let them kill my brother."

"Are you asking for help, Lady Ardella?" Kendra inquired.

"You said you were my friend. I need all the friends I can get, if I am going to make sure Rafe gets out of this alive."

"You may count on me," she said, "And, our common friend confirmed all my sisters in Metropolis are yours to command."

I smiled and thought. *How useful it is to be friends with the Queen of the Amazons.* "Tell our common friend and your sisters that I am eternally grateful," I replied.

Chapter 13

When once again I may hear my sister's sweet voice and know the warmth of her touch, then shall I join her in the land of the sun.

(last words spoken words by the God Apollo)
One thousand, seven hundred and twenty-two years Ab Terra Condita

"I AM IMPRESSED. Your hospital is easily as imposing as the one in New Athens—at least from the outside," I said as Alexander and I approached one of the most ornate buildings I had yet seen in Metropolis. The stone steps led up to large double doors of fine polished oak, while a wide portico with graceful Ionic columns ran the entire length of the front of the neoclassical structure.

"You will also find it impressive from the inside, Ardella," Alexander said, proudly.

"I am afraid I will not be able to make the comparison. I have never been inside Apollo's hospital in New Athens."

"Why did the Council not let you go to the hospital?"

"I am not sure exactly. They said it was concern for my

welfare. I never understood why Athena's Council believed entering a build could harm me, but they managed to make it forbidden all my life."

"Isn't it ironic that you have more freedom of movement as an exile in Metropolis than you did as a member of the Council in New Athens?" he mused.

It had occurred to me, but I decide to ignore Alexander's barb. I was too interested in finally seeing the inside of a hospital to rise to the bait.

"Apollodorus, may I introduce the Lady Ardella? I was hoping we could impress her with a tour of your hospital," Alexander said to the gentleman who met us at the door. Apollodorus was lean man with light brown hair, greying at the temples. His light blue smock emblazoned with the infinity rings of Apollo clearly marked him as a healer.

"Of course, Strategos."

We entered the heavy oak doors and found ourselves in the marbled entry. "Apollodorus is the man in charge of the hospital. He helped design it," Alexander said.

"It is a pleasure to meet you, Apollodorus. I look forward to the tour," I offered.

"Where would you like to begin?" he asked.

I knew very little about the inside of hospitals, but I did remember my mother having great admiration for the maternity ward of the hospital in New Athens. "Do you have a wing for new mothers? I know Hazell had her baby. I would love to see how they are doing," I replied.

"I am afraid all births in Metropolis happen at home. We send out trained midwives to assist since most of the women prefer familiar surroundings during the difficulties of giving birth," Apollodorus explained.

"What if there is a problem? I have heard of women who

had to be cut open to deliver their child."

"If the midwife suspects a difficult birth or if an emergency arises, then the mother is brought to the hospital for surgery," he replied.

I could feel his pride and confidence in his system that required only a few women to leave their home and family to give birth. It was very different than how things were done in New Athens—so I had been told.

"So who do you keep in this hospital? What do you treat?" I asked.

"Some people who become ill and need advance help to recover. Mostly broken limbs and other wounds," he said.

"That happen during raids?"

I felt Alexander as he tried to keep his irritation at my question from seeping through his defenses. He was not successful, but I decided to ignore his discomfort.

"Yes. We are very good a setting and treating bones to make them as strong as before. Most of our patients return to full use of their limbs," Apollodorus said.

"So they can go on the next raid," I said. Even in this testament to civilization and science the Hermian need to plunder reared its ugly head.

"Ardella," Alexander cautioned.

"Forgive me, Apollodorus. I meant no offense to you. I recall Apollo's hospital in New Athens had a research lab that often worked with scientists from the Academy. Do you have a lab in this hospital?"

Alexander nodded, giving Apollodorus permission to answer my question. "Yes, Lady Ardella. We have a fine research lab. I even have a microscope. Would you like to see it?"

"Yes, please. I have always wanted to look at the living creatures too tiny to be seen with our eyes. It is fascinating to realize there is an unseen world all around us," I replied.

"Follow me. I am glad you know about the microorganisms. You might find it interesting to learn that when a wound becomes infected, we have discovered there are large numbers of microscopic cells present that we think may cause the problem," Apollodorus said.

"Like a parasite. I recall my betrothed... Teldar mentioning a similar discovery by the Apollo sect last year. The healers of Heliopolis were planning to run a series of experiments to prove the microscopic cells caused the infection."

"I have no doubt my brothers are still testing and retesting this theory. They are very methodical. We have, however, moved on to trying to find substances that kill the microscopic cells without harming humans. It would give us a powerful tool in fighting infection, if such a substance could be found," he said.

"I think you are on the right track, Apollodorus. I remember reading something similar in a book from Athena's Archives. It was written over a thousand years ago by a healer of Apollo whose name escapes me. Garen, Garven..."

"You have read Galen?" he asked. His eyes widened with surprise.

"Yes, that was his name, Galen. He used to pour wine into the wound to treat infection."

"Wine such as you drink?"

"I remember thinking it was odd to use something that is made to drink to cleanse infections. How could something that doesn't harm us kill another living thing? I wish I could remember it more clearly. I have read too many books over the years. They begin to run together," I babbled.

"I think you have this confused, Lady Ardella. I have read all 12 of the books of Galen multiple times. I would remember a reference about using wine to fight infection."

"You are probably correct. I just ... Wait! You said you have read the 12 books of Galen, but I know for a fact he wrote 20 books on the art of medicine," I said.

"You are correct, but unfortunately the last 8 books were lost centuries ago in a horrible fire in the hall of records in Heliopolis. It is that lost knowledge we are trying to recreate with our research."

"Athena's archives have all 20 books. I have seen them with my own eyes," I cried out in excitement.

"Great Apollo. How could we have been so stupid? The Archive of Athena keeps one copy of every book ever written on Arcadia. All this time the knowledge was there waiting for us," he proclaimed.

I felt Apollodorus' sudden burst of hope while simultaneously feeling Alexander's growing suspicion and anger.

"You don't think the leaders of the Apollo sect knew about the books of Galen in the Archive?" Alexander asked. "Surely they asked for copies of the lost books shortly after the fire?" He paused for a moment to let us ponder his questions and then added, "I wonder why Athena did not provide them?"

I knew from my experiences with Athena's Archive that many books on Arcadia did in fact exist only as a single copy. "Athena prizes knowledge, especially knowledge that is unique," I said. I realized with horror the implication of that simple truth.

"But Apollo's healers use that knowledge for the benefit of everyone on Arcadia. Keeping it locked away as a prize would hurt all the sects, including her own," Apollodorus said.

"Ask yourself what is more important to Athena: her secret stores of knowledge or the lives of mere mortals?" Alexander speculated.

"That is not fair. Athena was not responsible for the fire that caused the books to be lost to the Apollo sect. She did not go out over her way to hurt anyone."

"No. She simply refused to help," Alexander suggested. He was quite sure the Goddess in question was at fault. I was not.

"Olympians are very temperamental. It happened centuries ago. We cannot be sure of the circumstances..." I argued.

"After everything she has done you still defend her," he said, exasperated.

"I served Athena for almost a decade, Alexander. I have had the unique opportunity to feel what she feels for her people and know the words she spoke were the truth. She is not perfect. She is an Olympian."

"She tried to kill us, Ardella."

"I once agreed to send an Amazon assassin to kill you, but I now know I was wrong. I will not make the same mistake again."

"That is good to know, but I am not sure Athena will ever admit she is wrong or change the way she does things."

"You may be correct, but, Athena is not the monster you believe her to be, any more than you are the monster I once believed you to be," I told him.

"I suppose this isn't an argument I can win, so Ardella, if you don't mind, while you look through the microscope in the lab I want to check on one of Apollodorus' patients," Alexander said. He turned to the healer, "Is he still in a coma?"

"There have been no changes since last time, Strategos."

Alexander frowned and headed down the far hall.

"Alexander knows someone in the hospital?"

"Therein was hit over the head with a staff by one of the metal warriors when your brother attacked the city. He has never awakened from that blow. We have done everything we can. If he doesn't awaken soon, his body will die," Apollodorus lamented.

"Oh." I was unsure of what else to say.

Fortunately, we reached the laboratory at that moment

and Apollodorus lead me inside. Here is our greatest treasure—a microscope that was once inside the walls of Heliopolis itself."

"How did the raiders manage such an important find?" I wondered aloud.

"They had a little help. It is the only raid I ever went on. It was strange seeing Heliopolis again as an outsider," Apollodorus said.

"I know your name, Apollodorus. You were the personal physician of the royal family. Prince Andros often complains about losing you."

The healer laughed. "I did serve the royal family of Heliopolis for many years. I happened to be visiting a hospital on the outer edges of the city when Alexander's raid took me prisoner."

"I do not understand why you would stay. Alexander said he gave all his prisoners the opportunity to leave when you had finished teaching the people of Metropolis the art of healing," I said.

"I considered it, but Alexander gave me the chance to build and run my own hospital. It was an opportunity I could not ignore," he said. I felt the strong stab of guilt in his chest and knew he was not being entirely truthful.

"There is more to it, Apollodorus," I suggested.

"Why do you say that?" he asked, suspiciously.

"Forgive me, but I can feel other people's emotions as clearly as you can see or hear. I cannot help but sense you holding something back," I replied.

"I have been told it is impossible to lie to you, Lady Ardella."

"Not impossible, just very hard," I laughed.

"You are correct. I chose to stay in Metropolis for a purely selfish reason—the love of a woman." With his simple confession I felt a rush of love and satisfaction.

"A woman forbidden to you in Heliopolis, even as a healer

to the royal family?"

"Exactly. My wife is a follower of Aphrodite. She was a temple maiden. I met her when I was a journeyman healer in New Corinth. We fell in love, but when I was ordered back to Heliopolis we had to say goodbye. I never thought I would see her again."

"It has to have been fate. How did she happen to come to Metropolis?" I asked.

"I am afraid I didn't wait for fate. I agreed to stay and build the hospital for Alexander if he raided the temple of Aphrodite and stole her for me."

"You asked Alexander to steal a woman from the temple of Aphrodite?" I asked, amazed.

"I asked him to steal the woman I loved," he replied.

"And how she feel about being kidnapped?"

"I think she forgave me. She married me and we have two healthy boys." He could not contain his pride.

"I would like to meet your wife, Apollodorus. She is lucky to have such a ..." I stopped in midsentence as a wave of pain and nausea drove through me like a lightning bolt. I felt as if my legs were on fire and I could barely breathe. I screamed as another wave of pain shot up my spine and I fell to my knees.

"Lady Ardella, what is it?" Apollodorus implored.

"It is not me. Someone nearby is in pain. Such terrible pain," I managed to whimper. The pain was horrendous.

I heard someone call from the doorway, "Master Apollodorus. There has been an accident. A cyclopean stone has crushed one of the workmen on the outer wall. It is very bad."

"Find the Strategos. He must get Lady Ardella out of the hospital immediately." Those were the last words I heard before I lost consciousness from the pain.

"How could you bring that woman into my home, Alexander?" I heard a female voice snipe. I don't know if it was the tone of her voice or the intense waves of anger she sent out that awakened me. I tried to open my eyes but could not seem to find the strength.

"There was an accident on the outer wall. A man was crushed. Apollodorus said as soon as his broken body was brought into the hospital Ardella screamed in pain and fainted. I had to get her out of there and your home was close by."

"What did you think would happen taking an empath into a hospital? It is a place full of people in pain. It would be a nightmare for someone with her gift."

"I didn't think about that. I knew the Athena sect had never allowed her into their hospital and I was trying so hard to impress her. I'm an idiot."

I could feel genuine regret in his tone and from his unshielded heart. I found I resented this woman with whom he felt no need to hide his feelings.

"Why would you be trying to impress her of all people, Alexander? Didn't you tell me she worked against us with Queen Lyessa and the Amazons? By the Sleeping Goddess, hasn't she sent assassins to kill you? It was her brother who attacked our walls and tried to destroy our city." The woman's tone was bitter.

"Everything you say is true, Galynda. I know she has been our enemy in the past, but can't you see the potential here. If we can win her over to our side, she could be a formidable ally."

"What if you don't convince her to join our cause? Then we are keeping a deadly viper in our midst that could destroy Metropolis from within."

"I can't explain it, but somehow this feels right. I am not

making this decision with my head, but with my instincts."

"Are you sure you are not making it with your heart?" the woman pried.

"I don't know what you mean," he protested.

"You forget, I was in the caravan the day you escaped from New Athens. I have known you longer than anyone. You were very lost those first few months. It was as if your heart had been broken."

"I had lost the world I had grown up in. I barely escaped with my life."

"It was more than that. You would spend hours staring into nothingness, living in your own dream world. Many of us wondered if you had left someone special behind in New Athens."

"It was so long ago. I left behind only possibilities," he sighed.

"But is the past clouding your judgment of the present?"

"No more than fear of the future is clouding your judgment, Galynda."

"I don't know why I bother to argue with you, Alexander. You must always have the final word."

He laughed at her comment, but his words were lost to me as I slipped back into oblivion.

⸻

"Alexander, she is waking." I heard Galynda call across the room.

I still felt the anger in her but it was more subdued now.

"Ardella, are you alright?" Alexander asked. His voice and his emotions were tinged with concern.

"What happened?" I asked.

"An accident victim was brought into the hospital. His body

had been crushed by one of the cyclopean stones. You fainted."

"I remember now. It was horrible. May the Goddess speed his way into the next world?"

"You pray for his death?" Galynda asked, irritated.

"I pray for an end to his agony. His pain was unbearable. I would not wish my worst enemy to spend his final hours in this world in such torment," I said.

"I saw the man's body, Galynda, it was beyond repair. It will only be a matter of time. If it helps, Ardella, I'm sure Apollodorus has done all he can to ease the man's pain and give him comfort as he leaves this life."

"I am sure he will. Apollodorus is a good man."

"There are many good men and women in Metropolis," Galynda said.

"I am coming to realize that," I replied.

"Ardella, I would like to introduce you to my adopted sister, Galynda. She was in the caravan that took me from New Athens."

The woman the Son of Ares called his sister was a stark contrast from the tall, dark Alexander. Galynda was smaller than most of the women in Arcadia. Her petite, feminine frame contained the right mixture of curves and softness to make her the perfect "damsel in distress". Most women would be jealous of the shiny red curls that flowed down the back of this Hermian beauty. In fact, I remembered the same wave of jealousy struck me the first time I saw her.

"We have met before," I said. I had spoken to her almost a decade ago, trying to arrange for Alexander's escape.

"I don't understand. When did you meet?" he asked.

Alexander was confused, but felt Galynda suddenly realized who I was. "You," she gasped in disbelief.

I felt the turmoil stir in her chest. Some of the anger was being replaced by doubt.

"I told you I arranged for the Hermian caravan to take you away from New Athens. I spoke to someone in the caravan. That person was Galynda," I explained.

"Is that why you took me in, sister?" Alexander asked.

"She asked me to look after you," she confessed. She then turned to me accusingly, "You told me he was your brother and he was being exiled from New Athens."

"I was afraid if I told you that you were helping the Son of Ares escape his death sentence you might ..."

"...refuse to help," Galynda supplied.

"I am sorry for deceiving you. I was trying to save his life."

"And then you spent the next ten years trying to kill him and destroy everything he built."

"Galynda," Alexander said.

"She is right, Alexander. I have been your enemy because I thought I had made a terrible mistake. I thought I had unleashed the Son of Ares on Arcadia through my naiveté. I felt guilt every time I heard you had raided another village or someone had been harmed. I became obsessed with stopping you."

"How do you feel now?" Alexander asked. Although his voice was quiet and without emotion, I could feel the fear that he tried to keep bottled inside.

"Confused," I said honestly. "I am beginning to realize that what I thought was the truth all these years was only my own perceptions and interpretations of events. I am no longer so sure I was right and you were wrong. I think the truth is somewhere here in Metropolis."

"All I ask is you give Metropolis a chance," Alexander said.

"Alexander," Galynda warned, "you need to stop to think about whether Metropolis will want to give their old enemy a chance. The loss of life is still fresh in everyone's mind. Don't rush this."

"Galynda, I think you underestimate the people of Metropolis," Alexander said, but decided not to continue the debate. Instead he turned to me, "If you feel you are able to walk, Ardella, perhaps we should head back to the citadel."

"Yes, perhaps that is best," I said. My head pounded as I rose, but I knew the intensity of the emotions in the room would soon make it worse. As we walked past the humble altar near the front door I saw a small wooden statue of a stag. Its significance was not lost on me. In my excitement, I simply blurted out my discovery. "You are a follower of Artemis?" I turned and asked Galynda.

I saw her look accusingly at Alexander. He shrugged. "I didn't tell her," he swore.

"It was the stag carving. The stag was sacred to Artemis. Have you seen the sacred stag in your dreams?" I asked.

"How could you know that I have seen a stag in my dreams?" She was suddenly wary.

"Like everything else I know, I read it in a book. It is said that Artemis would send the sacred stag to her followers in dreams to help guide them," I replied.

"Are you trying to tell me Artemis is aware of our efforts to worship her?" Galynda asked, astonished.

"The book says if you see a stag in your dreams it was sent as a messenger from Artemis, so she must be aware of you," I replied.

"What book are you talking about?" Galynda asked.

"*The Book of Artemis*. It was written by an Athenian historian almost a thousand years ago. Her name was Calysto and she tried to preserve all the knowledge of the Huntresses of Artemis. The book has a history of their last days, and includes descriptions of their religious rites, and..." My train of thought was interrupted by a sudden realization.

"What is it?" Alexander asked.

"Teldar said he brought all the books he found in my chamber. I think the *Book of Artemis* was on my desk. It may be here in Metropolis in the crates Teldar brought with him. We have to return to the tower and check," I exclaimed.

"I see why you like her, brother. I have never seen anyone but you get so excited about a book," Galynda chuckled.

"It is not just any book." My excitement was rising. "It has the lost secrets of Artemis, which her new followers could use to revive her worship."

"Are you saying this book tells how to awaken the Sleeping Goddess?" Galynda asked. I could sense her skepticism.

"I don't know for sure. I have not finished it. I do know it has the rituals and customs of the Huntresses."

"That alone makes it very valuable," Galynda said. Her suspicion of me grew. "Why would you want to share this knowledge with us?"

"Galynda," Alexander warned.

"It's a fair question, Strategos," Galynda retorted.

"It is a fair question," I agreed. "You expect me to say I would trade the knowledge for my brother's freedom."

"It had occurred to me," she replied.

"A few days ago that might have been my answer," I said, "but not now."

"You expect me to believe you have given up on your brother?"

"Certainly not. I will fight to my last breath to see that my brother's life is spared by Hermes' Council, but unlike my Goddess, I do not believe the withholding of knowledge to be a weapon."

"Your Goddess has used knowledge as the source of her power for thousands of years," Galynda said. "Why should you be any different?"

"Because knowledge is the greatest gift mankind gives to

each generation. It is bigger than you or I or even the Goddess Athena. Calysto recorded the last days of the followers of Artemis for the future, so someday that knowledge would be available if it were needed," I said, hoping my intent was clear.

"How do you come to think so differently than your Goddess?" Galynda asked.

"A wise man recently told me knowledge is important, but it is not as important as the application of that knowledge to improve the world as we know it," I said. I spared a quick glance at Alexander whose face did not show the spark of satisfaction he felt from having influenced my view of the world.

"Ardella may be willing to share this knowledge, but I want something from the followers of Artemis, if this book turns out to be as valuable as you two believe."

"Alexander, I ..." I started to say, but he cut me off.

"Galynda, I want you to help me make sure Ardella is given a fair chance in Metropolis."

Galynda looked over at me and then back at Alexander. "You win, brother. You have been right more often than you have been wrong in the past. If you say we need this woman, then I will support you—with or without the Book of Artemis."

Chapter 14

Love and hate. These are the two strongest emotions, yet they can both be shattered by a single act or event.

**Talon of the Athena sect from his work *On Emotions*
899 Ab Terra Condita**

WE WALKED THROUGH the streets of Metropolis without speaking. After our strange discussion at Galynda's, I was too uncertain about my feelings to try to make polite conversation.

I wondered if Alexander was having a similar dilemma.

I knew the strange void in his mind meant that he had again erected the wall to shield his feelings from me. Although his emotions were hidden, my empathy continued to sense to the feelings of the strangers we passed. Some were tired from a long day of work and happy to be headed home. Others carried around their anger or sorrow at recent events. Most had strong feelings of pride and admiration for their leader.

Some were curious about me, while others were hostile (I assume because they realized who I was), but no one said or did anything to betray their feelings in Alexander's presence. It was a tribute to their admiration for him that his very presence beside me kept his people at bay.

That held true until we were just outside the gates of the citadel. Suddenly, a woman ran into me as we rounded the corner and I fell backwards onto the hard paving stones.

"Forgive me. I did not see you," the woman said as she reached down to help me up.

It was at that moment her eyes finally saw my face. Daggers of anger and hatred burst from her mind, stunning me. If thoughts could in fact kill, I would have been dead at that very moment. "You," she spat, springing back from me as if I were some Arcadian viper intent on harming her, "How dare you walk the streets of Metropolis! Why aren't you locked up beside your accursed brother?"

I stared in disbelief as she drew a small knife from within the folds of her tunic. I felt the deadly intent in her mind, yet my limbs would not move. It occurred to me that I might well die at this woman's hands.

Alexander responded instantly. He struck her arm, sending the dagger clattering onto the stone beside me. "Watch yourself, woman. Lady Ardella is under my protection," Alexander cautioned. Although his command sounded cold and dispassionate, I felt his rage oozing from his icy emotional armor.

"Forgive me, Strategos. I did not mean any offense to you. But that woman and her brother are responsible for what happened to my sons – my Micah and Jonnas,"

I felt her deference for Alexander and her maternal instincts warring within her as she spoke.

"I lost both my boys to those horrible metal monsters! I want justice," she cried.

"It is for Hermes and the Council to determine Rafe's fate for his crimes against Metropolis," Alexander told her. His tone was firm and authoritative, but now that his walls were breached,

I could also feel his compassion for this woman.

"What about her? What will her punishment be?" the woman asked coldly.

"Lady Ardella has committed no crime. Despite her plea for her brother's life, no one believes she had anything to do with the attack on Metropolis." I was surprised by the conviction of his words. The Son of Ares had no reason to trust me, yet his emotions told me that he really didn't hold me responsible for my brother's crimes. Despite everything that I had learned about Alexander's Metropolis in recent days, that actually surprised me.

"My sons are in the land of the dead, while she walks the streets of Metropolis. How can that be justice?" the woman asked, her heart overwhelmed by grief.

I looked up at the distraught woman and could almost see her holding one of the lifeless bodies I had encountered upon my arrival in Metropolis. I felt the gaping hole in her soul from having her world ripped from her so abruptly. I felt tears run down my cheeks for her lost sons.

I glanced over at the dagger that lay beside me and made a fateful decision. I picked up the simple wooden-handled knife and offered it to the woman. "If it will bring your sons back to life, then you should kill me," I whispered.

"Ardella, no!" Alexander said. He reached for the dagger, but the woman was faster. In a heartbeat she took the blade and had it pressed against my neck.

"I will send you to the next life with my own hands," the woman growled.

I remained calm, however, because I felt her anger waiver. Despite her genuine grief, she was not a murderer. "Will killing me bring your sons back to you?" I asked her, nudging the doubt that was beginning to push at her rage, "Will it bring you peace?"

"It will bring justice," she insisted, but I could feel her

desperately struggling to hold on to the anger that was swiftly flowing beyond her reach.

"Will it?" I challenged.

As I had hoped, the woman paused for a moment to consider. She lowered the dagger just a fraction, and Alexander seized the opportunity. Once again he sent the dagger flying, while two nearby raiders in the crowd grabbed the woman and yanked her to her feet.

She struggled against their hold, the full fury of her rage returned, and she yelled "Let me go."

Her intense pain continued to bring tears to my eyes, but my first instinct was still to comfort her. "Please do not hurt her," I called loud enough for the raiders and Alexander to hear.

"Take her away. I will deal with her later," Alexander commanded.

"No!" I cried, rising from the ground. "Alexander, please! Do not hurt her. She has been through enough already," I said, weeping.

"I don't need your pity, my lady. I will never forgive – never!" the woman snarled. Although her words sounded harsh, my empathy told me she was once again losing her hold on her anger.

"It is not pity," I said as I met her pained gaze. "I am the only person in all of Arcadia who truly understands what you feel. I can feel it, too. Your sons have taken part of your soul with them to the next life. I will never be able to forget your pain nor forgive my brother for what he has done to you."

As our tenuous bonds of grief intertwined, I could feel her anger at last giving way. The pain was still there, but it could now fade with time.

I sighed with relief, until I realized Alexander's anger was still strong.

I moved to gently lay my hand on his arm. "Forgiveness is something we all must learn. It is the only way to break the maelstrom of violence that will shatter us against the Great Law of the Olympians."

"She tried to kill you, Ardella. If I let her go; she could try again."

"That is a risk I am willing to take. She is a distraught mother, Alexander, not a killer. Please! Let her go," I entreated.

I looked up at him and knew from his eyes that my words had reached him.

"As you wish, Ardella."

⁓

Hours later beneath the great oak overlooking Artemis' tomb Alexander and I sat in silence. I had tried when we first arrived to call forth the dryad Muriel to introduce her to the Strategos, but she was sleeping or unwilling to emerge from her tree. So we sat contently in the quiet of the early evening with the cool breeze gently rustling the leaves, and the sweet fragrance of the flowers floating in the air all around us.

"You are quiet," Alexander finally said.

"I like the stillness at the end of the day," I explained. I often sat in the Grove of the Dryads in New Athens at this time of day to enjoy a few quiet moments. It was a secret pleasure I had not shared with anyone, including Teldar. Even now I wondered why it felt so natural to be sharing it with a man who was supposed to be my enemy.

"I am sorry about what happened earlier," he said. Both his voice and his heart conveyed genuine regret.

I looked over at Alexander and could not help but notice that the fading light softened his features and, if possible, made him look even more handsome. His dark chocolate locks called to me. I clinched my fists to resist the urge to feel the silky strands tickle my fingers.

"I would never have forgiven myself if that woman had hurt you," he said, unaware of my wandering thoughts.

"What?" I murmured.

"I don't want you to think all of Metropolis feels as she does," he explained, misunderstanding my response.

"I did feel some anger and resentment towards me today, but she was the only one I sensed who actually wanted to kill me," I assured him.

"That is good to know." He sighed in relief. "I still don't understand what made you hand her back her dagger and taunt her to kill you."

I found myself slightly annoyed by the fact his emotions seemed to be that of a scolding parent. "I was not taunting her. I was trying to make her see her mistake," I replied. I was defensive, because I was pretending it had been a logical choice, when that was the furthest thing from the truth. *I let emotions—her emotions—rule over my own.*

"See her mistake?" Alexander laughed, "For pity's sake, Ardella she wasn't making a rational well thought out decision. She was a grieving mother."

"I knew that, but I..." I realized the only solution was to admit the truth. "I could feel her emotions. She was angry, but she was also in a great deal of pain. I felt her doubt. I did not believe she had it in her to kill."

"You knew for certain the whole time that you were in no danger?" he asked, incredulously.

"I felt sure that if I could get her to stop and think about her actions she would realize it was a mistake," I rationalized. The truth was I had almost let a woman kill me because her emotions had overcome my own self-preservation instincts, but I would never admit that to him.

"I have great respect for your empathic gifts, but this is too much. You were willing to gamble your life on someone else's ability to come to a logical conclusion in a moment of anger?" he asked. His feelings told me he was amused by my explanation.

"You make it sound ridiculous. You don't understand what it is like to be able to feel the emotions of the people around you. It colors your perception," I tried to explain.

"Your empathy does seem to influence you a great deal," he offered. "You act on your emotions, which is strange for a follower of Athena. Is that why you came running to Metropolis to save your brother?"

"Now you sound like my mother," I said.

I felt his sudden embarrassment at the mention of my mother and assumed it was from our encounter with her earlier.

"She wasn't happy to see us come into your room earlier. I wasn't sure if she was more upset there had been an attempt on your life or that you had spent the entire day with me," he laughed.

"She thinks you are distracting me from helping Rafe," I said.

"You should spend every day alone in your room waiting for your chance to speak to the Council?" he asked.

"I just should not spend time with you. She says you are a bad influence." I could feel his amusement at that statement and a hint of another emotion I didn't quite recognize.

"Do you think I am a bad influence?" he asked, leaning closer.

I felt my skin tingle where the warmth of his breathing caressed by shoulder.

"I think you have a strong influence on me. Only time will tell if it is good or bad," I said, "I really think you ..." I stopped in midsentence. I now felt a stronger wave of that strange new emotion, erupting from him. It made me shiver and my heart beat faster. An unusual tightness filled my chest. *Could this really be the emotion I thought it was? Did the Son of Ares desire* me?

Alexander was a strong and powerful man. His handsome features had turned more than one head as we had traveled through the city. I had sensed jealousy over my presence a few times. I was an average female more interested in books than men and yet his emotions made it clear that Alexander wanted me. The feeling was intoxicating. "Stop it, I cannot think when you do that," I muttered without considering my words.

"What did I do?" he purred. His emotions were pure male satisfaction. He knew exactly what he was doing.

"You know I can feel what you feel. It is very distracting to be able to feel your ..." I stammered as his manly scent tickled my nose and caused my breath to catch in my throat.

"Can you really feel everything I am feeling?" he crooned.

"Yes!" I hissed. I was already becoming caught up in the tide of emotions flowing around us, and he doubted my empathy.

"Tell me what I'm feeling," he encouraged. It was an absurd, yet ... The timber of his voice as he made the request called to something deep within me. I had no choice but to follow his command.

I found myself trying to share the moment as I perceived it. "Your heart is racing. Your breath catches in your chest. Your blood burns. I can even feel how your lips tingle in anticipation of a ...." His lips met mine. This time they were not soft and comforting but hot and demanding.

I felt little streaks of electricity flow between us and I parted my lips slightly in a soft moan of pleasure. It was all the encouragement he needed. His tongue slipped past and met my own in a fiery dance of passion. I could feel my heart and his racing as the passion coursed through our veins. My arms went around his neck and I instinctively pulled him closer. I felt his arms move down my back, gently exploring and caressing.

"Ardella," he whispered, breaking the kiss and looking down at me.

I felt pinpricks of guilt blunting his passion.

"If you don't feel the same, I should stop," he tried to offer, gently caressing my face. He was definitely not an empath, or he would know the flame of passion burned me as well.

In fact found I missed his lips on mine, so I reached up and pulled him back to me. As my lips touched his and I used my tongue to imitate his earlier kiss, I heard him moan and felt the strange pleasure/pain of his erection as if it were in fact happening to me. It was blissful discomfort that played havoc with my own senses.

"Strategos," a distant voice called. "Strategos, forgive me for interrupting," the voice said again. I finally realized the person speaking was standing right beside us.

"What do you want?" I heard Alexander growl as he too realized the raider was trying to gain our attention. My own embarrassment was over shadowed by Alexander's obvious irritation at the interruption.

"Forgive me, but Hermes and the Council are asking to speak to you immediately. They say it is urgent."

"You have delivered your message, Tomas. You may go. I expect you to remain silent about what you have seen tonight or there will be consequences."

The man's burst of fear left little doubt that Alexander's stern warning had been understood. Still, I was glad of the semi-darkness of twilight and hoped it might not be clear who lay entwined with the Strategos in a lover's embrace.

"Yes, my lord," the raider said and quickly departed.

"I'm sorry, Ardella," Alexander said as he gently caressed my shoulder. As his hand trailed down my arm, I enjoyed the tingling sensation it brought as well as the waves of disappointment I felt from Alexander.

I decided to try to lighten his mood. "Are you sorry you have to go? Or are you sorry for kissing me?" I hoped I sounded playful. To my amazement his mood changed at once, but not in the way I had intended.

"I...It just ..." Alexander started to say.

I felt his uncertainty tinged with doubt, and I couldn't help but smile. Where passion and desire were concerned he was a master, but the simple playful teasing of lovers was something he wasn't accustomed to.

"I was teasing." I said, putting my finger over his lips to end his attempts at an explanation. I could almost feel the relief and joy burst forth at my words. "You should go. The Council is waiting," I reminded him.

"Until tomorrow," he said. He stood up, extended his hand, and helped me rise. Then he placed a passionate kiss in my palm. It was the same gesture Teldar had made when we parted, yet the experience was not at all the same.

I felt the electricity shoot up my arm and leave my whole body tingling. My heart beat faster and my breath came in short bursts. *By the Goddess, what was happening to me?*

"I'll come by and help you look for the Book of Artemis. Perhaps we can turn the crates into shelving for your collection," he whispered against my skin.

"You are going to build me a bookshelf?" I chuckled.

"I have many talents, Lady Ardella," he said, huskily.

I felt a spark of desire shoot though my breast at his playful words. "Good night, Alexander."

"Good night," he said. As he turned to leave, I felt the strange jubilation that filled him slowly fade as he walked away.

By the Goddess if we ever did make love could I survive feeling everything he stirred in me and everything he too was experiencing simultaneously? I suddenly wondered where that thought had come from. Only a few weeks ago Alexander was my sworn enemy and if we had not been in interrupted just now I might just have allowed him an intimacy I had only shared with Teldar after almost a year of courtship. *Perhaps my mother had a point about Alexander being a bad influence.*

I watched him walk away until he was out of sight. I found that I missed his presence beside me and sighed. *This is getting absurd.*

Just as I began to leave the grove to return to my room, a voice whispered, "He is quite handsome. I think you could have convinced him to remain, if you have tried."

Now she makes an appearance? "Goodnight, Muriel." I said, leaving the grove. I decided I was not going to wait for Alexander, but would find the book of Artemis tonight before I slept.

I found the Book of Artemis in the second crate I searched and once found could not help myself, but began to read:

For almost a thousand years, the followers of Artemis and the followers of Hera had been closer than any other sects on Arcadia. Perhaps it was the similarity of their female dominated cultures that made them so comfortable with their fellow sisters. Although neither culture had a long- term place for men within their society, both had to occasionally make an exception for the sake of survival.

Procreation among the Amazons was seen as a necessary evil and every woman was expected to bare at least one female child while properly disposing of unwanted male offspring in the fires of

Hera. The Huntresses of Artemis had a similar philosophy about men, however many of Artemis' followers chose to actually remain celibate, like their Goddess, and did not bare any children.

This was a critical problem. The Amazons, because of the closeness of the two sects, chose to help their sisters by allowing the Huntresses of Artemis to adopt Amazon daughters. Thus, over the centuries, Amazons gave up their own children to see that the cult of Artemis did not die out. This bond of sisterhood drew the two cultures even closer together.

It happened that the Queen of the Amazons, Delilah, gave birth to twin daughters. She chose to give one child to the Great Mother of Artemis in a show of sisterly solidarity. Cynthia grew up in her new home and was selected by the blessing of Artemis follower her adopted mother, while her sister, Attia, grew up to become the Queen of the Amazons.

The two sisters knew of their heritage and spent as much time together as their respective roles allowed. They hunted together. They trained with sword and spear without fear of injury or death. They were even known to share the males who wandered through their lives without jealousy. It was a young man of the Aphrodite sect, however, that finally came between them. His name was Rowan and as it happened he was a Son of Ares.

It was in the summer of the twins twenty-second year that Rowan came to the grove of Artemis with many other young men from around Arcadia for the annual Great Hunt. In this particular hunt it was the young men who offered themselves as the hunted. The followers of Artemis and their sister Amazons hunted their prey by the light of the first full moon of the summer. It was a magical night intended to produce many new anonymous offspring for the daughters of Artemis and Hera.

As it happened, Cynthia was the first to catch Rowan, yet as they made love by moonlight a strange this happened: Cynthia fell *in love with the handsome Son of Ares and could not bring herself to leave his side: a great taboo. As dawn approached and the Great Mother Cynthia did not return from the forest, her sister Queen Attia of the Amazons became worried and went in search of her twin.*

Attia found Cynthia and Rowan sleeping in each other's arms beneath the branches of Artemis' sacred oak. Suddenly filled with a rage she could not explain, Attia drew her sword to stab the man who had tempted her sister to such heresy. Just before she struck the fatal blow however, Rowan opened his eyes and her hand faltered. Mesmerized by the arrogant young demi-god's handsome face, Attia's sword dropped harmlessly to the earth. At this Cynthia awoke and beckoned to her sister. Like so many times before they shared the affections of a male, but neither woman could have foreseen the consequences to Arcadia.

∽

"Good morning, Lady Ardella. Lady Lucinda," Deidra called as she entered my tower chamber. Yesterday Alexander and I had sent Deidra to spend time with her husband or perhaps visit the newest addition to her family. She had been with me almost constantly since I had arrived in Metropolis and we felt she could use a break.

"I understand you had quite a day," she said, "and I was not there to protect you as I promised to do."

"Alexander did a fine job protecting me," I offered.

"I have no doubt he held his own in knife fight, but what possessed him to take an empath into a hospital?" she asked.

I felt my mother's curiosity followed by anger from across the room. "That man dragged you into horrors of a hospital, knowing what it could do to you?" she bellowed.

"Alexander and I only told her about the attack, not my

fainting at the hospital," I whispered to Deidra.

"Sorry," she replied.

"What happened? Are you alright? Why did you let him take you to such a dangerous place?" my mother asked.

"We did not understand the risks, Mother. He invited me to tour the hospital because he is proud of it. He has been trying to show me all the things Metropolis has to offer," I said.

Her displeasure at Alexander's efforts to show me more of Metropolis was not a surprise to me. She ignored much of my explanation. "Why would you agree to go into a hospital?" she asked.

"Because I was never allowed to enter a hospital in New Athens. Everyone told me it was forbidden. I just wanted to see the inside—once." As soon as I uttered the words, I realized they sounded childish.

"I told you he was a bad influence. You were always high strung, but I hoped that over the years you had learned to let your head rule and had settled down. It is time to get you back to New Athens and married to Teldar. He is good for you. *That* man is not."

"Please do not tease me, Mother; you know I cannot go back. My engagement to Teldar is broken because of my exile," I said. Her shock and confusion enveloped me. By the Goddess, she was unaware of just how foolish her daughter had been.

"What are you talking about, Ardella?" my mother asked.

"I am sorry, Mother. I thought you already knew."

"What should I know, child?"

"I have been exiled by Athena. Teldar told me himself shortly after he arrived. Those boxes," I said, indicating the three crates my ex-betrothed had brought, "are all my worldly possessions. I cannot go back to New Athens. I am no longer welcome there."

My mother's confusion tore through her mind like a mad bull might rip through a field of tinder plants. My mother had always been a beacon of calm reserve, so being able to sense her inner turmoil was disconcerting. "I don't understand," she said. "You are the chosen of Athena. She promised her touch would make you cherished and protected for the rest of your life."

"Circumstances changed. She is displeased with me," I offered.

"What could you possibly have done? Surely Athena doesn't hold you responsible for what Rafe did?"

"No. Athena exiled me for what I did over ten years ago," I said.

When she didn't respond I continued, "In trying to free Rafe, I wanted to make everyone understand what had driven him to do such a horrible thing. I wanted to make them understand that it was not his fault." I paused as I felt the terror wheeling up in my mother's heart. I realized she was just as terrified of hearing the words as I had always been to speak them.

"I told them I was the one who freed the Son of Ares from his cell in New Athens and helped him escape with the Hermians—not Rafe. I admitted that I allowed my twin to take the blame for a crime I had committed and that my actions had shaped the man he became."

"You confessed to your brother's crime all those years ago to save his life?" she said, stunned.

I felt the desperation in her voice and heart. How is it that my own mother never suspected what I had done? I wondered. All these years she's truly believed that her son was guilty. What had I done?

"I confessed, Mother, because I am guilty. I released the Son of Ares all those years ago because I felt pity for his plight and in my naiveté I did not see him as dangerous," I said.

"You let them exile your twin brother for a crime you knew he did not commit and said nothing in his defense," she cried.

"I tried to tell Minister Tressa when I realized what they planned to do to Rafe, but she told me I was being a silly child. She said that trying to save my brother by confessing would only send our whole family into exile," I whined like a child caught snatching cookies.

"The leader of the Athenian Council told you to lie?" she asked.

"She told me to remain silent or we would all suffer."

The silence was suffocating. The words would not stay in my throat.

"I was fourteen and scared. I believed her and said nothing," I confessed.

"But you never told me the truth," she, obviously hurt.

"I was afraid at first and then too ashamed of what I had done. I know it is not an excuse."

My mother's anger finally erupted. "You let me believe the worst about my son for all those years and never told me the truth," she spat.

"I always defended Rafe to you and anyone who would listen. I always said I knew that he would not release the Son of Ares."

"You knew because you were the one who committed the crime."

"Yes!"

"Do you know what you have done? Your brother is bitter because of his exile. He may even have gone mad—why else would he attack a city? Ardella, he faces death even now for what your lies drove him to do."

Her savagery caught me off guard. She was outraged by what I had done, and I felt guilt churning in my soul.

"Mother, I never meant for any of this to happen. Why do you think I came to Metropolis? I am trying to make up for what I did to Rafe," I pleaded.

"And when your new friend Alexander and his barbarians execute your brother for his crimes against Metropolis, will you step over his corpse to join their cause?" she spat.

I stood transfixed at her words, more because I could feel the hate and anger behind them. It was almost as intense as the woman who had tried to kill me yesterday, however, coming from my own mother made it unbearable. By the Goddess, if I could go back to change the past and take my brother's place I would, but nothing I could do in the present would ever fix the mistake of a fourteen-year-old girl. Nothing will ever change the consequences of my actions.

My mother turned her back on me and headed to the door.

"Mother, please...." I reached for her arm.

"Don't, Ardella. I am too angry to discuss this with you right now. I need to see your brother," she said. She stopped in the doorway and turned toward me. "Does he know the truth?" she asked.

My tear-filled eyes looked at her. "He has to suspect the truth. He knew I felt the Council was being unfair. He could have used that knowledge to implicate me, but he never did."

"If he dies, Ardella, I will never forgive you," she said and walked out the door. I had a terrible feeling I would never see her again.

I don't know how long I remained transfixed before Deidra put her arms around me. "She didn't mean those things, Lady Ardella. She is just angry," Deidra whispered. I could feel my friend's pity for my situation and her fear that my brother's death was inevitable.

"My head knows that she is angry and even understands, but my heart feels as if it has been ripped from my chest. I actually felt her rage. My own mother ..." I babbled.

Tears began streaming down my face. In a numb haze I allowed Deidra to lead me to my bed. I lay there for only a few minutes. For the first time in my life it was the intensity of my own emotions that overwhelmed my mind and sweet oblivion took me.

Chapter 15

Choices are like notes on a new lyre. Until the strings have been plucked and commitments made one cannot be sure if they will turn out to be right or wrong.

Queen Lyessa of the Amazons
Two thousand six hundred and forty-five years Ab Terra Condita

I AWOKE FROM the nightmare covered in sweat. I had just relived the fight with my mother for the third time that evening. As it had the first two times, the scene had switched from her discovery of my deception to Rafe's execution. I wished the dream were not so vivid.

I pleaded in vain with Alexander to spare my brother, but he laughed in my face. I heard myself scream as the axe man's weapon fell upon my twin's neck and his head rolled from his body. As I turn my face away from the gruesome scene, I suddenly saw my mother and the woman who had lost both of her sons to the metal men. Both women carry daggers in their hands and hatred in their hearts. As they advanced toward me I knew they intended to kill me to avenge their lost sons. Unable to move, I was frozen not by terror, but by guilt. I saw them lift the daggers to strike... and then suddenly found myself awake.

Since the incident with my mother that afternoon I had been lying in bed. Except for the original fainting spell, I had gotten very little rest. I felt more miserable and tired than when my head had first hit the pillow, but I could not seem to find the energy to rise or the peace of mind to sleep. Both Deidra and Alexander had come into my room to check on me but I feigned sleep. I was not yet ready to discuss this with anyone, or worse, have to pretend everything was fine when I felt like my heart had been ripped from my chest and trampled under my mother's feet.

I had to remind myself that her reaction was not unreasonable. I was the one who had lied to her—to everyone. I not only let my brother suffer for something he didn't do, I had allowed his own mother to believe the worst about him. I had no right to expect her forgiveness.

I heard the tolling of the citadel's bell marking the beginning of the midnight hour. I had been in Metropolis long enough to recognize it was the signal for the changing of the watch. There was no point trying to sleep. I had no desire to watch my brother die again. I found the energy to rise from the bed and walked slowly to the table and splashed my face with some of the cool water Deidra has left for me. It removed the last of the fog of sleep from my mind, but left a bone deep weariness.

I wrapped my plain woolen cloak around my shoulders and headed for the door. I decided to see if Muriel was in a talkative mood. I knew she would not press me to talk about things I wanted to forget and perhaps might even distract me from my misery with her friendly ramblings. As I descended the stairs, the absurdity of an ancient dryad, approaching senility, as the only person I could turn to in my hour of despair was not lost on me. I laughed aloud. I left my tower and turned toward the path that led to the grove of Artemis.

I heard two familiar voices. I didn't want them to realize I was there, so I slipped backward into the shadows.

"You cannot fix this, Alexander. You and I know that no matter what Ardella says, no matter how good her argument is, the Council will vote to execute her brother. There are too many dead in Metropolis for them to do anything else," I heard Deidra argue passionately. Even from a distance I could feel her regret at that simple truth.

"Perhaps if I argued for mercy they will consider simply keeping him imprisoned for life," Alexander suggested. His feelings were more confused. I could feel the inner conflict over this predicament.

"Is that really preferable to a quick death, Alexander? Besides, how would you justify your sudden feelings of mercy? How would Therin, Micah, and Jonnas, and the families of the others who died, feel about you asking for leniency for the man responsible for so many deaths?" Deidra was trying to make him face reality.

"I know you're right. I can't spare her brother's life, but I can't stand the thought of the pain that it will cause her," Alexander admitted.

Despite everything I had done to try to stop him and his dream for Metropolis over the years, he cared about me. *How I could have been so wrong about the Son of Ares?* As he spoke the next words I realized just how well he understood me.

"She has given up everything to try to save him. When he dies, I know a part of her will die as well. I don't know if I can just stand back and watch it happen."

"She made the decisions that brought her to this point in

her life, Alexander. You are not responsible for her pain," Deidra reminded him.

Although it hurt to hear her words, a part of me knew she spoke the truth.

"I doubt Ardella will see it that way," he said. "She came to me to save her brother's life. She came to me looking for mercy for her brother."

"And have you thought about why you want to grant her request so badly?" Deidra asked.

"What is that supposed to mean?"

"Do you really believe that Rafe does not deserve to die for his crimes against Metropolis or do you simply want to please his sister?" Deidra asked.

Alexander remained silent.

"Don't feel bad, Alexander," Deidra said. "I am becoming quite fond of her, too. It is hard not to like Ardella. She is not the unyielding, spoiled lady you described to me that first day."

"No, she isn't at all like what I had believed for so many years. It took me by surprise and I hoped …" he said and then fell silent.

Although he did not speak the words aloud, I felt his regret and resignation at what must be. He finally put into words the truth I had felt in his heart.

"I know I can't compromise all that I have built for just one person—including Ardella. What scares me is that a part of me wants to do whatever it takes to please her—no matter what the cost," he admitted.

"It is out of your hands, Alexander. Her brother is going to die," Deidra said.

Then they moved too far down the path to hear any more of their conversation. All thoughts of my visit with Muriel were forgotten. I knew that my brother's life lay not in my skills as an advocate but in my ties with the Amazons. I had to find the Medusa Tavern and the Amazon spy, Kendra. I had to get my brother out of Metropolis.

∽

The area of Metropolis in which the Medusa Tavern was located was not as well maintained as the inner ring and the Grove of Artemis where I had spent most of my time so far. The graffiti on the walls and refuge in the streets suggested that these residents of Metropolis did not have the same pride as their fellow citizens in their free society. Although the streets near the tower had been practically deserted at this time of night, the streets near the Medusa Tavern were teaming with lonely souls wandering in search of what would end their suffering. Some sought the companionship of strangers, while others had clearly decided to lose their troubles in the bottom of a bottle.

The painted Medusa outside the door of an otherwise nondescript building was the only indication that this was my destination. Staring at gruesome image of snakes coiling around the otherwise beautiful face, I hesitated . My dilemma was solved when the door opened and an inebriated raider stumbled outside. The hum of voices behind him indicated clearly that this was the Medusa Tavern where Kendra said she could be found.

Now the trick was to get past the hulking form of the drunken raider. It seems that he had decided I was waiting outside the door just for him.

"You're a pretty little thang. What ya doing out here all by yurself? I bet you were just waiting for ole Nemeus to find ya," he slurred and reached out to pull me into his arms. His words were amorous and I could feel the playfulness of his emotions, which meant I immediately assumed he was no real threat.

"I am meeting someone here," I suggested sidestepping his

advance. It didn't deter him as I had hoped. It simply aroused his curiosity.

"I can show ya a better time than he can," he said and finally caught hold of my arm, "Ya likes ta have fun. Nemeus is fun. He'll make sure ya have fun." I quivered with revulsion; although he seemed aroused by his own promise of making sure I had fun.

I realized I was in trouble. "Let me go. I am meeting someone inside the tavern. I have to go," I said.

I was frantic to get out of his embrace, but his grip only tightened. I could tell his feeling weren't malicious, but he was too drunk to take no for an answer. I had no choice but to make him understand I was not interested in the only way left open to me— force.

I had spent a good deal of time with Queen Lyessa over the years and had been trained in Amazon methods of combat. Ironically, this would be the first time I had put those skills to the test. As the drunk's hand lowered to grope one of my breasts, I took the opportunity to clamp on to the hand that held my arm. I bent my knees slightly and used the raider's own size against him by kicking out one of his legs and making him loose his balance. I then pulled as hard as I could on his arm and sent him crashing to the ground.

As he fell his instincts made him let go of my arm to try to stop his fall. It didn't help him, but I was free. I took several large steps backwards to make sure I was safe. His first emotion was anger and it was directed towards me. "So you wanna play rough, little girl," he snickered, trying unsuccessfully to rise.

"I want you to leave me alone," I stated. I had to diffuse his anger, but reasoning wouldn't work, considering his inebriation. I was at a loss.

"Nemeus, go home," I heard a voice from the doorway call. It belonged to an older gentleman who wore workman's pants and a short sleeve shirt covered by a large woolen apron. Although I didn't know him, he seemed to be coming to my rescue and so I took an immediate liking to him.

"I was just trying to show one of your girls a good time," the drunk whined.

"She is not one of my girls, and if you had been listening, you would've realized she isn't interested," the innkeeper contended.

"You know how women say no, but really mean yes." the drunk argued.

"You know my rules, Nemeus. The woman has to be willing," the innkeeper reminded him. I could feel his tightly controlled anger just under the surface. I suspected this was not the first time he had had to deal with this type of situation and it didn't sit well with him.

"Just give me a chance to show her how much fun I can be and she'll be willing," the drunk suggested with a laugh.

"Nemeus, you're drunk. If you plan to come back and drink here in the future, I suggest you go home and leave the girl alone," the innkeeper said. This put an end to the discussion.

Nemeus grumbled about somebody always spoiling his fun as he lifted himself off the ground. He stumbled away from the Medusa Tavern without a backward glance.

"Thank you, sir," I said.

"You shouldn't be wandering around this time of night, woman. You are just asking for trouble. Next time it may not be a harmless old drunk," he chided.

"I came here looking for a friend," I tried to explain, but the innkeeper wasn't impressed.

"You must be new to Metropolis, so let me make the rules clear. Don't wander the streets of the city alone at night. Too many of the raiders consider a woman alone an open invitation. Do I make myself clear?" he said. He turned to go back into the Medusa

Tavern. I was no longer his concern.

"I am looking for my friend Kendra," I called after him.

He looked back at me and I felt his amusement. "She's upstairs. Follow me," he said not bothering to wait to see if I did as he commanded.

The inside of the Medusa Tavern was brighter than the street and filled with the smoke of the many oil lamps. There was a young musician in the corner playing a cithara and singing a familiar ballad about two star-crossed lovers. A few customers sat drinking at various tables around the tavern and in one corner a group of younger men were playing a dice game.

The innkeeper walked to the base of the stairs behind the bar and indicated I should go on up. "Kendra's the last door on the right. I am not sure if she's alone, so knock first," he said. He then set off for two men at one of the tables who indicated they were ready for more wine.

I found the last comment a little strange, but began climbing the stairs. As I got to the upper landing and began moving down the hall, the very door I was heading for opened and a muscular raider with unkept sandy-brown hair stepped into the hall way.

I stopped dead in my tracks as the man leaned back to Kendra who now stood in the doorway and gave her a long, lingering kiss. "I have guard duty for the next three nights, so it will be a while before I can make it back," the man said.

I could feel his lust for Kendra, but what surprised me was the Amazon's absolute loathing for the man who was kissing her goodbye.

"I'll miss you," she whispered tenderly, but her total lack of any true feelings behind the words made it obvious to me that the reason she was intimate with this man was not mutual passion. I wondered how she could so effectively fake affection she did not feel. I moved back against the wall to allow the raider to pass.

Although there was plenty of room, the man managed to have to push past me and rub his body against mine. My instinctive revulsion to this action gave me a new appreciation for Kendra's acting ability.

Kendra started to close the door when she noticed me in the hall. "Lady Ardella?" she called to me in surprise.

"May I come in? I need your help," I started without preamble.

"You are always welcome." Kendra said, ushering me into her room. "What are you doing here so late at night? It isn't safe to be alone in the streets after dark."

"So the innkeeper has already informed me. He actually saved me from a drunk just outside the tavern who did not want to take 'no' for an answer," I told her. I felt her suddenly alarm again and wondered that a stranger would be concerned for me.

"You shouldn't have taken such a risk coming here at night. Surely Deidra told you about the dangers in Metropolis?" Kendra said.

"I could not wait until the morning. I overheard Deidra and Alexander talking. No matter what I say to Hermes and the Council, they are going to kill Rafe. I need your help to free him and get him away from Metropolis." The words rushed from my lips like the waters of a dam when the floodgates are open.

She sensed my desperation and guided me to a chair near the window of her room. "I wish I could say I am surprised, Lady Ardella. Although Alexander tries to keep this city civilized, there is a dark side to many of its citizens that the Strategos can't control. Even if the Council could be convinced to spare your brother, I have no doubt the good citizens of Metropolis would tear him limb from limb in their thirst for revenge," she told me.

"What can I do to save him?"

"I anticipated this possibility and am already working on a

solution."

I looked up at her in anticipation.

"Lucas, the man you just passed in the hall is one of Rafe's jailers. That should get me access to your brother."

"That explains it," I commented.

Kendra gave me a curious look.

"I could feel your revulsion for him from down the hall. Now I understand why you pretended to desire him."

"I have had to do too many things, which I find distasteful since coming to this accursed city. I look forward to returning to Amazonia," she said. Her emotions screamed the truth behind her words.

"I appreciate your sacrifice, Kendra," I said. "Do you really think you can get my brother out of his cell?"

"That won't be a problem. I can even get him out of the city, but where do we go? I am not sure he will be safe anywhere but with the Amazons.

Her statement confused me. "Are you suggesting taking Rafe to Amazonia? I would think New Athens would be a better choice. Perhaps Athena can be persuaded to relent...."

"I have been thinking about it. New Athens is where everyone will think we are headed. When the Hermians discover Rafe has escaped, they will send out search parties," she explained.

"If they are able to catch up, then you and Rafe would be recaptured," I speculated.

"If the raiders catch up to us, they will likely just kill us outright," Kendra suggested.

"Are you suggesting we try to trick them into searching the wrong direction?"

"We need to make it difficult for them. It will take us almost two days to reach the safety of Amazonia by horseback. Alexander's raiding ships travel at three times the speed of horses,"

Kendra informed me.

My mind raced as a horrifying plan formed in my mind. I had witnessed the love the citizens of Metropolis had for their leader. Perhaps we could use their devotion to our advantage.

"What if we kept the search parties from being sent out at all?" I suggested.

"What do you have in mind?"

"If they believed we held Alexander hostage, do you think they would let Rafe go without incident?" I asked.

"Are you suggesting we threaten Alexander's life to keep the Hermians from sending out their search parties?"

"If we leave a message making it clear that Alexander will be killed if we see even one caravan ship, do you think the citizens of Metropolis will obey?"

"I think the citizens of Metropolis will avoid any actions that might harm their Strategos, but Alexander is too dangerous to drag on horseback all the way to Amazonia. He would do everything he could to stop us with or without the search parties."

"That is why he is never leaving Metropolis. I will keep him captive right under their noses."

"You would need to keep him captive for several days," Kendra reminded me.

"You have another suggestion?" I asked.

"It might be safest to just ..." she hesitated. I felt rage in her heart. I had once seen a similar look in Counselor Tressa's eyes. Thank the Goddess looks cannot kill.

"If you are suggesting we harm him, I do not believe that is wise. I think a sleeping potion should do the trick, and I can use him to negotiate, if you and Rafe are captured," I said.

"I suppose you're right. You're a much better strategist than I would have expected. You would have made a fine Amazon, Lady Ardella," Kendra replied.

"So Lyessa keeps telling me," I mused. I then turned to a part of the plan that still bothered me. "Are you sure Queen Lyessa will allow Rafe to be sheltered in Amazonia? Men are not usually long term guests on your island."

Kendra looked wary and guilt gripped her heart. "I haven't had a chance to ask my queen about that yet."

"Perhaps I can take care of speaking to her. This is delicate and needs to be discussed in person."

"I don't understand?"

"It seems Alexander wants me to go to Amazonia to negotiate a peace treaty."

Kendra's laughter filled the starless night and washed away the last of my trepidation. With the Amazon's help I could save my brother.

◈

The rosy fingers of the dawn were just filling the sky as I approached my tower room. As I went to open the door, I felt him within. *I'm not ready for this encounter.*

I had just spent over an hour taking the longest route possible back to the tower to try to figure out what I was going to say —I still didn't know.

I hoped that I could act normal in his presence until it was too late to stop the plan Kendra and I had set in motion. It was time to find out how good an actress I was. The man waiting for me inside my room was worried and frightened and frustrated all at once. The feelings were too intense. I opened the door quietly and saw Alexander pacing. He looked up at me and I felt intense waves of relief flow from his body.

"Ardella, by the Goddess, where have you been?" he asked. He crossed the room and wrapped me in his arms. I felt I brief moment of guilt over where I had been and what I had been doing but I suppressed it, reminding myself that I came to Metropolis to free my brother no matter what the cost.

Despite my mind's rational voice telling me that driving away Alexander was the cost for my brother's life, my heart leapt for joy at the sweetness of his embrace. *How is it that my world has changed so much so quickly? When did I come to care for the Son of Ares?* I suddenly wished that I could make time stand still and that the future where I betrayed this man would never come.

"I've been so worried," he whispered against my ear.

I knew he was expecting an explanation, and so I gave him a reasonable story. "I was having trouble sleeping, so I went for a walk," I replied, deciding to stay as close to the truth as possible.

"I awoke early and decided to come to check on you. When I found you missing, I didn't know what to think. Between the attempt on your life and the incident with your mother I was afraid that..."

"Forgive me. I did not mean to worry you. I just needed to get some air to clear my head."

"Walking the streets of Metropolis after dark is not exactly safe, Ardella. Something could have happened to you."

"And you would not have been there to save me," I teased.

His fear for me was tangible. "It is not funny, Ardella. I don't know what I would do if anything happened to you," he said.

I could feel the tightness in his chest at these words and a blooming intensity.

"I was terrified," he confessed.

"I felt that through the door before I even entered the room," I offered. I hoped that the reminder of my empathy would raise his defenses as it had in the past. I had just agreed to kidnap and drug this man. I had to put some emotional distance between us, if I was going to save my brother. As usual, Alexander didn't cooperate.

He gently took my face between his hands and caressed my lower lip with the pad of his thumb. My body thrilled at his touch and my heart skipped a beat, but my emotions were hardly discernible compared to the tidal wave that swept from his heart to mine. I felt the desire, passion, and concern for me shoot through his chest, and then I felt LOVE. I couldn't help but think of the ancient Earth legend of Cupid and his magical arrows that caused mortals to suddenly fall in love. It was an absurd story, but perhaps I had discovered its origin. As I tried to wrap my mind around this incredibly intense feeling that flowed between us, my eyes widened and my breath caught in my throat.

"You felt that?" he whispered.

I only nodded wordlessly. I felt his joy mixed together with frustration.

"It seems unfair that you know how I feel about you in the same moment I realize it," he grumbled.

"I cannot help being what I am, Alexander," I said.

"I wouldn't have you any other way, Ardella," he said and pulled me closer.

A voice inside my head tried to tell me this was wrong, that I had to remain detached from Alexander if I were to save my brother, but it could not compete with the roar of sweet pleasure that flooded over me. Nothing could compete with the feeling of being loved with such intensity.

"Ardella, are you awake?" I heard Deidra's voice call from the other side of the door just before it opened.

I felt Alexander's frustration as he pulled away from me just as Deidra entered the room. When she saw Alexander standing so near, she experienced only embarrassment, not surprise. She already suspected. *Why did that not surprise me?*

"I didn't mean to intrude. I can come back later," she stammered, moving to close the door.

"No," Alexander and I called simultaneously.

"We were just..." I began at a loss for words.

"I just came by to check on Ardella..." Alexander interrupted.

"You don't have to explain. It is none of my business," Deidra said. She turned to leave.

"Please, Deidra, you do not have to go," I whispered.

She finally stopped and turned back to me. "I just came by to see how you were feeling," Deidra said.

"I am so tired, but I could not sleep last night," I replied. "My mother's words filled my dreams and turned them into nightmares.

"I'm not surprised. What your mother said yesterday haunted my dreams as well. You have to realize they were only words of anger," Deidra said.

"Just because they were spoken in anger does not make them any less true. It was worse because I could feel the intensity of her pain and disappointment. I wonder if she will ever forgive me," I tried to explain.

"I think I better tell you something," Alexander interrupted. "When Teldar and Tannis departed late yesterday for New Athens, I ..."

His hesitation gave me pause, but he finally gathered up the courage to continue.

"...I sent Lady Lucinda with them. She didn't want to go, but I insisted. My only defense is that I was angry."

I shook my head in disbelief.

"I really wanted to lock her up next to your brother, but I didn't think you would approve."

"So you sent my mother home?" I began to laugh. I was relieved that I didn't have to worry about her. Alexander had done me a favor.

"Does this mean you are not angry?" he asked.

"I will prove to you I am not angry," I laughed. "I have decided to go to Amazonia to negotiate your treaty."

Chapter 16

*One should be careful as to just how high one aspires.
The further up you go, the further you then have to fall.*

Titus Caesar, Son of Ares
Two thousand, one hundred and forty-eight years Ab Terra Condita

THE COOL BREEZE caressed my flesh while drawing strands of hair from my customary bun to send them dancing before my eyes. The chilled air and spray of the ferry's wake caused me to shiver and sent goose bumps creeping up my arms. Logically I should go back into shelter of the caravan ship, but didn't want to miss our first glimpse of Amazonia. At least I was not alone in my desire to see the shores of the Amazon capital come into view. Deidra stood beside me gripping the railing so hard that her knuckles were white. I could feel fear, joy, hope and sadness spinning around within her like water caught in the whirlpool of one of Poseidon's great sea storms. I wondered how long it had been since she had seen her home.

"I can't believe we got past the ferry this time," Captain

Arius sighed as he came up to stand beside us at the railing. Captain Trenton Arius was the commander of the caravan ship that brought us to Amazonia. His rough demeanor and unshaven face hid his true age and perhaps even a handsome appearance. It was hard to tell. From this leather pants and swashbuckling shirt to the colorful cloth he wore on his head Captain Arius brought to mind the tales of pirates from ancient earth. I never found the courage to ask if the likeness was on purpose.

"How many times have you tried to get this diplomatic mission to Amazonia?" I asked suddenly realizing there was more to the story than Alexander had shared. I knew from Deidra's guilty reaction that the Strategos had forgotten to mention the previous attempts on purpose.

"Is this the third or the fourth attempt, Deidra?" Arius asked oblivious to the taboo nature of the subject.

"This is the third time Metropolis has sent a delegation to negotiate a treaty with the Amazons. Neither of the two previous transports was allowed passage on the ferryboat to take their message to the Queen Lyessa," Deidra supplied, obviously deciding truthful answers would serve best at this point.

"I do not understand how you can get to the Amazonian villages for your raids without some means of transport across Lake Hera," I pondered. Both Captain Arius and Deidra found my question amusing.

"We usually borrowed a ferry to get our transport back and forth across the lake." Arius responded. When I raised my eyebrow in amusement, he quickly added, "We always returned them when we're done. We aren't thieves."

The Captain seemed confused when Deidra and I burst out laughing.

"It didn't seem prudent to use that method for a diplomatic mission," Deidra explained. "But when you have to ask permission, then you take the chance of being turned down – twice."

"So Alexander did not need my negotiating skills, he only needed me to get past the front door," I speculated.

"He did seem to think Queen Lyessa would allow you access to Amazonia, if only out of curiosity," Deidra said.

I laughed.

"I am afraid your diplomatic skills are wasted on this mission, Lady Ardella. This whole treaty is a fool's errand. The Amazons won't be interested in anything the Son of Ares has to say," Deidra offered sagely.

∽

The light drifted down through the tall windows of the bibliotheca. In the long silence that followed my explanation for coming, I found my gaze wondering to the interaction of the colors and textures on the shelves behind my friend Lyessa's head. I could feel her confusion and I didn't know how to explain my actions, because I wasn't certain myself.

"You are the last person I expected to see as a representative of Alexander and Metropolis," the tall and beautiful Queen of the Amazons said carefully. "I have always thought of you as an honorary Amazon, Ardella." Lyessa was only a year older than I was, yet the golden diadem she wore gave the effect of a more mature woman. At sixteen, Lyessa had been the youngest Amazon to ever assume the throne, but even her most vocal critics had been silenced by her decisive decision-making and conservative policies. Queen Lyessa was a traditionalist who was passionate about preserving the Amazon way of life. I knew she was well loved by her sister Amazons.

"I will admit old friend that this is not a place I ever saw myself, but I am here none the less."

"So Ambassador Ardella, what does Strategos Alexander want from my Amazons?" Queen Lyessa asked in a tone just tinged with sarcasm.

"He wants to form an alliance with the sect of Hera," I said softly.

"What? Is this a trick?" she scoffed, "Or is alliance just his new term for surrender?"

"Alexander does not want any more conflict with the daughters of Hera," I replied.

"He started this conflict, so why does he suddenly sue for peace?" Queen Lyessa asked skeptically.

"The Amazons are one of the most powerful fighting forces on Arcadia, and a cause of great concern for Metropolis. You have worked long and hard to bring an end to the new capital of Hermes, but your efforts have been in vain. It would require one... (my voice broke) or both of you to break the Great Law of the Olympians to remove the other from power. It is quite possible the remaining Olympians would destroy both Hera's and Hermes' followers for the transgression."

"So now Alexander is worried about the wrath of the Olympians?" she scoffed.

"Alexander is concerned for the future of his people," I offered.

"So what terms does Alexander suggest for this alliance?" she asked.

"He simply wants a non-aggression pact," I explained.

"That's all," she laughed turning toward the windows that looked out over the royal gardens. I felt her confusion intensify. "We cannot attack him now because of the Great Law of the Olympians, what is the point of putting an existing arrangement on paper?" she asked suspiciously

"Alexander wants ALL forms of aggression to stop. He would

make sure the raiders no longer bother any of your settlements and you would stop sending spies and assassins." I paused, "and stop supplying arms and training to the other sects."

"He is asking us to stop helping our neighbors defend themselves and make it easier for the Hermians to raid them."

"Essentially," I said.

"Helping our neighbors fight was your idea, Ardella. You now think it is a good idea to leave them on their own?"

"It would leave you in peace," I said carefully, and then added "but your neighbors are likely to suffer for it." I had decided on the way to Amazonia not to lie to my old friend, even for the sake of my brother.

"You are not a very good negotiator, Ardella," Lyessa observed.

"Actually I am. I convinced the Son of Ares to send me exactly where I wanted to be and he thinks it was his idea," I revealed.

"What exactly did you have to promise the man?"

"I agreed that I would present his proposal to you. It is his mistake if Alexander thought I would try to influence an old friend into agreeing to it."

"Now that is the Ardella I know," Lyessa laughed but I felt her mind in turmoil. "What bothers me, however, is that the offer seems logical and makes sense for the Amazons. I wish I could figure out the trap."

"If it makes it any easier, I know this offer is genuine and he plans to live up to his end of the bargain." I replied.

"Your ability to detect deceit has always been a useful talent. I am surprised, however, that Alexander let you use your empathy on him," she said.

"His defenses are stronger than most, but even the Son of Ares cannot suppress all emotions. Besides, I made it clear that the only way I would agree to do this was if he proved to me he was telling the truth," I said.

"You sound like you truly believe him when he says he wants peace. Surely you have not forgotten that Alexander is a monster who you and I swore to destroy?" I cringed at her use of the word "monster" and the vehement tone of her voice. *Had her attitude toward the Son of Ares been my own only a few weeks ago? How did I make my best friend understand my change of heart?* The truth.

"Being close enough to feel what he feels makes him more of a man than a monster, Lyessa. I admit I am beginning to have trouble thinking of him as the enemy," I said giving voice to the uncertainty that has been nagging me since I had come to Metropolis.

"Remind yourself of the massacre at Argos next time you forget. The Son of Ares and his raiders were responsible for the slaughter of 15 people including 6 of my Amazons," Lyessa reminded me. I felt her fresh surge of anger at the outrage as if it were only yesterday. I hoped it would help her to understand the truth.

"Argos was a mistake," I said softly.

"Is that what he called it, a mistake?" she spat.

"He called it a tragic accident," I explained. "He did not expect to find your Amazons there during the raid in Argos. His men were inexperienced, so rather than being intimidated, they felt threatened. Even Alexander says they reacted poorly to the resistance of your Amazons and regrets what happened."

"I don't care how he rationalizes it, 15 people died," she said.

"Twenty-two citizens of Metropolis died in my brother's attack," I said softly, "I saw first-hand the bodies being burned and the families grieving. In the grand total of death and destruction I think we are actually ahead."

"We didn't start this, Ardella. You are letting him twist the facts to suit his purposes," she replied.

"I have seen Metropolis with my own eyes. It is not the den of evil and oppression we were told." A strange silence filled the air and I felt Lyessa's cry of guilt to my very core. "But you already knew this."

"My spies told me as much."

"And you never bothered to share this information?"

"You never approved of my sending Amazons to Metropolis, Ardella. It would have been difficult to provide you with such information without revealing the source," she rationalized, but I could feel her doubt.

"That is just an excuse. I only objected to your assassins, my friend. I was shocked by what I found in Metropolis. I was expecting slaves."

"People can be enslaved without putting chains upon them. Metropolis enslaves the people by putting heretical ideas in their head, making them dissatisfied with their lives so they act against their own self-interest."

"Metropolis offers them something the Olympians cannot – freedom to choose."

"Freedom is just a word, Ardella. They have freedom, but at what cost? The citizens of Metropolis have the freedom to steal from their neighbors and kill people just trying to defend their homes. Their precious freedom harms others."

"The citizens of Metropolis are not all bad. I saw people there who just wanted what the Olympians would not allow. A physician of Apollo married to a priestess of the Temple of Aphrodite. A son of the Earth not forced to work in fields of Demeter and able to marry..." I almost said an Amazon, but stopped myself.

"And these mortals took it upon themselves to reject the ways and customs of the Olympians because they believe they are wiser than the Immortals."

"They just want things that the Gods of Arcadia do now allow."

"The Olympians have guided mankind for almost two thousand years – I would not see the rejects and rebels of our world topple the perfection that is Arcadia. The Olympian rules are intended to protect us from each other and ourselves. They are necessary and unalterable."

"Yours is a very traditionalist point of view."

"I thought you were a traditionalist as well. You are the daughter of Athena."

"I am not sure any more."

"So you have decided to take Alexander's side?"

"I am not on his side, but now I know he is not evil."

"He may not be evil, but he is wrong. Metropolis is a place of anarchy and false promises. Arcadia belongs to the Olympians, not mankind. We are the servants of the Olympians, and to allow people to believe otherwise is cruel. It can only end badly."

"What about those rejected by the Olympians? Alexander created a place for the outcasts and exiles of the other sects."

"Now you are actually defending him, old friend! You are letting him cloud the issue. Remember you let your emotions rule your head once before and came to regret it. Don't make that mistake again."

"So you have heard about my confession to the citizens of Metropolis all the way in Amazonia."

"Yes. I have often suspected it might have been you who allowed Lysander to escape New Athens," Queen Lyessa admitted.

"Why would you suspect such a thing?"

"Rafe. He was adamant that he didn't do it, but always became circumspect when I would ask him who he thought was actually responsible. His silence always suggested he was protecting someone."

"Oh!"

"Who would he have any reason to give up his life to protect - except you?"

"And suspecting such a secret you would still call me a friend?"

"We all make mistakes, Ardella. Your unrelenting drive to see Alexander brought down spoke of a quest for redemption."

"That does not make up for what I did. How could I have let my twin brother take the blame for my crime?"

"You were only 14 and scared. I am sure you didn't plan for him to take the blame."

"No, that was the Council's idea, but I could have tried to stop it."

"Do you think standing up to the Athenian Council really would have made a difference?"

"I will never know. I kept the secret. I will always be haunted by that one terrible mistake. How could he ever forgive me for allowing him to be exiled?" I lamented. For a few long moments the silence hung in the air all around us. I could feel Lyessa's sadness, but it was only a pale reflection of my own sorrow. I had made a terrible mistake – one I would never be able to change.

"Did you ever think about the fact that Rafe kept the secret, too? Why?" Lyessa whispered into the silence. Her words felt like the first drops of rain on a hot summer's day.

"I am not sure," I admitted as the soft shower of compassion began to fall on my soul.

"You have to know why he didn't try to stop what happened either, Ardella. He loves you. Where there is love – there is forgiveness."

"You know my brother very well," I said. I felt her unease, but she showed no outward signs.

"How is Rafe doing?" she asked genuinely concerned.

"Rafe is the real reason I have come to Amazonia, Lyessa. I need your help."

"Anything, my friend."

"Do not make any promises until you hear what I propose. Kendra and the other Amazons in Metropolis have a plan to help Rafe escape."

"And," my old friend prompted.

"And Rafe will need a place where he will be safe."

"You want me to give him shelter here in Amazonia?"

"I know long term male guests are not normally allowed, but ..."

"Say no more, my friend. It is against tradition, but you and your brother are allies of the Amazon nation and very dear to me. I will consult with Hera immediately. I believe she will allow me to shelter Rafe in Amazonia," Lyessa assured me, but I felt the turmoil of her inner core. She may sound confident, but her heart was filled with trepidation. I hoped she could sway her Goddess to our cause. "I can also shelter you, Ardella."

"I cannot thank you enough, my friend, but I will not be leaving Metropolis with Kendra and Rafe. Kendra fears the raiders will try to recapture Rafe after the Amazons help him escape. Part of the plan is for me to drug Alexander to keep him from communicating with his men until Kendra and Rafe can reach safety. With him as my hostage the citizens of Metropolis will have no choice but to let my brother go."

"That could be dangerous for you," Lyessa said concerned, although I could feel a suddenly sense of anticipation at the prospect. Her strong emotions took me by surprise.

"And an advantage for you somehow," I suggested wondering what the Amazon Queen had in mind.

"You don't usually use your little mind games on me,

Ardella!"

"I cannot help it. I can feel there is something you want from me very badly."

"I wouldn't even suggest it, but ..."

"Yes?"

"If you have Alexander in your power, it would be a simple matter to end the conflict once and for all. I know it is not in your nature, but you are closer to the Son of Ares than any of my Amazons have ever been."

"If you are suggesting I kill him, I am not capable of that."

"Of course, but..."

"We need him alive in case Rafe and Kendra are captured and I need to negotiate for their lives."

"I just..."

"Beside, Lyessa, we need him to continue as the ruler of Metropolis. His death would harm our cause more than it would help it."

"I don't believe that."

"Then you are wrong. Alexander is not a cruel tyrant who rules his people with fear and hate. After Athena's destruction of the citadel, I watch his people rally around him and draw their strength from him during the crisis. In that he reminded me a great deal of you. He takes responsibility for the people he rules. He will always do what is necessary to protect and preserve Metropolis." There was a long silence. "But you knew this as well."

"My Amazon spies agree with your assessment that Alexander is not by nature evil, but a determined man driven by his passions."

"And yet you still seek to destroy him."

"It does not matter if the man is good or evil. He is the Son of Ares sent to cause distrust and chaos. The ideas he promotes are wrong. Metropolis is a cancer upon the face of Arcadia. If it is not stopped, it could destroy the very fabric of our civilization. I am Queen of the Amazons. I took an oath at my coronation to preserve the ways of Hera and the Olympians."

"I believe Alexander is a good man, Lyessa, and a strong leader."

"But his ideas are dangerous."

"Is it so wrong for men to want to make decisions for themselves rather than always be guided by the hands of the Immortals?"

"The Olympians are our loving parents who only want what is best for us. We must follow where they lead for the sake of all Arcadia."

"Now you sound like my mother."

"Our mothers, and their mothers, and their mothers before them have followed the Gods of Arcadia. It is a long and proud history of peace and tranquility. Who are we to question two thousand years of tradition?"

"And yet Metropolis exists. It is in our best interest to have a strong leader there who tries to control all the desperate factions of the city. Alexander keeps the peace. He will do everything in his power to make sure his followers do not transgression the Great Law of the Olympians. If you succeed in assassinating him, can you say that about the next leader?

"No," she said softly. My empathy told me she was disappointed, yet I felt her real concern when she continued, "You do realize that given the chance the citizens of Metropolis are likely to kill you for your part in Rafe's escape."

"I have thought of that possibility. I do not want to die, but if I leave Metropolis with Rafe and Kendra there is a very good chance we will all be captured and killed. It is a risk I must take for the plan to have any hope of success."

"May Hera bless you in your mission, Ardella," Queen

Lyessa said handing me a goblet of Moonwine. I took the cup from her hand with a newfound sense of hope.

"Here is to the day you and I and Rafe may offer our thanks to the Goddess safe and together in Amazonia," I toasted.

༄

"There you are, Deidra," I said.

"She spent the entire time in the transport," Captain Arius offered.

"I don't care for Amazonia," Deidra said quietly. No doubt she had to be careful not to be recognized.

"More like she doesn't care for Amazons," Captain Arius suggested.

"Every wife in Metropolis lives in fear of an Amazon killing her man while he is on a raid. They are disliked by more than just me," Deidra said.

"Maybe so, but you should've at least come into the city. So many beautiful things to see," Arius suggested.

"Are you talking about the sites or the women, Arius?" she asked.

"Both. It was a thrill to be one of the only men in a city filled with beautiful women," he replied. His strong feelings of lust seem to flow off of him in waves and I found myself blushing. Deidra's heart, on the other hand, was filled with anger.

"Did you ever stop to think about why there are no men? They are not allowed. You could not live here even if you wanted to. Men are forbidden," Deidra pointed out.

"There have to be few men around. I mean they would need them to... well" he seemed at a loss for words, "they do need children."

"They host the annual Great Hunt. Men from all over Arcadia

come to participate. When that is not sufficient they borrow the Sons of the Earth or seduce a male from one of the other sects," she said.

"Oh my," he said suddenly looking a world away. I felt his guilt even before he asked, "Does that mean I am going to be a father?"

"Arius, you didn't? What were you thinking?" Deidra scolded.

"I wasn't really thinking. I've never had two beautiful women interested in me."

"Two?" I asked.

"At the same time. It was ..."

"No details, please. As to your impending fatherhood, don't worry about it. If it is a girl then her mother will keep her and raise her as an Amazon. You will never even see the child," Deidra said.

"What if it is a boy?" Arius asked with a slight tremor in voice.

"Then it will be left on the doorstep of Metropolis in the middle of the night - like a piece of unwanted garbage," she replied vehemently.

"Oh," he said once again lost in his own private thoughts.

"Elusian orphanages are full of Amazonian rejects – ask my husband Kern," Deidra spat.

"You seem to know a lot about Amazons," he suggested. There was an awkward pause.

"I am probably as much of an expert on the Amazons as Lady Ardella. It is wise to know the ways of the enemy to understand them better," Deidra said.

"Those are the words of an early Amazonian Queen, are they not?" I asked.

"It was Hippodamia, Titannia's grandmother who said that about the last of the native wildmen living in Amazon territory, just before they exterminated them," she replied.

"You do seem to know a lot about your enemy. So why not go into Amazonia itself to learn more?" Captian Arius asked.

"There is nothing in Amazonia I needed to see. I would never even have come on this journey, if Alexander hadn't ..." she trailed off unsure how to continue.

"asked you to keep an eye on me," I suggested.

"Something like that," she admitted.

"Were you supposed to make sure I returned to Metropolis?"

"I don't understand," she said softly, but I could feel her unease and knew it to be a lie.

"It never occurred to Alexander that Queen Lyessa might offer me sanctuary in Amazonia, or that this could be a one way trip for me?"

"Alexander realized that was a possibility, but my orders are that the decision was to be yours. If you choose to stay, I won't try to stop you."

"But any chance of freeing my brother would be lost."

"The reality is that you are the only person in all of Metropolis who will fight to free your brother. If you stay in Amazonia, then..."

"He will die."

There was a long awkward silence finally broken by Captain Arius, "Lady Ardella, I am going to have trouble reporting to the Stratagos how the negotiations went, since I was not allowed attend any of the meetings."

"No one but Lady Ardella and Queen Lyessa attended the negotiations. I am sure it made people on both side uncomfortable - not knowing exactly what was being discussed," Deidra added.

"Well you can tell Alexander that Queen Lyessa does not like him at all, but she is considering his proposal for the sake of her people. She will get back to him with Hera's answer."

"I will admit I am surprised at Lyessa's sudden open mindedness."

"You are being too hard on her. I have also worked against Metropolis in the past and I am open minded enough to consider I might have been wrong about certain things," I offered.

"Yes, but the truth about Metropolis was kept from you. Queen Lyessa has spies in Metropolis. She has known the truth for some time and still works against us."

"She is a traditionalist. She serves the Olympians faithfully," I offered.

"She is smart and courageous, but so scared to offend Hera that she lets it cloud her every decision."

"I am beginning to think you must get your information from someone who has spent time in Amazonia. Your insight into Amazon society and the personality of its queen are quite good."

"I knew an Amazon named Deianeira," she offered quietly, but I didn't need my gift to know that she was lying. I suspected I now I had her Amazon name, but continued to play along with her ruse.

"Does that mean there are Amazons living in Metropolis?" I speculated.

"Other than Queen Lyessa's spies and assassins?" she scoffed. When I did not reply, she continued, "No, and even if there were, they would keep their true identities a secret."

"Understandable. There is a punishment for breaking the oath to Hera and leaving Amazonia."

"The offending Amazon would be dragged back to Amazonia in chains and spend the rest of her life in slavery. It is the law of Hera and a fate worse than death," Deidra replied trying unsuccessfully to hide the spear of fear that pierced her heart at thought of the Amazon reprisals.

"Lyessa would hate having to do such a thing to a sister

Amazon."

"On that we agree. The queen is passionate in her concern for her sister Amazons, but she is a traditionalist. She follows all the Amazon strictures no matter how barbaric."

"You make her sound so harsh. The woman you describe is very different than the one I know."

"She is a servant of the Olympians."

"I served Athena for over a decade. How are Lyessa and I that different?"

"The Amazon queen would never have defied her Goddess for ANYONE. If it had been her brother in Alexander's prison, Queen Lyessa would have left him there," she pointed out.

"She might have made the sacrifice for a sister Amazon."

"Perhaps, but would the Queen of the Amazons have been able to let go of her hatred for Alexander and see the man for who he truly is?"

"I am not sure that is fair. I have felt Alexander's guilt over what happened in Argos and his real desire to forge a peace agreement to keep it from happening again. My empathy makes it easier for me to trust."

"While we are discussing the truth, I think there is something you should know. Kern once talked about how the incident at Argos had haunted Alexander. The Strategos felt that he had not trained the men well enough and that their reaction was his fault. I remember seeing unshed tears in his eyes as he ordered the execution of Rennin," she said.

"Rennin was the commander of the raid?" I asked stunned.

"Yes, and he paid for his mistakes with his life," Deidra said sadly although her feelings said justice had been served. It was unfortunate that the rest of Arcadia has no knowledge of any of this.

"I had no idea," I said, then asked, "What happened to the

other men?"

"He put them in charge of the defense of Metropolis. He told them the other sects would retaliate against us for what they did in Argos. He was right. It was only two months before your brother and the metal men attacked. All seven of the survivors of Argos were killed on the plain before Metropolis that day trying to atone for what they had done. Two of them were the sons of the woman who attacked you."

I realized in that moment the true scope of the massacre at Argos and its cost to both sides. I could not change the past or lessen the pain it had caused, but I would do everything I could to make sure Argos never happened again.

After Deidra left I settled down to read more of the Book of Artemis. It took only a moment to find my place in the story of the last days of the daughters of Artemis.

As the sun rose the three young people celebrated the miracle of new love beneath the sacred oak of Artemis. It was an experience of fulfillment and joy that neither sister had ever experienced before and it clouded their judgment. As a child of Ares raised by the followers of Aphrodite Rowan knew just how to manipulate the newfound feelings he had evoked in the twins.

Thus began their year-long love affair. Cynthia and Attia had a house built on the border between the lands of Hera and Artemis for Rowan to live. The house of Rowan lay in valley created by the Saren and Galadian Rivers in the foothills between Amazonia and Luna, the City of Artemis. It was made of stone and had many rooms including a kitchen, a bath complex and sculpture garden – all for the love of a man. Despite the gossip this caused for both young queens, neither was willing to send Rowan on his way as their custom demanded. It was under pressure from her subjects that Attia visited Rowan less and less often and only in secret. Cynthia, however, refused to listen to the warnings of the other followers of Artemis and became more and more obsessed with the Son of Ares.

When it became clear that Cynthia was going to have a child with Rowan, Attia tried to reason with her sister and remind her that there was no place in either society for fathers and he should be sent away. Cynthia refused to listen and encouraged by Rowan became estranged from her sister and the Amazons. Although many of Artemis' followers did not agree with the Great Mother's decision, she was the leader through the blessing of Artemis. Until the Goddess withdrew her support for Cynthia or admonished her actions, most felt that it was their duty to obey, even when they did not approve. They had no way of knowing that their Goddess was on hunt far across Arcadia and unaware of the situation.

Unable to convince her sister, Attia waited until Cynthia was away and approached Rowan. She tried to reason with him explaining that his continued presence could cost Cynthia her place among the followers of Artemis. Attia even suggested that if Rowan loved Cynthia he would do what was best for her and leave. Rowan laughed in her face. He taunted her by revealing that he was the Son of Ares sent to divide the followers of Artemis from the followers of Hera. His purpose was to come between the two closest sects on Arcadia by coming between the sisters who were their queens. He crowed that even if Attia tried to tell Cynthia about his treachery she would not be believed.

Attia was enraged by Rowan's boast and drew her sword and stabbed him through the chest just as Cynthia returned to the house. Grief stricken by the loss of her lover Cynthia refused to listen to Attia's explanation or believe what her sister told her about Rowan's deceit. She instead called upon Artemis and the spirits of the wild *places to curse her sister's womb and keep life from growing there. As one blessed by the Goddess the dryads of the sacred grove obeyed the Great Mother's request without question. Again Artemis was too preoccupied with her hunt to realize what was happening.*

Still estranged from her sister, five months later Cynthia gave birth to twins naming the girls Dyanna and Artemesia. Meanwhile Queen Attia unable to have children of her own thanks to her sister's curse became obsessed with the twin daughters of Rowan and Cynthia. She convinced herself that Cynthia was an unfit mother and that Artemesia & Dyanna would be better off being raised among the Amazons and formed a plan to kidnap her sister's children.

Chapter 17

I travelled the great savannah in search of the elusive shadow cat – a panther of such skill and stealth that few (even its prey) ever caught sight of it. I tracked the beast with every hunter's skill I possessed to the exclusion of every other thought. Then after almost three years at last it fell to one of my arrows. I returned home in triumph - only to discover the world I knew was no more.

The Goddess Artemis
One thousand, seven hundred and twenty-two years Ab Terra Condita

AS THE WALLS of Metropolis came into view I let out a sigh of contentment and realized I was looking forward to returning home. *Had I really come to think of my tower in Metropolis as home?* While examining my newfound emotions for this place, I had to admit there was also a person I was looking forward to seeing as well. I actually missed Alexander.

As if my longing alone could bring him to me, I looked up to see Alexander standing alone before the great gates of Metropolis. As the caravan ship came to a halt before the Strategos, my heart sang with joy. He had come to meet our ship rather than wait for us to report to the citadel. Perhaps he could not wait for news of his peace treaty with the Amazons, or perhaps he missed me as well.

I moved to follow Captain Arius and Deidra as they exited the ship to greet the Strategos.

As the door of the caravan ship slid open with a hiss, I realized my heart was pounding with anticipation. Suddenly unsure, I stayed back in the doorway as Arius and Deidra joined Alexander on the paving stones glistening in the early morning sunlight.

"We made it into the city this time, sir. Your little lamb there did the trick to get us in the gates just like you said she would," Captain Arius said proudly. I saw and felt both Deidra and Alexander cringe at his words, but neither made any attempt to correct him.

"I am pleased by your success, Arius. How did the negotiations with the Amazons go?" Alexander asked.

"You better ask Lady Ardella about that. You just told me to get her to Amazonia. I didn't really talk to too many Amazons," Arius said.

"You talked to at least two of them, Arius." Deidra commented.

"I wouldn't exactly say we did much talking," Arius replied.

"That is the point. Aren't there rules against what you did?" she asked.

"This wasn't a raid. I didn't force anyone. Those two Amazons came to me asking ..." Arius flustered becoming irritated with Deidra for bring this up in front of the Strategos.

"Perhaps we need to modify the rules for diplomatic missions. I trust you not to take advantage of a female during a raid or you would not be captain of my best transport," Alexander said. Captain Arius beamed, while Deidra sighed in defeat, but the Strategos wasn't finished. "However, Deidra is correct, Arius. Sexual encounters, if that is what your cryptic little exchange is all about, with the people we are negotiating with is NOT appropriate. It could be misunderstood and work against the best interests of Metropolis. In the future you will be more careful."

"Yes, Strategos," Captain Arius replied turning back to his transport, but stopping suddenly to add, "By the way, if Deidra is right and a baby boy is dropped off on our doorstep in about 10 months, make sure someone lets me know. I plan to take responsibility for any kids the Amazon mothers don't want."

"Mothers?" Alexander said trying to hide his sudden smile, "I will be sure to make your wishes known to the watch," Alexander replied, "And Arius, thank you for your help with this mission. I know it wasn't profitable like raiding, but ..."

"You don't have to thank me, Strategos. I know what this mission means for Metropolis and I was proud to be a part of it. I just hope I didn't screw it up."

"You are my best raiding captain. I chose you for this mission because I trusted you to handle whatever happened."

"Thank you, Strategos," Captain Arius beamed.

"It was more the Amazons' fault than yours," Deidra offered. "They knew what they were doing; you didn't understand the consequences."

"I will admit Amazons aren't so bad when they aren't trying to kill you," Arius laughed.

"I think I will have to take your word for that. I have never met an Amazon who didn't want to kill me," Alexander scoffed. Deidra's laughter filled the air. I wondered again how the former-Amazon had come to be a part of the Son of Ares inner circle.

"I think I should be going. I don't believe I have ever been away from my home for five days before," Deidra said.

"You won't find your husband at your home, Deidra. Last time I saw Kern – just after dawn – he was pacing the ramparts watching for any sign of your caravan ship. Your husband has been a nervous wreck for the past five days and none too happy with me for sending you on this mission in the first place," Alexander said.

"Perhaps it will do Kern some good to know how I feel every time he goes on a raid. I get tired of his taking my concern for nagging," Deidra said.

"I think both of us have a better understanding of what the women of Metropolis have been complaining about for the past few years. Raiding is a necessary way of life, but it is hard to watch the caravan ships disappear over the horizon taking those we love towards uncertainty and possible danger," Alexander said. As he said these words his eyes caught mine and I could not look away. I knew that he was talking to me and admitting in words what he and I had felt the night before I left.

"That is the most romantic thing I have ever heard you say, Strategos. There is hope for you yet," Deidra laughed. Alexander looked at her as if suddenly realizing that she too had been present to hear his confession and blushed. "I think I should find Kern and put him out of his misery," she added and then moved swiftly toward the gate.

"Ardella," he said but did not move any closer. I saw him swallow and then he asked "How was your trip?" I couldn't help but giggle at his rather formal tone. Did he forget I could feel the raging need he was trying to hold inside? Even now I could almost feel his arms crushing me to him, yet he stood like a statue trying to sound casual.

"Do you really want to hear about my talks with the Amazons right now?" I teased as I moved toward Alexander.

"No!" he hissed as the flood gates finally broke free and he surged forward to take me in his arms and swing me around from sheer joy. It was an incredible feeling to be wrapped in his arms and surrounded by his love. "I missed you!" he whispered in my ear.

"May Athena help me, but I missed you too, Alexander," I replied.

His happiness was practically exploding from his chest. "I didn't know if I would see you again," he said quietly with a strong sense of relief that I did not understand.

"I was in no danger. Why would you think ...?" I started to ask, and then the realization hit me. "You thought I would stay in Amazonia with Queen Lyessa."

"It occurred to me that you might," he admitted, "I would have understood."

"She did offer."

"Why didn't you?" he asked.

"I still have to save Rafe," I answered honestly. I felt his disappointment at my answer. Drawn by his pain, I reached up to touch his face. "And I am beginning to care for the people of Metropolis."

"Good," he said as his lips touched mine. For a few moments there was just the two of us in the world with no past or future or obstacles between us, but it could not last. I felt the nervousness and fear from the young man even though I could not see him. I also felt the single minded determination and knew our reunion was about to be interrupted. "I think the young man behind me needs to speak to you, Alexander," I whispered in his ear.

"What are you talking about?" he started to ask, but then looked up to see the young man in question, "Oh! Nice trick - when you aren't using it on me," he stepped out of our embrace and turned toward the young messenger, "What do you need citizen?"

"Strategos, Phoebus sent me to find you – to tell you ..." the messenger stammered, "It is Therin, sir. He died just before dawn. He never woke up." The words felt like a hammer that had just shattered our perfect moment.

"Thank you for bringing me the news. Tell Phoebus to prepare the body for a hero's funeral at sunset," Alexander told him and he hurried away. I had felt the pain the messenger's words had brought him and the distance it suddenly place between us. I looked out across the open plain that had been littered with bodies when I had first arrived in Metropolis and realized that the deaths my brother was responsible for might always be there between us – especially when the Amazons and I rescued Rafe from the justice Metropolis had in mind. For the first time I experienced a twinge of doubt about my plan to save my brother. It was all too apparent that I was having to choose between Alexander and my brother and that Rafe's cause was losing ground. *I had to get my brother away from Metropolis before I was tempted to change my mind.*

As we began to walk slowly into the city, Alexander was quiet – too quiet. He made little effort to hide his pain, but I decided to give him privacy for his grief and didn't say anything. "Your brother wants to talk to you," he said finally breaking the silence. When I looked at him questioningly, he continued. "Apparently your mother told him you were here."

"Oh!" I replied.

〜

My first thought as I entered my brother's small, but airy prison cell was that it was compassionate of the Hermians to provide him with such accommodations while he awaited his fate. In New Athens I had pictured my brother in a dark, vermin-infested hole chained to the wall with untreated wounds. In fact as I looked over at the man I had turned my life upside down to save, I had to admit that he was not being mistreated. Staring at the lowered head of my twin, I could not help but think of another time and place.

I couldn't quite reach the next branch and I had stretched as far as my little arms were able. I sighed in resignation and lowered my arm.

"Come on little sis, you aren't even half as high as me," Rafe called to me from higher in the poplar tree that stood beside the garden wall just behind our home.

"I am not your little sister! We are twins!" I informed him. "I cannot reach the next branch, Rafe."

"We are twins, but I am almost two inches taller than you, Ardella. And everyone thinks girls are superior to boys," he scoffed.

"That is not true. Mother says we are all equal in the eyes of the Goddess."

"It's always Mother says or Mother wants. You value her opinion more than Father's. Why is that, Ardella?" he asked but never gave me a chance to respond, but continued, "Why is Mother's position in society greater than Father's – they are both professors at the Academy?"

"That is just the way the Goddess wishes it. It does not mean woman are superior to men."

"Doesn't it, little sister? Why is every member of Athena's Council a woman?"

"Ah, little sister, Alexander has finally decided to let you come visit your poor condemned brother," Rafe said acerbically from where he sat on a bench in the corner of his cell. I found myself surprised by his tone. The brother I remembered was not so bitter or cruel, but perhaps the strain of his imprisonment was responsible for his mood.

"I have been out of the city, Rafe. I just arrived back in Metropolis," I responded trying to reassure him. He looked up at my response and I realized suddenly that the eyes I was now looking into were unfamiliar. They were wild and bright with an inner fire I had never seen before. They frightened me.

Unexpectedly I discovered I felt none of his emotions. He had never blocked them from me before. I didn't even know he could block his feelings from me. I had always believed that was an Olympian trait , but first Alexnader and now Rafe managed to do it just fine. Perhaps I was wrong.

"So you are free to come and go as you please from Alexander's capital," he reflected, "isn't that interesting." His insinuation and insulting tone was not like the brother I knew, but I took a deep breath and reminded myself that he was facing his mortality and I should try to be understanding.

"I was visiting Queen Lyessa and the Amazons," I told him.

Suddenly I felt his heart jump but he put up his wall again almost as quickly and skillfully as Alexander. He stood slowly and asked, "And how is the beautiful queen of the Amazons doing these days?"

"She is concerned about you, Rafe. So am I," I replied. For a brief moment the brother I remembered appeared before my eyes and the sadness I saw there was unbearable, but it was gone like a candle flame extinguished by a cold burst of wind.

"As well you both should be. I fear my days are numbered," he replied, but with his emotions hidden, his words sounded cold and hollow.

"I came to Metropolis to ...." I began as tears filled my eyes, but Rafe cut me off.

"Did Alexander happen to mention how many days I have left, sister dear?" he scoffed. The sarcastic tone of his voice began to grate on my nerves.

"You and I will be allowed to plead your case before Hermes and the Council soon. They will decide what happens from there."

"Oh what an excellent plan, little sister. Like two brave citizens of New Athens we are going to talk our way out of our troubles. I am sure Athena must be so proud," he mused.

"Athena has nothing to do with my efforts to save you, just like she had nothing to do with your attack on Metropolis in the first place. We are on our own, Rafe."

"I am not surprised Athena abandoned me, but I thought she might actually care for her precious empath."

"I have not given up yet."

"So what is our defense strategy, Ardella? Throwing yourself at Alexander's feet and begging for mercy?" he pondered, but then broke out laughing. I felt my heart tighten at his derision, and fought back tears as he scoffed, "I hear that your little stunt when you first arrived backfired on you."

"It was not the best plan."

"It is sad when the raiders pity the Daughter of Athena."

My patience snapped at his caustic remark. "What is wrong with you, Rafe?"

"I could say that I had just learned my own sister had betrayed me and caused my exile from New Athens," he offered sarcastically.

"But that is not true," I replied, although I was guessing since his emotions were still hidden from me. I felt a wave of scorn escape his icy wall.

"Yes, little sister. I have known from the beginning."

"I suspected. I wanted to ask, but ..."

"Do you know why I let them exile me without defending myself?"

"You were trying to protect me?" I whispered. Rafe's laughter was cold and cruel.

"I am not that selfless, Ardella," he retorted and then smiled at me as my heart sank in my chest. "I did it because Athena told me to. She sent me out of New Athens on a mission and then saw to it that I was blamed for what you did," he informed me. My heart froze in my chest. Lyessa had been wrong about Rafe's motives. He had been forced to keep my secret. Athena had known all along. Her recent anger at my confession was just a pretense.

"I did not know."

"Of course you didn't. Athena destroyed my life to save her precious empathy, and you were oblivious."

"I should have said something. I ..."

"You were afraid of the consequence for what you did."

"Yes," I whispered.

"Better me than you – right?" Rafe laughed.

"No, but I am only human. Forgive me."

"Too late for that, little sister!" he snorted. "How does it feel to be an exile like me?"

"How does it feel?" I echoed.

"I'm afraid Athena didn't bless me with the gift of empathy, so to know what my dear sister is feeling, I must have you tell me. So how does it feel to be exiled - to know you will never again see Athena's tower, or the Academy, or Mother?"

"Angry!" I shouted to cut off his tirade. "I am angry."

"Who are you angry with, little sister?"

"Who am I angry with?" I pondered, "With myself I suppose."

"Be honest," he said seriously and as I looked into his eyes I saw myself reflected there. I didn't like the vision. I didn't see the youngest member of Athena's Council or the leader of the resistance against the Son of Ares, but a stupid, gullible pawn of the Goddess of Wisdom. Athena cursed me with the gift of empathy; Athena told Rafe to take the blame when I allowed the Son of Ares to escape; Athena tried to kill me and possessed my body just to kill the Son of Ares; Athena was the monster in this tale.

"I am angry with *her* for encouraging you to attack Metropolis; it was such a foolish risk," I finally whispered, grateful to finally say the words aloud.

"Really, just her?"

"What do you want me to say?"

"Who are you angry with?" Rafe growled. Suddenly seeing the bodies of the dead on the plain of Artemis, I realized my guilt was causing me to make excuses for acts that were unexcusable.

"You! I am angry with you because you are the one who put us in this indefensible position. What were you thinking attacking Metropolis? Why did you let *her* put such a crazy idea in your head?"

"You think Athena convinced me to attack Metropolis?"

"She as much as admitted it to me, when she told me you have been captured by Alexander."

"Then for once Athena is not as clever as she thought."

"Attacking Metropolis was your idea?"

"I took steps, necessary steps, that no one else – mortal or Olympian - was willing to take," Rafe said proudly.

"You went to Athena with this plan?"

"I knew Athena would appreciate my ambitions. I had a way to stop the chaos created by the Son of Ares."

"You tried to end the chaos by attacking a city? That doesn't even make sense."

"It was the only way to get Alexander's head."

"And you were willing to have Hephaestus's metal warriors kill every man, woman and child in Metropolis to reach the Son of Ares?"

"If necessary, yes."

"Are you listening to yourself? You sound just like Athena. I think your obsession with stopping the Son of Ares has driven you mad."

"Since when is wanting to stop the Son of Ares madness? Haven't you wanted the same thing for years?"

"This is not about Alexander. It is about the city of Metropolis and its right to exist. You would not attack New Athens or Amazonia. Why did you attack Metropolis?"

"Metropolis is an abomination. A city of full of captives from all over Arcadia forced to serve their Hermian masters."

"You are wrong about Metropolis. We have been wrong about what Alexander was doing here all these years."

"You deny that the raiders carry off unwilling people in their raids of other sects?"

"No, but most of the people in Metropolis are here of their own free will. No one forced them to come or forces them to stay."

"I suppose Alexander told you this."

"No! The citizens of Metropolis told me this. This is not a city of oppression and slavery. Just look at your surroundings, Rafe. You are the most hated person in all of Metropolis and yet they feed and house you like a guest."

"Except for the locked door."

"You killed 23 people in your attack on this city. It is amazing that they are offering you a trial rather that the point of one of their spears."

"So you think I deserve to die?" his tone was deadly calm, yet I could feel the despair creeping out from beneath his defenses. Just that brief glimpse at his inner turmoil took my breath away.

"No! I do not want you to die, Rafe. That is why I am here. I came to save you," I said softly, but felt compelled to ask, "but do you feel the least bit of guilt over the lives that were lost in your attack?"

"Get out!" he spat.

"Rafe, I ..."

"I don't need a lecture from you of all people."

"What are you talking about?" I asked.

"We are twins Ardella. We were born on the same day into the same family and yet you were chosen for great things and I was ignored. How do you think it feels to be overshadowed by your own twin?"

"You were not overshadowed. You served in the temple of Athena just as I did. You were a guardian."

"And you were the chosen one – the empath. You got a seat on Athena's Council and I got to be your servant. She always preferred you to me, she even sacrifice me to save you."

"Athena should never have asked such a thing of you."

"Is that pity I hear in your voice? There is no need to pretend with me, dear sister," he murmured as a burst of anger ventured forth from his emotional shields.

"I am sorry for what I let happen to you. I was scared and if I could go back and..."

"Don't!" he spat. "Don't try to make up for everything that has happened in the last ten years with pretty words and apologies. I don't want them."

"I am just sorry that ..."

"I said enough. I don't want your apology. I don't forgive you. I won't forgive you – ever." Lyessa's words 'where there is love there is forgiveness' haunted me. First my mother and then my twin brother – would everyone I love come to hate me?

"Rafe!" I cried.

"I asked you here so you would have to face the consequences of your actions this time. I wanted you to see the suffering you caused."

"Please!"

"Go on to your new life in Metropolis. Don't let the death of your brother ruin your chances at a bright new future," he spat.

"Stop it. Why are you saying these things, Rafe?"

"Because I know I should have had a destiny greater than yours. You are the chosen one of Athena, but I am important, too. My name should live on in the history books that talk of the glory of the Olympians, but history will only talk of you and Alexander. If you knew the truth ..." but his words were cut off by a sudden painful mental blast that knocked us both to our knees.

"Rafe," I whispered. "What was that?"

"Nothing," he hissed, and then burst out laughing. "Just part of going mad, little sister."

As the sunlight danced in through the window around us, I faced a man that I truly didn't recognize. The man I had given up my life to save wasn't my twin brother, but a dangerous stranger. "What happened to you?"

"*You* happened to me – a long time ago. I am just tired of pretending." A cold unnatural anger seeped from the body of the man who I had once called my brother. It was not just the strong emotions of a deranged man, but something else. That burst of pain has been too deep and too powerful to originate with Rafe. It almost felt – Olympian, but I didn't have time to contemplate further. As the anger coming from Rafe became more and more intense, I had the instinctive need to escape before it overwhelmed me. As I fled my brother's cell, his cruel laughter followed me into the hall.

༺

I don't remember how I got from my brother's cell to the waterfall at the edge of the grove of Artemis, but I know what drew me there. The soft cascade of water was soothing and the dancing colors created by the sunlight were a joyful display of the wonders of nature. As I sat staring at the simple beauty of the cascading water, I let it wash away some of the turmoil churning in my psyche.

I sat there for a long time trying to clear my mind of my brother's cruel words and the pain they brought. I wondered at the strange other worldly anger I had felt and decided it had to have been my imagination.

I realized I had lost track of time when I heard Deidra say, "Lady Ardella, is everything alright? I was told you have been sitting here for hours."

I looked up at Deidra and sighed. "Has it been that long?" I replied.

"Do you need anything? Can I help?" Deidra asked moving to sit beside me. Her concern for me covered us both like a soft, warm blanket.

"You know about my conversation with my brother?" I guessed.

"I know that the guard said you ran from his cell very upset," Deidra said. "Do you want to talk about it? Can I help?"

"I did not know the man you are holding in that cell. He is not my brother," I murmured.

"Was the man who attacked Metropolis impersonating Rafe?" Deidra asked misunderstanding my words.

"No. I wish the man in the cell were an imposter. The body belongs to my brother, but his mind is gone. He is so lost in his madness and obsession I cannot see even a glimpse of the brother I knew," I said allowing my fears and regret to be put into words as tears streamed down my face.

"I am sorry, Ardella." Deidra said as she hugged me. I felt her concern tinged with pity even more strongly. I knew she meant well, but it wasn't helping. I pulled away from her embrace.

"In my sorrow I was drawn to the soothing nature of the waterfall. I guess I lost track of time. I did not mean to worry you.

I hope you were not pulled you away from your husband to deal with my problems," I said.

"Kern was understanding. When Alexander sent word to me about what had happened, I thought you might need a friend."

"Thank you. I am in very short supply of friends ... and family these days. I have never felt quite so alone in my entire life."

"You are not alone, Ardella. I am here for you, and although I know you may not believe it Alexander cares for you as well."

"I know he does. He seldom hides his emotions from me anymore," I said and then laughed as a strange thought occurred to me.

"What?" Deidra asked.

"I was just thinking about Rafe and Alexander. Although Alexander is the Son of Ares his emotions always feel strong and rationale. That is not what I would expect from a demi-god controlled by Ares."

"Are we sure that Alexander is in fact the Son of Ares?" Deidra asked.

"The Athenian Council determined that over a decade ago, even before he became leader of the Hermians."

"Did it ever occur to you that if a man were told he was the Son of Ares, it might influence his behavior – even if he were just an ordinary mortal?"

"You may be the first person to ever suggest Alexander may not be the Son of Ares."

※

Later that evening as all of Metropolis attended Therin's funeral, I heard a soft knock on my door. "Come in Kendra," I called softly. I felt her surprise through the door and knew my guess about the identity of my visitor had been correct. Considering the limited number of people I knew in Metropolis, it hadn't been that difficult a guess.

"Lady Ardella?"

"I have been expecting you. Our mutual friend sends her greetings."

"So the plan to rescue your brother may proceed?"

"With her blessing"

"I am glad, although I had little doubt that the queen would wish to help Lord Rafe."

I raised an eyebrow at her statement and she added, "The queen has always shown strong appreciation of your brother's efforts in the struggle against Metropolis." Considering I had begun to suspect the Queen of the Amazons was in love with my brother, I found her assessment fair.

"So how do we proceed?" I asked.

"Let me meet with the other Amazons. Now that we have the queen's permission, we should be able to arrange to rescue your brother within days."

"Good. The period of mourning will be over soon. I think we need to act before the trial begins. Once they pass sentence, security will be much tighter."

"I agree. They won't be looking for an escape attempt before you are given a chance to appeal for Rafe's life."

"Everything I have said and done so far should make them believe I am stupid enough to trust their promises of a fair trial."

"You are being too hard on yourself, my lady."

"No. It is just ironic that my naivety will finally prove to be a benefit."

"Do you want me to find a place in Metropolis for you to hold Alexander?"

"I actually have an idea to get Alexander out of Metropolis entirely. I should be able to keep him away for several days."

"Are you sure it is a place the Hermians won't find him?"

"No one has been there in a thousand years. It should be perfect." I said thinking about a passage I had found in the book of Artemis on the way home from Amazonia.

The house of Rowan lay in valley created by the Saren and Galadian Rivers in the foothills between Amazonia and Luna, the City of Artemis. It was made of stone and had many rooms including a kitchen, a bath complex and sculpture garden.

As our caravan ship travelled through those foothills on our return trip from Amazonia I spotted the stone ruins referred to in the book. I doubt anyone remembered it even existed. It was at least a day's journey from Metropolis and should be just the adventure to spark Alexander's interest. Once we were out of the city the Amazons could work their magic and release my brother from his captivity. The only task left was to win Alexander's trust and convince him to leave the city with me without telling anyone where we were going.

Chapter 18

The laughter of children is magical. It cannot help but touch even those with hearts of stone.

Tendaria (a follower of Aphrodite)
Two thousand, one hundred and fifty-six years Ab Terra Condita

THE NEXT DAY as I walked in the grove of Artemis I was again drawn to the waterfall by an incredible bubble of joyful energy. The noise of children's laughter greeted me as I came to the pool formed below the natural spring that fed the cascade of water. It was a hot day and the children were splashing in the water and enjoying its cooling relief. I had always loved to be around children playing. Their innocent happiness always drew me to them. Unlike the children of New Athens, however, the youth of Metropolis had not been trained from birth to allow their heads to rule over their hearts and so the intensity of their unbridled joy held me mesmerized.

"Ardella, what are you doing?" Alexander asked from behind me. It was a testament to the intensity of the children's emotions that I had not even noticed his approach. As I turned toward him I was met with a look that was a mixture of curiosity and amusement.

"I was just watching the children play," I offered.

"You are doing more than just watching them play, Ardella. You looked as if you were in a trance as I approached. Is everything alright?" he asked. I hadn't seen him since the encounter yesterday with my brother. Although I am sure Deidra reported to him after our conversation by the waterfall, (well maybe not our speculation about whether he was really the Son of Ares), I found it comforting that he was still concerned.

"I am fine. I just ..." I let my voice trail off. I suddenly realized that I didn't feel the aching buzz at the back of my head that had plagued me since my conversation with Rafe. The children's joy had finally washed away the residual anger and pain. "I cannot explain the children's effect on me to someone who does not feel what I feel," I offered vaguely.

"Tell me what you feel," he whispered drawing nearer. I would normally feel his emotions at such a close range, but the joyful bubble created by the children was overpowering.

"Their joy is so intense. All playing children create a bubble of happiness that I can sense even from a distance. But these children do not try to rein in their emotions like children do in New Athens. It is incredible. I can even feel the coolness of the water on their skin. It is intoxicating."

Alexander laughed. "You mean to tell me that you are standing beside a beautiful waterfall on a hot day and experiencing it only vicariously through the children."

"Well, I am not sure I would have put it quite that way. You cannot feel what ..." I tried to explain but he cut me off.

"Did it ever occur to you to step into the pool and enjoy the refreshing water for yourself?"

"I am a grown woman, Alexander. It would be inappropriate for me to be playing in a public fountain like a child."

"Perhaps in New Athens, but not in Metropolis," Alexander said lifting me in his arms.

"Alexander, what are you doing?" I exclaimed as my arms clasp his neck for support. Although surprised by his action, I could not help but notice just how nice it felt to be in his arms once again.

"It is time you stopped living through other people, Ardella. Just because you can feel other people's emotions doesn't mean you should stop experiencing life for yourself."

"Put me down. You cannot mean that you are taking me into the fountain."

"Since you enjoy the children's play so much, I am certain you will enjoy it even more at closer range," he said as he stepped over the edge of the pool into the knee deep water. Although technically he was the only one wet at this point, I knew from the intensity of his emotions that I would soon be, too. I started to struggle in his arms, but quickly realized that there was nowhere to go except into the water. Perhaps the Son of Ares could be reasoned with.

"Alexander, please. This is absurd. We are too old to be playing in a public fountain with the children. You are the Strategos of Metropolis. What will your citizens think?" I pleaded, but he only grinned at me. It was a wicked, mischievous grin that told me just as clearly as my empathy that the Strategos was having too much fun to be swayed by my protests. As we reached the base of the waterfall where the cascading water enters the pool he stopped and looked down at me curiously.

"Ready?" he asked smugly.

"Alexander, please ..." I attempted one last time to change his mind, but was stopped suddenly by the frigid deluge that enveloped us. Although part of me still couldn't believe Alexander had done such a thing, another part of me had to agree with him that experiencing it first hand was much better than just watching.

"Now that was refreshing," he said stepping out of the waterfall and at last putting me down into the pool.

"I do not believe you just did that. Alexander, we are not children. We have no business splashing around in the park's waterfall," I chided.

"You're not in New Athens anymore, Ardella. This is Metropolis. Here anything is possible."

"So I am beginning to understand," I replied. "Now may I go change into something dry?"

"You are hopeless, Ardella. We are going to have to work on your concept of fun," he replied, but I had already turned and started to huff off. Although trying to exit with some dignity, I did not anticipate the slipperiness of the stones. Without warning my feet flew out from beneath me and I found myself sitting in an undignified heap in water up to my waist.

Alexander looked down at me; the laughter clearly showing in his eyes. I had had enough of his amusement at my expense for one day. "Since this is all your fault, you could at least help me up," I said haughtily.

"Of course," he said offering his hand gallantly. As I reached up to accept the assistance, another thought popped into my head. I smiled sweetly and took his hand. Rather than pulling myself up, however, I pulled down as hard as I could knocking Alexander off balance and landing him in the water right beside me.

For a few moments he just looked at me in utter shock. I saw the sparkle enter his eyes just before he began splashing water at me. Before I knew it we were racing around the pool and splashing with the children who found the addition of two adults to their game highly amusing.

As I stood beside the waterfall a few minutes later catching my breath, I found myself staring at Alexander standing there with his wet clothes clinging to his very masculine body. His eyes met mine, and I realized that something in the game had changed. As Alexander moved towards me, I felt his desire and I knew that he intended to kiss me. Unfortunately I also felt the curiosity of those around us and realized we had an audience to our sudden lapse in decorum.

"Alexander, there are too many people watching," I tried to warn him, but he either wasn't listening or didn't hear. As the warmth of his lips met mine I found myself lifted in the air and pulled against him. I wrapped my arms around his neck and held on for dear life.

Somewhere beyond the world created in his arms I heard applause and cries of approval from the crowd around the fountain. I heard a voice that sounded like my mother instruct me that we were causing a scene, but the unrestrained joy I felt (my own emotions, not the feelings of those around me) drowned her out.

When Alexander finally ended our kiss, I found myself still held tightly within his arms staring into his deep blue eyes. "I have never felt like this before," I said breathlessly.

"You never allowed yourself to feel this way, because it is frowned upon in Athenian society. You have had to keep your spirit and passion bottled up to fit in in New Athens. You don't have to hide that part of yourself here, Ardella. In Metropolis you may enjoy life and live every day to the fullest. We allow passion here. We want passion here," he said ending his discourse by once again kissing me. This time I wasn't taken by surprise and kissed him in return.

"Strategos! Lady Ardella!" a voice called to us. I recognized it as the messenger who had interrupted us in front of the gates yesterday.

"What do you want, Derek?" Alexander looked over at him

and barked.

"Hermes sent me to ..." the messenger began, but Alexander cut him off.

"Tell Hermes I will come to his tower as soon as I have put on dry clothes," Alexander informed him.

"But Strategos..." the messenger began hesitantly.

"What? Why haven't you departed to inform Hermes that you found me?"

"Hermes did not send me to find you, Strategos. He wishes to speak to the Lady Ardella."

⁂

My hand trembled as I reached for the ornate iron door handle that led into the inner sanctuary of Hermes. From the outside, the Tower of Hermes had appeared no different than the ones Alexander and I occupied. In fact my first instinct upon realizing where the guard was leading me was that there was some mistake. No Olympian would dwell in such a humble abode.

The mark of Hermes was evident, however, as soon as I opened the outer door. A rush of cool air struck me in the face. The sweet smell of lavender filled my senses, and the soft strains of a harp floated into my ears. Despite the soothing atmosphere flooding out of entrance, my mind was as turbulent as the violet storms of the southern swamp. *What did Hermes want?*

"Great Hermes, I come into your presence as you requested," I intoned softly, even though I could not yet see the God in the dimly lit room.

"Ah, it is the white Athenian rose," a deep baritone voice beckoned from an overstuffed chair in the far corner of the room. The melodious timber of the sound washed over me and gently caressed my skin. A strange sense of peace dissipated the cloud of doubt and tension that had been building since my summons. "Come here child," he called as a head of blond curls peered around the side of the chair.

I glided across the room in a daze, unable to stop my forward motion, even if I had wanted to. When I finally stood before him my breath caught in my throat at his immortal countenance. He was one of the most handsome men – mortal or immortal – I had ever seen. His face was a pleasure to behold, but what touched me most were his eyes. His eyes were magical. It was as if I there was something about them that drew your gaze and would not allow you to turn away. "You wished to speak to me?" I managed to ask.

"Yes, Ardella. I wanted to make sure you had been made comfortable here in Metropolis," Hermes began.

"Comfortable? Yes. Alexander has seen that I have everything I need," I replied.

"Surely he has not left you in the white robes of Athena all this time?"

"Oh no! Deidra found me more suitable clothing the first day I arrive, but that dress was wet and my white robes were dry. I intended no offense," I replied.

"I am not offended. I was just curious as to your choice of wardrobe. Your other dress was wet, you say. I must be spending entirely too much time inside this tower. I was not even aware that it had rained."

"It has not rained. In fact it is sunny and hot. I am afraid I was too close to the edge of the fountain in the park and ... I slipped."

"That is very tactful of you. As I heard it my Strategos picked you up and carried you into the waterfall like a mischievous school boy," Hermes mused.

"That is fairly accurate. May I inquire, if you already knew how my clothes got wet, why the charade of asking me what happened?"

"As the Olympian patron of this city, I try to know everything that goes on here. Forgive me if I pretend otherwise and enjoy the unfolding of the conversation."

"I understand. As an empath I must often ignore the emotions of others and try to focus only on their words," I replied, but suddenly felt compelled to add a *caveat*, "But Hermes, keep in mind the illusion is broken when you suddenly contradict the other person's version of the story with the truth."

Hermes laughed softly and like his hypnotic eyes the sound was magical. It suddenly occurred to me I would never have said something so impertinent to Athena and she certainly wouldn't have been amused. *Why was I being so cavalier with this Olympian?*

"I like you my sweet Athenian rose, but I don't think white is your best color. Perhaps red," he said touching the sleeve of my robe.

I watch fascinated as the color of my robe slowly changed from white to red.

"How did you do that?" I gasped.

"Transmutation," he replied. "It is a simple enough trick. All the Olympians can do it."

"I served the Goddess Athena for almost ten years and I never recall seeing her do anything like that."

"I am not surprised. My sister likes to pretend she is one of you - just a wise and wonderful mortal who wants to guide her people to a better world. She is, however, an Olympian with all the supernatural abilities and passions of her siblings."

"I have witnessed her Olympian passions up close and personal."

"That you have, my dear, and lived to tell the tale." Hermes agreed.

Again I was shock by my casual bantering with an Olympian.

It was totally out of character.

"You are very different than the other Olympians," I commented.

"What do you mean?" Hermes asked. I could feel his curiosity at my observation.

"When I must speak with other Olympians, I often feel anxious - like a child speaking to an adult who might scold them at any moment."

"I am sure that is the way my siblings want mortals to feel."

"I cannot explain it. My natural anxiety seemed to melt away as I came into your presence. I find myself speaking before I think. That is not normal for me."

"The calming effect you have noticed is another Olympian gift, although I believe this one is unique to me. I like the fact it makes everyone comfortable enough to be themselves around me."

"Does that mean the other Gods have unique abilities, too?

"Why do you ask, child?"

"I have spoken with the Goddess Athena many times. Often it seems as if she knows what I am feeling and thinking. It was so similar to my ..." I trailed off.

"go on." Hermes prompted.

"It was just so similar to me. I often wondered if she too has the gift of empathy she gave to me."

"You never asked her?"

"I would not presume to question the Goddess. She would not ..."

"Appreciate your curiosity?"

"It is better to be ignorant but in favor."

"A wise decision," he said. "To answer your question - my sister is excellent at reading other people, but she has no powers of empathy. She has just had millennia to study human nature."

"Oh."

"I cannot even imagine my sister wanting to know what the people around her were feeling. It might interfere with her stoic reserve."

"It is not easy being dispassionate, when you can feel the passions of those around you. It is especially difficult here in Metropolis where everyone is so free with their emotions."

"Is that what you were doing in the fountain – letting other people's passions get the better of you?"

"Not this time. If you must know, I ended up in that fountain because your Strategos thought I needed to have a little more fun," I joked. Again Hermes magical laughter tickled my ears and sent waves of joy through my body.

"That is good to hear. That boy is too serious and stuffy."

"Really? That has not been my experience with him. He is full of passion for life. It is hard to believe he was born Athenian."

"Alexander is reserved and dignified when the occasion calls for it. He can also be strong and ruthless when the need arises. The Son of Ares is more than just a simple man."

Although I had come to agree with his assessment, I made the mistake of once again getting lost in Hermes gaze and losing my train of thought.

"That reminds me of the reason I called you here. I have learned that you feel some guilt about being the one who release Alexander from his captivity in New Athens," Hermes said.

"Perhaps I feel responsible for the changes in your society. I was the one who introduced him into one of your caravans."

"Then you may stop feeling guilty. If you had not brought him out to us, I had given the leader of that caravan instructions to go in after him." My mind spun with this new information. The God Hermes wanted the Son of Ares released?

"I do not understand."

"You didn't wonder at the coincidence that one of my caravans just happened to be camped outside of New Athens at the perfect time to facilitate Alexander's escape?"

"I never really thought about it."

"That caravan had been staying there for almost three weeks. They were just waiting until you had identified the Son of Ares, so we could come in and steal him away. You did us a favor by bringing him out to us, but he would have ended up in that caravan either way." A sudden burst of irritation filled my soul and cleared away a little of the effects of Hermes calming magic.

"Why would you want the Son of Ares?" I asked gruffly.

"Athena owed him to me. A hundred years ago the last Son of Ares was born to one of my followers. He had the potential to do great things for my people as other incarnations had done for my siblings, but Athena had other plans. When she learned that the Son of Ares had been born, she arranged a fatal accident. The boy was only 12 years old. There was no reason to kill him."

"Perhaps she thought she was saving your people from the corrupting influence of Ares?"

"So she claims. But I knew her true motivations and I waited patiently for a hundred years to get my revenge."

"What other motivation could she possibly have had?"

"Do you know the story of Gidian the Great?"

"Of course. He is the only man to ever rule the Great Council of Athena. He is a legendary figure who brought about many reforms and is considered one of our greatest leaders."

"He was also the Son of Ares."

"That is not possible. He was wise and compassionate and …"

"Strong, ruthless and very charismatic. He was not given the leadership of Athena's Council. He took it through careful manipulation. Toward the end of his reign he even became a little paranoid and unstable. Many of the changes he brought to Athenian society were against his Goddess' wishes."

"I had no idea. I have never seen even a hint of that story in any book I have ever read about Gidian – even the ones from Athena's private collection. Why could such an important fact have been kept out of our history books?"

"Your Goddess preserves knowledge for the power it gives her. Can't you image that she might also destroy knowledge when it suits her purposes?"

"I suppose it is possible. But what does Gidian the Great have to do with your stealing Alexander from New Athens?"

"The reign of Gidian was five hundred years ago," Hermes explained. "Ever since that time Athena has been hunting down and eliminating the Son of Ares upon each incarnation. She has become obsessed with saving Arcadia from the corruption of Ares."

"That is what she has always claimed she was doing."

"But she had no right to destroy my Son of Ares. I wanted his strength and personality to help united my people and push them forward. The Son of Ares is about promoting progress. Athena had no right to impose her petty views on my people, so I stole her Son of Ares for myself and have encouraged him to do anything and everything to annoy my sister."

The warm flush of anger cleared my mind for a moment and I found myself asking, "Is that what Metropolis is – a chance to annoy Athena?"

"Certainly, but it is something even more important. It is a chance to reignite the spark of humanity. That is why we brought Ares with us to Arcadia in the first place, even when we left Zeus behind in the ruins of Earth. It is the conflict spawned by Ares that fuels the inner strength of mankind. When the necessity arises, the intellectual and technological potential of your race has proven to be something wondrous to behold."

"Are you saying you want the conflict caused by Ares?"

"Many of the Olympians did, but mother Hestia had other plans. She didn't want Ares to have influence on Arcadia, so she imprisoned him and imposed the Great Law upon us."

"Hestia imprisoned Ares and imposed the Great Law? I thought it was a pact among all of you to save us from the conflict of war."

"Conflict does keep life from getting boring. Besides, one generation every hundred years isn't going to send mankind spirally out of control as it did long ago on Earth. It worked until five hundred years ago when Athena convinced some of the other Olympians that the conflict caused more harm than good and began secretly killing the Son of Ares as he appeared each century. She has caused mankind to stagnate and cannot see the harm this is doing to our future."

"Why you are telling me all this," I asked.

"Perhaps to annoy my sister. She has gone to great lengths to manipulate the situation and then hide the facts, so she might pretend they unfold without her knowledge. No doubt she manipulated your poor brother on his suicidal attack of Metropolis."

"Athena had nothing to do ..." I began.

"Spare me your defense of New Athens. I have no intention of holding them responsible for the actions of one person- even it if is my Olympian sister. But keep in mind that I have been matching wits with the Goddess of Wisdom for a very long time. I recognize her machinations when I see them." His words struck the wounded corner of my soul that still smarted from my own recent experience with Athena's manipulation, but the pain of betrayal was muted this time by Hermes calming effect.

Even as my body felt numb, my mind recognized that I

should be upset by Hermes revelation and I managed to ask, "Is that what the last ten years have been – a game the Olympians are playing with mortals as their pawns?"

"No matter how much we care about mortals, your existence is from our perspective, well - fleeting. You will never be our equals, so you will never have a place at our table. You will always be pawns upon the game board."

"That is exactly what Athena said."

"I am surprised she admitted the truth. You are the Daughter of Athena - I would think she would want to keep your belief in her love for you alive and strong."

"Athena has exiled me and made several attempts on my life. She is not concerned about what I think about her."

"That is where you are wrong. She will always be worried about what you think," he said with a mischievous grin that reminded me of Alexander. "It is much easier to manipulate the pawns, if they believe you care about them."

My mind fought to hold on to the spark of irritation that his comment inspired, but it was fleeting. "Your frankness is a little disturbing."

Hermes laughed. "You have no idea how frank I can be."

"Does Alexander know what you just told me?"

"Alexander knows all of this and more. He finds the games of the Olympians …"

"Frustrating," I offered.

"Yes. He would see the power of mankind reasserted. To that end I have let him have his way in Metropolis. It is good to allow the human race to grow and regain some of what has been lost since our departure from Earth."

"What do you mean?"

"Has there ever been a time in your life when you wanted to do something, but was denied to you by the Olympians? Didn't you feel frustrated and resentful? That is human nature."

"You are talking about free will."

"I suppose I am," he said. Again the nagging suspicion that had always been in the back of my mind burst forth into the light of day. Athena had as much as admitted humans had free will that could not be taken away by Gods of Arcadia.

"Then free will is not a gift of the Olympians to mankind?" I asked.

"More like the greatest curse for us immortals. We can control and transmutate anything in nature, but not the human race. You are independent of our grand designs. The human spirit is perfect and beyond our control."

"Then the Olympians did not create mankind."

"No. Your ancient cave dwelling ancestors existed on Earth even before the birth of Hestia – the mother of the Olympians."

"The Academy teaches that the Olympians created mankind on Earth and gave us the gift of free will."

"A lie. You are not our creation, and we cannot control your actions. We Olympians are all powerful, but with one terrible flaw. We have lived with your kind side by side for so long, I doubt we could go on without human followers." I felt the sadness tinged with fear in his words. I knew for certain they were the truth. The existence of the human race was independent of the Olympians.

"The human race could survive without the Olympians?" I gasped.

"Your brothers and sisters that we left behind on Earth do so even now."

⸺

I left the Tower of Hermes in a daze. I sat for a while on the cool stone bench beside the tower as the calming haze caused by Hermes presence slowly dissipated. It was so bizarre to reflect on the conversation I had just had and feel as though it was just a story I had been told. As the words replayed in my head, the emotions were belatedly evoked, and the implications of their significance finally reached me.

"We are just pawns to the Olympians," I murmured as a wave of anger tore through my heart.

"Don't let him upset you, Ardella," a familiar voice in my head offered sympathetically.

"Athena."

"My brother is just trying to use you to get to me."

"Hermes had some very interesting things to say."

"Hermes is the God of liars and thieves. You can't trust anything he says."

"Then there are not humans living without the Olympians on Earth?" There was dead silence. "Or perhaps Gidian the Great was NOT the Son of Ares?" I added.

I felt the tremors of frustration through the tendrils of our mental bond. She wanted to deny it, but suspected I would recognize it for a lie.

"What if he was?"

"Your obsession with stopping the Son of Ares each century is some misguided anger over being unable to control Gidian? Everything you have done is to avenge yourself on a mortal dead for over 500 years?"

"You are taking this far too personally, Ardella. You are not even..."

"not even important enough to consider."

Athena was silent, although I could feel her irritation.

"Hermes may believe that mankind has free will, but it is all an illusion," I sighed.

"Yes it is. Mankind will never be free to choose as long as they live under Olympian rule. Mortals may live on Arcadia, but

this world belongs to us." A peal of thunder shook the walls of Hermes Tower and the Goddess of wisdom was gone.

Why did my encounters with Athena always leave me feeling small and insignificant? What was the point of free will, if the Gods of Arcadia simply manipulated us into doing what they wanted? It was all a game to them. My whole life, everything that had happened - just an Olympian game!

Never again! Frustration and self-pity bubble up from deep within my soul. In my anger I wanted to lash out – to destroy. I don't remember picking up the hoe that had been left by the bench; I only remember using it to strike at the well-ordered foliage of the tiny garden again and again. I cursed each and every Olympian as I stabbed the hoe into the earth sending the colorful flower petals flying in rain of dirt and debris.

As I swung the hoe again and again, I poured all the negative emotions filling me into that selfish act of destruction. I burn off the frustration with my violence. My anger spent I crumbled to the earth and began to cry. That is where Alexander found me.

"Ardella?" he asked softly. "Are you alright? What did Hermes say?"

"Your God is despicable. I hate Hermes, and Athena, and all the other pompous Olympians who presume to..." but I couldn't seem to finish the thought, but instead crumbled in his arms.

"What did he say to you, Ardella?"

"We are nothing more than pawns to them. My whole life has simply been moves on an Olympian chessboard."

"What did he say?" Alexander urged again.

"He said that ten years ago his caravan was outside New Athens to rescue you. That if I had not released you, then his followers would have. That one decision changed so many lives and Hermes said it did not even matter." There was a long silence, but I felt a strange longing in Alexander's heart.

"It mattered to me, Ardella," he whispered. I could feel his love and something else – gratitude. "I never got a chance to tell you how much what you did meant to me. I was full of despair and anger from waiting in that tower for my fate. The fact it was you that released me made all the difference in the world. You were the Daughter of Athena, yet you chose to go against your Goddess to do what was right – I knew then that there was hope for mankind. It was in that moment that Metropolis was born."

"Really?"

"Really."

"Thank you for telling me this."

"If it makes you feel better, I understand your frustration."

"I suppose you do. Hermes said he allows you to raid in order to annoy Athena."

"So he tells me."

"What will happen when he gets tired of fighting with his sister?"

"Hermes will be in for a very unpleasant surprise, Ardella. Metropolis is not the capital of Hermes – it is the capital of mankind. Do you think all of our citizens will simply go back to their parent sects and once again become devout followers? Hermes may think Metropolis only exists to annoy Athena, but he has underestimated the determination of the humans."

"Hermes said free will was the greatest curse of the Olympians. He said there are humans back on Earth who do not live under Olympian domination."

"One day Metropolis will be the home for men on Arcadia who do not wish to live under Olympian rule."

"Be careful, Alexander. The Olympians are likely to destroy Metropolis if they realize what you intend."

"Let them try."

Hours later I lay awake on my soft bed in my tower room. My conversations with Hermes and Alexander were spinning round in my head. I knew there was no chance of my sleeping, so I found the Book of Artemis.

After Attia the Queen of the Amazons successfully kidnapped her twin nieces Aremesia & Dyanna, the Great Mother Cynthia called upon her sisters, the children of Artemis, to help her take back her stolen children and make her sister and the Amazons pay for their crimes. Although most of the followers of Artemis were sympathetic to their Queen's anguish, many were beginning to question her sanity. There was great debate in Luna over whether the children of Artemis should follow Cynthia in her reckless path. Many pointed out that attacking the Amazons to get back the children might bring down the wrath of the other Olympians.

Some of the foster daughters of the Amazons raised in Luna came to the Great Mother and announced that they could not fight and possibly kill Amazons, the women who had given them life. In anger Queen Cynthia ordered all foster daughters to be removed from her city and return to the Amazon nation – where she taunted their hearts truly lay. This edict broke apart families and brought great despair to Luna. It also ended all open dissention.

The foster daughters took their possessions and their weapons and headed for Amazonia, but for some reason the Amazons guarding the border mistook their march home for an attack and they defended their homeland with deadly force. The waters of the Saren river at the edge of Amazonian territory ran red with blood and only a handful of the foster daughters survived. Terrified and covered in the blood of their sisters they returned to Luna for shelter. Having suffered the loss of their daughters, the children of Artemis were at last ready to follow their livid queen in her quest for revenge. The Huntresses took up their weapons and made war upon the Amazons.

※

Many hours later when I was finally able to sleep, Athena came to disturb my rest.

I walked through the familiar halls of Athena's archive. I reached up and let my hand run over the rough leather backing of one of the ancient tomes. It felt hard and cold beneath my fingers. I looked more closely at the gold embossed letters that read "The Biography of Gidian the Great."

"He is manipulating you," Athena whispered.

"Who?" I asked.

"Hermes. He twists the tale to further his own agenda."

"And you have never done that yourself?"

"I am protecting all of Arcadia by destroying the Son of Ares. You have helped me in my cause."

"Because I did not understand the whole truth."

"So now you would side with my brother?"

"I do not take sides. I have stopped playing the game. I will not be just a pawn on an Olympian chess board."

"Now, Ardella, you must admit..."

"No, Athena. I am done with your game!"

"It is not your choice, Ardella. You are done, my child, when I say you are done!"

Chapter 19

Who is to say if evil comes from the heart of a man or if the seeds of evil are planted deep in our soul waiting for the precise event which will bring it forth into gruesome bloom.

**Minister Tressa, High Counsellor of Athena
Two thousand six hundred and thirty years Ab Terra Condita**

"WOULD YOU MIND telling me why the latest raid from the villages of New Athens has returned with three honeysuckle plants for you?" Alexander asked from the door of my tower room.

"Tannis," I exclaimed as I moved to inspect the plants. "He remembered my request. How sweet." I felt Alexander's irritation with my comment, but he replied without revealing any hint of anger.

"That explains it. My raid commander said a young farmer simply walked up to him and presented him with the honeysuckle cuttings telling him they were for Lady Ardella," he said.

"Tannis must have left them for me knowing you would eventually raid that particular village."

"You frown upon our raiding for food and necessities, but you asked Tannis to send you honeysuckle?"

"It is not for me, Alexander. It is for Muriel."

"Muriel?"

"You worked in the Grove of the Dryads, surely you remember how much they like honeysuckle."

"Are you trying to tell me your story the other night about an ancient dryad in the Grove of Artemis was the truth?"

"Why would I lie about something like that? Surely Deidra told you about our encounter with Muriel when we took the children to the grove?"

"It seems she forgot to mention it. But the other night when you called for the dryad, I didn't see or hear anything."

"Are you sensitive to dryads?"

"I knew quite a few dryads in New Athens," he laughed. "I did work in their grove."

"I have no idea why Muriel did not come out to speak to you. She did make her presence know just after you left. In fact, she said you were handsome."

"I think I am going to like this Muriel."

"Well, shall we go?"

"Go?"

"You do remember how to plant seedlings, right? I think it is time to bring Muriel her gift."

～

Just over an hour later, Alexander and I had the three honeysuckle vines planted at the base of the large oak tree that Muriel called home. Although we had been there over twenty minutes planting the honeysuckle, Muriel had yet to make an appearance.

"I am beginning to think this dryad is a figment of your over active imagination, Ardella. We have been planting the honeysuckle for a while now and no sign of your Muriel. I have never met a dryad who could resist honeysuckle."

"I do like honeysuckle. I had forgotten how sweet its aroma can be," Muriel said finally making her presence known.

"It is about time," I said.

"I thought you two might want to be alone, but if he is not going to kiss you again, then I would like to come out and enjoy the honeysuckle," Muriel announced.

I burst out laughing as Alexander turned an odd shade of pink.

"Be nice Muriel. We brought you honeysuckle," I said.

"It is nice to meet you, Muriel," Alexander offered.

"He is sensitive to dryads. If you want to come out of your tree, he can see you." I suggested.

To my surprise Muriel's ethereal form shimmer from the tree directly behind Alexander. "Boo!" she said loudly. Alexander jumped at the sound but bravely turned to face the ancient dryad. I had never seen her be so playful or go out of her way to tease anyone.

"Was that necessary?" Alexander said in a huff, more of embarrassment than anger. I suddenly realized that the playful man from the waterfall was not with us today. I almost laughed as I realized Alexander was much more like the stuffy Athenians than he would care to admit. I was not surprised that Muriel agreed.

"Your clothing says that you are the ruler of the Hermians, but that can't be right. You have no sense of humor," Muriel observed. "You must learn to have a little fun."

I could not help but laugh at her words, so similar to his directed at me during our adventure in the fountain.

"I need to learn to have more fun?" Alexander murmured looking at me accusingly.

"Alexander was born in New Athens. He became a Hermian

as an adult," I offered.

"That explains it. The children of Athena were always so stuffy. They don't know how to play and have fun. The Hermians on the other hand are the most playful of all the Olympian children. They even outshine my own sweet daughters of Artemis," the ancient dryad rambled in her nostalgic way.

"How old are you, Muriel?" Alexander asked suddenly.

"I was young when the Goddess Artemis willed herself into her eternal slumber. Ardella tells me that was a thousand years ago," Muriel replied.

"You remember the followers of Artemis and what happened to them?" he gasped in amazement. I cringed at the question unsure of Muriel's reaction. I was startled to realize I had avoided any mention of Artemis or the destruction of her followers in all my conversations with Muriel.

Since I had encountered the ancient dryad in her lost and confused state, I had been treating her like an elderly grandmother in need of protection. In his usual practical and straightforward manner the first words out of Alexander's mouth had been to learn about one of the most monumental events in the history of Arcadia. I just hoped the event that not so traumatic for the ancient dryad that to even think about it would cause her to lose touch with reality. I should have known better.

"I miss the daughters of Artemis. I miss the songs they would sing at the coming of the full moon. Their voices would fill the night and stir the magic of wild places," she reflected in a tone that I was gratified to know was firmly rooted in the here and now rather than lost in her memories of the past.

"What did they sing, Muriel?" I asked softly.

The dryad sang a simple haunting melody:

Come one, come all ye children of night

Diana's moon is calling.
Come sing, come dance, come celebrate life
before the day is dawning.

Come Huntresses, Amazons, sisters of light
Come servant girls and ladies
Diana's moon she calls to you
You must not keep her waiting.

"That was beautiful, Muriel," I whispered.

"Who is Diana?" Alexander asked.

"It is what an ancient culture on Earth called the Goddess. They were a militaristic race called ..."

"the Romans." Alexander supplied.

"Yes! Diana is the Roman name for Artemis. You must have studied history at the Academy, young Athenian," Muriel said.

"I didn't go to the Academy, but I spent a lot of time reading about the wars of the ancient Earth and the cultures of Greece and Rome. I even took my new name from one of the Hellenistic rulers," Alexander said calmly. Although the emotions were not easy to bear, I was glad the Son of Ares no longer felt his pain must be hidden from me.

"Alexander the Great of Macedonia," Muriel supplied. "He was a very successful conqueror on Earth. You know that he was the Son of Ares, the God of War," she continued.

"Since I am the Son of Ares as well, I picked an appropriate name," Alexander offered.

"You are not the Son of Ares. You are too agreeable. Rowan was the Son of Ares and you could feel something no quite right in the air when he was near," Muriel commented.

"I ..." he faultered. I too found myself at a loss for words. Still searching for a way to explain, we waited too long and Muriel lost interest in the subject.

"Would you like to hear more songs of Artemis?" she asked. It suddenly hit me what an incredible wealth of knowledge this dryad possessed. I was a fool not to have realized it earlier.

"That would be wonderful, Muriel. May I invite others to listen, too? There are new followers of the Goddess in Metropolis who would be very interested to learn her sacred songs," I said.

"New followers of Artemis, you say. I would like to meet them and teach them all I know about the worship of the Goddess," Muriel said. "They must learn to call forth the wild magic at the full moon."

I turned to Alexander who was looking a little bewildered by the change of topic. "Go get your sister and tell Galynda to bring as many of the followers of Artemis as possible. They will want to hear what Muriel has to say. And then try to find a follower of Apollo who knows how to notate music. We will also need paper," I said in rapid succession. When he started to protest, I added, "There is no time to argue. This is too important. These are songs that have not been heard by human ears in almost a millennium. I have never seen Muriel so focused and lucid before. We must learn everything we can while there is still time." With this he admitted defeat and went off to do my bidding. I sat down beneath Muriel's tree as she once again began to sing:

>   Starlight, starbright
>   The veil of night is falling.
>   First star I see tonight,
>   Diana's moon is calling.
>
>   Come one, come all my sisters awake
>   The night is yours til the morning
>   We shall not pass this way again

Diana's moon is calling.

Many hours later I returned to my tower room amazed by what had taken place. Muriel had shared four more songs used by the followers of Artemis to celebrate the coming of the full moon. Galynda and the eight other followers of Artemis sang with the dryad dutifully practicing each melody until they could sing if perfectly. I recorded all the words on the precious paper Alexander provided.

Unfortunately the Strategos had been unable to find a musician among the followers of Apollo, but he had stood nearby and watched and listened to the proceedings nonetheless. I looked up several times during breaks in the singing to find Alexander staring at me intensely. Unfortunately there were so many people around with strong emotions that his feelings were clouded and unclear to me. I could guess at his thoughts, since more than once during the evening I found myself just watching Alexander, and had had to ask Muriel to repeat what she had just sung. I wanted so badly to go over to stand beside him and feel what he felt, but I never got the chance. Even when Muriel began to show signs of fatigue and our choral practice ended, Alexander walked away with his sister and the other followers of Artemis as they left the park. He didn't even come over to say goodnight.

I watched him go willing myself not to run after him asking him to stay with me. I wasn't sure exactly when or how it had happened, but I had little doubt that I was falling in love with the Son of Ares.

I stood out on the balcony of my tower room gazing out at the tomb of Artemis and the dark, deserted park. I had tried to sleep, but my body had been too restless. Every time I closed my eyes I saw Alexander's face. I had tossed and turned unable to find rest, until I had given up trying to sleep. The gentle breeze touched my aching body and I found myself remembering his kiss and the feel of his hands on my skin. *By the Goddess, if this is what loving Alexander was going to do to me, how was I going to survive?*

Perhaps if I went to him; if I could see him and touch him the ache would stop. I sighed. I didn't even know where he was. He might still be with Galynda or perhaps already asleep in his tower. I felt a sudden surge of frustration. *How dare he sleep contently when he had caused such chaos in my life!*

My heart jumped as I heard the door softly open. I could feel his presence in my mind. Alexander! He was here. He had come.

"Ardella?" Alexander whispered. The longing in his voice touch my very soul and I knew instantly that he was restless as well.

"Out here," I managed to reply despite the unexpected dryness of my throat. Suddenly I felt a wall of desire more intense than anything I had ever experienced slam into me. My body quivered in response and my heart beat faster. By the Goddess, I knew in that moment that Alexander was here to make love to me and that was exactly where I wanted him to be.

Cocooned in the sensual embrace of Alexander's desire, I flushed with satisfaction as his arms went around my waist and he pulled me against his hard, masculine body. "I was on my way home from Galynda's, when I found myself standing at the base of your tower instead."

"Perhaps this is where you wanted to be," I suggested.

"I don't suppose I have to tell you what I am feeling?" he

whispered softly against my ear.

"I felt your desire from across the room. It is a tangible thing floating in the air all around us. It is the most incredible sensation I've ever felt," I told him breathlessly.

"The night is young," he murmured kissing his way down my neck.

"Alexander," I sighed.

"I want you, Ardella," he said between kisses. "I suppose I should ask if …" he started to say, but I distracted him when I reached back to run my fingers through his hair.

"I want you, too," I said softly, thinking he was asking for my consent. His soft chuckle confused me.

"I already knew that, my love, even without the gift of empathy," he said, "I wanted to ask you about Teldar."

"Teldar?" I repeated, my mind too muddled with desire to comprehend what he wanted to know.

"How long were you two engaged?"

"Engaged? Almost two years." I replied still unable to see what this had to do with our current situation.

"Then you two have been… intimate?"

"I do not understand," I said. "What difference would that make? Is this jealously?"

"No," he said adamantly, but then paused. "Well, perhaps a little. But my reason for asking is that I need to know if you have done this before. I mean …. If this is your first time, then I must be careful, so I won't hurt you," he said calmly and logically, although I could feel a twinge of fear in his heart. The great and powerful Son of Ares was scared. What could he be scared of? Then it hit me. He was scared that he might not be able to be gentle. The primal woman deep within my soul surged forth answering Alexander's desire in kind.

I turned in his arms and let my hands move up slowing

exploring the hard plane of his chest, his broad shoulders and finally the long black hair that framed his face.

"There is no need to gentle," I replied and then pulled his lips to mine.

∽

The first rays of sunlight slipped through the window of my tower room and fell softly upon the man sleeping in my bed. I lay there staring for a long time wondering if it had been a good idea to allow my heart to rule my head. I was here to free my brother and I couldn't turn back now. My heart ached as I looked at him. How was I going to betray him, when just thinking about the deed made my chest hurt and my heart beat faster?

"Alexander," I called softly. "It is morning." No response. I gently shook him and his eyes fluttered. "Alexander."

"Good morning," he said with a grin. I don't think he had ever looked more handsome.

"How did you sleep?" I inquired.

"Quite well, considering."

"Considering," I prompted.

"This bed is soft enough, Ardella, but it is not the right size for two to sleep comfortably."

"We did not sleep all that much, but I guess I should complain to my provider and see if I can get a bigger bed."

"As your provider I would suggest that next time we try this in my bed, which is significantly bigger."

"That would seem to be a good suggestion, although you will have to give me directions to where you live."

"It is the tower next to Hermes, but you've been there."

"That was Athena. I do not remember anything about how I got there."

"You have no memory of how you got to my room?"

"The first thing I remember is sitting on your chest holding a knife to your throat."

"Really?"

"But that does bring up an interesting point - how did Athena know where to find you? Had she been watching you before I arrived or is it an Olympian power?"

"Don't go there, Ardella. It will make my head start pounding."

"I suppose some things are better left a mystery."

"I guess I should go before Deidra arrives," he said with a sigh.

"Too late," I retorted. "Her sudden burst of surprise at finding us is what woke me."

"Oh dear!" he sounded truly alarmed at this development.

"I suppose she will have to report our conduct to the Strategos," I teased.

"I am going to get a long lecture on taking advantage of you."

"Taking advantage of me?"

"She told me about your concerns that I was your provider and what expectations I had for you?"

"Ah."

"I assured her I had no ulterior motive for providing for you and no expectations. Now she is going to think I was lying."

"I would imagine Deidra of all people would have sympathy for thinking with the heart instead of the head."

"You don't understand. She is the defender of all the women of Metropolis. Even the fiercest of the raiders behave in fear of what she might do."

"I overheard her tell a particularly mean bully that 'you know what I do to men who abuse the women they are supposed to protect'. I am curious – what was she threatening to do to the man?"

"Deidra is a legend in Metropolis. Many years ago there was a nasty bully named Tragor among the raiders. He raped a number of women and threatened to kill their providers if they told anyone what he had done."

"That is horrible."

"He made the mistake of trying to rape Deidra."

"I think I know where this is going."

"She beat him senseless and threatened to castrate him, if he touched another woman."

"So that is why the men of Metropolis fear her?"

"Exactly."

"Did he behave after that, or did she have to castrate him?"

"I doubt he would have stopped, so I took the steps necessary to end it."

"What did you do?"

"He stood trial. Twenty-two women testified against him. He was the first man I had to execute as the Strategos of Metropolis." The haunted look in his eyes no longer surprised me. I had come to understand that despite his ruthless reputation Alexander was not a killer by nature.

"I will assure her that you did not take advantage, so perhaps she will go easy on you," I laughed trying to lighten his darkening mood.

Suddenly his look was serious, too serious. "I swear that I will provide for you without any expectations," he said gently reaching to caress my cheek.

I felt the tears fill my eyes at the love I experienced through that simple touch. "I already knew that," I assured him touching his hand with my own.

"I don't suppose last night really changes anything between

us?"

"My purpose in Metropolis has not changed," I admitted.

"You are still intent upon saving your brother."

"And it is still your duty to see that he is punished."

"Hermes' Council could decide in Rafe's favor." Alexander said, although his feelings of doubt were intense.

"When Poseidon walks upon the land again."

"What are you going to do?" he asked.

"The same thing you will do – what I have to do," I replied as guilt rose in my throat.

"I guess I should be going. I wish ..." he began, but let his voice trail off. I could feel his conflict between desire and duty. It hurt me almost as much as it was hurting him.

"What do you wish?" I prompted softly.

"That we had met in a different time and place."

"That would have been wonderful," I said hugging him. After a few moments he pulled back from the embrace. Rising he dressed in the black robes of the Strategos of Metropolis and moved to the door to begin his day.

He turned just as he was reaching for the door and offered joyfully, "The priest of Apollo here in Metropolis will be leading the ceremony of the dawn at sunrise tomorrow. Would you like to come with me?"

"I would like that. Thank you."

⁓

Many hours later I found myself in the small garden that I had destroyed after my interview with Hermes. As a suspected there was a young woman there patiently replanted the plants that could be salvaged from my rage. For years I had lived in the tower of Athena with servants to care for me. Although I tried to show gratitude for their service to me, I never once stopped to help one of them in their duties or take responsibility for myself. It wasn't the way things were done, and it never occurred to me to do so. I decided this morning to live like a citizen of Metropolis and help clean up my own mess.

"Hello," I offered softly.

"Hello," the young woman responded.

"I have come to help in the garden."

"How much do you know about gardening?"

"A little, but I have no practical experience."

"And you are new in Metropolis."

"Yes," I replied. *Praise the Goddess – she didn't realize who I was. I loved that about Metropolis.*

"So the Strategos sent another one?"

"Sort of," I began, but then realized her assumption would smooth the way. "I am a quick learner," I added.

"We'll see," she said. "Start at the far end of that bed. Find as many savable plants as you can and put the rest in that basket for the compost pile. To be viable they must have roots and at least two intact leaves. Clear enough?"

"I think so," I said as I moved to the end of the bed and began sorting plants. I was saddened to realize how much of the delicate foliage I had destroyed in my anger at Hermes and Athena. We worked in silence for a long while. When I came upon a plant with complete roots and numerous leaves, I cringed, for it also held a beautiful yellow bloom that dropped off as I lifted the plant.

"I wish I could save the flower, too," I muttered. The young woman looked over at the mangled vegetation in my hand and took pity upon us.

"I suppose Demeter wouldn't mind," the young woman said taking the small plant from my hand and gently picking up the yellow blossom. She carefully laid it where it had grown on the stem and bowed her head. I watched in awe as a warm golden glow enveloped her hands and the tiny plant she cradled. After a few moments she lifted the plant and the bloom was once again attached.

"That was incredible. How did you do that?" I asked.

"I have the gift of Demeter. I can make plants grow. It is a simple thing to make the broken stem regrow and save the flower."

"Why are you in Metropolis?"

"What do you mean?"

"Women with the gift of Demeter are highly revered in Elusia, are they not? You are the nobles of your sect who can have anything they desire. Why would you leave Elusia to come to Metropolis?"

"I was given everything I desired, except the right to marry the man I loved. Because he was a son of the Earth he was not considered good enough for me."

"So you came to Metropolis to be together?"

"I wish we had. Hugo and I could not help how we felt about each other and we were certain no one knew about our late night rendezvous. But the elders discovered our secret. Hugo was executed for daring to touch a daughter of Demeter. The very next day I ran away to Metropolis."

"That is terrible. I am sorry."

"Every day I use my gift in honor of Hugo. I make something grow to spite the Elusian Elders and their unjust laws."

"You do not fear Demeter's wrath?"

"I did at first. I even welcomed the day she would strike me down and I could once again be with Hugo in the afterlife. But it never happened. I have been in Metropolis almost a year and every day I use her gift - not once has Demeter objected."

Interesting.

"Ardella, are you ready?" Alexander's voice called softly from the other side of the door.

His announcement had not startled me, despite the early hour, since my empathic powers had felt his excitement as he climbed the stairs.

"Come in, Alexander," I replied. The first thing I noticed as he entered was the lack of black in his wardrobe this morning. Instead he wore light beige pants and a soft white shirt that he belted with a simple leather band. His hair, which he normally wore tied back, flowed down his back and danced on his shoulders. He laughed at the surprise in my eyes.

"I try to blend in during the ceremony," he responded to my unspoken curiosity. I looked him over again and realized nothing in his attire gave any hint that he was the Stratagos of Metropolis or the Son of Ares, although I doubted a man with his handsome face would easily blend into a crowd.

"I have been ready for a while. I was too excited to sleep. I have never attended Apollo's ceremony for the rising sun."

"Then we should hurry. It is almost dawn," Alexander replied taking my arm and escorting me down the stairs.

We walked quickly down the path towards the Grove of Artemis. The darkness was heavy all around us and I shivered in cool breeze that gently played with the folds of my now red robes. I could feel a hint of the mystic energy that was building in the air around us. I was so enthralled by the sensation that I made no effort to ask Alexander any of the questions about the ceremony I had intended to. He must have felt the strange calm as well, because we reached the crowd of Apollo's followers without ever speaking a word.

Suddenly from the darkness there was a bright light. It

originated from a globe atop a golden staff, and I knew from my books that it was powered by the life energy of the priest who held it.

"Children of the Sun. Welcome to the ceremony of the dawn," the priest of Apollo said in a deep, commanding tone that hushed the crowd that had gathered for the ceremony. "At dawn every third day the followers of Apollo gather to honor our silent Olympian who stands even now in the harbor of Heliopolis in his eternal vigil."

"Praise to Apollo!" voices in the crowd cried out.

"Praise to Apollo!" the priest said, "Apollo who is beloved of the sun and the inspiration of the arts. We thank him for the blessings bestowed upon us and we long for the day when Apollo once again will walk among us to witness the miracle of the dawn."

"Return to us, great Apollo. Your children are waiting," voices in the crowd called out.

"All praise to Apollo, lord of the sun!" the priest shouted. "Give us another dawn!"

"All praise to Apollo, lord of the sun! Give us another dawn!" the crowd replied in unison. Just as the sound died away the first pink rays of dawn shot into the darkness. The soft, white edge peaked over the horizon. "Praise Apollo!" the crowd shouted.

In a strong, baritone voice the priest began the anthem of Apollo.

> Rise up spirit of life and light
> Fill our hearts with peace
> Banish gloom and fears of night
> Your children still believe.

After a few moments other voices joined in until the waning

night was filled with the enchanted melody.

> Be with us now as we face a new day
> Grant our troubles are few
> Apollo we cast our doubts away
> Your children believe in you.
>
> Apollo be with us in each new day
> Your children are waiting for you.

As the music filled the dying night it stirred the positive emotions in the crowd. Hope joy, and peace pour forth from the multitude and created a bubble of euphoria I suspected even non-empaths could sense.

As the song ended and the sun climbed high enough to fill the Grove of Artemis with light, no one in the crowd spoke or moved. It was as if time had stopped and everyone savored the moment of wonder. The soft melody from the lyre the priest played finally broke the spell and everyone began to disperse toward the mundane world.

Alexander took my arm and led me back toward my tower room. After a few minutes he asked, "What did you think?"

"It was beautiful. Thank you for inviting me."

"I thought you would like it. It is a little less frenzied than the Bonfire of Demeter, but just as magical."

"So Deidra told you that she invited me to the Bonfire of Demeter?"

"Yes, and that you felt with your gift it would be a good idea to attend."

"Actually I did see it."

"Really?"

"I watched from atop your cyclopean walls. I could see the

dancers whirl and leap in and out of the shadows of the bonfire. It was an exciting spectacle."

"Without the entanglements of the strong emotions often associated with the Bonfire. Very clever."

"So were you among the dancers that night?"

"Actually I was. I try not to miss a Bonfire."

"And do you participate in all the activities?"

"If you are referring to the couples who sneak off into the woods to continue the celebration the answer is no – not since ..."

"not since?"

"Several years ago the dancer who tried to pull me off into the woods turned out to be an Amazon assassin. I have had to be much more careful about such things ever since."

Chapter 20

The lotus plant is a wondrous herb with a large variety of medicinal properties. In small doses it calms a troubled mind or removes unwanted anxiety. In slightly larger doses it can induce sleep even in the most resistant patients.

**Exerpt from the 20th volume of the *Arcana Medicinae*
by Galen the Wise of the Apollo sect
One thousand, two hundred and thirty-six years *Ab Terra Condita***

I WASN'T SURE how she would react as I knocked upon Galynda's door. The midday sun beat down upon paving stones which in turn warmed my sandaled feet. I glance up at the star that gave life to Arcadia and thought of the sunrise ceremony for Apollo. As I waited for the door to open, I suddenly remembered a story I had read in one of the many books from Athena's archive. It was from the classical mythology of ancient Earth and it told the story of how the god Apollo drove the chariot of the sun across the sky. I smiled as I tried to imagine the handsome giant standing silently in Heliopolis' harbor guiding magical horses pulling the sun behind him. Our ancestors on Earth had such primitive beliefs.

I remember mentioning the story to Teldar who was also puzzled by such a fantastic tale. The Olympians were immortal and had many powers that might seem magical to primitive humans, but where had they come up with such a fantastic tale as Apollo pulling the chariot of the sun across the sky or the seasons being caused by Demeter's anger. I finally became so curious, I asked Athena herself.

She explained that the Olympians had lived together on Mt. Olympus far removed from the people in Greece who worshiped them. It had been a mistake, because the people made up stories about their Gods called myths. The stories stuck and the Olympians didn't see the harm in such tales until centuries later when they were used by skeptics to suggest the Gods did not really exist. It was the dark period of unbelief on Earth that had shaped the nature of Arcadia.

Here each Olympian lives with their followers, so the people would never doubt the Gods were real. No one on Arcadia would make up or believe such fantastic tales as the myths of ancient Greece, because they have seen the Gods with their own eyes. Living among humans, the Olympians have been able to shape our societies and guide our footsteps like a trusted parent. And keep a closer eye on us so we don't stray into the darkness like our ancestors on Earth.

"Lady Ardella?" I heard Galynda's voice ask from the doorway. I had been so lost in thought I not even heard the door open and it took a moment for me to come back to the present and the reason for my visit.

"Lady Galynda, I was hoping to speak to you," I said.

"Just Galynda," she replied with a hint of annoyance in her voice and in her mind.

"What?" I asked unsure of what had caused her irritation with me.

"I am a citizen of Metropolis like any other. I have no title or rank," Galynda explained.

"I meant no offense," I murmured. "I just assumed since you were the sister of the Strategos you would addressed with a title of respect due your role in the ruling class of Metropolis."

"You are a long way from New Athens, Lady Ardella. There is no ruling class, or scholarly class, or servant class here. Everyone in Metropolis is equal."

"Of course, Galynda. I am just learning the ways of Metropolis. Please forgive me for my lack of knowledge," I offered sincerely and I felt her irritation give way to guilt.

"I'm sorry, Lady Ardella. I didn't mean to be rude," she said honestly. "Please come in."

"Thank you," I said entering her home.

"I am very proud of the way of life we have established here in Metropolis. I must learn not to be so sensitive," Galynda explained, her feelings of pride strongly flowing from her heart.

"I have felt a similar sense of pride in many of the citizens of Metropolis. It has been a surprise for me to learn about the nature of your city firsthand."

"Most of our society and its customs are based upon the traditions of our ancestors on Earth that Alexander learned from your crystal reader."

"Are you referring to the crystal reader with the better part of the Academy library stored on it that your brother stole from me?"

"I would love to hear that story," Galynda laughed.

"Perhaps another time, Galynda." I sighed softly. I took a deep breath and continued, "I have come to you with the first excerpt of the *Book of Artemis*."

"Wonderful," she exclaimed joyfully, "Does it tell us how we might awaken the Sleeping Goddess?"

"No so far. The parts I have translated are the history of the conflict between the Amazons and the followers of Artemis. I am only about a third of the way through the book, though, so have no idea what the rest might contain," I said handing her the pages.

"Thank you. I look forward to reading the pages. I can return them to you when I have finished."

"The pages are yours to keep and share with the others. There are also copies of the words to the songs Muriel sang for us. Unfortunately I could not find anyone from the Apollo sect with the skills to make note of the melody."

"You have done more than enough, Lady Ardella. Thank you."

"I want the new followers of Artemis to have access to all the knowledge about their Goddess. I will keep translating every chance I get."

"And you are certain there is no payment required for this knowledge?"

"For the knowledge? No! I could, however, use some additional paper on which to translate."

"I believe I can arrange for the paper," she said smiling. After a moment her brows furrowed and she asked, "What does that mean 'translate'?"

"Oh! Let me show you." I said pulling the *Book of Artemis* from my bag. I handed the small leather-bound tome to Alexander's sister. I watched as she opened the book and a puzzled look crossed her face. I felt her surge of confusion and suspicion.

"I recognize the letters. Why can't I read the words?"

"It is in an ancient Earth language called Latin. Very few people on Arcadia can still read it."

"I don't understand."

"On Arcadia today we all speak and write in a common tongue. The Olympians wanted it that way to facilitate communication among our sects. Our ancestors on ancient Earth, however, had many different cultures and many different languages."

"And the Olympians preserved one of these ancient languages?"

"Athena did. I learned to read Latin in an advanced course at the Academy after I became a member of Athena's Council."

"The Athenian sect has a secret language no one else on Arcadia can even read."

"Most common citizens in New Athens can't read it either. It is the language of the scholarly elite. Some of the books in Athena's archive are written in Latin to keep their words from being understood by anyone outside the elite."

"So translating is writing the words of the book in our common tongue so all might understand them."

"Exactly."

"I am still not sure why you are doing this for us."

"Because I am the only one with the book, the knowledge, and the motivation to do this for you. That makes it my destiny."

"And will Athena be displeased that your destiny is to translate the *Book of Artemis* and shared her secret knowledge with others."

"I have no doubt she will be very displeased."

"You are starting to talk like a citizen of Metropolis."

&

I paused outside the large doors of the Metropolis hospital. My heart was racing as I contemplated entering to find Apollodorus. I knew logically that the odds of the incident from the last time repeating itself were minimal, but fear gripped my heart and I could almost feel the horrible pain of that dying man. I had to go inside in order to obtain the lotus blossom powder I needed for the plan to free Rafe. I just had to find the courage to open the doors and enter.

"Lady Ardella," I heard a voice behind me ask.

I turned to find a very beautiful woman in her early thirties. Her auburn hair flowed down her back while her dark green eyes sparkled in the sunlight. She was dressed in a simple homespun garment like the other women of Metropolis, but there was something about her face and manner more suited to the silk robes of the temple of Aphrodite. I knew my suspicions were correct as I looked closely at her face and saw the faded tattoo of dove beside her right eye.

"You must be Apollodorus' wife," I said giving voice to my intuition.

"How could you know that?" she asked startled.

"Your husband told me you were a follower of Aphrodite," I explained.

"Is he still telling that story about having the raiders stealing me away from the Temple?" she asked smiling. I could feel her love for her husband like the warm touch of campfire on a cold winter's night.

"He made it sound quite romantic and sweet," I told her smiling back.

"Men! He forgets the part where I was terrified out of my mind at being taken by strange men whose intentions I did not know," she scoffed, but her emotions held none of the irritation here words would suggest.

"You seem to have forgiven him." I prompted, suspecting there was more to the story.

"I forgave him the day our first child was born and I did not have to give it up to the Temple Elders to be raised in the ways of Aphrodite. I never dreamed I would someday be able to keep and raise my own children."

"I didn't realize training began so early in New Corinth.

The children of Athena's followers are not required to go to the Academy until the age of ten."

"Training begins at seven for followers of Aphrodite. But I was a temple maiden. Because of the nature of our role, we do not marry or raise the children we bare. They must be fostered by others so we may fulfill our duties to the Goddess," she said with just a hint of sadness.

"It sounds like your Goddess asks a great deal from her temple maidens."

She laughed softly and the sound tickled my ears. "She also gives a great deal. You have no idea the bliss of just being in her presence," she sighed.

But I did know what she meant. I smiled as I recalled life in the Tower of Athena. How many times had I done my research in the cramped cubicle on the highest floor of the Archive beneath her private chambers, rather than my comfortable study just because I felt closer to the Goddess there? Even through the metal and stone between us I could sense her presence within her apartments opening my mind and enhancing my intelligence. "There is something otherworldly about the presence of the Olympians," I offered.

"Yes. Just being near them makes you feel..."

"Special."

"And loved," she whispered her voice raw with emotion.

"That must be a trait of Aphrodite. I have never felt love in the presence of Athena – wiser, but not loved."

"Aphrodite makes all her followers feel cherished. She even gives beauty and long life to those who serve her. I thought I would attend her my entire life."

"Do you miss your Goddess?"

"Sometimes. I wish I could once again just stand in her presence."

I wish my sons could witness the Dionysiac – it is an incredibly vibrant and spiritual pageant."

"I have read about Aphrodite's procession to visit Dionysus each year. I have been told it is a wonder to behold."

"It is a wonder to see, hear, touch, taste and smell. Sometimes I dream about the colors and sounds," she said and I could feel her joy and pleasure at imagining the scene.

"I can feel your awe just remembering the Dionysiac," I said caught up in the moment. Suddenly her joy was overshadowed by a different emotion – suspicion. I had felt it many times before as the person I was talking too suddenly realized that I knew what they were feeling.

"Apollodorus told me you were an empathy," she said quietly.

"Yes. I'm sorry if I ..." I tried to apologize. So many people felt my reading of their emotions was a violation of their privacy – despite the fact I could not control it.

"Don't apologize, my lady, for being who you are," she said earnestly. "My husband told me about what happened last time you were here. Could you really feel the dying man's pain?"

"I felt everything he did, but only for a few moments before I fainted."

"It is a miracle you would want to return to this place under the circumstances. Did you come to the hospital to see my husband?"

"Yes, I was planning to go in as soon as I could work up the courage to enter the front door. Apollodorus was going to let me look through his microscope."

"I was just coming to bring him food. Shall we go in together?"

"Thank you,... I just realized I never learned your name."

"Celestia."

∽

Later that day a quiet knock proceeded Kendra's entrance into my tower room.

I gave her half the lotus blossom powder I had stolen from the hospital. Hers was for Lucas and mine for Alexander. Lucas was on guard duty for the next three nights, so the perfect moment was at hand. My time in Metropolis was growing to a close. *Why did that make my heart ache?* Why did it hurt to know that if I freed Rafe, I could never be welcome again in Metropolis.

I could make a difference in this place. I had spent almost a decade intoxicated by Athena's Archive and drinking in all the knowledge my mind could hold. Yet in all that time I never stopped to wonder what I could do with what I learned. Metropolis had opened my eyes to the possibilities I had never considered before, and yet I would never have the chance to fulfill any of these dreams.

I shivered as I realized that although I had come to understand the manipulations of the Olympians, I could not seem to escape them. My fate was all too clear. In order to save my brother I would have to betray a man I had come to love and a place that had begun to feel like home. I had no choice in my own future and no chance at a happy ending.

For the first time, I truly understood why people were drawn to Metropolis and its promise of freedom from Olympian oppression. Even if I could never live within its promise and hope, I knew it was more important than ever for Metropolis to endure – for all the mortals of Arcadia.

∽

Later that night as I sat in the dining hall of Alexander's tower sharing a meal with Diedra, Kern, Apollodorus and Celestia I found myself staring at each of them in turn trying to memorize their faces for the dawn when I would have to leave this place forever. The only one in the room I could not look at was Alexander. My eyes became blurry every time they rested upon his handsome face. *Who would have ever believed that I would have fallen in love with the Son of Ares?*

"Do you two ever agree on anything?" Alexander asked with a chuckle. His words caught me by surprise, and I realized I had not been following the dinner conversation as I should have. Across the table from me Apollodorus had been telling tales of his tumultuous courtship with his wife, Celestia.

A knowing look passed between his guests before Apollodorus replied thoughtfully. "I am afraid such a thing has never come to pass."

Celestia's radiant smile filled the small dining room with warmth like the first rays of sunlight on a cold winter's day. "Now dearest, you make it sound like a scientific impossibility." She patted his hand gently. "There have been rare occasions when we were of a like mind."

He raised one eyebrow and challenged her claim. "Name one."

"Let's see." Celestia tilted her head and closed her eyes as if replaying the events of their lives searching for an answer to her husband's challenge. Finding what she sought, her eyes opened suddenly. "There was the name for our oldest son – Titus after my father."

Apollodorus shook his head. "As I remember it, I wanted to name our eldest Memnon after the great king of Heliopolis and you vetoed my suggestion – rather adamantly."

"Ah yes, Titus was a compromise, wasn't it?" Celestia mused, but quickly added. "Perhaps you would consider our marriage a mutually agreed upon event?"

He smirked at her. "How many times did you turn me down before you finally accepted my proposal?"

A gentle pout rounded her lips. "Three," she admitted.

"Four, if you count the time in New Corinth."

"Proposals from guests to the Temple of Aphrodite were far too common. That one does NOT count." Celestia shook her head in dismay. "What about the honeymoon?"

"What about it?"

"That first evening as we lay in the emerald grotto watching the sun set into the sea, you and I agreed that the view was the most beautiful thing in all of Arcadia." There was a long silence. A slight blush crept up Apollodorus' neck. "Really? You are going to deny the words you spoke on our honeymoon?" she huffed.

"No, my dear. I did say the view was the most beautiful thing in all of Arcadia, but ..."

"But?" she prompted clearly irritated.

"I wasn't looking at the sunset," Apollodorus explained lifting his wife's fingers to his lips. "I was looking at you."

"Really!" the former priestess of Aphrodite countered less than generously, but it was all an act. Celestia's heart soared in her chest and her contented smile spoke louder than words could of her feelings for her husband. Even without my gift I knew that she loved him. She looked radiant. "I concede, my darling. You seem to be correct. Our mutual agreement on any given subject is an impossibility."

"We are living proof that opposites attract," Apollodorus mused and they both laughed.

"What about you two?" Celestia asked looking curiously at Kern. "How did you meet, Deidra?"

I felt Kern's flush of panic at the mundane question and I

wondered what strange events had brought together a son of the Earth and a wayward Amazon. Despite his inner turmoil, Kern simply smiled and began his tale. "Deidra and I both had the same Amazon trainer teach us to fight. We spent a great deal of time together practicing and one thing lead to another."

"Your Amazon teacher must have been very good. I have seen your wife fight," Celestia suggested coyly. "Are you as skillful, Kern?"

"I'm not sure how to answer that," Kern replied looking over at his wife, who was trying unsuccessfully to hide her smile.

"Now, my dear, I am sure that is too personal a question for dinner conversation," Apollodorus scolded softly.

"And discussing the microorganisms that cause wounds to fester was making polite dinner conversation with the Daughter of Athena?" Celestia countered.

All eyes were suddenly on me. "I really enjoyed looking through the microscope. It was so nice to be able to do something so special and not just read about it," I said in Apollodorus' defense.

"You have to come again soon, my dear. You are a natural. You should consider helping me with the research," Apollodorus said. My first reaction was excitement to be included in something so important, but then I remembered tomorrow.

I felt my heart sink and the blood rushed from my face. For a moment the room seemed to spin. *I was never going to get to help Apollodorus with his research. I was never going to see any of these people again.*

"What's wrong, Ardella?" Alexander asked reaching over to touch my arm. A silent scream of guilt roared in my ears and had tears threatening my vision. I could feel the concern of everyone around the table and I clasp my fingers together to try to stop the trembling in my hands.

"Forgive me," I managed to whisper. "I am just tired." I felt the group's relief wash over me, and I thanked the Goddess that none of them were empaths who could detect my clumsy lie.

"I'm not surprised. You were up before dawn," Alexander said softly rubbing my hand. "Perhaps it is time to call it a night."

"You don't have to end the dinner just because ..."

"I'm tired, too, Ardella," Deidra offered.

"Yes, it has been a long day," added Apollodorus.

"Then it is settled. I wish you all a safe journey home," Alexander offered a traditional Hermian farewell as he rose from the table. Each couple bid the Strategos goodnight and departed into the night, but as I moved to do the same, Alexander reached out to stop me.

"Where do you think you are going?" he asked huskily.

"I was going to my tower - to my bed," I teased.

"I thought we decided this time we would spend the night in my bed," he reminded me as his lips met mine.

⁂

I listened to Alexander's soft, rhythmic breathing and felt the warmth of his body pressed against mine, yet still sleep eluded me. Something strange was in the air. I couldn't quite identify why my nerves were on edge, but the night was filled with an unseen energy. A distance peal of thunder from an approaching storm finally brought my uneasiness into focus.

I rose from the bed carefully to avoid pulling the Son of Ares from his slumber.

"Athena," I whispered into the dark.

"*Greetings, my daughter,*" a familiar voice in my head replied.

"*How long have you been watching?*" I queried, careful to only think the question rather than speak it for fear of waking

Alexander.

"Long enough. I am impressed by your determination. I would never have thought of seducing the Son of Ares," Athena remarked.

"I am so glad I finally impressed you," the voice in my head offered before I could stop it.

"Don't be difficult, Ardella. You are my child and I have always been proud of your tenacity."

"Proud of my tenacity?"

"I remember how scared you looked that day in the Council Chambers when you stood up to Tressa over whether or not Alexander's raiding broke the Great Olympian Law."

"I knew Minister Tressa was wrong. I had to speak," I insisted.

"Exactly. You stood up to her despite your fears. I was proud of you."

"Is that why you took my side in the debate?"

"That was part of it, but I saw the potential in your interpretation of the events."

"My interpretation?" I scoffed.

"I had no desire to see the punishment of the Great Law imposed upon another Olympian sect. Your more flexible interpretation kept that terrible price from being imposed."

"And prolonged your little chess game with Hermes."

Her soft laughter filled my mind. "*I am coming to enjoy your impertinent attitude. It has been centuries since a mortal stood up to me. It is refreshing.*"

"It has been five centuries since a mortal stood up to you, has it not?"

The Goddess sighed. "*Gidian. I have never loved or hated a mortal more than that man. I still miss* him," there was a long pause, "*just as I miss your presence in New Athens.*"

"Does this mean I may come home?" my inner voice suggested impishly before I could stop it.

"I'm afraid that is out of the question, unless..."

"Unless," I asked as goose bumps stole down my arms.

"If you were to return to New Athens with Alexander, then how could I turn you away?"

"What about Rafe?"

"What about him?" Athena replied.

"Would he be welcome in New Athens, too?"

"It doesn't matter to me one way or the other, but if it is important to you."

"And what would you do with Alexander, if I brought him to New Athens?" I asked warily.

"The Son of Ares was from New Athens originally. Perhaps he would like to see his mother and sister again."

"You really expect him to just walk into New Athens because you invite him?"

"No, I expect him to come because you invite him," Athena scoffed.

"Or drug him and bring him against his will?"

"I didn't suggest that, but if you feel that is the only way to..."

" I am not interested in returning home under those conditions," I replied cutting off her offer.

"Now, now. Don't be too hasty, Ardella. Everything that has happened could be called a misunderstanding. New Athens is your home."

"Your price is too high," I replied as another peal of thunder shook the sky.

"What if I promised not to kill him, just keep him imprisoned to stop the spread of his chaos? Would that appease your mortal sensibilities?"

"Have you thought this through, Great Athena? Or are you so caught up in your desire to win that you do not realize the situation has changed?"

There was a long silence. Finally Athena whispered, "*Go on.*"

"*What do you think would happen if Alexander came to New Athens and Metropolis was left leaderless?*"

"*Hermes followers could finally...*"

"*Metropolis is not just Hermes followers anymore. It is made up of the mortals from every sect on Arcadia. They are there because they were rejected by their Olympian. They do what they must to survive. You think the raiding is bad under Alexander. Imagine what chaos would pour out of Metropolis without the Son of Ares controlling all the outcasts.*"

"So I should just let the Son of Ares reign continue, because the alternative might be worse?" Athena mocked.

"Yes," I replied. "*The Son of Ares wants what is best for his people. He can be reasoned with and guided by his nature. He is after all a child of the Goddess of wisdom by birth. I guarantee Metropolis without Alexander would spiral out of control into something far more dangerous to all of Arcadia.*" Athena was silent for a long time.

"*I love the ingenuity of the human mind. This is an interesting dilemma, Ardella. I will have to ponder this for a while,*" Athena said and then she was gone.

As I tried to decide what that last comment meant for myself and Rafe, the sky opened up and Athena's storm drenched Metropolis.

Chapter 21

Curiosity is a double-edged sword. It can lead you to wonders beyond imagination or get you into a great deal of trouble.

Lokuri, a follower of Hermes
One thousand, eight hundred and eighty-six years Ab Terra Condita

THE NEXT MORNING back in my own tower I continued my translation of the Book of Artemis.

The followers of Artemis took up their weapons and marched upon Amazonia. They overwhelmed the border guard who had mistakenly slain their daughters and showed no mercy. Still in the throes of a bloody rage, they took control of the port of Lake Hera and travelled across to the capital.

From inside her palace Queen Attia struggled with how to react to this breach of the Great Olympian Law. Could she and the Amazons defend themselves or would that condemn her sect to the same fate as their sisters? Her fellow Amazons wanted revenge for their fallen sisters and daughters, but Attia forbid them to act.

Finally she commanded her Amazons to defend the city. However, Queen Attia alone walked forth to meet her sister on the field of battle.

Standing before both the Amazons and the Huntresses of Artemis Queen Attia declared:

> I am Attia Queen of the Amazons. The anger that brings us all here today began as a quarrel between two sisters. I say that it must end here. No more of our sisters on either side should have to die. Cynthia, I challenge you to single combat. Let us settle this once and for all.

Both the followers of Artemis and the Amazons roared their approval as Queen Cynthia stepped forward to meet her sister. A hush fell over the crowd at her words:

> I am Cynthia the Great Mother of Artemis. I accept your challenge. I will prove to all here that my cause was just and this conflict was your fault.
> I will fight to win back the children you have stolen.

As the battle between the two sisters began the heavens shook with the roar of thunder. From high above the battle field a divine voice was heard. Hestia the greatest of the Olympians issued her verdict upon the offending mortals.

In a voice that roared across the island home of the Amazons and shook the vault of the sky the greatest of the Olympians spoke to the doomed mortals:

> I am Hestia, mother of the Gods of Arcadia. Every

> *Olympian obeys my commands. Long ago I decreed that the terror known as war would forever be banned on Arcadia. No exceptions. It is forbidden for any Olympian sect to make war upon another Olympian sect. For a thousand years the Gods of Arcadia have respected my wisdom and obeyed this command, yet two mortal sisters have dared to presume they may settle their differences by spilling blood. They have allowed Rowan, the Son of Ares, to trick them into teaching Arcadia what it means to make war. For that they and their followers are both doomed.*

Horrified at what they had done, Cynthia and Attia both fell to their knees supplicating themselves before the Goddess Hestia and begging her to show mercy to the children of Hera and Artemis.

There was a long silence, but at last Hestia spoke:
> *Because I am benevolent, I shall give each sister an opportunity to save her Goddess' followers. The winner of this single combat between the queens stays the death sentence for her sect. Know, however, this is a battle to the death. To save your people, you must kill your twin sister.*

As the last word rang across the field of battle, as stunned silence filled the air. Every daughter of Hera and Artemis held their breath as the two sister began their contest. Their entire lives these two queens had trained together with sword and shield and no two mortals on Arcadia were so evenly matched. No one, even the Great Hestia, could predict the outcome for certain. Every woman there understood that the Olympians were watching and the fate of an entire sect hung in the balance.

I slammed the *Book of Artemis* closed unable to continue reading. My hands shook as rage stole up my spin. It had all been Hestia, the mother of the Gods of Arcadia. It was alarming to realize how long the Olympians had been trifling with mankind. I had always been horrified that an entire sect had paid the price for breaking the Great Olympian Law, but Celestia's account made it clear that that had not really been the case. The destruction of the Huntress had not been because they were at fault and the Amazons innocent. The obliteration of the follower of Artemis had been at the whim of fate and set in motion by the arbitrary decree of the Goddess Hestia. *Why would Hestia do such a thing? She was the most elusive of the Olympians who had not bothered to interact with mortals for centuries.*

Unfortunately, I could no longer dwell on the past, but had to begin taking the steps that lead to my future. I went in search of Alexander.

"I found it, Alexander," I exclaimed enthusiastically as I came into the Strategos' office in the tower of Hermes.

"What did you find?" he asked turning to me. His arms came around me as they often did these days and I experienced a twinge of guilt at what I was about to do.

"I know where to find the House of Rowan mentioned in the *Book of Artemis*. I saw ruins on my return from Amazonia," I said trying a little too hard to sound excited. "I didn't suspect then, but I just read the passage again. They are exactly where the book said they would be," I said in rapid succession.

"Slow down," Alexander said amused.

Thankfully, I could already feel his curiosity becoming

engaged and my fake enthusiasm was beginning to bleed over into his emotions as I hoped it might. I had to get him to make his decision with his heart and not take too much time to think about it.

"The House of Rowan - no one had been there in a thousand years. Most of Arcadia does not even remember it existed."

"That sounds... fascinating."

"So, you will come with me," I asked with a burst of joy that I hoped would sway him.

"Come with you ..." he began but suddenly stopped short and his eyebrows drew together. "You want to go to the ruins of the House of Rowan?"

I could feel his emotions in turmoil. His first instinct was suspicion and doubt, but his love for me fought to push his mind toward trust and acceptance. I suppressed my guilt at manipulating him this way and added one more emotion to the mix - desire.

"Aren't you curious? The House of Rowan is not too far from here," I said trying to make my longing evident in my tone.

"Sounds interesting," he replied.

"It is a day's journey there and then a day back plus the time to explore the ruins. We would be all alone for three whole days. Nothing to worry about. No one to interrupt," I said, wrapping my arms around his neck and placing a soft kiss on his lips.

"The idea is starting to sound better and better," he said as the mischievous smile I had come to love appeared on his face, "When do we leave?" he asked enthusiastically.

Victory! I smiled wickedly up at the man I loved; the man I was about to betray. "How about right now?"

"Kern!" Alexander bellowed for Deidra's husband and the Son of Ares closest advisor.

Kern appeared instantly in the doorway his mind and body at full alert. "What it is, Strategos?" he inquired.

"Would you inform Hermes and the Council that I will be unavailable for the next three days?"

The wind whipped through the narrow mountain pass stirring my long red robes and causing the loose tendrils of hair to tickle my face. All around me the colors of nature wove an intricate tapestry of raw beauty. The greens and browns of the Forest of Artemis wrapped around me like a child's blanket, offering safety and serenity. High above the last stage of the sun's daily journey was turning the cloud filled sky a stunning mixture of mauve and orange.

The rhythmic sway of the horse below me and the scenic beauty of the mountains we travelled through were hypnotic. I smiled as I realized Alexander's exhilaration matched my own and it had begun to win out over the worry and suspicion he had tried to hide from me for most of the trip.

I couldn't say I blamed him. Alexander was too much the strategist to not see the potential for danger in this situation. Even if he had decided to trust me, he could not help but see that this would be a perfect opportunity for the Amazons to finally kill him.

As each hour passed without incident I felt him become more and more at ease. At least his worrying about a possible Amazon attack kept him from suspecting the truth - Kendra was going to free Rafe from his cell tonight.

"Ardella, I think I see the ruins," he called. As my horse climbed the next rise to stand beside Alexander's mount, I had a breath-taking view of the House of Rowan. The structure must have once boasted unbelievable mountain vistas from every window and balcony. Even in ruins its simple majesty was still obvious. A complex of buildings and ornamental gardens, the dark stone buildings now lay in various stages of disrepair, while the garden plants had long since escaped their civilized boundaries and begun to consume their surroundings.

"It is incredible," I gasped.

"We should be able to get down there well before dark – plenty of time to set up camp."

⁓

Staring into the dancing flames I found myself lost in thought and fighting off the pangs of guilty that pricked at the edges of my consciousness. Even as Alexander and I sat beside the warm glow of the fire, I knew that Kendra and the other Amazons were freeing Rafe from his prison cell in Metropolis. Once again I was at a crossroads and this night would forever change the path of my life.

"You are quiet, Ardella."

"Sorry. I guess I am just tired. It has been a long day."

"I was afraid something was wrong," he whispered as his arm encircled my waist and his waves of concern washed over me. A stronger stab of guilt shot through my heart.

"Have you suddenly become an empath, Alexander?" I scoffed, trying to make light of his comment far too close to the truth for comfort.

"No chance of that, but I have gotten pretty good at reading your moods. It is more than fatigue. Something is wrong."

"I was lost in thought worrying about tomorrow," I offered truthfully.

"Tomorrow will be here soon enough, Ardella. It is pointless to waste time or energy worrying about it."

"I know you are right. I just wish …" I tried to explain, but wasn't sure how to tell him that my heart felt like it was being torn in two without admitting what I had done.

"What do you wish?" he asked softly snuggling closer.

I felt the longing behind his question and I succumbed to my need to unburden my soul.

"I wish that life wasn't so complicated and that I could just enjoy being here without worrying about the future," I said wistfully.

"I thought that was what this trip was all about, Ardella – to get away from all our troubles and be alone."

"So why did our troubles follow us? Why does it feel like the world is closing in all around me?" I whispered as a single tear rolled down my cheek. I felt his love surround me even as his arms squeezed me comfortingly.

"I promise I will not let anything bad happen to you, Ardella. I will protect you with my life," Alexander proclaimed.

How could I betray this man? My heart was pounding and the guilt threatened to drown my heart.

"Don't say that!" I whispered. "Don't make that kind of promise."

"Why not? I love you, Ardella. I want to protect you."

"I cannot let you protect me if it puts you in danger. I would never forgive myself if anything happened to you because of me," I told him softly. I felt his surge of relief and joy. I knew that even now part of him must be expecting an Amazon ambush. He wanted to trust me, but he had lived for so long having to be on guard every minute that it had become part of who he was.

"Could it be that you are beginning to care for me?" Alexander laughed.

I felt the intensity of his love flow in and around us and its warmth washed away all other feelings – his doubt and my guilt were carried away in the floodwaters of joy leaving me with the aching truth.

I could not help myself. The words just poured out of my heart. "I have fallen in love with you, Alexander. No matter how hard I tried to fight against it. Being around you is like being caught in a raging river that pulls me into its wake."

"So now I am a force of nature," he laughed.

"And so very humble," I replied, turning in his arms to smile up at him. I saw in his eyes the moment his mind truly comprehended what I had said.

"Did you really just say that you loved me, Ardella?" he asked with a joyful longing in his voice.

"I think I did," I replied.

"Say it again," he demanded.

"I love you, Alexander," I whispered.

"I love you, too, Ardella, and I will protect you."

"If you love me, do not make that promise. You may not always be able to protect me."

"Why?" he asked as his suspicion returned in full force. The silence that followed hinted at what I could not say. "What's wrong?" he asked.

For a moment my heart took control. *Perhaps if I told him the truth and asked for his help, there was a chance for our future together.*

"I ... I..." I stammered, but could not find the words as tears flowed from my eyes. I found myself trembling in his arms, overwhelmed by the fear of what my confession might destroy.

My distress was so great that Alexander began to rock me gently and murmured, "It's alright, Ardella. Everything will be alright. You don't have to tell me now!" he comforted.

"I must tell you...," I tried to explain.

"No!" he said putting his finger to my lips.

I could feel his love and contentment surging to control the dread blooming in his heart. "Save confessions for tomorrow," he pleaded suddenly as fearful of the future as I was.

He was right. Telling him the truth now could not change what I had done. I smiled and kissed away his doubt. Tomorrow would come soon enough. Tonight was all we had left and I could not bring myself to ruin it.

Alexander must have felt the same, because for a long time we cuddled together by the fire in blissful silence. There was no need for words for we both knew this time together was precious and must be savored. As the sky above us darkened, one by one the stars appeared bringing with them their mystical celestial magic.

"The stars are beautiful tonight," Alexander crooned in my ear.

I sighed contently. "I have always loved star gazing," I replied.

"Is that why you studied Astronomy at the Academy?" he asked smugly.

"How would you know my focus at the Academy?" I inquired.

"The Amazons aren't the only ones who have spies, Ardella."

"Of course," I laughed. The end of my training at the Academy had been exhilarating, but lonely. Because of my gift, the Council of Athena had decided I could not return to the Academy to finish my studies. Instead, my professors came to me in the Tower of Athena for private tutoring. That is when I had learned to think of books as friends and my fascination with Athena's Archive began. "To tell you the truth, I was torn between Arcadian history and Astronomy," I informed him.

"So how did you decide?"

"I never did. I convinced Head Mistress Leanna I needed to take advance courses in both. My official focus was Astronomy, but my capstone project was the History of the Council of Astronomers and the Establishment of our Constellations and Calendar," I said leaning back into his arms.

"That sounds..."

"Boring – I know, but it gave me access to the Celestial Telescope and Athena's Archive."

"I envy you getting to work in the Planetarium at the Academy. I remember the outside of the building was covered in such beautiful mosaics of stars and planets that seem to move and change as you stared. I always wondered if it was as magical inside?"

"Would you be surprised to learn that I have never been inside the Planetarium either?"

"But then how did you use the Celestial Telescope?"

"The Academy does not have the only Celestial Telescope on Arcadia, Alexander."

"Really?"

"Athena has a smaller one on the roof of her Tower."

"You used the Goddess Athena's personal Celestial Telescope for your research?"

He actually sounded surprised.

"A few times the Goddess even came to look through it with me," I replied.

"Athena really thinks of you as a daughter?"

"Yes, in her own way," I whispered as a wave of sadness washed over me. I thought of all the things I loved in New Athens that I would never be able do again. I ached for all the people who I would never see – even the Goddess of wisdom.

"Ardella," Alexander whispered as his arms tighten around me comfortingly. *He may not be an empath, but he certainly seemed to be able to read my moods.*

"Sorry, I just started thinking ," I started to explain and then reconsidered my words. There was no point wasting time or energy on things I cannot change. I had many happy memories of

New Athens and that is what I wanted to remember. "I did love looking through the Celestial Telescope. Do you know I may be the only mortal on Arcadia that has seen Sol?"

"Sol?"

"Sol is the star of Earth – the home world of our ancestors and birthplace of the Olympians. It is not visible to the naked eye, but I discovered the instructions on how to find it with a telescope during my research."

"Really?" I could hear the wonder in his voice and feel the growing bloom of joy in his heart. *He loved to learn new things as much as I did.*

"I was terrified I would get in trouble, but I was too curious not to look," I whispered conspiratorially, as if just admitting my transgression might bring down Olympian wrath. Alexander's laugh reminded me that I was no longer under the thumb of the Gods of Arcadia. "I was a little disappointed. It is just an ordinary yellow star. It is hard to believe it nourished the planet that was the cradle of our civilization."

"Now I am tempted to raid New Athens just to look through their Celestial Telescope. I would like to see Sol," the Son of Ares announced boldly.

"That may not be necessary. You only need a small handheld telescope. Look up at the Gemini during the month of Demeter and it is about fifteen degrees to the right in the constellation of the Plow."

"I will need your help with that. I'm afraid Athena didn't think gardeners needed a working knowledge of astronomy."

"You cannot find the constellations in the night sky?"

"No," he replied nonchalantly.

He tried to pretend it was not important, but I could feel the ache in his heart. I knew the little boy in him had never really gotten over his being excluded from the Academy. I fervently wished I could take away that raw whole in his soul and give him his heart's desire. Perhaps there was one last thing I could do for him before I had to leave.

"Then we are going to change that," I offered. I smiled at his protest when I rose from his lap.

"What are you doing?"

"I am going to teach you the basics of Arcadian Constellations. Come on. We need to move away from the light of the fire to see the stars better."

I felt Alexander's anticipation and it fueled my own enthusiasm at sharing one of my favorite subjects.

"Where do you suggest we go?" Alexander asked, rising.

I looked around the ruins and spotted a still intact tower to our right. "Up there!" I shouted and took off toward the stone stairs leading up.

"Wait for me!" he called, chasing after me. Out of breath yet exhilarated at the top of tower, I felt Alexander's boisterous energy surround me moments before he himself arrived on the landing. "So what is my first lesson?"

I thought for a moment, and then replied, "Find the Gemini."

He turned in a slow circle looking up at the starry sky. "There," he said pointing to the two brightest stars in the sky.

"Very good. Now the Gemini are fixed points in the sky. Each month the constellation for that Olympian will be in the sky directly above them. As we move from one month to the next the stars of the constellations move across the sky on the Celestial Wheel."

"How can stars move across the sky?"

"The movement is just our perception. It is actually the planet Arcadia moving in orbit around our sun."

"Oh," he replied. I saw the light in his eyes just before he questioned, "and why are the Gemini fixed points?"

"That is because the two bright stars that appear on the northern horizon every night are not stars at all," I explained and then paused to let my words have the greatest impact.

"Then what are they?"

"The Gemini are the ships that our ancestors used to travel here from Earth."

I felt his whirling storm of awe and wonder at this knowledge and smiled as I realized it match my own reaction to this discovery many years ago in Athena's Archive.

"There are two derelict ships in orbit around Arcadia?" Alexander asked shocked.

Oh, it is even better than that! I mused. My smile became smug as I anticipated the Son of Ares reaction to the truth. "There are two still functional ships in stationary orbit above the northern pole. They are maintained by Hephaestus' automatons. Athena even has a control room to monitor them from her tower."

"Athena controls the two space ships that brought mankind here from Earth?"

"How do you think she influences the weather? That was Zeus' ability back on Earth, but when the Olympians left him behind Athena had to get creative."

"Then Athena's lightning bolts..."

"Are generated by the ships, but directed by the Goddess."

"Just when I thought the Olympians couldn't possible surprise me," Alexander admitted quietly and his eyes became introspective.

I felt his awe begin to mix with dread, and I knew it was time to distract him. "Perhaps we should get back to the lesson on the constellations," I suggested.

"Yes," he replied. I could almost feel his need to change the dark direction of his thoughts.

"This is the month of Hestia, which means Hestia's

constellation is dominant in the sky. See there are two red and two yellow stars that form a sort of diamond. That is the flame of Hestia."

"I see them."

"The month of Dionysus is fast approaching, so look just to the left and you can see his constellation on the rise," I said pointing upward.

"You mean those four white stars."

"Yes, those are the cup and the two smaller ones below them form the stem to make it a goblet of wine."

"Of course Dionysus' constellation would be a goblet."

"No doubt filled with Dionysian Red." We both laughed.

Alexander recovered first and placed one hand under his chin thoughtfully. "So since the month of Poseidon just passed, his constellation should be just to the right of Hestia's."

"Exactly."

"What am I looking for?"

"Try to guess," I replied and he shot me a bemused glance.

"Something from the sea?" he guessed.

"Try his symbol of power."

"Ahh. I'm looking for a trident."

"Very good. They are four blue stars that form the three points of the trident and two smaller white ones that form the handle."

I watch him search the night sky and felt his excitement and determination. Unfortunately, astronomy is not always an easy skill. "I don't see them."

I could feel his disappointment.

"There," I said softly pointing toward the brightest of the blue stars. As Alexander's gazed followed my indicated direction I saw his eyes sparkle.

"I found it," he replied enthusiastically.

"You are a natural."

"So since there are eleven Olympian months, there are eleven constellations that move across the sky like a giant wheel."

"Basically - although there are actually twelve Olympian constellations."

"Oh."

"Even though he does not have his own month, Ares does have a constellation."

"He does? Where?" he asked curiously.

I moved in close to Alexander and could not resist running my hand down his arm until our hands touched. Forcing myself to ignore the pull of desire that sparked between us, instead I lifted his hand to point at the constellation in question. "See the three red stars in a row?"

"Yes," he replied calmly, although I could sense the spark of desire had been felt by us both.

"That is the Sword of Ares."

Chapter 22

I have never witnessed a more beautiful sight than the opening of a sunflower at the first rays of the dawn, or heard a more magnificent sound than that of a woman's first sigh of passion.

The God Apollo
Four hundred and ninety-one years Ab Terra Condita

MUCH LATER AS the coals of our small fire slowly burned themselves out a strange blue glow filled the night. It came from sunken area just across the courtyard where the enclosing wall was still intact.

"What do you think it is?" I asked softly.

"Perhaps we should go found out," Alexander replied rising from his place by the fire. My first instinct was to protest that it could be dangerous, but I realized the voice I heard in my head sounded suspiciously like Mistress Tressa. Shuttering at the idea the High Councilor of Athena could still be controlling my life, I let Alexander help me up intent on marching into the unknown just for spite.

Moving around the wall and through the ruins of an iron

gate we came into a private bathing chamber and a mysterious pool filled with glowing blue water. To be specific the walls of the pool were studded with large blue glowing crystals that gave the water of the pool its particular glow.

"Is it my imagination or are those crystals on the walls of the pool glowing?" Alexander asked.

"Could they be moon crystals?" I speculated thinking of the rare gems I had read about in Athena's Archive.

"Moon crystals?"

"The legend says they are crystals with magical properties that were created by the Goddess Artemis for her followers," I replied.

"So that would mean these moon crystals have to be over a thousand years old," he whispered in awe. "And they still shimmer in the moonlight. It is incredible." Reaching down Alexander dipped his hand in the crystal blue water. "It is warm," he said softly. "It must have been their private bathing pool."

"It is lovely."

"And very inviting," he said starting to take off his shirt.

"What are you doing?"

"Going for a moonlight swim," he said tossing the shirt on a nearby rock. "Care to join me?"

"The night air is too cold to swim."

"The water is quite warm."

"Alexander, we cannot," I protested. A shiver of fear accompanied Mistress Tressa's voice in my head this time, and I knew a decade spent in the shelter of the Tower of Athena was not so easily overcome.

"Why? Who is stopping us?" Alexander asked perceptive enough to ask just the right questions.

"I do not think that ..."

"Stop thinking so much. Try letting your heart lead. Do you

want to come for a moonlight swim with me?" he asked huskily. My heart leapt at the prospect.

"Yes, very much." I admitted and let my fears flee. I don't recall shedding my clothes, but suddenly feeling the warm water splash against my skin. The contrast of the cool night breeze and the warm bubbles of the moon pool caused goose bumps to rise on my skin.

I closed my eyes as I lowered myself into the warm crystal water and felt the pleasure of its relaxing touch. As the water surrounded my limbs I felt a peculiar tingling, as if tiny hands were massaging and caressing my skin. "This is pure bliss," I sighed. "Thank you."

"You're welcome, Ardella. Thank you for bringing me along on this adventure. It is good to get away – if only for a little while."

"*If only we could get away from everyone and everything else forever,*" a petulant voice in my head sighed. I tried not to let my guilt bubble up and ruin the moment, but it would not be stopped. I swam across the pool to try to distract myself.

"Why are you feeling guilty?" Alexander asked suddenly.

"What?" I replied shocked that he would even suspect my inner turmoil.

"You are feeling guilty," he said with authority.

"How do you know what I am feeling?" I asked suspiciously.

"I'm not sure. It is like I am feeling guilty, but I know I'm not the source. How can that be?"

His question shocked me. I knew the answer, but that was not possible. "You are describing what my empathy feels like?"

"Why would I suddenly be an empath?"

"I do not know. I have never met another person with empathy."

"Could it be the moon crystals? You said they had magical properties."

"That is just a story."

"But it is possible?"

"I am not sure," I replied casually, but my mind soared with the possibilities.

"Now you are feeling curious and excited."

"I know what I am feeling, Alexander!" I replied unreasonable irritated by his comments. I had never really understood why people considered my reading their emotions and invasion of privacy until now.

"Now you are uncomfortable and irritated with me."

"I do not need your commentary telling me how I feel."

He laughed. "Now you know how we poor mortals feel around Athena's empath."

"This is not a joke, how can you suddenly be an empath?"

"I don't know. Perhaps the crystals transferred your power to me somehow. How is your empathy working, Ardella?"

I realize with a start that I had not felt his emotions since I had lowered myself into the soft, warm waters of the moon pool. To be certain I reached out to learn what Alexander was feeling and found nothing. My empathy was gone. "Your feelings are blocked," I suggested desperately, hoping I was wrong.

"I'm not shielding my feelings, Ardella," he informed me and then gave me a few moments to contemplate what that meant. "Your gift seems to be missing."

"That is not possible. Athena said she could not take back my gift. How can it be gone?" I began stammering in my panic.

"Ardella, it's alright," Alexander said calmly putting his arms around me. "I am sure it's just temporary."

"I cannot remember what it was like before I could feel the emotions of the people around me. I feel like one of my senses is suddenly missing and I am …."

"your terrified."

"stop that! This is…"

"wonderful. Do you know how many times I envied your gift? Your empathy allowed you to touch a part of me no one else on Arcadia ever could. I always wondered how it would feel to be able to touch you the same way."

"Alexander."

"I can feel your emotions, Ardella. This is incredible, although fear and confusion are not so much fun. Perhaps I should work on changing your mood," he said as his hands and his lip began exploring my neck and shoulders. I shuttered as desire flared and I heard his husky reply, "Much better."

༄

Just before dawn I heard a soft hum of the touchstone in my saddle bag. My heart raced as I realized it was Kendra with word about Rafe's escape from Metropolis. *Did everything go according to plan? Were they even now on their way to the safety of Amazonia?*

Slipping out of Alexander's arms and rising, I wrapped my cloak around my body to shield my shaking limbs from the cool morning air. Gently removing the touchstone from the bag, I looked back at Alexander to be certain he was still sleeping. I felt no emotions from him and was certain he was unaware of my movements. (He had been correct that my empathy returned as soon as we left the moon pool.)

The gentle pink light of the rising Dawnmoon danced around him and my heart ached as the sight of his dark brown curls caressing his aquiline nose in the soft breeze. The common people of our world believed that the light of Arcadia's second moon, which only remains is the sky for a few minutes just before dawn, had magical properties. If you made a wish in the light of the Dawnmoon, it would be granted by the sleeping Artemis. *If only a wish could make a world where I did not have to betray my own heart.*

"I came to Metropolis in order to save Rafe," I reminded myself as a single tear of sorrow escaped. "I did what had to be done."

Looking down at the touchstone I wondered if this had been the only way. I wanted Rafe to be safe without losing Alexander; if only that had been possible. Suddenly I knew the burden of Alexander's confession to Deidra not so long ago beneath my tower in Metropolis. I could hear his voice filled with regret and resignation that tore at my heart, "I know I can't compromise all that I have built for anyone, including Ardella. What scares me is that a part of me wants to do whatever it takes to please her - no matter what the cost." He had had to make the same choice I had – duty over love. *But did either of us really have a choice?*

My mind screamed at injustice of it all. The fates were not kind. They tantalized us with glimpses of other paths and other destinies, but made the price too high and left us with nothing but regret. Perhaps that was the price of not being simple mortals. We were both children of the Olympians – pawns in the eternal game of the Gods of Arcadia.

"So is that the Amazons?" I jumped as I heard Alexander ask from behind me. I turned to find him standing silently in the cold morning air. I still sensed none of his emotions and felt my heart sink that he had once again built an icy wall to keep me out of his mind.

"What?" I gasped.

"The message on your touchstone is from the Amazons, isn't it?"

"I..."

"It's the touchstone you brought back from Amazonia."

"How did you know that I..." I started to ask and them the

truth came flooding into my mind. I hadn't fooled the Son of Ares. He knew. "You had Deidra search my belongings?"

"Don't get all pompous about our going through your things. You brought a secret communication device back with you from Amazonia – for what purpose?"

"Queen Lyessa gave it to me. She was anxious about my safety in Metropolis."

"So the message is a friendly greeting from the Queen of the Amazons?"

"I have not played it yet, so I cannot be certain who…"

"Don't let me stop you, Ardella. It is not as if I don't already know this is all a trap."

"A trap?"

"The ironic part is that I sent you to Amazonia. It should have occurred to me that Queen Lyessa would convince you to help them capture me to trade for your brother."

"Trade you for Rafe?"

"At least you didn't kill me yourself, or is that coming later?"

"I could never kill you, Alexander, and there are no Amazons coming for you. I swear it. I did not trade you for Rafe."

"Prove it," he hissed. I felt his rage despite his defenses and I knew it was time to share the truth.

I activated the touchstone and suddenly a tiny hologram of Rafe stood in my palm. "Ardella," he said softly. "Kendra tells me I have you to thank for my rescue from Metropolis. After what I said to you in my cell, I wouldn't have blamed you for leaving me there," his voice cracked. "I didn't mean it. I'm sorry," he whispered and sighed.

The tear rolled down my cheek unbidden. My emotions were in such turmoil that I am not sure if it was a tear of joy or a tear of sorrow. I wanted to hug my twin brother and be glad he was safe, but I also desperately craved the embrace of the man standing coldly beside me - a man whose touch I might never feel again.

"We are making good time and there have been no signs of pursuit from Metropolis. Your idea to hold the Son of Ares hostage seems to have worked," Rafe's hologram continued. "Ardella, promise me you will be careful with him. Don't take any unnecessary risks, and don't trust him. We have to keep moving, but there's one more thing I need to say. I heard you offered to trade your life for mine. Thank you. Sis. I ... Be safe." There was a long pause before he whispered, "I love you."

As the image faded the lonely tear was joined by a flood, and I felt the core of regret I had carried for what had happened to Rafe so long ago melt away in a burst of joyous relief. My twin was free and on his way to safety.

My joy was short lived, however. As I looked back up at Alexander I could see the spark of anger in his eyes, even if his Herculean will kept his emotions shielded from me. In the instant before he spoke I felt a glimmer of relief seep through the tiny cracks in Alexander's armor. "So you didn't sell me out to the Amazons," he commented, "This was all about setting your brother free."

"You knew from the beginning that was my reason for coming to Metropolis."

"Yes. I let myself forget that. It seems you never did," he commented as the ache of loss broke free of his control – spiraling all around us.

"Alexander, I am sorry I..."

"You don't have to apologize. I suspected something was wrong since you agreed to go to Amazonia. Then every survival instinct screamed that this sudden trip to the House of Rowan was a trap, but I ignored them. I have let myself be blinded by my desire and now..."

"What are you going to do?"

"Now that is an interesting question. Considering what I just heard I should be furious with you. You pretended to love me to lure me away as part of the Amazon's plan to free your brother."

My heart was torn by his words. "You know I was not pretending."

"Really?" he replied in a sarcastic tone I had not heard in his voice since my first day in Metropolis. It suggested we were once again adversaries debating in the citadel – that we were strangers. I knew that was not true.

"You possessed my gift of empathy last nigh. You shared what I felt for you, Alexander. You know that I love you."

"I know. I felt your love for me last night in the moon pool, but that all seems like a dream."

"A lost dream," I whispered.

"It doesn't matter. You made your choice."

"How much choice would you have had if Hermes Council had ordered my brother's execution? Love would not change what you had to do, only make it harder."

"I'm sorry falling in love messed up your plan."

"I am not sorry I fell in love. I just wish I ..."

"We seldom get what we wish, Ardella."

"No we don't. My whole life has been dictated by the whims of the Olympians. I have never been more certain that free will is just an illusion."

"No! You don't get to blame this on Athena or Hermes. You made your choice knowing the consequences of your actions."

"And I should have let you execute my brother, so I could stay in Metropolis with you?"

"You should have trusted me to help find a way out of our dilemma."

"Rafe was my responsibility, not yours. I could not take a

chance with his life. I owed him too much to ..."

"I know. A life for a life."

"That brings us back to the question – what are you going to do?"

"What I have to," he replied opening his hand to reveal a tiny vial. I recognized it as the one holding the lotus powder I had planned to use to put Alexander to sleep.

"That proves I did not plan to harm you."

"Just keep me asleep," Alexander postulated. "Apollodorus was beside himself when he discovered the lotus powder was missing. He didn't want to believe you had stolen it."

"It seemed the easiest way to keep you here until I knew Rafe was safe. I was going to wake you this morning with a cup of tea dosed with the powder."

"Well that part of your plan didn't go too well – did it?" he mused, but then a felt a burst of clarity rip through his defenses. "If you were going to drug me this morning, it means Rafe and the Amazon need one more day. There might still be a chance to capture them," he hypothesized.

"By the time you get back to Metropolis and send your raiders out to search, Rafe will be beyond your reach," I countered.

"You think so. You don't imagine I came here alone, do you?"

"What do you mean?"

"I was expecting an Amazon ambush, Ardella, so I brought along a caravan ship full of my best raiders. They are camped just beyond that copse of trees."

My eyes widen with fear. I had never considered the possibility that Alexander would have a secret plan of his own. "But you only have one raiding ship. Which direction do you send it to look for my brother?" I asked hoping to keep him from doing anything that might ruin my brother's chances of freedom.

"There are only two real possibilities New Athens or

Amazonia."

I did my best to remain calm despite his very accurate assumption. "I will not tell you where Kendra and my brother are headed."

"You don't have to. I just have to look at who is helping you to answer the question of Rafe's destination. Either the Goddess Athena relented and agreed to allow you and your twin back in New Athens or the Queen of the Amazons is going to hide you in Amazonia."

"I am the Daughter of Athena."

"Even so, it is far more likely that a mortal queen could feel pity for you and Rafe. Your brother is headed to Amazonia."

"You cannot know that for certain. He could..."

"It is almost dawn. If they left Metropolis last night on horseback, they will soon be nearing the Valley of Tarsus. It is the fastest way from Metropolis to Amazonia."

"Alexander." The word was a plea torn from my throat.

"I think my raiders can arrange a welcoming party for your brother."

"No! Please!" I begged reaching out to the Son of Ares. The touchstone dropped forgotten to the ground as I wrapped my arms around his neck and pressed my body against his. I felt the familiar pull of desire that always sparked between us as my skin touched his.

"Ardella," he groaned and I felt the heat of his emotions melt away the wall around his mind and heart. Pain, hope, anger and love spewed forth from his soul like lava covering my body and burning my heart.

"Please. Take me back to Metropolis if you must have someone to appease your people. Do whatever you have to do, but let Rafe go. Please," I begged as tears of desperation blurred my vision.

"Ardella," this time the word was a prayer whispered against my lips. The roar of passion filled my ears as his kiss drew me from our raw reality into a sensual world of promise and hope. His lips played against mine sending shivers spiraling to every part of my body. I tasted the saltiness of my tears as his tongue caressed and teased mine, while the wondrous masculine smell that was Alexander seemed to float all around me. There was no time, no Olympians, no past and no pain. All I felt in that moment was hope. *Everything will work out as it should.*

The sweet thrill of that kiss stole my breath away – no it was the hands around my neck that cause the world to spin out of control. *No, not again!* I tried to scream in vain. Just before the darkness took me I knew the awful truth – the Son of Ares had finally won!

Chapter 23

Love is the greatest strength known to mankind. It can make the impossible come true. It can topple cities and empires, and even bring down Gods of Arcadia.

Alexander, the Son of Ares
Two thousand six hundred and fourty-five years Ab Terra Condita

THE BRIGHTNESS OF the sun forced me to squeeze my eyes shut once again. I knew I had been unconscious for a while, because my body ached from lying on the hard ground. Unsure of where I was from the brief flash of light and unwilling to repeat the experience just yet, I decided to attempt to use my other senses to try to determine my current location.

I heard the melody of birds and the whispers of tree branches swaying in the wind. I could smell the sweet aroma of the flowering grasses and the lingering smoke of a campfire. I suspected I was still lying in the ruins where I had fallen and wondered if I was alone. The sound of voices near me startled me and confirmed my worst fears. The Son of Ares was near.

"Do you want me to stay until she wakes up?" Kern asked softly.

"I think I can handle the Daughter of Athena alone," Alexander replied.

"I'm not so sure. This has to be difficult for you."

"You have no idea."

"Once you were able to turn an impossible situation into a future for Deidra and I. I wish I could do the same for you now."

"There is no happy ending today, Kern, but thank you."

"The latest word from Deidra is that there is rioting all over Metropolis. We must return as soon as possible. I believe seeing you alive and unharmed will lessen the citizens' anger."

"As soon as she awakens we will leave – I promise."

"You aren't planning to bring her back to Metropolis?"

"No. I don't think she would be safe there. I am going to leave her the two horses and enough supplies to get to Amazonia. I have no doubt Lyessa will give her shelter."

Slowly I opened my eyes and found the two men standing some distance way with their backs to me. I felt my anger burst into bloom as our last conversation came flooding back. *What had he done to Rafe?*

Rising I launched myself at Alexander's back and slammed by fists against his shoulders. "What have you done to my brother?" I felt Alexander's shock even before he turned. I should have been moved at the love shining in his eyes, but I felt nothing but fear. I just began to pound his chest until his hands caught my arms.

"Enough, Ardella," he said softly.

"Where is my brother? What have you done to Rafe?" I cried struggling against him.

"Kern, would you get the touchstone for Lady Ardella," Alexander requested calmly.

"Tell me what happened to him!" I shrieked as panic tore

through my chest.

His quiet sigh took me by surprise. "Because I don't know what happened to your brother."

I froze. "What?"

"You had another message from the Amazons a few minutes ago. Hopefully that will ease your mind," he explained. No longer struggling in his arms, I looked up into his cerulean blue eyes. Finally I allowed myself to see and feel the truth – Alexander's eyes and heart were overflowing with love. I let the warmth of that sweet fire calm my mind and allow hope to creep back into my chest. By the Goddess, was there a chance Alexander had spared Rafe?

As he loosened his grip and I turned toward Kern who was holding out the touchstone. My hands trembled as I reach for the crystal and the answer that would change my world forever. I tapped it once and miniature image of Lyessa rose from the crystal.

"Ardella. I have wonderful news. Rafe and Kendra arrived safely in Amazonia a few minutes ago. They are exhausted but otherwise unharmed. Kendra tells me they saw no raider ships in pursuit, so it seems your plan worked." I tapped the crystal to pause the playback and looked questioningly up at Alexander.

"What about the raiding ship?" I asked confused.

"Since I couldn't be sure where Rafe was headed, I had no idea which direction to send the ship," he replied. I didn't need my empathy to know he was lying, but I was shocked when my gift registered no surprise from Kern at this pronouncement. He had lied to his own men. Alexander could have recaptured my brother, but he hadn't done it. My heart soared. The Son of Ares really had let my brother go.

"Now that the Lady Ardella is awake, we need to return to Metropolis," Kern reminded them calmly even as his concern and frustration screamed in my head.

Alexander looked at me nervously. "We have to get back. There is..."

"Rioting," I finished for him. "I overheard you and Kern discussing it."

"It seems your threat to harm me if the raiders tried to recapture your brother was played for the Council of Hermes before a gathering of citizens in the citadel. They were not pleased and you are not the most popular person in Metropolis at the moment."

"So I am responsible for the riots and more innocent people getting hurt?"

"I'm afraid so," Alexander sympathized. He understood my regret and although I could feel his desire to offer comfort, he made no move toward me. "The passionate nature of most of our citizens tends to make these kinds of things happen often. I must get back before too much damages is done or anyone else is killed."

"I understand," I murmured as a strange emptiness bloomed within my chest. I just stared at Alexander's unruly chocolate locks and sad smile unable to look away.

"Are you going to play the rest of the message?" he asked startling me from my revere.

"The message – yes."

I tapped the touchstone and Lyessa continued, "Be careful when you release Alexander. The Son of Ares is going to be ... upset. Perhaps I can give him a reason to let go of his anger. Tell him that I will negotiate a peace treaty with Metropolis under one condition – you must be our arbitrator. That means you must arrive safe and unharmed in Amazonia or there is no deal."

"She is a shrewd negotiator," Alexander commented.

"Great minds think alike," I laughed.

"Which should make negotiating this peace treaty between

us easier for you," he suggested.

"Oh Ardella, I almost forgot," Lyessa's holographic image continued unaware of our commentary on her message, "I just received word from the High Council of Athena. Your Goddess has decreed there will be no more assassination attempts on the Son of Ares. It seems she has decided the serpent we know is preferable to the unknown chaos of his absence. I couldn't help but notice it sounded a lot like the argument we had when you were in Amazonia. You never cease to amaze me. I will see you soon, Ardella. Safe journey."

The laughter that sprang from my lips could not be stopped. It shook my whole body and stole my breath until I collapsed on the cold dawn earth still cackling.

"What did you say to Athena?" Alexander asked kneeling beside me.

"Would you believe I stopped trying to please her, and simply told her the truth? Who would have known that was how to influence the Goddess?" I replied still trembling with mirth.

"Thank you for convincing her to leave me in peace," he said softly.

"Oh she will not leave you in peace, Alexander, but at least there will be no more attempts on your life."

He smiled at me, but the joy didn't reach his eyes. The love that had shown there had been replaced by sadness. We knew this was goodbye. To his credit none of his sorrow could be detected by my empathy. He had once again erected that cursed wall to keep me from touching his soul, but this time he had done it to protect me.

"Strategos, we need to go," Kern reminded us softly.

"I know." Alexander sighed.

"I will wait for you at the ship," Kern said.

"I'll be right there," Alexander replied.

"Kern, wait." I called rising to my feet. "Please tell Deidra goodbye for me. Thank her for everything."

"Of course," Kern replied.

"Oh, and give her this," I said throwing the touchstone to him. "I will ask Queen Lyessa for its counterpart when I reach Amazonia. Perhaps I could tell her tales of my adventures with the Amazons and she could share stories of life in Metropolis." I looked into his eyes as I added, "Perhaps there is someone in Amazonia she would like for me to visit?" His eyes widened and then he smiled.

"I am sure she would appreciate that, Lady Ardella. Goodbye."

As the Son of Ares most trusted advisor walked back toward the raiding ship, Alexander rose as well. His hand reached out to gently touch the mark on my neck. "I'm sorry," he offered.

"Why did you do it, if you did not plan to go after my brother?"

"I had every intention of going after Rafe," he replied.

"What stopped you?" I asked.

"I blame you for that," he retorted.

"You chose me over the citizens of Metropolis?" I asked as a warm flood of hope filled my soul.

"My heart wouldn't let me make any other choice."

"A few weeks ago I would have been shocked that the Son of Ares even had a heart, but now I know how wrong I was. I was blind to the real you," I admitted, and added silently, "*and now it is too late.*"

"Does that mean you might forgive me for doing this again?" he mused once again touching the bruise on my neck.

"You want me to forgive you for today or for the day you stole the crystal reader after I had just saved your life?" I replied.

He was silent for a long time. "I'm sorry. I shouldn't have

asked you to..."

"I forgive you, Alexander, f" I said softly, "because I understand why you did it."

His joy shattered the wall around his heart as his arms went around me.

"You needed the knowledge of Athena to create a place of hope and freedom," I said enjoying the sensation of warmth and safety I always found in his arms.

"Metropolis," he whispered.

"Your haven for the rejects and exiles of Arcadia, and the hope for the future of the human race," I laughed.

I felt his wave of surprise, and realized he had misunderstood me as well. After all, he was only human. I pondered my reflection in the cerulean pools of his eyes, and had to admit I was pleased by what I saw. I knew that I was a better person than the one who had stormed into the citadel to free my brother.

"Metropolis has changed me. You have changed me," I informed him.

"So you have decided I am not a monster?" he laughed.

"Alexander," I sighed. That word had haunted him too long. Instinctively I wanted to comfort him. My hand reached up to caress his check, but instead I found myself pulling his lips to mine.

I felt his love burst forth and mingle with my own until we were encased in a bubble of joy that blocked out the rest of Arcadia. In that moment there were no past betrayals to forgive. There were no obstacles keeping us apart. There was only the timeless joining of two souls who had found the one who made them complete. Unfortunately, it was a fragile bubble too easily broken.

The ache as his lips left mine allowed reality to come flooding back into my heart. In that sorrow the words could not be held back. "I love you, Alexander, Son of Ares."

He laughed. "Since you can feel what I do, I guess there is no point in telling you that..."

I gently placed my finger to his lips. "I like to hear the words."

The mischievous twinkle in his eyes tore at my heart. "I love you, too, Ardella, even if you are the Daughter of Athena."

"What we need is a place that would allow the Son of Ares and the Daughter of Athena to live together in peace," I suggested.

"That would be wonderful, but where would we even begin?"

Like the pieces of a jigsaw puzzle coming together to form a larger image, all the revelations of the past few weeks coalesced in my mind. I hadn't even realized until that moment the answer had been right in front of me all along. I knew what had to be done. At last I understood why Hermes had sound awed by the potential of mankind. We had the power to defeat the Gods of Arcadia.

"You already have," I informed him excitedly.

One eyebrow shot up and an impish grin stole across his face, but he didn't speak a word. He didn't have to. His growing curiosity was all the encouragement I needed.

"Your peace treaty with the Amazons is the first step, but cannot stop there. I think a peace treaty with the Elusians should be your next endeavor."

"I like it, but Demeter is unlikely to listen to anything I have to say."

"True, but she might listen to me. I simply have to show her a way to stop your raids once and for all."

"Ardella, you know I want to stop raiding, but we must have food for the people of Metropolis."

"What do you think Demeter would give to stop your raids on her villages? What price would the Goddess of the Harvest be willing to pay to protect her children?"

"Anything, but there is nothing I want from Demeter. All we need is food. If the Goddess would just allow us to grow our own grain in Metropolis then we..." he stopped suddenly and I saw the spark of understand in his eyes. "You really believe Demeter would give her permission for us to plant crops in Metropolis?"

"I believe I can convince her it is the best way to stop the raids. It should be possible - as long as she believes I am doing it for her benefit and not yours."

"Are you suggesting some sort of conspiracy?" he asked.

"Secrecy is vital. No one can know we are working together. I can only manipulate the Olympians as long as they believe we are still adversaries."

"I am beginning to see your plan, and I like it," he said with a chuckle.

"After Demeter, we should work on Aphrodite. If she is convinced, then Dionysus will be no problem at all. Athena will be one of the hardest to convince, but once I am back in New Athens I should be able..."

"Wait, you were exiled from New Athens. What makes you think you will be allowed to return?"

"Athena said she misses me," I informed him. "She already offered to pardon me."

"So why are you on the way to Amazonia instead of New Athens?"

"I refused her offer. The price was too high."

"What was Athena's price?" he asked.

"It was too high."

"Ardella," Alexander insisted.

"She wanted me to drug you and bring you back to New Athens. I refused."

"You wouldn't sacrifice me to save your brother for Athena or the Amazons?"

"My heart would not let me make any other choice."

"Ardella," he whispered as his lips met mine. Knowing it might well be our last kiss, I held nothing back. I allowed my passion to take control and shattered the barriers of my reserved Athenian upbringing. I poured my very heart into the joining of our lips and felt my love magnified as it was absorbed and reflected by Alexander. We touched the ageless spring from which mankind's power sprung – a place no Olympian could ever find.

Silence filled the air long after our lips had parted. Still entangled in each other's warm embrace, Alexander asked softly, "You really believe we can defeat the Olympians?"

I pulled away just far enough to catch his gaze. "You and I can weave Metropolis into the canvas of this world, so it will live on as a haven for mankind long after we are gone."

I felt the tiny seed of hope bloom within the storm of fear and doubt that filled his heart. "I don't know if ...?"

I was startled by the passion that filled me as I imagined the future of Arcadia. Alexander had carried the fragile seed of freedom solo for too long. "You are not alone anymore, Alexander," I said gently touching his face. "I believe that with the Son of Ares and the Daughter of Athena working together anything is possible!"

Epilogue

Often it is not the events themselves, but the intent or motivation that is the driving force of history. One man or woman with the vision and the ambition can change the world, even if no one realizes they are doing it.

Lady Ardella of Metropolis
Two thousand six hundred and fifty-two years Ab Terra Condita

I FINISHED THE last words and laid down my pen. A single tear slipped from eye as I realized I there was nothing left to write. This was the true story of how it all began, not the version that we told Arcadia. Until this moment it had been a secret shared by Alexander and I, but one day it would be part of our history.

"Lady Ardella, the children have begun arriving," Deidra said softly from the doorway of my study.

"Already? I thought there were still several hours until classes began," I replied.

"You have been cloistered in your study writing for hours, Ardella. You didn't even eat the lunch I left for you," she said as she entered the room and looking disapprovingly at the tray of cold soup, dry bread, and wilted fruit on one corner of my desk.

"I seem to have lost track of time, again. No matter. I finished it, Deidra. The tale is finished."

"What will you do with it now?"

"I will have copies placed in the archives of New Athens and Amazonia. The original will go into the archives of the new library here in Metropolis when it is finished. Each one will be sealed with instructions to open them on the one hundredth anniversary of my death. That should be long enough that nothing I reveal could harm anyone."

"But what is the point of writing book no one will read for a hundred years?"

"Truth is the point. Someday future generations will look back at this moment in our history and seek to know what really happened. This book will teach them the truth."

"Perhaps that is necessary for you or Alexander, but I don't understand why you asked me to write down my story for your book. I did not help build Metropolis, so how is my story important?"

"Your story in the most important one, Deidra. Your tale will reveal why Metropolis was necessary at this moment in history and might even inspire future generations of Amazons to change the rules of their sect to be fairer to all – without hurting you or your new family," I said nodding at her belly swollen with the child she would bare in a few weeks. She smiled.

"I will trust your judgment on the needs of the future, although for now I think we should concentrate on the first day of school at Metropolis' new Academy."

"Growing up I always thought I would become a teacher like my mother before me. I guess we shall find out today if ..."

"Ardella! I sent Deidra to fetch you, and I find you two here visiting. The children have begun arriving. You are both needed," Alexander said with mixture of anxiety and irritation.

"We are coming. Not even Athena's thunderbolts could stop Metropolis' new Academy from opening its doors today," I laughed.

"That is not funny, Ardella," Alexander snapped.

I smiled. "Muriel is right, Alexander. We need to work on your sense of humor!"

FINIS

** Deidra and Kern's love story will soon be available for readers. Please go to www.godsofarcadia.com and leave a message, if you would like details.**

You can also email Andrea Stehle directly at magistrastehle@yahoo.com

Gratias tibi ago

There are so many people who have inspired and help me during the creation of the *Gods of Arcadia: Daughter of Athena*. I could not have done this without you.

Monica – my daughter who finished her first novel at 14 and inspired me to try one more time to write a novel of my own.

Amanda – my daughter who is the inspiration for Ardella and the one who listened to every word of the story before it was published.

Linda – my daughter who's bickering with her sister gave me lots of ideas on how Alexander could annoy Ardella

Vicky Alvear Shecter and Sasha Summers – two incredible authors who share my love of mythology and the classical world and who encouraged me to follow my dream.

San Antonio Romance Authors – the group that took me in, taught me what it really means to be a writer, and who celebrated my success with me each step of the way.

Mindy F. Reed – my editor who improved my words without changing what I wanted to say.

Howard David Johnson – the artist who created the incredible cover of the book.

Heather Brown and Noel Castaneda – two former students who read the story and gave me useful feedback

Sandra – my mother and the first person to read the story from beginning to end. She gave me my love of reading and had always encouraged my desire to write.

Gary Miller - my friend who said the story was "too girly" and made me realize that sometimes love does conquer all

From the Author

I hope you have enjoyed Ardella's story. Please visit my website to learn more about the world of Arcadia, ask questions, and for a preview of the next installment of The Gods of Arcadia – The Son of Ares.

www.godsofarcadia.com

This is my first novel. I have loved mythology all my life and have enjoyed sharing my Post-mythical world with you. I earned my degree in Classics at the University of Texas and currently teach Latin in San Antonio. I would love to hear from my readers.

magistrastehle@yahoo.com

Made in the USA
Charleston, SC
18 May 2015